Praise for the novels of Hester Fox

A Lullaby for Witches

"Weaves a spell of darkness that's mysterious and magical, and binds it with a knot of deathless love."
—**Susanna Kearsley,** *New York Times* **bestselling author**

"A spine-tingling blend of paranormal and historical fiction that feels gothic, gloomy, and perfect for winter." —*BuzzFeed Books*

"With unexpected twists aplenty, this is sure to keep fans of paranormal fantasies turning the pages. It's a multilayered, haunting tale."
—*Publishers Weekly*

"Fox deftly navigates the overlapping borders of romance and the paranormal."
—*Kirkus Reviews*

"A haunting story full of long-buried secrets… Fans of Louisa Morgan and Susanna Kearsley will want to pick this up." —*Shelf Awareness*

"Both timelines are compelling and readers will enjoy this blend of paranormal, gothic horror, romance, and historical fiction." —*Booklist*

The Widow of Pale Harbor

"A gothic romance with the flavor of Edgar Allan Poe, this is also a suspenseful mystery novel… Highly recommended." —*Historical Novel Society*

"Sophy is a strong gothic heroine." —*Publishers Weekly*

The Witch of Willow Hall

"Steeped in gothic eeriness, it's spine-tingling and very atmospheric."
—**Nicola Cornick,** *USA TODAY* **bestselling author**

"*The Witch of Willow Hall* offers a fascinating location, a great plot with history and twists, and characters that live and breathe. I love the novel and will be looking forward to all new works by this talented author!"
—**Heather Graham,** *New York Times* **bestselling author**

Also by Hester Fox

The Witch of Willow Hall
The Widow of Pale Harbor
The Orphan of Cemetery Hill
A Lullaby for Witches

THE LAST HEIR TO BLACKWOOD LIBRARY

HESTER FOX

GRAYDON
HOUSE

GRAYDON HOUSE®

ISBN-13: 978-1-525-80478-6

The Last Heir to Blackwood Library

Graydon House
22 Adelaide St. West, 41st Floor
Toronto, Ontario M5H 4E3, Canada
www.GraydonHouseBooks.com
www.BookClubbish.com

Recycling programs for this product may not exist in your area.

Printed in U.S.A.

In loving memory of DJF

THE
LAST HEIR
TO
BLACKWOOD
LIBRARY

PROLOGUE

Yorkshire, England, 1349

They bricked her up on Saint George's Day.

An expansive blue sky stretched over the rolling moors, the distant bleating of sheep echoing through the valley as Matilda had taken her vow of solitude and entered confinement as an anchoress. It was an auspicious day, given Saint George's patronage of books and England, and then a sheep had passed a bezoar, and the nuns had passed the smooth, polished stone between them, marveling at its singular beauty. Father William had immediately hailed it as a blessing from God himself, a cure for the plague which was spreading throughout the world, creeping ever closer to the remote abbey of Blackwood. But the sisters of Blackwood were in good spirits, and even reports of the Black Death could not dampen them as they helped Matilda prepare by dressing her in a simple white robe and headscarf.

Mellow sunlight filtered in through the small porch window, enjoyed equally by the sparrows that flit about the gardens and the languid abbey cat watching them. The breeze carried with it the sweet scent of lavender and the ringing of the Terce bells. Matilda dutifully knelt at her *prie-dieu* and recited her prayers. Then, rising, she arranged herself at the small desk that would be her confessional, her anchor, and her oasis for the decades to come.

The bishop had blessed the cell, swinging his pendulous incense and filling the small room with the intoxicating scent of myrrh and other exotic spices. Her fellow sisters had queued to say their goodbyes, kissing her smooth, unlined cheeks and leaving her humble gifts befitting an anchoress, such as pots of ink, candles, and hard cheese. They might have still resided under the same roof as her, but henceforth Matilda would be as a stranger to them, a ghost of a woman who once was, confined to the small cell. As soon as the last brick was in place, her only contact with the outside world would be the food and gifts left by the pilgrims who would come to seek advice from the porch window. This would be the last time she would feel human touch, join her sisters in song and worship. Afterward, only Sister Alice had lingered, her sweet blue eyes wet with tears, and Matilda had had to look away, lest she lose her resolve.

But the truth was, the world was as large as one allowed it to be. The four walls of her cell might have been no more than a fingertip's reach in each direction, but Matilda's horizons were broader and brighter than those of the lord of Blackwood, who lived on a vast estate yet never bothered to look up from his account books. A single oak leaf blown in through the window was a wonder to behold, the delicate veins an intricate and divine network unrivaled even by man's highest cathedral. The birdsong that carried on the breeze was as rich and haunting as any *Te Deum* or devotional, a celestial hymn composed by God himself.

Matilda's world had not always been thus. As a child, she had fallen ill with a fever from which the physician had told her parents she would never recover. While on her sickbed, she had received visions of Christ on the cross. But rather than being frightening or grotesque such as the carvings in the church might have her believe, Christ appeared content, ebullient, even. After all, he was a harbinger of eternal life, joyous in the prospect of offering her such sweetness, such happiness in the hereafter as she could not even comprehend. When she had arisen from her sickbed, Death held no power over her, for she knew what came next, and would welcome it when the time came.

And as for the days in between those visions and her last mortal breath? Well, she would fill them with learning, with joy, with humble exultance of the beautiful world created by a beneficent God. She would walk into the Kingdom of Heaven knowing that she had not wasted nor taken for granted one precious moment.

So she had taken orders and given her earthly body over to Christ. But still, it was not enough. There were so many distractions, such petty squabbles within the Church and among the nuns. How could she devote her mind and time to the beautiful questions of the universe if she constantly had to attend to bureaucratic nonsense?

It was no small thing to become an anchoress, and it had taken some persuading on her part and more than some prayerful intervention on God's part, but she had finally convinced the bishop that having an anchoress in Blackwood would elevate their small abbey, and bring in much-needed funds. She would dispense wisdom to pilgrims who would come to hear of her visions, and the sisters would sell them charms and badges, proof that they had made the journey and received the word of God from his humble vessel.

As the years stretched on, the gentle passage of time left its mark. She had no looking glass, but touching her fingers to her face, Matilda could feel the softening of her skin, and she smiled as she traced the contours of time across her cheeks and under her eyes. Learned men and women traveled from afar to hear of her visions, and in return, they brought her knowledge from all corners of the world. She learned of crusades and battles from the men, philosophy and advancements in medicine. New ways to measure time, including a mechanical horologe from the East. Machines that could do sums greater than the human mind could conceive. But it was the women who brought her the most valued knowledge—that of herbs and plants, little miracles that could cure most any ailment if one knew how to apply them properly.

When she had exhausted her studies of herbs and plants and the creatures that lived among them, Matilda still had a keen hunger to learn more. So every clear night, when the bells for Vespers had ceased ringing, Matilda would look to the sky.

What she saw there astounded her. It was not a static mural, but an ever-changing mosaic of dark and light, celestial players forever dancing and gliding on the stage. Every living thing on earth had a part to play, and it was the stars that guided their courses. Such strange flowers bloom at night in the shape of stars, she mused. Therein lay the answers to the questions that so captivated man—life and how to extend it, cures and remedies for almost any ailment, and most importantly, a map of what was to come. Stars, just like seasons, never died completely, simply slumbered for a cycle to be born once again. World without end, indeed. She spent endless hours charting plants and their blooming times, the migration of birds, the changes in weather, and the stars that shone above them all.

But such knowledge immortalized on parchment was powerful, and power in the wrong hands could be dangerous. Too many men had come to her window under the guise of seeking some remedies for their wives and lovers, and she had seen them for what they were: wolves, hungry for knowledge that would harm rather than help. John Webb had been such a man. Mild-mannered and unassuming, he had a constellation of pox scars across his temples and drooping eyelids. With a gift of candle wax, he had beseeched Matilda for her help in easing his wife's pain caused by stones in her stomach. He had prayed to the Virgin Mother to no avail, and his wife was suffering, both bodily and spiritually. Would Matilda help him? Could she help his wife along to the loving arms of Christ? She should have known that a man asking for help on behalf of a woman was suspicious, but even with a proxy, Matilda would not deny being of service to another woman. So against her better judgement, she agreed, and gave him instructions to make a tisane that would ease his wife into eternal slumber.

Not one fortnight later, the seeds of her charity bore fruit. Even in her cell, she could feel the reverberations of excitement, the whispers running through the abbey. When the little kitchen maid had brought Matilda her nightly meal, Matilda grabbed her hand through the slot, staying her.

"What has the abbey in such a clamor?" she had demanded.

"'Tis John Webb's wife," said the maid. "She's been found dead, and John Webb is crowing that she took her life into her own hands, leaving him a free man."

Matilda had let the startled maid go, rocking back on her heels in thought. God forgive her, she had blood on her hands.

So she would record everything she learned, but she would put safeguards in place, just as the quail hides her eggs in the abandoned nest of another bird. Who might find her work after her aching hands had set aside her pen for the last time?

She hoped Alice would someday read her words, would understand why she had made the choice she had, but there were generations beyond her to consider. Someday, perhaps, the right woman would find Matilda's life work and share it with the world, illuminating long-forgotten secrets.

Matilda ran her hands over vellum as soft and pure as buttermilk, a gift brought to her by pilgrims from the Levant. Inks in oyster shells and bottles lined the desk, each painstakingly ground from beetle shells and dried flowers, plants and ores. Yes, the room was small, but the world spread before her, vast and full of promise. Dipping her nib into the black ink, she set quill to parchment, charting the bounds of knowledge.

1

London, 1925

Ivy trudged down the soggy gray street, abandoning any pretense of trying to stay dry. Women selling flowers stood under dripping awnings, and a bus rumbled by in a splash of crimson, street water sloshing in its wake. Men sat on the wet ground, the world flowing around them like rapids around a rock. Some had signs and cups, but most just sat, eyes glazed, faces set. A twinge of guilt ran through her as she hurried past a man with one leg, his trouser tucked around the missing appendage. He had fought for his country in the Great War, and now he was reduced to begging for change on the street, as invisible as the pigeons that flocked around the city. Would that have been James, if he had come back from France? No, of course not. He would have had Ivy. She would have taken care of her brother, no matter what.

Plunging her numb hands deeper into her pockets, Ivy put

her head down against the rain. Miserable rainy days were meant for curling up inside with a cup of hot tea and a good book, not tramping across the city with only one's thin coat for protection. Never mind that the interior in question had leaky windows and a cranky landlady, and everything perpetually smelled of mildew. Inside was always preferable, simply by virtue of there being books.

If she'd had the fare money, Ivy would have taken the Underground, but curiosity and more than a little apprehension propelled her through the driving rain and the busy Piccadilly sidewalk. Her hand curled around the paper in her coat pocket, the unexpected missive's words already seared into her mind.

Miss Radcliffe, your presence is respectfully requested at the reading of the late Lord Hayworth's last will and testament.

Signed,
Mr. Cecil Duncan, Esq.

Most things in life could be distilled down into a simple pattern, and there was comfort in that. Whether it was walking the same route to the employment office to receive the same answer every week, or eating the same tinned herrings and biscuits every night, predictability was something Ivy did not take for granted, not after the last few years. But letters like this did not simply appear out of the blue. She didn't know any Lord Hayworth, and certainly not well enough to be included in a reading of his will. Perhaps the solicitor had the wrong Ivy Radcliffe. Well, she would go and clear up the misunderstanding and fall back into her pattern. She skirted a line of men snaking around the front of a benefits office, hats pulled down low over their faces. The wind chased her down a respectable street with modest homes and offices, well-kept front gardens and pubs boasting flowering window baskets.

She stopped in front of a row of brick offices. Checking the soggy note one more time, she took a deep breath and let the brass knocker swing.

The door cracked open, and a small, hawk-nosed woman with spectacles on a chain around her neck peered out into the rain. She looked Ivy up and down, her shrewd gaze taking inventory of Ivy's worn coat and battered shoes. "You have an appointment with Mr. Duncan?"

Ivy shifted her weight, trying to appear respectable despite the rain plastering hair into her eyes. "Yes, ma'am."

The woman nodded for Ivy to follow her and led her into a blessedly dry and warm office. "Have a seat. He'll be right in."

Gratefully, Ivy lowered herself onto a chair and removed her soggy hat. After the damp of the street, the small office was like heaven, with leather chairs and cheery electric lamps, the carpet plush beneath her wet shoes. There was a comfortable, lived-in feeling, with piles of books stacked haphazardly on every shelf, and teacup rings staining the varnished desk. No sooner had she peeled her gloves off and tucked her straggling hair back, than the door opened and a jowly middle-aged man with receding brown hair and a healthy paunch bustled inside.

"Miss Radcliffe, thank you for your patience." He stuck out his hand and she rose to accept it. "I'm Cecil Duncan, solicitor and executor of the Hayworth family," he said in a slightly nasal upper-class accent. "Nasty day out, isn't it? I do hope you didn't have to come too far."

His introduction did little to illuminate any questions she might have had about why she had been summoned. Taking her seat again, Ivy watched him settle behind his desk. "You'll have to forgive my confusion," she said, when he didn't say anything, "but you see, I don't know any Hayworths."

Mr. Duncan had produced a thick envelope from the desk drawer and was in the process of leafing through the contents. At her words, he looked up over his half-moon glasses. "I don't suppose you do, Miss Radcliffe. But the fact of the matter is, you are actually a distant relation of the great family, the last living relation for that matter."

She absorbed this, as he resumed rifling through papers, then shook her head. "I still don't understand. I received this letter, asking me to come here. How did you even find me?"

"Oh, we have our ways." At her dubious expression he broke into a smile. "Your address was publicly listed."

"And this family...the Hayworths, who are they exactly?" Her friend Susan religiously read the society and gossip pages, but Ivy couldn't bring herself to care about the lives of people far above her, and how they spent their time and wasted their money. The Hayworths might have had their name splashed across the pages every week, and Ivy would have been none the wiser.

Setting aside the papers, Mr. Duncan leaned back in his chair, a kindly expression softening his already-round face. "You'll forgive me, Miss Radcliffe. Sometimes we lawyers forget that not everyone operates in the same circles that we do, and that what might be standard procedure for us, is in fact, a life-changing event for someone." He tented his fingers, sighing, and Ivy resisted the urge to leap across the desk and shake the answer from him. "I will do my best to explain it simply," he said finally. "The late Lord Hayworth of Blackwood, Yorkshire, passed away leaving no issue. Tracing the lineage back, it appears that your late father was..." He broke off as he peered down his glasses at the paper in front of him. "Ah, here it is. Your late father was a third cousin of Lord Hayworth's." He paused, as if waiting for Ivy to confirm the impossible story that she was now hearing. When she didn't say anything, he continued. "Of course, the line would pass to your elder brother, but I believe that he is likewise deceased?"

Ivy cleared her throat, her mouth suddenly dry. "Yes."

"My condolences," Mr. Duncan murmured. "Usually in these circumstances the estate would then revert back to the Crown, but I am not sure if you are aware that the laws of investiture have recently changed, meaning that under the new law, women can now inherit titled land."

A faint buzzing began to build at the base of Ivy's neck. Mr. Duncan leaned forward in his seat, his eyes locking on hers over the rim of his glasses. "Miss Radcliffe, you are the sole heir of Blackwood Abbey, seat of the Hayworth family in Yorkshire."

If there was a pattern to everything, then the pattern of Ivy's life was one of deaths and disappointments, and by the age of twenty-five, she had resigned herself to an existence of poverty and struggle. Surely, she would have heard about a wealthy relation before, however distant? Possibilities whizzed before her eyes: being independently wealthy, not needing to beg for a job or find a husband. Comfort. Stability.

"Miss Radcliffe? You look very pale." The lawyer rang a bell and a moment later the spectacled woman appeared again. "Mrs. Harvey, please bring a cup of tea for Miss Radcliffe, she's received some very startling news."

Mrs. Harvey shot a curious look at Ivy before retreating and closing the door behind her. A clock on the mantel ticked. Mr. Duncan was going on about bloodlines and titles, something about a stipulation in the will which required she live at the abbey. But Ivy hardly heard him.

Her eyes drifted closed. How very far away from her monotonous life in the East End she was. She stood, teetering on the edge of a gilded world, cold and hunger and want at her back. What would her parents think if they could see her now?

The plan had been for her mother to emigrate to England and land herself a peer; her American money paired with a revered yet impoverished bloodline. The only problem—and luckily for Ivy—was that she never made it to the altar. Instead, she met and fell in love with a handsome young man who shared her passion for the written word, and happened to be a destitute professor. She sold her train ticket, wired home that she would *not* be wedding a lord or earl or what have you, and was promptly disowned without a penny.

Ivy's family often teased that Ivy had inherited her American mother's sentimentality. But that was the joke; her mother was pragmatic and unreserved, someone who would make the journey across the Atlantic to the unknown. It was from her father that Ivy inherited her romantic notions, the gentle slant through which she viewed the world. Ivy knew that the Radcliffes were an anomaly, a tightly-knit group that considered themselves friends as well as family, and who enjoyed spending time together in the evenings reading and laughing. No boarding schools or being sent off to work for the Radcliffe children. If they struggled, they struggled together.

What might have been minutes or hours passed when the door opened again, and Mrs. Harvey brought out a tray with wobbling teapot and cups. Ivy received the teacup with shaking hands. She had little appetite after the news, but she wasn't about to pass up something hot to drink.

"There now, that helps, doesn't it?" Mr. Duncan was regarding her with something between apprehension and pity. "Do you have any questions for me? Is there any way in which I might put your mind at ease?"

She thought of her friend Susan and the flat they shared, all the things they'd been through together. Between Ivy's small war pension and Susan's dancing money, they got by, but they were always one missed rent payment away from destitution. Susan insisted that she had no interest in marrying, and Ivy was of the same mind, but how long could two young women realistically survive in a world that closed all the doors to employment to them? Jobs were for the war heroes, the boys who came home. Women might have stepped in to do their bit during the war, but now that it was peacetime, it was back into the kitchens and bedrooms for them.

"You said I would be expected to live in Yorkshire?" Ivy managed to ask. The place brought to mind bleak moors and howling winds, summer heather and castle ruins. Romantic maybe, but far from everything that was familiar to her.

The shadow that flitted across the solicitor's face was quick, but Ivy caught it all the same. "Erm, yes. There is a stipulation in the will that the heir live on the premises."

"Is that normal in these types of situations?"

"It's a little unusual, but not unheard of. It won't be as daunting as it sounds. I believe prior to Lord Hayworth's death, the abbey was being used as an infirmary for the wounded in the war. Many landowners are finding that selling some of the land, or letting the buildings as hotels is more financially judicious. Of course, the house is not what it once was, but it is an abbey of some significance all the same. My firm would be more than happy to help you, perhaps by finding tenants for cottages. Regardless, it should be a pretty source of income for you."

Rain smeared down the window, casting London in dreary monochrome. Automobile horns blared at each other, and she could practically hear the disgruntled mutters of pedestrians navigating their way around ankle-deep puddles. Perhaps a change of scenery would be good for her. Her mother was buried in a small churchyard in Bethnal Green, and her father lay on some anonymous field in Europe where he had fallen. As for James, Ivy didn't know where he was. What did it matter if she mourned them from her flat with the peeling wallpaper, or a cold, empty estate in Yorkshire? She wondered why she had never heard of her relations before. Had the Hayworths lived like kings the whole time her family had been scraping by? Why had they never reached out? Had her parents even known about them? Well, Ivy intended to find out.

Nodding, she reached for the pen. "Where do I sign?"

Mr. Duncan's brows rose. "To accept the bequest? Are you certain you don't want to read everything first? I would hardly be doing my due diligence if I didn't make certain you understood exactly what you are signing."

But she shook her head. Reading the giant packet of papers would only give her time to second-guess herself.

With obvious discomfort at her rash decision, Mr. Duncan flipped through the pages, indicating the lines where she needed to sign. By the time she'd finished, her hand was cramped and smudged with ink.

She sat back in her chair, heart racing. Mr. Duncan scanned over the last of the papers before looking back up. "Congratulations, Miss Radcliffe. You're now Lady Hayworth, sole owner, proprietor, and heiress of Blackwood Abbey."

2

Thoughts as jumbled as the London traffic ran through Ivy's head as she bid Mr. Duncan goodbye and left the warm office. He'd sent her off with a small envelope containing a letter of introduction and enough money for train fare. Back in the rain with her shoes quickly soaking through again, it was as if the surreal meeting had never happened. A warm shop window boasting rows of books shone like a beacon in the dreary gray afternoon, stopping Ivy in her tracks. She lingered briefly, debating whether to go in and browse before meeting Susan. But books were dear, and if she didn't have the money for the soldiers, she certainly didn't have the money for something as frivolous as books. Perhaps once she was lady of Blackwood she would be able to afford books, fill a library with them. But until then, she would have to make do with what was left of her father's collection, which lived in a trunk beneath her bed.

Susan was waiting for her in the bow window of their favorite tea shop, a warm cup already in her hands. Ivy's friend was enviably untouched by the London weather, her dark bob immaculate, her light brown skin powdered and glowing. In a sea of dark coats and somber expressions, Susan stood out like a brightly plumed bird with her orange cloche hat and red lipstick. A quick glance at her reflection in the window told Ivy that her own blond bob was irreparably tousled, and no amount of makeup or clever styling would do anything for her drowned-cat appearance.

Ivy sat heavily down in the chair, her sopping coat dripping onto the linoleum floor. Steam curled invitingly out of a teapot, and Susan pushed a cup toward her.

"Bless you," Ivy said, gratefully wrapping her frozen fingers around the cup.

"Well?" Susan looked at her expectantly from kohl-lined eyes. "How did it go? What did the solicitor say?"

Ivy took a long sip of the hot tea, gathering her thoughts before responding. She was further spared having to answer right away by a diminutive woman drowning in a white apron, who set down a bowl of sticky toffee pudding with a clatter.

"Two spoons, if you please," Susan said.

The woman scowled. "It's thruppence for a second."

"Never mind, we'll share," Susan said breezily.

The woman stalked off, and Ivy accepted the spoon, dipping it into the sticky toffee and savoring the eye-watering sweetness.

"Well?" Susan prompted her after she'd relinquished the spoon. "What happened? What was the meeting about?"

"It seems…" Ivy paused, the situation still too extraordinary to be true. "It seems I've inherited an estate and title in Yorkshire."

Susan set her cup down, tea sloshing over the sides. "I'm certain I didn't hear you correctly. Say that again?"

"The solicitor said that I'm the last surviving member of the Hayworth family, and that I'm next in line for inheriting Blackwood Abbey in Yorkshire." Even saying the words out loud sounded preposterous. She was sitting in her favorite tea shop, talking with her best friend, and the streets of London marched on with their day. But she was not just Ivy Radcliffe anymore, she was the heir to an ancient name and title. Somehow, in the grand scheme of the universe, she was a lost puzzle piece that had finally found its place.

"Are you saying that you've been a duchess this entire time?"

"A viscountess," Ivy answered absently, stirring her tea.

Susan reached out and took Ivy's hand in hers, bringing her out of her thoughts. "Ivy, you're going to move to Yorkshire?"

Her friend's dark eyes shone with excitement, but there was also a shadow of something like hurt lurking there. Ivy brought her other hand to clasp Susan's. "I don't know yet, I think so. I…" She trailed off. How did she explain that the news had opened her eyes to the dark cloud under which she had been living these six years? Everything in London was a reminder of her sacrifices, of the family she had lost. She was not alone in her loss, but everyone here wore their grief like great overcoats, wrapped around them so tightly that they couldn't see each other. If Ivy stayed, her options were trudging to a job at a typewriter—that is, if the employment office deemed her worthy—or worse, shackling herself to a bore of a man. And that was if she could even find a husband; an entire generation of young men had been decimated, wiped clean off the earth. As for her dreams of continuing her father's work, well, no one would hire a woman to work in a university studying medieval manuscripts.

Across from them, a mother and her young daughter were sitting, sharing a plate of biscuits and sandwiches. The girl was rosy-cheeked and dressed in a darling pinafore, giggling when the milk from her cup clung to her upper lip like a little mustache.

Susan turned to see what Ivy had been looking at, then softened when she turned back. "Maybe there will be men there," she said. "Eligible men."

Ivy took a sip of her tea. "Maybe." But if there were no men in London, it was not likely that there would magically be any more in a tiny Yorkshire village. Not that she made much of an effort to meet anyone. Sure, she went to the occasional dances with Susan, but the men there weren't the serious type. Even if they were looking for something more than just a dance or a kiss behind a curtain, she suspected they weren't the sort she'd be happy spending her life with. Ivy had all but accepted that she would never have a family of her own, that her childhood had been an anomaly, and her one chance at happiness. Susan was the closest thing she had to family, and now Ivy was going to be moving across the country.

She squeezed Susan's hand. "Come with me," she said on impulse. "It would be good for you, for both of us. We can start fresh in Yorkshire. You know I'd be hopeless at running an estate, and you have such an eye for design and decorating."

Susan gave her a sad smile, slowly extricating her hand from Ivy's grasp. "You know I can't," she said. "My aunt is here, and she needs me. Besides..." Susan flicked her gaze to the window, where rain ran down in thick rivulets. "There are more opportunities in London for a single woman. What would I do in Yorkshire? Where would I go dancing? Goodness, can you imagine me doing the Charleston or Black Bottom in a village hall?"

Ivy had to concede the point. Susan was vivacious, loved dancing; she was made for the stage, trying new things and meeting new people. It was hard to imagine her thriving in a small Yorkshire town where nothing ever changed. The determination Ivy had felt holding the pen and scrawling her name on the line was quickly fading.

As if sensing her dwindling confidence, Susan patted her hand. "I'll come visit—you won't be able to keep me away. You're going to be brilliant, I just know it. I'll read about you in the society pages."

Ivy's lips kicked up into a weak smile. If only she had her friend's confidence in herself. She had thought that she would have felt lighter somehow, as if years of grief would have simply sloughed off her as she stepped out of the solicitor's office; after all, she was a new woman now, at least in name. But instead, she felt as if she'd just shackled herself to a dark and uncertain future, one where she would be completely alone with her ghosts.

3

As the London buildings rushed past, and heavy smoke clouds were replaced with trees and fields, Ivy struggled to settle into the plush train seat. Her book lay tented and forgotten on her lap as she stared sightlessly at the passing landscape. Just as with signing the will, her preparations had taken place at breakneck speed, so as to leave little room for creeping doubts or second guesses. Sparse belongings were piled into her trunk, enough money to cover the rest of the month's rent was left with Susan, and then she was off. Now Ivy was bound for Yorkshire, and the abbey that was to be her new home.

A man in a tweed suit sat across from her, his newspaper proclaiming in uppercase bold fonts that unemployment rates were going up, some insufferable nonsense about the Eugenics Society claiming that birth rates were dropping among desirable populations, and that there were rumblings of German discontent. Ivy swept her gaze back to the passing landscape, a patchwork of rolling green hills and meandering stone walls. When was the last time she'd been out of the city? It would have had to have been when she was a child, a family trip to Brighton most likely. Cramped lodgings in a flat shared with two other families. Salty bathing excursions and sweet ices shared on the pier. Back when she didn't know that they were poor. They had been together, and so they had been happy. Every mile that the train gobbled up was another mile lost between her and her memories, her mother's grave, her grief.

"Excuse me, miss?"

The sound of the man's voice snapped Ivy from her thoughts. "I couldn't help notice your book there," he said, nodding to the volume that lay forgotten in her lap. "What are you reading?"

The book was a battered copy of *Northanger Abbey*, gifted to her by James. It had seemed like an appropriate choice for the trip, given her destination. James had always encouraged her love of reading and respect for books. He hadn't been the bookish type himself, much preferring nature hikes and woodworking, but that was the wonderful thing about James—he was full of surprises, nothing like you would expect.

Ivy closed the book, tucking it under her arm. Sharing even the title felt like giving away a piece of her brother. "Nothing...just a book."

"Must not be a very interesting book, you looked as if you were miles away."

And yet you thought it a good idea to strike up a conversation with me, Ivy thought.

"I'm being terribly rude," the man said, sticking out his hand. "I'm Ted Martin." When Ivy didn't return the gesture, he raised his brows in a prompt. "And you are...?"

Ivy glanced down at her finger and the narrow gold band that she wore. It had been Susan's idea, of course. "A ring on your finger is as good as being invisible to a certain sort of man." She hadn't needed to elaborate which sort of man that might be. Grateful for the armor, Ivy managed a smile, and extended her hand so that the ring shone. "Mrs. Radcliffe," she said.

The shift in his demeanor was instant. "Mrs. Radcliffe, a pleasure," he said stiffly. "I hope I didn't bother you."

"Think nothing of it."

The last hour of the journey was spent in blessed silence, the steady chug of the train's engine a comforting background. Ivy's eyes were just drifting closed when the train began to slow, and the muffled voice of the conductor passed through the cars. Shaking herself awake, she peered out the window. A heavy mist wreathed the land, but dark stone spires were just visible, piercing the clouds.

"Where are we?" she asked the man across from her.

He ducked his head, squinting out the window. "Blackwood," he told her. "That's the old church. Gloomy old town, I wonder that they even have a train station." He looked surprised when Ivy rose and began to gather her bags. "I hope your husband is meeting you at the station," he said, a glint of accusation in his eyes. "Nasty weather for a woman to be out alone."

"I'll be fine, thank you for your concern," she said curtly. Would she though? She had assumed that there would be cabs, but as the small station grew closer, it seemed unlikely.

The porter helped her off the train with her bags and trunk, then gave her a short nod. "Good luck, miss," he said, before hopping back on the steps of the slowly chugging train. Ivy frowned, not certain why he thought she would need luck. Only a handful of other passengers had disembarked, and already they seemed to have faded into the mist, meeting loved ones and being whisked away in automobiles. A lone bench sat in front of the station, a closed kiosk boasting of ices and cakes shuttered beside it. Susan had been right: this was a far cry from London.

"Lady Hayworth?"

It took her a moment to realize that whoever was speaking, was speaking to her. She was Lady Hayworth now, the last living member of an ancient and revered bloodline. Ivy spun around, coming face-to-face with a white placard bearing her name. She slowly raised her gaze, traveling up until she met the eyes of the man holding the sign. He was tall with a strong, stubbled jaw, and intensely dark gray eyes. Dressed in a duster coat, muddy boots, and a wide-brimmed hat, he looked more like a highwayman than a chauffeur.

"You're Lady Hayworth, aren't you? I'm here from Blackwood Abbey, to collect you."

Her shoulders slumped in relief. Of course she didn't need to worry about a cab or making her way to the abbey by herself; she was mistress of a great house now, and as such an auto would be sent round for her. "Oh, yes."

The man gave a curt nod, tucking the sign beneath his arm as he leaned down to collect her luggage. She didn't have much—just her trunk of books, a valise, and a carpet bag with her clothes. All the same, she resisted the urge to help him; a woman of her class wouldn't be expected to carry her own luggage.

But when she noticed him walking with a pronounced limp, Ivy hurried to relieve him of one of the bags. Up close, he smelled like coal smoke and leather and windswept moors. "Here, let me manage that one at least," she said, grabbing her valise.

His grip on it tightened. "That won't be necessary," he said gruffly, and she got the impression that she had injured his pride. Limp or no, his long strides still accounted for every two of hers, and she had no choice but to jog to keep up with him.

The car that waited outside the station was black and sleek, and looked as if it had been recently polished. The chauffeur opened her door, then loaded her luggage into the back. A moment later they were rolling out onto the cobbled street and Ivy craned her head to see out the window. "Pity it's so foggy out—I would have loved to see more of the town."

She caught him glancing at her in the rearview mirror. "You won't see much of the sun this time of year," he told her. "Fog and wet is what we have here in Blackwood." His Northern accent was thick and deep, musical, but hard to understand.

Disappointed, Ivy sat back in her seat, the little village crawling past them as the rain picked up. "I'm so sorry," she said suddenly, "I'm afraid I didn't catch your name?"

The dark brows in the mirror rose. Was a lady of the house supposed to ask for the chauffeur's name? She wasn't certain, but it seemed rude not to.

"Ralph," he said shortly.

"Your full name, Mr...?" she prodded.

A heavy pause. "I go by Ralph."

His tone didn't invite further conversation, so Ivy pretended to be absorbed in the shrouded landscape that they passed. They had left the jumbled streets of the village, and were now winding along a lonesome road, broody moors stretching out around them, the only landmarks the occasional crooked tree or cairn of old stones. She would have almost certainly been miserably lost if she'd had to find her own way.

By the time they pulled up to a gravel driveway, the rain was coming down in sheets. So much for exploring the grounds of the abbey. The car came to a stop in front of an imposing facade with marble steps, chimneys disappearing into the gray sky. Through the rain and the mist, Ivy was able to make out the impression of a heavy fortress made of dark stone with rambling additions. It must have once been a staunch defender of civilization amidst the moors, though it appeared a weary sentry, with its crumbling stones and overgrown grass. From the crenelated windows to the stately battlements, it certainly delivered everything that a Gothic abbey ought to. Yet it was a graceful decline, dignified and suited to a castle on the wild moors.

Ralph turned off the engine, then jumped out, flipping up the collar on his coat. "I've no umbrella," he said as he opened her door. "You're going to have to make a run for it."

Used to navigating the rainy streets of London, Ivy held her scarf over her head and made a dash for the marble steps. Behind her, Ralph followed with the luggage. Just as Ivy was about to pull on the iron knocker, the door swung open, revealing an older woman in a navy-blue service dress looking as startled as she.

"Oh, forgive me, my lady! I didn't realize you had arrived. I was just coming with an umbrella to meet you." She stepped aside, her long skirt skimming the stone floor.

Ivy hurried inside, grateful to be out of the rain, though the chill of the November day seemed to be just as pervasive in the house as it was without. Inside was much like the outside, opulent on a grand scale, but fraying at the seams when inspected closely: tapestries worn, carpets patched, and chandeliers missing candles. Behind Ivy, Ralph set down her luggage with a heavy *thud*.

The woman closed the door behind him, before turning back to Ivy. "Welcome to Blackwood Abbey, my lady. I'm Grace Hewitt, head housekeeper."

Everything about the woman was neat and tidy, from her tightly coiled dark hair to her crisply ironed dress. If not for the firm set of her lips and slightly aloof gaze, she would have looked almost motherly.

Ivy stuck out her hand. "How do you do, Mrs. Hewitt?"

Looking at the outstretched hand as if Ivy had offered her a slimy toad, the older woman reluctantly returned the gesture. Ivy added not shaking hands with the service members to her list of things she wasn't supposed to do now that she was a lady.

"You'll have to excuse me," she said, shoving her hands in her cardigan pockets. "I'm not used to any of—" she broke off, looking about the grand hall "—this. I hope that you'll help me find my footing at Blackwood. I clearly have a lot to learn."

It was the right thing to say. Mrs. Hewitt gave her a tight nod, drawing up her chin with obvious pride. "I've served four generations of Hayworths," she said, "and I intend to provide you with the same unparalleled service. Begging your pardon, my lady, but how exactly are you related to the late Lord Hayworth?"

"He was apparently a distant cousin on my father's side. I never met him, and didn't even know we were related until the solicitor informed me that I was his only heir."

Mrs. Hewitt's lips pressed tighter. For some reason, this did not seem to be a satisfactory answer. "I see. Well, there will be time for all these details later. Ralph," she said, looking past Ivy's shoulder to the doorway. "Take Lady Hayworth's luggage to the blue room, won't you? Just follow Ralph, he'll show you the way," she told Ivy. "I will give you a tour of the abbey, as well as introduce you to the rest of the staff once you are changed from traveling and settled in. I'll have Agnes bring up some tea in the meantime."

With that, Mrs. Hewitt was gone in a swish of skirts, her heels clicking away down some unseen corridor. Feeling as if she'd failed some sort of test, Ivy turned to see Ralph gathering up the luggage again. Now that he had shed his hat, she could see the gold threaded in his brown hair, the way the lamplight caught shifting flashes of gray in his dark eyes. He couldn't have been more than a couple of years older than her—James's age, had her brother lived.

"Follow me, my lady," he said gruffly.

"I really wish you would allow me to help," Ivy said, hurrying to catch up with him as he mounted the stairs. "I can certainly manage my own valise."

Ralph grunted. "Determined not to be a proper lady, are you?"

"I only became 'a proper lady' a few days ago with the stroke of a pen," she informed him. "And as I told Mrs. Hewitt, I have a lot of learning to do. Besides," she added, "I don't really believe in class distinctions." Perhaps it was her American heritage or her father's liberal views, but her parents had always been adamant about instilling in her the notion that the accident of one's birth should not determine their place in the world. They had been careful that while they had made sure she was literate and well-spoken, she never looked down on those who were not.

A snort, and it was clear that was to be the end of their exchange.

Despite Mr. Duncan's warning that the great house was in less than pristine condition, it was still easily the grandest place Ivy had ever been. The carpets might have been a little threadbare in places, and there was a persistent chill that clung to the echoing hall, but the marble staircase was magnificent, and giant tapestries in muted tones hung from the second-story gallery. Everything was neat as a pin, proof that Mrs. Hewitt did indeed take her job seriously.

They reached the second landing, and Ralph headed down a long hall, lined with heavy oil paintings and more tapestries. Goodness, there was even an armory, complete with mounted crossed battle-axes and silver suits of armor. Jane Austen would have no doubt found it all a little too on the nose for satire on abbey living.

Coming to an abrupt halt, Ralph nudged open a door with his knee, and then gestured Ivy inside. "This will be you, then," he said, dropping her bags at the foot of an ancient four-poster bed. "Water closet is through there, and bellpull right there will connect you to the kitchen if you need anything."

Entranced by the grandeur, Ivy moved through the room, gaping at the oil paintings that hung on the wall, the fine china basin and flocked blue wallpaper. Ralph made no movement to leave, rather, his gaze on her sharpened as she reached out to touch a velvet drape.

"I can't believe this is real," she whispered.

"You're married," Ralph said from behind her. There was no surprise in his voice, just a statement of fact.

"What?" She glanced down at the ring on her finger. "Oh, no."

Something like pity crossed his face, softening the hard lines of his jaw and brow. "A widow, then?"

"No, that is, I just wear it in town, so that men don't..." She felt her cheeks growing hot. Ralph was still fixated on the ring. Twisting it clumsily off her finger, she switched it to her other hand. Ralph had been in the war, that much was clear from his limp and the dark, glassy look that haunted his eyes. And here she was, pretending that she was a widow, so that she didn't have to talk to strange men.

Ralph looked back to the door. "Well, if that will be all, then..."

Belatedly, she realized he was waiting for her to release him. "Oh, yes, of course. Thank you, Ralph."

"No need to thank me," he said, his voice gruff. He looked only too grateful to finally escape her.

When the door had shut behind him, Ivy threw herself down on the bed. Susan would never believe this. The thought of her best friend brought an ache to her chest. Later, she would have to see if there was a telephone somewhere in the abbey and give the boardinghouse a ring. She let her gaze wander around her new room. Amidst all the grandeur and finery, though, there was a want for something familiar. At least London had boasted all the places she had shared her childhood with her family, but here was vast, unexplored territory that was void of memories and familiarity. Well, she would just have to make her own memories. After all, a fresh start was only fresh if one embraced the changes that came with it.

4

As easily as she could have fallen asleep on the soft bed after her journey, Ivy forced herself to get up and change into a fresh skirt and cardigan. She was certain Mrs. Hewitt had something else in mind when she'd suggested that she change, but Ivy was no grand lady, and these were her warmest clothes.

As promised, a few moments later there was a knock on the door and a dark-haired girl stuck her head in. "M'lady? I've brought tea," she said in a broad Yorkshire accent. "May I come in?"

Ivy beckoned her inside. The girl wore a blue service dress with a white pinafore and lace cap, the sort of outfit one would expect to see in a posh London tea house. Setting the tray carefully down on a table near the fire, she dropped a curtsy. "If that will be all, m'lady?"

"Yes, thank you." The girl turned to leave, but Ivy changed her mind. "Sorry, that is, would you stay a moment, please?"

Darting an uncertain glance at the door, the girl returned to the tableside. "Yes, m'lady?"

Ivy bit back the urge to tell the girl she didn't need to address her in such a fashion. "What's your name? And what is your position at Blackwood?"

"My name?" The girl wrinkled her nose as if she'd never been asked such a question before. "Agnes Miller. I'm an all-about maid. I live in the village and come in for day work."

So some of the staff just came in for the day. That would make sense, given that up until recently there had only been one person living in the old house.

"Do you like it here?"

Agnes shifted her weight in her leather work shoes. Ivy had a pair just like that. "I like it well enough, I 'spose. Never saw much of the old Lord Hayworth—he mostly kept to his room. During the war I came with me mam to help look after the soldiers. The abbey 'as a bit of a reputation around the village, but aside from being dark and gloomy, it's not bad."

"What kind of reputation?" Ivy asked, intrigued.

"Oh, I don't know," Agnes said, shifting her gaze as if she was sharing confidential information. "The usual sort of stories about spooks that rise up from an old place like this."

"Do we have a resident ghost, then? Or maybe more than one restless spirit?" She was half joking, but Agnes looked deathly serious.

"Bein' as it used to be an abbey, there's stories that the ghost of a monk haunts the house. Never seen anything of him myself, and I wouldn't pay them no heed if I was you, m'lady."

Ivy gave the young maid a smile. "I won't. Thank you, Agnes."

After Agnes had beat a hasty retreat, Ivy poured herself a cup of tea, and, wrapping her hands around the warm cup, ventured out to explore her new home.

Some of the doors along the corridor were locked, but most opened easily, revealing bedrooms with furniture draped in white dust sheets. When it became clear that most of the upstairs rooms were vacant, she made her way back downstairs to the great hall where she had first entered the house. Mrs. Hewitt had turned on the lamps, and even though it was still dark Ivy could see how the abbey could be a comfortable, even homelike place with the right touches. It still seemed surreal that she was the one responsible for those touches now. So many of these grand old estates seemed not to have survived the war, or had been converted into hotels as Mr. Duncan had said. The weight of the responsibility to keep the abbey running settled heavy on Ivy's shoulders. Where would she even start to learn about the duties and protocols that guided her new station in life? She didn't know the first thing about overseeing a staff or keeping accounts of a large estate.

Leaving the hall behind, Ivy chose the right-hand corridor, following a wide hallway lined with more paintings and empty vases until she came to the dining room. Generations of Hayworths peered down at her from their heavy gilded frames, some in fancy ruff collars, others in romantic gowns with windswept landscapes behind them. She shivered under their haughty gazes. *So, this is the girl to whom all of our fortunes have led,* they seemed to say as they looked down their noses at her. Hugging her tea, Ivy tried to imagine the cold room once boasting great feasts and parties, glittering with crystal and filled with lively conversation. Now the chairs were covered in dust sheets and pushed up around the edges of the room, no longer needed for entertaining on a grand scale.

Retracing her steps to the hall, this time she took the corridor branching off to the left. This was where she had seen Mrs. Hewitt disappear. The hall came to an abrupt end, with only two options leading off of it; one was a narrow staircase that presumably led down to the kitchen and cellar, and the other was a heavy set of double doors.

There was a low humming emanating from behind them, as if a machine were running, or perhaps it was the buzzing of electricity. She tried both handles of the ornately carved doors, but they were locked fast. Pressing her ear against the wood, Ivy strained to hear better. It was so faint, just the suggestion of sound, that she wasn't certain if she were really hearing something at all, or if it was just the heightened buzzing of silence. She shook the handles again, putting all her weight into it. They didn't budge. She would have to ask Mrs. Hewitt for all of the house keys if she wanted free run of her new home.

Downstairs, Ivy followed the sound of voices to the kitchen, where she found Mrs. Hewitt, Ralph, and an older man sitting around a long, rough-hewn table all drinking tea. Mrs. Hewitt was knitting, her needles flashing fast and sharp. At Ivy's entrance, they all bolted up, Ralph taking a little longer to get to his feet.

"Oh, I'm so sorry, I hope I didn't interrupt your tea."

"Quite all right, my lady," Mrs. Hewitt said with a tight smile. "I was just going to fetch you, but it seems that you've already taken it upon yourself to explore."

"Yes, I was anxious to have a look around."

"I was just leaving," Ralph announced, more to Mrs. Hewitt and the man than to Ivy. "There's wood needs chopping out back."

Ivy stepped aside from the doorway as Ralph's sleeve brushed her on his way out. He gave her a nod and then was gone.

Mrs. Hewitt turned to the man, a hand on his arm. "My lady, this is Hewitt, head butler of Blackwood Abbey."

The spare, graying man gave a short bow from the waist. He had a neat mustache, and impeccable posture, the picture of British dignity and comportment. "A pleasure, my lady. I hope you will let us know if there is anything we can do to make you feel more at home here at Blackwood."

So, the butler and head maid were married. Ivy wasn't sure if that was standard practice in a house like this, but she liked the idea of it. Mrs. Hewitt was far from welcoming, but Hewitt had a certain warmth about him, and for the first time since setting foot in the old abbey, she allowed herself to feel as if this might really be her home.

"Thank you, I certainly will," she told the butler.

He gave her another short bow, and then excused himself, leaving Ivy with Mrs. Hewitt and the remnants of the servants' tea.

"Since you are here now, would you care for a cup of tea?"

Ivy looked down, realizing she was still clasping her cup, the contents now cold. "A top-off would be lovely."

She seated herself at the table, and Mrs. Hewitt poured her a fresh cup. A clock in the corner ticked, and somewhere outside a rooster crowed. Though the kitchen was large, it felt cozy, a far cry from the damp, echoing house above it. Through the small ground-level window she could see Ralph heading out onto the grounds, an ax in hand. Ivy nodded toward the retreating figure. "I didn't realize Ralph did more than just driving."

"We all do more than strictly our roles, otherwise nothing would get done," Mrs. Hewitt said. Her tone made Ivy feel as if she didn't understand what a hard day's work entailed. "Ralph drives, tends the horses, and does most of the groundwork. He's a good lad," Mrs. Hewitt added, her eyes softening.

Ivy thought of the way that he had rebuffed her help, and then his concern when he assumed she was a widow, and shame flushed through her anew. "He fought, didn't he?"

Mrs. Hewitt, her back already plank-straight, seemed to stiffen further. "Yes," she said shortly. "He did."

"Where did he serve? How was he injured?" She knew she was overstepping polite conventions, but in the absence of answers about her own family, every story, every anecdote helped her understand what James and her father had gone through. It felt like they had all been in a story together, a book, but her father and brother had gotten to the ending without her, and she needed to fill in the blank pages.

A long moment stretched out before Mrs. Hewitt finally answered. "The Somme," she said. "And he was injured by a mine. But never ask him about it," she hurried to add. "He doesn't remember, and it would only serve to upset him."

"Of course not," Ivy murmured. "Mrs. Hewitt," she asked suddenly, "is there a telephone here I might use? I'd like to make a call."

The housekeeper looked surprised. "Telephone? Of course not. Whatever need would we have for a telephone?"

Ivy could think of quite a few things, but decided to keep them to herself. She had so badly wanted to hear Susan's voice, to let her know that she had arrived safely. "Do you know where I might find one?"

"I believe the post office in town has one."

So another car ride to the village would be required. The sky was already darkening; it would have to wait until tomorrow. "Very well. Would you be kind enough to show me about the abbey now?"

"Of course," Mrs. Hewitt said, rising stiffly. "If you will follow me."

Mrs. Hewitt gave her a cursory tour below stairs, including the old servants' quarters and an empty wine cellar. "There is no need for you to plan menus or advise on meals. We have a plain cook from the village come every morning and make a hot breakfast and prepare a simple luncheon. Dinners are prepared by myself," Mrs. Hewitt told Ivy over her shoulder as they made their way up the stairs. "We have simple fare here, however, it is your prerogative as lady of the house to change something if it isn't to your liking."

"I'm sure it's all wonderful," Ivy murmured, just grateful that she didn't need to ever worry about where her next meal would come from. At the top of the stairs, Mrs. Hewitt made to go straight, but Ivy stopped.

"What room is behind those doors?" she asked, gesturing to the double doors ahead of them. "I thought I heard something in there."

"Nothing of interest," Mrs. Hewitt said without turning. "You must have imagined it. It was used as an infirmary during the war. If you will follow me this way, we'll pass through the main hall and go to the dining room."

The infirmaries in London had been overcrowded, soldiers lying on the ground when no bed was available, and diseases tearing through the wards with horrifying efficiency.

"What soldiers came here?" she asked. "I mean, how were they chosen?"

"Heavens, how should I know," Mrs. Hewitt said. "Come along this way, if you will."

A shiver ran down her spine. Luxurious or not, it had still been an infirmary and it was possible that men had died behind those doors. With one last lingering look, Ivy fell into step behind Mrs. Hewitt who was setting a brisk pace.

"The original structure dates back to the thirteenth century, when it was founded as a nunnery and then a Cistercian abbey, and is listed in the Domesday Book. After the dissolution of the monasteries, King Henry VIII bestowed it upon the Hayworth family."

They arrived in the great hall, and Mrs. Hewitt pointed out some of the more notable portraits.

"Where is the late Lord Hayworth?" Ivy asked her. She was more than a little curious about her predecessor, the man who supposedly provided her delicate link to this illustrious family.

Mrs. Hewitt led her to a modestly sized portrait of an average-looking man with graying hair and a receding chin, perhaps in his middle forties. Nothing about him looked particularly aristocratic, and there was certainly no family resemblance to the Radcliffes.

"How did he die?" she asked.

After a heavy moment of silence, Mrs. Hewitt began walking again. "Dementia," she said. "Now, over here we have the Bordeaux tapestries. These tapestries have been in the abbey since Sir Gerald Hugh Hayworth brought them back from a campaign in the seventeenth century. I don't suppose you care much about the history, so I won't bore you with the particulars."

"On the contrary—I am very interested in medieval history," Ivy told her, excitement bubbling up. "My father was a professor and I find this all terribly interesting."

Mrs. Hewitt's lips pressed into what Ivy was beginning to suspect was the only line of defense against some rather cutting words. "Of course you do," she said, as they continued to the dining room.

"Is this where Lord Hayworth took his meals?"

"He took his meals in his room toward the end of his life," Mrs. Hewitt told her. "Of course, you are free to do the same if you choose. Hewitt will be happy to arrange it."

Grateful that she wasn't expected to eat by herself in the echoing room, Ivy murmured her assent.

"This has always been the family's preferred sitting room," Mrs. Hewitt said, leading her into the parlor through the sliding door. It was comfortable enough, with a large fireplace lined with bookshelves, and heavy red velvet drapes. Yet Ivy couldn't see herself sitting in one of the overstuffed chairs on a rainy evening, reading or composing a letter. It was still larger than any single place she had ever lived, and it would just be her, alone.

"Is there a gramophone or wireless?" she asked hopefully.

"I believe there's a gramophone somewhere, but it hasn't been used for years," Mrs. Hewitt answered. "There is no wireless."

"Maybe we could purchase one." The idea of living in the great abbey with no music, no friends, no sound other than the driving of the rain and howling wind was becoming increasingly disheartening.

Mrs. Hewitt turned to Ivy, her face etched in hard lines. "You will find that I run a very tight ship here, my lady. We operate on a threadbare budget, and are happy to do so, but there is no room for frivolous purchases. If you are interested in making improvements, might I suggest flower arranging or perhaps reupholstering some of the furniture."

Brought back down to earth, and by her housekeeper no less, Ivy kept quiet for the rest of the tour. After a time, all the endless halls and empty rooms blurred together, and she was fairly certain that she would never remember how to get anywhere in the abbey. They ended back by the great stairs, and Mrs. Hewitt stood with her hands clasped in front of her waist. "I hope that you will be comfortable here, my lady, and that you will be satisfied by the service of myself and the rest of the staff. If you need anything, you may always ring for one of us. Now, I must get back downstairs to see about dinner. I will have Agnes bring you up a tray at eight."

Before Ivy had a chance to thank her, Mrs. Hewitt turned on her heels and clicked away down the hall.

Slowly, Ivy made her way back upstairs to her room. The tour, rather than making her feel at ease in her new home, had overwhelmed and somehow disappointed her all at once. How was she supposed to fill her time now that she not only didn't have to work, but was expected to live a life of leisure? She didn't care for the blood sports that the aristocracy seemed to favor, and she had no friends here with which to host gatherings. She didn't like the feeling of being watched, whether it was from the portraits or empty suits of armor, and she didn't like feeling as if she was simply the latest tenant to an indifferent landlord. She was mistress of her own house—and not just any house, an *abbey*—so why did she feel instead as if she was a prisoner?

A tap at the door, and Ivy eagerly went to answer it. Maybe it was Agnes, she would keep her company. But when she opened the door, there was no one there. She stood, staring out into the empty hall.

"Hello?"

There was no answer, but there was a heaviness in the air, as if someone were just out of sight, watching her.

Ivy gave the empty hall one more sweeping gaze, then quickly closed the door and threw her body weight against it as if that would keep out whoever had knocked. It had probably just been one of the servants moving about in a room down the hall.

Then came an icy gust sweeping across her skin.

Every hair along her neck lifted, and in the stillness that followed she was hyperaware of the texture of the carpet, the condensation gathering on the windowpanes. For a moment everything stood still, the air charged with quavering energy. Something was wrong, very wrong. She knew it the way a roe deer knows when it is in a rifle's cross hair before a shot is even fired.

Then in the time it took her to blink an eye, a hairbrush flew off the vanity, whizzing past her ear and slamming into the wall. It clattered to the ground, the silver handle glinting as it rocked back and forth gently until it came to a complete stop.

Heart pounding loud and hot in her ears, Ivy yanked the door back open and threw herself into the hallway, running at breakneck speed.

When she reached the stairs, she let her body sag against the marble balustrade and gulped down huge breaths of air. The unicorns and lions in the dark forests of the tapestries regarded her with unsympathetic eyes. How did one explain a hairbrush flying across the room? And how was she supposed to set foot in her room again, let alone sleep there? There had to be dozens of bedrooms in the house; she would ask Mrs. Hewitt about preparing another one and moving her things.

With shaking legs, Ivy made her way downstairs. She would have given anything to be back in her old room, sharing a bed with Susan, teasing her about her icy feet. But instead, she was trapped in an old house with an indifferent staff, nothing to fill her time, and the uncanny feeling that she was sharing her home with something that very much wanted her gone.

5

The nightmares were always the same.

A ditch, dirt pouring down from above her, unable to grasp the fingers that desperately reached out from the soil. Muffled voices begging for help. A London hospital, the floors slick with blood, each sickbed occupied by a skeleton eternally waiting for a nurse that would never come. Searching for the face of her brother, a telegraph clutched in her sweating hands. *Missing in action*, it says. But every time she leans over a bed, the sheet falls away to reveal a tangle of disembodied limbs, blood everywhere. Then she awakens with a gasp, sweat trickling down her neck.

From somewhere just beyond Ivy's consciousness a clock struck the hour, and she was released from her nocturnal torments. Any moment Susan would flounce in and jump on the bed, tickling Ivy awake and demanding that she get up and read the morning gossip pages with her.

A rooster crowed. *Why was there a rooster?* When Ivy cracked her eye open, it wasn't the water-stained walls of their room that greeted her, but the mahogany posts of a grand bed, and walls with decadent blue wallpaper. A seam of dim light shone through the gaps in the heavy velvet drapes.

She sat up. She was in Blackwood Abbey, and she was no longer Ivy Radcliffe, but Lady Hayworth.

Her head felt fuzzy, as if she'd had too much to drink. Swinging her legs out of bed and going to the window, she drew back one of the heavy curtains. A gray, blustery day greeted her, the shrubs and trees surrounding the estate swaying in the wind, white sheep dotting the rocky green landscape beyond. The pressing sense of dread from her nightmare lingered, like a heavy weight sitting in her stomach.

A knock at the door brought her back into the present, and a moment later Agnes was wheeling in a cart with silver-domed trays. "Good mornin' m'lady," she said as she brought the cart to the foot of the bed. "Cook 'as sent up some nice hot breakfast for thee."

Removing the silver lids, Agnes revealed plates of kippers, eggs, porridge, and thick slices of country toast. Ivy's mouth watered. No more breakfasts of thin oats and tinned herrings for her.

"Thank you, Agnes," she said as she pulled on a cardigan over her nightgown and helped herself to a plate. Agnes bobbed a curtsy and turned to leave. "Wait." Ivy stopped her. "Will you stay a little? Have some tea with me?"

Surprise and unease warred on the girl's face, but she took a tentative seat on the edge of a chair, and accepted the cup that Ivy held out to her. Ivy desperately wanted to tell her about the hairbrush and how it had flown across the room, but she didn't want Agnes to think her foolish. Instead, she said, "I was thinking of going into town today. I don't suppose there are any bookshops?"

Ivy wasn't exactly clear how her new finances operated, but she still had her pension and, if nothing else, now that she didn't need to worry about room and board she could use that money for books and other luxuries that she had thus long gone without.

"Oh, no, m'lady. We don't have anything like that here." Agnes tilted her head in consideration. "Munson, two towns over, now I 'appen they might have one."

Of course, a little town like Blackwood wouldn't have a bookshop. "Well, no matter," Ivy said brightly. "I'd still like to explore the village." She turned her attention back to the toast, slathering it with butter and trying not to eat too fast in front of her maid.

"If that will be all, m'lady?"

"Oh, yes, thank you, Agnes," Ivy said. "There's no need for this 'my lady' business," she added. "Between you and me, I'd much rather just be called Ivy." Agnes couldn't have been that much younger than her, and aside from an unbelievable stroke of good fortune, not much separated them.

Agnes looked uncomfortable at the request, but nodded. "If you insist, m'lady. I mean, Ivy."

Ivy offered her an encouraging smile. "I'd like that, thank you, Agnes."

With a hurried curtsy, Agnes hastily collected the dishes and disappeared with the cart.

After washing and dressing, Ivy made her way downstairs. She had kicked the hairbrush under the bed, unable to bring herself to handle it after what she'd witnessed. Her hair was short enough that she could run her fingers through it, pin it back without too much fuss.

The house was quiet. It must have been a lonely existence for Lord Hayworth when he was living here. An old man with dementia and a skeleton staff that seemed more concerned with keeping to themselves than anything else. She wondered how he had passed his time, if he had moved with ease through his aristocratic life, or if he had been cowed by the legacy that he carried.

Mrs. Hewitt had said that she thought there was a gramophone somewhere, so Ivy made her way to the north wing where most of the rooms were used for storage. The sheer scale of the abbey still astounded her. It must once have been a dynamic home, bustling with servants and families full of children and governesses. And before that it would have been busy in a different sort of way, with monks gliding silently down the halls, bells chiming, hymns drifting across the lawn.

After a few minutes of trial and error, Ivy found the old ballroom. Aside from the mysterious double door downstairs, few rooms in the abbey were locked. The door creaked open, and she tiptoed in, as if she might be interrupting some ghostly soiree. The ancient curtains were mercifully pulled back, allowing in what little daylight there was. Like most of the other rooms, the ballroom was largely empty, with its remaining furniture pushed to the sides and draped in sheets.

The air was stale and heavy with dust as Ivy carefully navigated the shrouded shapes. Snagging her stocking on a protruding nail, she cursed; stockings weren't cheap, and she only had three pairs to her name. She was just bending to inspect the damage when behind her the door swung closed, and there was the soft patter of footsteps.

Ivy spun around. "Hello? Mrs. Hewitt?"

No one answered; the room was just as empty as it had been when she'd come in. She shuddered. She wouldn't have been surprised if there were rats or something even bigger like feral cats in an old wing of a house like this.

But there was no scurrying of paws, no animal squeaks. The hairs along her arms stood up, and the story Agnes had told her about the monk that supposedly haunted the abbey came back to her. Here, in this distant wing of the house with the moaning wind outside and stillness pressing around her, it was easy to imagine herself in the company of ghosts.

She stood frozen, waiting for something though she didn't know what. Her breath came in deep, even measures, her ear trained on the door. Gradually, when her legs were starting to grow stiff and numb, the sensation faded. She was on edge, jittery from the hairbrush, and now she was imagining things that weren't there. The more she thought about it, the more she wasn't even certain it hadn't been a dream.

Returning to her search, Ivy gently lifted the cloth from a hulking shape and was rewarded with an old gramophone. It was dusty and needed a good polishing, but it looked to be in working order. She would have to enlist Ralph or Hewitt to help her move it into the other wing, but already she was in a better mood, anticipating being able to listen to some music.

Wiping her dusty hands on her skirt, Ivy retraced her steps back to the door and gave it a good yank. God only knew how it had managed to swing itself closed in the first place.

Turning down the hall, Ivy nearly collided with Mrs. Hewitt.

"Oh! Excuse me, my lady." Her gaze dropped to the dust on Ivy's skirt. "Doing some exploring, were you?"

"I found the gramophone."

"Did you now." Mrs. Hewitt looked less than pleased. "Well, if you'll excuse me, I should be getting back downstairs." She moved to step around her, but Ivy stopped her.

"You're actually just the person I was hoping to see," Ivy said.

Mrs. Hewitt's look turned wary. "Is there something I can do for you?"

"I'd like a different room."

"Is your room not to your liking? I assure you it is by far the best room in the abbey, and I oversaw the cleaning of it myself. If—"

"No, it's not that. It's…" Ivy tried to put her thoughts in order, squirming a little despite herself under the housekeeper's steely inspection. "It's just that, there was an incident."

"An incident?" Mrs. Hewitt repeated, her brows raising.

"Yes. That is, a hairbrush. It went…it flew across the room."

There was no amount of confidence that would make the assertion sound dignified, or anything short of sheer fantasy. But Ivy waited anyway for Mrs. Hewitt to respond.

After a painfully long pause, Mrs. Hewitt sighed. "My lady, I'm not sure what you saw, or what you think you saw, but a different room will hardly change it. Of course, if you insist I will air out another room and have Agnes clean it. We will have to wash the linens and scrub the water closet…" Mrs. Hewitt made a show of wringing her hands.

"All right, Mrs. Hewitt. Never mind all that." It was a battle that Ivy didn't think would benefit her in the long run. Maybe she had just imagined it, and even if she hadn't, Mrs. Hewitt was right; there was no guarantee that it wouldn't happen in another room.

"Very good," Mrs. Hewitt said, impassive once again. "Will there be anything else, my lady?"

"As a matter of fact, I was hoping to go into the village. I'm afraid the weather was too uncooperative the other day for me to be able to remember the way. Could you point me in the right direction?"

The housekeeper looked as if Ivy had suggested traveling naked on horseback. "You mean to walk? Oh, no, my lady. The way is much too long."

Ivy's heart sank as another little piece of her freedom fell away. "Surely I will need a way to be able to get about?"

"You can always ask Ralph, and he will drive you where you need to go."

Relying on the mercurial Ralph for a ride did not strike Ivy as ideal. But she gave Mrs. Hewitt a tight smile. "Do you know where I might find him?"

Mrs. Hewitt pointed her in the direction of the stables, and then continued down the hall, walking as if she couldn't get away fast enough.

Ivy found Ralph mucking out an empty stall, sleeves rolled to the elbow, sweat darkening the hair at his neck. Like the stables of most wealthy families, it must have once housed race-horses of the finest bloodlines, but was now home to only a couple of plow ponies, a donkey, a big brown nag, the other end converted into a garage for the abbey's autos. The animals swung their heads over the stall doors, greeting Ivy with soft snuffs and inquisitive, velvety brown eyes. Though she'd never ridden a horse, she'd always felt a sort of affinity with the carriage horses of London, wild creatures that were broken and shackled, forced to exist in a habitat far removed from the green pastures they were used to. Ivy put out a flat palm, and the mare nuzzled against it, soft lips searching for food.

"Can I do something for you, m'lady?"

Ivy startled, not realizing that Ralph had heard her come in. He was leaning against his rake, watching her with an interest that made her cheeks heat.

Returning to stroking the nag's long brown face, she focused on regaining control of her erratic heartbeat. "I didn't realize we had any horses at Blackwood. Are they riding horses?"

"No, Minnie here came from a slaughter auction," he said. "Her owner said she was ornery and wont to bite, but I think she was just in the wrong hands."

"Will you break her in? Put her to the plow?"

Ralph had come up beside her, and the mare transferred her attention, eagerly nuzzling into his palm. "I have no interest in breaking her," he said, running his hand over the horse's neck with long, soft, strokes. "But I will tame her, accustom her to the harness. She could make a fine lady's horse."

Realizing that he was looking at her, Ivy's blush stupidly deepened. "Oh, I can't ride."

"Mm. Well, I assume you didn't come here to pass the time with the horses."

"Yes, that is, I was hoping to go into the village. Mrs. Hewitt said you would—"

"I can drive you," he told her, fetching his cap from a hay bale and pulling it on.

"I'm so sorry to interrupt your work," she said as she hurried to follow him down the corridor and out into the mist. She was also sorry to leave behind the warmth; the stables felt safe and snug in a way that the abbey didn't.

His broad shoulders fell in a shrug. "Driving you *is* my work," he said without turning.

She bit her lip. Ralph was still dressed in his stable clothes, his boots muddy and pants smeared with dirt. "I can wait if you need to…that is, your clothes…"

At this he finally turned and raised a brow at her. It was the closest thing to a smile she had seen on him since coming to Blackwood. "Embarrassed by a little dirt on your chauffeur, are you, my lady?"

"What? No! Of course not. And you really don't have to call me that," she informed him, crossing her arms. "I'm not some high-born lady, you know."

Continuing his loping walk to the front drive, Ralph gave a shrug again. "If you say so, my lady."

Unsure of how she had somehow been made to feel as if

she was in the wrong, Ivy ignored the mocking bow Ralph executed as he opened the car's door for her.

They pulled up in front of a small stone building with a post box and bench outside. "Post is in there," he said nodding toward the building. "Pub is next door, and if you need any essentials there's a small shop across the road. I'll be here when you're ready to leave."

"You're going to wait in the car?"

"Aye. Take your time." With that, he leaned back in his seat, and pulled his cap down over his eyes.

"Well, now I won't be able to," Ivy grumbled as she got out of the car. Really, she was expected to do her errands while he waited for her like a dog? It felt as if she were being guarded, watched.

Leaving Ralph to his nap, Ivy took her time walking to the post office. Blackwood was quaint, the quintessential English village complete with banners for a harvest festival hanging over the main thoroughfare, and red-and-blue bunting fluttering in the breeze. Susan would have been horrified at the lack of cinemas and department stores. The thought of her best friend propelled her inside the post office, where the promise of a telephone waited. But after calling only to have Mrs. Beeton inform her that Susan was out, Ivy felt restless and defeated.

She returned to the car. "Would it be possible to drive to Munson?" she asked through the window. "Agnes said there was a bookshop there."

Ralph stared at her, his jaw set, and she was sure he was going to say no. But he gave a nod, and got out to open the door for her. This time the drive seemed much shorter, the landscape less alien now that she had seen it before. When traveling through London, there was always some spectacle, whether it was a policeman in a bare-knuckle fight with some street tough, a dog upending a cart of fruit, or a sea of grim-faced men in a labor march. Here, the landscape was vast and beautiful, but every crooked tree and rocky outcrop they passed looked the same. Brown heather and overgrown grass stretched endlessly with only the occasional farm or derelict gate to differentiate them. She tried to think of something to ask Ralph and start a conversation, but the yawning moors didn't spark so much as a question.

"Let me guess, you'll be waiting right here for me?" she asked as she got out in front of a small bookshop, the double-paned glass windows boasting rows and rows of books.

"Now you're getting it," Ralph answered, settling back into his seat, his long legs folded under the steering wheel.

"If I were you, I would bring a book with me at least. That way I would have something to do while I was waiting."

"You aren't me, thank God," he said with maddening nonchalance.

Insufferable, was what he was. Well, she wasn't going to waste any more time trying to strike up a conversation or a friendship; the promise of new books awaited.

Munson was still small by London standards, but it was infinitely more varied than Blackwood. Shoppers bustled along the streets, motorcars navigating around them. Several tea shops and restaurants boasted chalkboard signs advertising their menus. But most importantly, they had a *bookshop*, and so anything lacking could be easily forgiven.

The bell tinkled on the door, and Ivy closed her eyes as she stepped into the shop, the familiar scent of books and leather welcoming her. Whether it was London or Munson, it didn't matter, a shop full of books was a refuge, a quiet place away from the storm of the world. A spectacled man gave her a nod of welcome from behind a book-lined counter, and an orange tabby came and wound round her legs. With a sigh of happiness, Ivy began browsing the shelves, every once in a while taking down a book and tenderly flipping through the pages. She found herself in the local history section, searching for anything having to do with Blackwood and its abbey. If this was to be her new home, she wanted to learn as much about it as possible, and Mrs. Hewitt didn't seem eager to tell her much beyond the basics she had imparted during her tour.

A book of Norman abbeys and churches in the area caught her eye, and soon she was so lost in the pages, that she didn't notice the bell at the door, or the new customer that had entered.

"Keen to learn about local history?" The voice came from right beside her, and was polished and clipped, not like the broad Northern accents that surrounded her. When Ivy looked up, she found a well-dressed young man of about her age, standing close enough that she could smell his expensive cologne. He had a movie-star look about him, dark hair, defined jaw, and a confidence that could only come from having been raised knowing one could have whatever one wanted.

"I'm keen to learn about any sort of history," she replied, wary at this unexpected overture.

"A woman after my own heart." He flashed a brilliant smile, and stuck out his hand. "Sir Arthur Mabry. How do you do?"

"Ivy Radcliffe," she said automatically. "Well, I suppose now Lady Hayworth."

To her surprise, he didn't look the least bit nonplussed. She had expected that he would have scoffed or raised a brow at her usual workaday clothes. But he didn't bat an eye at her wool skirt or worn-in cardigan. Instead, he gave her a broad smile that illuminated his clean-cut face. "You don't say! A woman has inherited Blackwood Abbey!" Almost sheepish, he quickly added, "I apologize. It's only that my father was very good friends with the late Lord Hayworth, and we wondered who was next in line for the title."

"That would be me." She cast him a sidelong glance. Any other time she would have regretted taking off her gold band, but there was something inviting and easy about this young man, and truth be told, she was finding her new home to be a lonely place without the hint of a smile or friendly face. Besides, this wasn't a stranger on a train, this was someone who had come into a bookshop, seeking the same sort of refuge as she.

"Well, welcome to Blackwood, and I daresay, Yorkshire?"

"What gave me away?" she asked. "The accent, I suppose?"

"Might as well have a sign around your neck saying you're from London," he said, a wink gilding his bluntness. "What luck that we should bump into each other like this, and in a bookshop of all places. But I must say, I wouldn't expect the lady of Blackwood Abbey to be perusing a bookshop, not when the abbey boasts one of the finest libraries in the county, if not England."

The book she had been holding nearly fell from her hands. "The abbey has a library?" She was certain she hadn't seen one on Mrs. Hewitt's tour, and she definitely would have remembered if anyone had mentioned it. He couldn't possibly be referring to the few bookshelves that lined the fireplace wall in the parlor, could he?

A finely shaped brow arched. "It most certainly does. Don't tell me that you haven't seen it yet?"

"Well, no. That is, I only arrived the other day. I haven't had much time to explore." The house was large—huge, really—so it stood to reason that she wouldn't have seen every corner yet. But a library was hardly an old bedchamber or water closet. Why hadn't Mrs. Hewitt mentioned anything about it?

"You have an enviable task in front of you then."

"I haven't much else to do, so I suppose so." She hadn't meant her words to come out quite so pathetic sounding, but they were out before she could stop herself.

"I should say so." Sir Arthur was regarding her with a thoughtful tilt of his head, and she waited for him to excuse himself from the conversation. But instead, he surprised her. "Listen, if it's not too forward of me, I'd love the chance to show you around, introduce you to some of the society here in Yorkshire. I can't imagine what a shock it must be to come from London and be thrown into an entirely new life. What do you say?"

A loneliness that was deeper and older than she could fathom swirled and eddied around her, threatening to pull her down into its depths. Ivy, who wore the wedding band to avoid conversation. Ivy, who was content to share her world with only one other person. Ivy, who had never left her little corner of London. Is that who she wanted to be? She worried at her lip. What had started as an innocent conversation was quickly slipping past her control. But there was a hopefulness in Sir Arthur's voice, and he seemed genuine enough. Better yet, he liked books and anyone that liked books had to be, at the very least, a decent person.

He must have felt her indecision. "How about this—let's have lunch at the King's Head next Monday, right in the village. We can compare our reading lists and chat about the inanities of country life. If you find my company tolerable, perhaps we can go from there." He stuck his hand out. "Deal?"

Ivy found herself smiling at the young man in the bookshop who had successfully swept her off her feet. "Deal," she agreed, shaking his hand.

6

"Did you know that Blackwood Abbey has a library?" Ivy had hardly slid into the back seat and deposited her new stack of books on the seat beside her, when she bombarded Ralph with the question.

He started the engine, a jerky puttering that soon smoothed into purring as he shifted gears and pulled away from the shop. "Is that so?" he asked without the slightest hint of interest.

"Yes, apparently quite a grand one. I wonder that Mrs. Hewitt didn't mention anything about it," she added, more to herself. It had to be through those locked double doors at the far end of the hall—the only place Ivy hadn't seen for herself. Mrs. Hewitt had said that room had been used as the infirmary during the war. Maybe it had suffered damage or become disorganized, and the housekeeper hadn't wanted Ivy to see it in such a state. Well, no matter, she would assure Mrs. Hewitt that she didn't mind a little mess.

The car had barely rolled to a stop when Ivy threw open the door and let herself out, ready to find her library.

"M'lady. Wait."

Ivy turned to find Ralph standing beside the car, fidgeting his cap around in his hands. "Yes? What is it?"

Ralph glanced about as if checking to make sure no one was around, and then he was swiftly closing the distance between them, drawing her around the corner and out of sight of the front door. "What are you—"

Taking her by the shoulders, Ralph brought his face down to her level. His breath smelled like cinnamon, and his body radiated heat. Too stunned to resist, she stood there, letting him handle her as if she was a doll, and not lady of the house.

"Listen to me. You get out of here, my lady. Get as far as you can and don't come back."

His fingers dug into her shoulders, but she just blinked at him. "What?"

"It's only going to get harder to leave," Ralph told her. "You'll start forgetting, and then before you know it there will be nothing left of you. You should leave, today. Christ, I should have put you back on the train as soon as you arrived."

"What are you talking about? Ralph!"

Her voice seemed to snap him from his agitation, and he drew back, dropping his hands.

"I don't know what you're talking about, but you're never to touch me like that again. Do you understand?" Her face was flushed, her heart racing, and she didn't like the way that her skin was tingling where his fingers had been. "Do you understand me?" she repeated.

"Aye, I understand," he said darkly.

She hurried back to the house, but not without one last glance behind her. Ralph stood, hands in pockets, making no secret of watching her retreat.

Best not to dwell on whatever had just happened. She raced to the double doors at the end of the hall. They were locked, as she had expected. Finding the nearest bellpull, she rang for Mrs. Hewitt as if the house were on fire.

The poor woman appeared from thin air, wiping her hands on her apron. She looked around, bewildered. "My lady, are you all right?"

A little sheepish that she'd made such a fuss, Ivy cleared her throat. "I'd like to see the library, please."

Mrs. Hewitt blinked. "The library?"

Ivy faltered. Had Sir Arthur been mistaken? "I was told there was a library. I believe it's behind these doors."

"I see." Mrs. Hewitt had regained her composure, her back straight, her hands folded at her waist. "I told you, my lady—that room has not been opened in some time and is not in a fit state at the moment."

So there *was* a library. Her heart beat faster. "I won't be put off by a little dust, I promise you," Ivy told her. "I spent my childhood in libraries among some of the oldest, dustiest books."

Mrs. Hewitt looked as if she wanted to say something else, but Ivy preempted her. "Please open it, Mrs. Hewitt," Ivy said, in what she hoped was her most authoritative tone.

Irritation twitched at her lips, but Mrs. Hewitt heaved a sigh and rummaged for a key on her belt. Ivy held her breath as the housekeeper unlocked the doors, and slowly pushed them open.

It was dark inside, the only light coming from the fading twilight filtering through a set of tall, crenelated windows at the far end. Mrs. Hewitt swept inside first, fumbled at a switch on the wall, and a moment later dim electric lamps dotting the walls buzzed to life. Ivy sucked in her breath. Even in the poor light it was magnificent.

"Why is it kept closed up?" she asked without tearing her eyes from the soaring bookshelves that lined the walls.

Behind her, Mrs. Hewitt shifted, a floorboard creaking under her shoes. "There's no reason to keep it open. We don't have the staff to keep it dusted and in order."

Books sat spine to spine, all hues of red and green and deep brown leather, the occasional glimmer of dusty gilt titles winking in the dim light. Marble busts of great men sat sentry along the walls, their vacant eyes once white but now grimy and gray. It rivaled the libraries at Cambridge and London, and it was all hers. The air was a little stale and there was the unmistakable whiff of mildew, but it was hardly in the condition which Mrs. Hewitt had implied. It was not unfit, it was simply unused.

"Well, I think it's a shame," Ivy said. "From now on, please keep it unlocked. It doesn't matter to me if it's dusty or mildewed. I'll take care of it."

"Very good, my lady," Mrs. Hewitt murmured, though her tone indicated she thought it was anything but. "The electric in here is very old and unsound, and I would not recommend coming in after dark as the strain on the system could ignite a blaze. Candles are likewise a great risk of fire."

Ivy hardly heard her as she moved further into the library. This would be her safe haven at Blackwood, a domain in which she finally felt comfortable. The dark wood shelves and familiar smell of leather and paper wrapped around her, safe and cozy. Above her, a narrow gallery ran the length of the vaulted ceiling, a reminder of the building's ecclesiastical history. If she closed her eyes and breathed deeply, she could almost feel herself transported back through the centuries. Every book held not just the story written in its pages, but a secret history of the hands that had touched them, had loved them. Hers. This was all hers. A lifetime of learning and scholarship lay before her, something that would have otherwise been closed to a woman like her.

Though she wanted more than anything to start a fire in the fireplace and curl up with a blanket and a book, she felt a headache coming on and Mrs. Hewitt was waiting impatiently at the door, her hand hovering over the light switch.

"It's no wonder," Mrs. Hewitt said when Ivy mentioned her headache. "You've hardly sat still for more than five minutes since you got here. I will send your tray up shortly."

Throwing one last wistful glance at the library, Ivy followed Mrs. Hewitt out. She couldn't help but notice that Mrs. Hewitt discreetly turned back, locking the doors behind her after all.

7

Voices fade, photographs are just tricks of lights and mirrors, and touch is a passing phantom. But scent lingers, and even long after the last particle of someone's essence is gone, the faintest smell can bring all the memories rushing back.

If she closed her eyes and put her nose to the soft, pilled wool of her favorite cardigan, Ivy could just make out the merest suggestion of roses and lilies. In a cold, unfamiliar place, the cardigan was like wearing the warm embrace of her mother. But then, she couldn't really wear something with loose buttons and holes around the cuffs to dine with a peer. Slipping instead into a wool tweed skirt and her best blouse, she tied a kerchief over her hair and ventured out to the stables.

She tiptoed through the abbey, still feeling more like the proverbial city mouse visiting the country mouse than a lady in her own home. In London, she could walk everywhere or take the Underground, free and untethered in her anonymity.

But here she was isolated, and at the mercy of someone else if she wanted to leave. She again had the sensation that she was forever being observed, watched, though she supposed that was how ladies lived. She had exchanged the constraints of poverty for the gilded bonds of wealth.

In the stables, Minnie greeted her with a soft whicker, and hopeful eyes searching for a treat. To Ivy's immense relief, Ralph was nowhere to be seen. Ever since his bizarre outburst he'd seemed to be avoiding her. Luckily there was an old bicycle leaned up against the wall, a little rusty and cobwebbed, but with inflated tires and working pedals. Brushing away the webs, she wheeled it out of the stable, checking to make sure Ralph wasn't about.

The landscape that had whizzed by in a blur of dreary hills in the motorcar now crawled past her, and by the time she reached the village, her hair had come loose and her skirt hem was worse for the wear. Ivy hardly looked like a lady, but something told her that Arthur Mabry wouldn't mind. He was different from how she'd expected someone from the gentry to act, kind and warm, self-deprecating.

Wheeling the bike to the side of the pub, she leaned it against the stone wall and gave her hair a quick pat. Inside was warm and boisterous, much like a pub in London except most of the clientele were in waders and tweed caps. Old men lined the bar, ruddy noses deep in pints of ale and cider, and a spirited game of darts was taking place in the corner. Second after a library, a pub was a haven of warmth, and Ivy had always enjoyed spending an afternoon with a hot drink away from the polluted and cold streets of London. They might not have been strictly the most appropriate places for a woman, but as long as she and Susan had acted as if they belonged and didn't cause any trouble, no one had ever bothered them.

Sir Arthur was already seated at a table in the corner. Ivy

still had a chance to back out, to pretend she hadn't seen him and leave. In London, she never would have accepted the invitation of a strange man, so what was she doing here? Turning in his seat, he caught her eye and gave her a bright smile, putting an end to her last-minute plans of absconding.

He stood to greet her. "Lady Hayworth," he said with a warm handshake and an old-fashioned kiss on the knuckles. "A pleasure."

She'd had to haul out a dusty copy of *Burke's Peerage* the night before just to find him and figure out how to address him properly. "Sir Arthur," she returned, unable to keep her own lips from pulling up into a smile. It all seemed so absurd to be rubbing shoulders with the son of an earl, meeting for lunch at a pub as if they were old friends.

He moved over on the bench, but she sat on the chair across from him. He was terribly charming and friendly, but what did she really know about him?

Unfazed, he flagged down a middle-aged woman carrying a tray.

"Sir Arthur," the woman said by way of greeting. "We've missed you 'round here. Do hope your father is in good health?"

"You know the old man," he told her with a wink. "A Zeppelin couldn't carry him off."

When the woman had taken their order, Arthur leaned back in his seat, his posture carelessly elegant. He was dressed casually, in a well-cut suit and crisply starched collar. "How are you finding Blackwood?"

She chose her words carefully. "I'm in awe of its size and the grand scale of everything, so I'm also a little surprised by its lack of modern amenities." She leaned in and whispered, "Do you know, there's no wireless?"

Arthur leaned in to meet her. "How barbaric!" he exclaimed in mock horror.

Ivy Radcliffe of Bethnal Green, London was not a giggler, so she was more than a little surprised when she discovered that Lady Hayworth giggled at this. "There is a gramophone at least, though it hasn't been used in some time. I think I should have died if I couldn't have music in that drafty old house."

"Is Mrs. Hewitt still head maid? Tough old girl, that one," he said, with something like admiration. "Blackwood Abbey could use some young blood, shake things up a bit though."

The food arrived, two big plates laden with thick, golden chips and steaming hot pie. "So," Arthur said, as he tucked into his pie, "did you find your library after all?"

"I did," she said. "Mrs. Hewitt seemed very reluctant to admit me, and it was in a bit of disarray, but goodness! I never imagined anything so magnificent."

"It's something, isn't it? I daresay she wasn't keen on having to add it to her daily cleaning schedule." Arthur paused, his fork hovering over his pie. He started to say something, then closed his mouth again.

"What is it?" Ivy asked.

He gave her a self-conscious grin, then shook his head.

"Tell me!"

"Well, you're going to think me terribly rude or forward, or both."

"Maybe, but you won't know until you ask."

He gave a sigh and pushed his plate away as if she had him cornered. "The truth is, I would love to get into the library and see it for myself. My father speaks fondly of visiting years ago, and I'm terribly keen on old books."

Maybe it was the cider, warming her from the inside, or his good-natured conversation and earnest love of books. Either way, Ivy was inclined to agree to anything Arthur asked. "Of course, you must come and see the library," she told him. "You probably have a better understanding of what's in there than anyone else in the house, if your father has been there before. I would love to know more about it."

Arthur's dark eyes lit up. "I would be more than happy to be at your service in such an endeavor."

They ate, conversation and laughter swelling and flowing around them. Arthur was easy to talk to, and Ivy found her attention wandering to his face every time he became animated as they discussed books. It wasn't just that he was handsome—though he certainly was that—but there was a sparkle, an undeniable charisma about him. His conversation was soft and silky, a comfortable yet luxurious blanket that eased her mind and made her want to settle in and stay forever.

But then he grew somber as the subject shifted, and he started telling her about a memorial that the Munson village board was planning for fallen soldiers. "It's too easy for the world to forget, to move on," he said. "Our heroes should not be relegated to just names on a plaque, but it's better than nothing. There will be a large stone and a garden bed cared for by the Ladies' Auxiliary as well as several benches for quiet contemplation."

"Did you serve?" she asked cautiously. She'd learned to recognize the shuttered horror imprinted on the faces of returned soldiers, the reluctance to speak about the war, but she didn't see that in Arthur. He seemed altogether untouched by the grief and traumas of the world, a golden child in a bubble of light and laughter.

His eyes clouded. "No," he said bitterly. "A lung condition kept me from enlisting. Otherwise, I would have been at the front, showing those Krauts a thing or two."

She winced at his language. It prickled the pride of men not to be able to go fight, though Ivy wasn't sure why. She would have given anything for James to have had a medical excuse that kept him from being shipped off to some godfor-saken muddy field.

"My father is the soldier of the family, a decorated general," he continued. "It was always expected that I would follow in his footsteps, but..." He trailed off, pushing the potatoes around on his plate. "And you? Did you have anyone in the war?"

Ivy nodded, tears pricking behind her eyelids. It seemed that tears were always just one memory away. She pushed the lump in her throat down. "Both my father and my brother," she told him. "My mother died shortly afterward from the flu."

She felt rather than saw him nod. "So you're all alone," he said quietly. There was no pity in his voice, thank goodness, just a resigned statement of fact. "Tell me about them, about your childhood."

Thrown off guard by his direct question, she folded her fists into her sleeves, as if she could make herself smaller, beyond notice, like a turtle retreating into the safety of its shell. "Why?" she asked warily. "What do you want to know?"

He shrugged, downing the last of his pint and motioning for another. "To be frank, I've never met anyone like you," he said with an appraising gaze. "We've had vastly different lives, but something tells me we have more similarities than we have differences. Besides," he added, "I like you. I want to know more about the girl sitting across from me."

Arthur leaned forward on his elbows, his dark eyes locked on Ivy, and gooseflesh sprang up along her arms. Some of her reserve melted away under the warmth of that gaze. No one ever asked about her. Aside from Susan, no one ever really looked at her.

"Well," she said, drawing in a deep breath, "my father was a professor. I spent most of my childhood in the library with him, or at home helping him catalog and index his research sources. We managed well enough. It wasn't until he lost his job, that things became...difficult."

The day was still sharp in her mind, her father coming home, the whispered conversation between him and her mother in the kitchen while she pretended to be absorbed in her book. After that, it had been different. It wasn't the creeping poverty, but the emptiness in her father's eyes, the way he went through the motions of life, but didn't seem to be fully present. Whatever had caused him to lose his job was never spoken of, and Ivy could only imagine that it had something to do with her father's progressive way of thinking, his refusal to pander to the wealthy sons of peers who came through his classroom. Soon after that, they had lost the neat little lodgings in Cambridge, and moved to a dreary flat in Bethnal Green where her father tutored a handful of students, and her mother could take in laundry.

"My mother was an American, the daughter of a wealthy banker," Ivy continued.

Mina Radcliffe had thrown herself into the role of wife and mother and still had found time to campaign with the women's suffrage movement. Their home had been cozy and safe, a refuge. Mina had given up all the comforts of her old life, but she had forged a new one, where everything she did was for her children. The only relic of her old life that she had managed to keep was her harp, a big golden thing with twinkling strings that sat in the corner of the parlor. Ivy's father refused to entertain the idea of selling it, even when they were desperately in need of the money it could have brought in. Late at night, after the cooking and dishes and endless chores of the day were done, Mina would take her callused fingers to the strings and coax the most ethereal music from them. As a little girl, it had been like watching a fairy queen sitting on her throne and holding court.

"She was beautiful," Ivy added in a whisper.

"And your father?" Arthur gently prodded. "What was it he studied, exactly?"

"Medieval history, esoteric manuscripts in particular." There was more to it than that, but her father's work felt sacred, and she wasn't certain that Arthur would understand the intricacies of his brilliance. "There's even a manuscript he discovered named after him. He could read a dozen different languages, including dead ones. And he was generous with his knowledge, never put himself above anyone else. His students loved him."

"He sounds like an incredible man," Arthur said softly. "How lucky you were to have a father like that."

Ivy could only bring herself to nod. She had been lucky, but it had made the loss all the more keenly felt.

"I am not fortunate to enjoy such a relationship with my parents. My mother died when I was very young, and I am a great disappointment to my father." He was forging ahead, carelessly knocking back the rest of his drink before Ivy had a chance to absorb this strange turn of conversation. "He makes no secret of the fact that he believes I should have been at the front to see action."

She hesitated, parsing out the right words. "Does he really believe that, even with your lung condition?"

Arthur's expression hardened. "Of course he believes it, and he has every right to."

His response surprised her, and she paused, her glass lifted halfway to her lips. "What do you mean?"

"I was born to follow in my father's footsteps. I played soldier as a little boy, was in the Scouts. And of course I wanted to make my father proud, what son doesn't? But I was sick as a child, and my blasted lungs never recovered so now I have to live with the knowledge that I sat at home while my countrymen went out and sacrificed their lives. I would have given anything for that glory." He ran his finger over the rim of his glass, his fair face darkening.

Ivy's gaze skimmed over the people absorbed in their own conversations around them. She was unused to speaking confidentially with other people in the room. "War is not so glorious," she said, keeping her voice low out of habit. "I would have given anything for my father and brother to remain home. No one thinks of glory when they are in the mud, dying far away from everything and everyone they love."

Arthur regarded her for a long moment with an unreadable expression. "Well, we all had to do our bit, didn't we?"

Everyone had done their bit, and some more than others. Everyone had darned socks and knitted hats, rationed, and stood in bread lines. But some had also sent their brothers, their husbands, their fathers to the trenches to be injured or killed. Yes, Ivy had done her "bit," and then some.

"I've made you sad," he said, the clouds lifting from his face, his good humor returning. "You mustn't mind me. I daresay my father gets in my ear sometimes."

"Not at all," she said, only too glad to escape to a different topic. "May I ask you something?"

"I'm an open book," Arthur said, leaning back and spreading his palms. "Ask me anything."

"You said your father knew the late Lord Hayworth, did you ever meet him?"

"Oh, let's see. A handful of times, perhaps. Kept to himself mostly, and I believe he was quite sick toward the end of his life."

Ivy pushed her pie around, trying to hide her disappointment. They finished their meals in silence, until Arthur glanced at his watch. "I hate to do this, but my father is expecting me for a club meeting and I completely lost track of the time." He paused, running a speculative gaze over Ivy. "You should come."

There were only two kinds of clubs in London: gentlemen's clubs, and those that had drinking and dancing. Ivy had liked going dancing with Susan, but she had a feeling that wasn't what Arthur was talking about. "What sort of club?" she asked.

"Oh, it's all very informal. Just some of the scholarly-minded local gentry. We discuss literature and host lectures... that sort of thing. I can't say women usually attend, but then, you are something of an anomaly. I mean that in the most complimentary way," he quickly added. "I'm sure they would be very keen to hear about your father's work."

Ivy glanced down at her cycling attire, and then out the window where dark clouds were gathering. Discussing literature did sound lovely, but was she ready to take her place in a society comprised of earls, lords, and other aristocracy? How would they accept her, a young woman from the wrong part of London who had miraculously ascended to their class overnight? She didn't even have a fit dress.

"Another time, perhaps," she said, with a warm smile to let him know that the invitation was appreciated.

Standing, Arthur brushed her hand with a kiss. "Lady Hayworth, it was a pleasure. I look forward to exploring the library with you." He let his gaze sweep over her, then linger at her mouth, before excusing himself.

A rush of heat ran through her as she watched him weave around tables, all fluid grace, exchanging friendly greetings with some of the men at the bar. It had been a long time since a man had looked at her like that, and she'd forgotten the little thrill of it.

Retying her kerchief and slipping into her coat, Ivy left the warm pub, and hopped on her bicycle. Raindrops were starting to fall, and the few pedestrians in town were hurrying for cover. With any luck, she could make the ride back to Blackwood before it got worse.

But the gods were not on her side. Rain began to fall fast and heavy, picking up with breathtaking speed. Bloody brilliant. The ride into the village had been mostly downhill at least, but now she was working against a gradual incline as well as the wind.

Her skirt was stuck to her thighs, and any protection her flimsy coat offered had long since given way. Miserable rain. Even in London the weather wasn't usually so unforgiving, and if it was, there was always an awning or shop to duck into. Thunder cracked and a moment later a flash of lightning illuminated the sky. A lone tree, crooked and bare, stood behind a wall and Ivy started to head for it, until she remembered there was something about trees and lightning storms. She would have to take her chances on the road.

Mud sucked at the bicycle wheels, and she wrestled to free them, throwing her weight against the stubborn contraption. Her feet went out from under her, and she found herself on the ground, cold quickly seeping in through her skirt as pain shot through her leg.

She closed her eyes, wishing very much that she had taken Arthur up on the invitation to his club. If she allowed herself to indulge in self-pity, she might have come to the conclusion that she was going to die here, wet, cold, and alone at the side of the road, all because she had been too proud to ask her chauffeur for a ride.

Ignoring the throbbing in her leg, she scrambled to her feet. Riding was out of the question, so she doggedly righted the bicycle and began pushing. As if to punish her efforts, the wind kicked up, a gust nearly knocking her back over. Step by limping step, she put her head down against the wind and began the long walk back.

The sound of an automobile motor cut through the deluge, and Ivy navigated the bicycle to the side of the road to get out of the way. Except that the car didn't pass, it slowed down and drew up beside her, mud splattering her already drenched skirt.

The window lowered, and Ralph stuck his head out. "Get in, my lady," he ordered.

As if her afternoon couldn't have gotten any worse, here was Ralph of all people to witness her plight. Even with the miserable weather and dismal state of her clothes, his demand abraded her.

"I am perfectly fine," she countered, making to push her bicycle from the rut of mud where it was caught again. If she conceded defeat, she would lose the only sliver of independence she had.

Ralph pulled his head back inside and for a moment she thought he was going to keep driving and leave her there. But then there was a slam of a door, and he was coming around to her side. He easily disengaged her hands and lifted the bicycle, stowing it—muddy wheels and all—in the back. The rain made quick work of obscenely slicking his sleeves to his leanly muscled arms. Ivy tore her gaze away as Ralph stood before her, hands on hips, rain dripping from the brim of his cap. "Will you get in yourself, or would you like me to put you in as well?"

Glaring at him, she allowed him to open the door for her. The warm leather seats felt decadent, and she could have leaned back her head and fallen asleep right then if not for her pride.

Ralph slid into the driver's seat, wiping rain out of his eyes. Pressing his foot to the pedal, he muttered a colorful stream of curses as the car heaved itself out of the mud and onto the road. The windshield wipers worked frantically to clear the rain.

"You should have asked me for a ride into town," Ralph said, once they were back on the road.

Ivy crossed her arms in an attempt to appear unflustered, despite shivering from head to toe. "I have a bicycle, I didn't need you to drive me."

An unimpressed grunt. "What was so important that you had to pedal into town by yourself?" His gaze flicked up into the mirror to meet hers, a flashing hint of interest behind the indifferent façade.

"If you must know, I was meeting a friend at the pub."

"Who do you know in Blackwood?"

"You certainly ask a lot of questions for someone who has made it clear that you don't like me."

Ralph's brows gathered in a frown. "Why would you think I don't—"

But Ivy didn't want to hear it. "I met a man named Sir Arthur Mabry at the bookshop the other day and he invited me to lunch at the pub."

There was silence for a moment, and Ivy thought that was the end of it. But then Ralph let out a soft curse. "And you thought it was a good idea to meet a man by yourself, a man you don't even know?"

The censure in his voice caused her to stiffen in surprise. "Do you always speak so directly to your employer?"

"And here I thought you said you weren't a 'real lady' and didn't believe in, what was it? 'Class distinctions'?"

Ivy bristled. "I don't. That is, I'm not. But you certainly have a way of getting under one's skin. In any case, pope, chauffeur, or the king himself, I don't see how it's any of your business with whom I converse."

If Ralph had a witty rejoinder, he kept it to himself as he swung the automobile onto the winding drive. Rain droplets obscured the landscape, but the outline of Blackwood Abbey was just visible as they pulled up. The gray stones were stained black with rain, and Ivy couldn't imagine a less inviting place to come home to.

Ralph stopped the motor, and for a moment, it was just them in the silent car, rain pelting against the metal and glass. "You be careful of Sir Arthur, my lady," Ralph said suddenly. "I know it's not my place, but I also know that you haven't any friends here yet, and I don't want to see you fall in with a bad lot."

"Thank you, Ralph. Though I'm certain the son of a decorated war hero and peer can hardly be considered a 'bad lot.'"

"All the same, I shouldn't trust him."

"And I suppose I should trust you and take your word as the final one on the matter?" she retorted. "After all, I don't really know you either."

Her words hung in tense silence. "Listen to me," Ralph finally said, his voice so low that she had to lean toward the front seat. "You shouldn't trust me. You shouldn't trust anyone here."

Another cryptic warning, and this one no more coherent than the first. "What? Why?"

Ralph didn't elaborate, though the hunch in his shoulders and tightness in his jaw told her he had more thoughts on the subject. Finally, he heaved a sigh. "Don't get out yet," he instructed as he dashed out, opened an umbrella, then came around to her door and let her out.

"Oh, thank you," she said, surprised at the chivalrous act, though really, he was just doing his job.

He saw her to the door, then went back for the car. Ivy trudged up to her room, drew herself a warm bath, and indulged in a long soak. A truly impressive bruise was starting to blossom on her thigh where she had fallen in the rocky mud, and her muscles ached with cold. With the rain pounding against the windows and storm clouds racing along the moors, she felt small and young. Alone. She couldn't expect to be able to get to the village on her own, and now it seemed that even if she did, she'd quickly be found out. What had Ralph been doing in town, anyway? Driving about, looking for her? The thought only made her feel more like a prisoner.

A draft of cold air blew in from somewhere, and she shivered, wishing that she'd secured the windows before getting in. Settling deeper into the tub, she let the warm water soak away some of her anger. But her eyes flew open when there was a long, slow creak, as if someone was walking across the floorboards, trying not to be heard. Ivy sat very still.

"Hello? Agnes?"

There was no response. Then footsteps, the soft sweep of fabric, like a dress trailing along the floor. Ivy had put the unsettling incident with the hairbrush out of her mind, but now she wondered if she'd dismissed it too quickly.

"Hello?" she whispered again, this time chancing a look over her shoulder back into her room.

Nothing.

James had always teased her for believing in ghosts, but to believe in ghosts was to believe in an afterlife. And there had to be an afterlife, there just had to. Otherwise Ivy would never see her family again, and without that distant promise, life would simply be unbearable. During the war, spiritualism had swept the nation, as mothers and wives, desperate for closure, had flocked to séances in the hopes of reuniting with their men, even if only for a moment. Susan had once dragged Ivy to one, where the table lifted and bangs and moans could be heard coming from the walls. The medium—an ancient woman draped in strands of pearls and dressed in black lace— had claimed to have sensed the presence of a man in military uniform. Every woman present had gasped, certain that it was *their* loved one come back from the battlefield. But Ivy had seen the strings attached to the table legs as they were leaving, and ever since then her romantic notions of ghosts had been tarnished.

She gripped the sides of the porcelain tub, her body wracked with shivers as the air grew colder. This wasn't the dramatic commotion of a séance; this was quiet, a building sense of dread, as if she was sharing space with something that wasn't human.

"What do you want from me?" Her voice came out cracked and small.

Closing her eyes, Ivy held her breath, feeling the air move about her. The smell of incense and warm herbs tickled her nose. Bells tolled in the distance—or were they in her mind?—reverberating through her bones. When she finally had the nerve to open her eyes again, the movement had stopped, the sensation vanishing. The water had grown cold, and her fingers were pruned with wrinkles.

She hurriedly clambered out of the tub and wrapped herself in a towel. Everything was just as it should be, the windows closed and locked, the door firmly shut. If she had been disappointed by the séance, then she was downright disturbed by the confirmation of her beliefs. Something supernatural had occurred—she was sure of it—but rather than being comforted, all she wanted to do was escape somewhere safe and warm and filled with old friends.

It was time to explore her library.

8

The lock had been easy enough to pick.

Ivy and Susan had found themselves on the wrong side of Mrs. Beeton's front door plenty of times after staying out past curfew, and a hairpin was all it took to pop the locking mechanism of the abbey's library doors. She had only felt the smallest twinge of guilt as she stood on her knees and jimmied the pin until it had clicked. But she *had* asked Mrs. Hewitt to leave it unlocked and it *was* her library after all.

With a steaming cup of tea, warm lights casting shadows across the wood-paneled walls and a fire crackling in the marble fireplace, Ivy snuggled deeper into the plush velvet chair by the window. The battered copy of *Little Women* had been a gift from her mother, and Ivy could open it to any page and happily slip into the March sisters' lives. No ghostly footsteps or strange changes in the air, just books and the sound of wind racing across the heather outside. This had to be heaven, and it was all hers. Ivy hadn't needed to marry a man to gain her wealth or security. Besides, what man could have ever provided her with such a treasure as this?

Her reverie was interrupted by clipped footsteps and the clearing of a throat. She looked up from her book to find Mrs. Hewitt standing with clasped hands, a deep line of dismay etched into her temples.

"Good afternoon," Ivy said. "Is there something I can do for you?"

Mrs. Hewitt looked taken aback to be asked. "It's only that I noticed you are in the library," the housekeeper said, stating the obvious. "And what with the dark weather and the electric lights needed..." She trailed off, wringing her hands.

"Surely the wiring cannot be as bad as all that?"

"Unfortunately, it is, my lady," Mrs. Hewitt said.

"Oh dear, we can't have that. Perhaps we should have a man in to look at the wiring? Or, do you think Ralph would be able to? He seems awfully clever with automobiles and that sort of thing."

"My lady, I—"

"Mrs. Hewitt," Ivy said gently, stopping her. "I know that you worry, but this is my home now, and I intend to use the library. I'll ask Ralph tomorrow if he can look at the wiring, and if he can't, perhaps he can recommend someone in town who knows what they're doing. In the meantime, I'll be very careful, and turn off the lights at the first sign of trouble."

The housekeeper's neck went red and her lips tight, but she only gave a nod and then stalked out. Ivy had pulled rank, and Mrs. Hewitt had no choice but to fall in line.

True to her word, when dusk fell and the weak electric lights couldn't adequately penetrate the darkness, Ivy reluctantly turned off the lamps and brought her book upstairs with her. It was just as well; a powerful headache had taken hold, and her eyes were starting to go fuzzy. It was time for another lonely dinner in her room, with only the sound of rain for company. Ivy had never been able to muster much sympathy for rich people who complained of unhappiness or really much of anything at all, but as she spooned up her creamy soup and nibbled at the soft white bread, she could understand how loneliness could chip away at a soul, wealthy or not.

Ivy was not keen to track down Ralph and ask for his help with anything, not after their encounter in the rain the previous day. Everything about him prickled her sense of pride and independence, from the way he never seemed to be more than a few steps away, to the manner in which he regarded her from behind heavy lashes, as if cataloging her every movement. Never mind that he also seemed intent on driving her from her home with his strange warnings. But she was desperate to spend more time in the library, and Ralph was her best chance at addressing the problems with the wiring.

It was a cool, gray morning, still damp from the previous day's storm, and the smell of woodsmoke hung in the air, the distant bleating of sheep echoing across the moors. No motor engines, no honking buses, no street vendors hawking their wares. The quiet allowed Ivy to hear her own breath, and the crunch of gravel and leaves underfoot, reminding her that here in the countryside, she was more than just another face in a sea of humanity. Following the sound of an ax chopping wood, she found Ralph behind the stone barn, sleeves rolled to the elbow as he lifted an ax over his shoulder and let it fall, splitting a log neatly in two.

She cleared her throat, but he continued chopping. "Ralph?"

Each punishing chop sent splinters flying as he took some primal anger out on the wood. Edging her way around the gravel path, Ivy tried again to catch Ralph's attention.

Lifting his head for his next ax stroke, he caught her gaze

and nearly lost his grip. There was something wild in his eyes, a fierceness that transcended mere concentration, or even anger. Then it passed and, cursing, he stumbled backward. "Don't sneak up on a man like that," Ralph snarled.

"I'm sorry. I didn't realize—"

"I could have hurt you, killed you even," he said, giving voice to the flash of fear she'd felt coming upon him like that. Wiping the perspiration from his temple, he seemed to collect himself. "What are you doing out here?"

"I—I needed to ask you something."

Some of the wildness in his eyes dimmed, giving way to his usual guarded expression. Chest still heaving with exertion, he chucked the ax to the ground, either an invitation to continue, or a hint that she shouldn't bother him.

Assuming it was the former, Ivy hurried on. "Mrs. Hewitt said that there is bad wiring in the library, and that it isn't safe to have the lights on there. Is that something you would be able to look at?"

Ralph stared as if she were speaking a foreign language, his gray eyes boring through her. "The wiring?"

"Well, yes. It's faulty or old, I'm not certain the exact problem."

Squinting up at the clouds, Ralph ran a hand through his hair. "Aye."

Ivy waited for more. "What does—"

"I'll look at it," he said, cutting her off. Throwing a tarpaulin over the woodpile, he set off for the house.

It seemed Ivy was always running to catch up to him. "Right now?" she asked, hope mingled with confusion.

"Said I would, didn't I?"

Ivy bit her lip to keep from smiling, jogging to keep up. Ralph might have been as surly as a cat awakened from its nap, but she was beginning to think there might be something decidedly more agreeable under all that bite.

Mrs. Hewitt intercepted them in the hall, as if she had been watching them from the window. "Ralph, a word please?"

Ivy pretended not to listen as Mrs. Hewitt drew him aside for a conversation of hissed whispers. Whatever they were talking about, Mrs. Hewitt was adamant, but Ralph only nodded and then raised his shoulders in a shrug. He was a good head taller than the housekeeper, but Mrs. Hewitt was staring him down all the same, and Ivy was glad it wasn't her on the receiving end of the housekeeper's cutting lectures for once.

A moment later Ralph broke away and headed for the library. Ivy wasn't sure if he expected her to follow, but she didn't want to be left alone with the disapproving Mrs. Hewitt, so she took off after him again. But at the end of the hall, he turned to go downstairs instead of the library.

"Wait, where are you going?"

Ralph stopped, turning abruptly so that she nearly skidded into his chest. He still smelled of wood chips and exertion. "To get my tools. Is that all right with you, my lady?" he asked, a mocking edge of condescension in the last two words.

"Oh. Yes. I mean, of course."

Ivy fidgeted at the top of the stairs until Ralph returned with his toolbox, then she trailed after him like a lost puppy to the library. He got to work right away, taking out his tools and setting up a ladder against the wall. When it became clear that watching him wasn't going to make him work any faster, Ivy decided to do some work of her own by the light of the windows.

There should have been a catalog of the library's contents, but thus far she had not come across one. Who knew what treasures were hidden there? Creating one would not only benefit the library in the long run, but would be a way to keep busy, keep her mind from dwelling on the shadows of the past. She'd never really had a purpose before, or rather, she had but the world and society at large would not allow it. Her parents had never exactly told her outright that a university education was out of the question, but it was clear enough from the way her father's colleagues were all men—and besides, education, a good one, was a privilege of the wealthy. But now she had the time and the means to lose herself in her work, and the title and position so that no one could question her.

The shelves, at least, seemed to be arranged in some semblance of order. There were novels, natural histories, encyclopedias, and every manner of classical text. But the deeper she ventured into the library, the stranger some of the subjects became. Memoirs by people she'd never heard of, texts in unrecognizable languages. The bulk of the shelves lined the room, but there were also a handful of freestanding shelves tucked in the back corner, away from the windows. Wiping away a thick layer of dust, Ivy revealed a vast collection of the genealogy and biographical history of the Hayworth family, each labeled in a neat hand. Were the Radcliffes mentioned somewhere in a footnote? Or perhaps they had had their own straggly branch on the family tree? She was just pulling down a volume when Ralph's voice cut through the silence.

"There's your problem."

Ivy let the book slide back into place, and looked back to where Ralph was holding up a fistful of wires.

Wiping dust from her hands, she hurried over. "What is it? Can you fix it?"

"Mice—or something—chewed clean through these."

"Oh, well that's easy to fix, isn't it?"

Ralph nodded. "Will just take a trip into Munson to get the right parts."

Ivy watched as he carefully climbed down the ladder. "Do you think that you could go today?"

He gave her a long look, and she knew that she was trying his patience. But he just nodded. "Aye. I can go."

Perhaps Ralph wasn't so disagreeable after all, or perhaps he just wanted Ivy to stop pestering him. Whatever the reason, she knew better than to look a gift horse in the mouth. After she'd thanked him profusely amidst his grumbles, he left. Ivy hugged her arms to herself. It felt as if she'd been in a stand-off between herself and Mrs. Hewitt, and she had just scored a major victory.

"My lady?" Hewitt stood at the door to the library. She had almost forgotten about the butler, so rarely did she see him around the abbey. "A parcel has arrived for you. Shall I bring it into the parlor?"

Had Susan sent her something already? Ivy couldn't imagine who else would have known where she was, let alone thought to send her something.

She followed Hewitt to the front door where two men in work coveralls were wheeling something large draped with burlap. Her curiosity built until one of the men removed the burlap and looked about the parlor. "Where would you like it, m'lady?"

The wireless radio was beautiful, encased in gleaming mahogany and embellished with an unfurling leaf motif where the sound came out. It was a far cry from the wireless which Ivy and her family had gathered around in their old flat, which had been broken and repaired so many times that it had been little more than a patched wooden box emitting distorted sounds. Hewitt sprang into action when it was clear that Ivy was too stunned to direct them.

"It came with this note, m'lady," the other man said, handing her an envelope.

Ivy fumbled to unfold the thick ivory paper and caught her breath.

A little welcome-to-Yorkshire gift. My hope is that this will fill your abbey with music and news from the outside world, dispelling any ghosts that might linger there. Warmest regards,

Your friend,
Arthur M.

If Ivy had any doubts about Arthur's intentions, this grand gesture certainly banished them. How on earth had he arranged for this to come so quickly? She watched as the men fit the wireless between the window alcoves, and went about fiddling with dials until it crackled to life and a lively foxtrot began playing. She hadn't realized how gloomy it was, how lonely, until music began pouring through the old house. Closing her eyes, Ivy let the music wash over her, her chest lighter, her breath easier. Dispelling any lingering ghosts, indeed.

True to his word, Ralph had gone to Munson and gotten the parts needed to fix the faulty wires in the library, and made quick work of repairing the lighting. But it seemed that the universe conspired against Ivy. Every time she sat down in the library, a terrible headache would come on, and her head would go fuzzy, her eyes unfocused. The mildew must have been worse than she'd first thought, or perhaps it was eye strain. More than once she even fancied that she was being watched as she tried to catalog the books. Was Mrs. Hewitt spying on her, disapprovingly watching from the upper gallery, or behind a shelf? Or had she enlisted Agnes to watch Ivy? The young maid was eager to please, and Ivy could imagine her being easily manipulated. Though whatever the staff thought they would find was beyond her.

Irritated beyond measure that another cozy day in the library had been thwarted, Ivy stalked off to find Ralph and ask him for a ride into the village. She would telephone Susan, and hearing her friend's voice would make her feel better, she was sure of it. Ivy would tell her about Arthur and how he was throwing everything she thought she knew about her inclination for solitude into chaos. As the golden-brown moors rolled by outside the automobile's window, Ivy's thoughts circled back to the library, and all the treasure that awaited her there once she had figured out the source of her headaches.

"Thank you for attending to the library wires so quickly," she told Ralph, breaking the silence.

A grunt was his only reply.

Ivy's irritation grew. No matter how hard she tried, Ralph was determined to be rude and distant. She'd been mistaken in thinking that he was kind and good underneath his gruff exterior.

"Maybe you could teach me how to drive? That way you wouldn't have to chauffeur me around all the time."

"I'm a chauffeur. That's my job," he said with infuriating evenness.

They had arrived in front of the post office, and Ralph turned off the engine. The truth was, though she and Ralph didn't get along, there was at least a pattern to their bickering, and there was comfort in that. Mrs. Hewitt and the rest of the staff treated her as if she were a different species from them entirely, and seemed to avoid her at all costs.

Sighing, Ivy allowed Ralph to open the door for her, and then got out. "Enjoy your nap," she told him.

"I always do."

The man behind the counter glanced up at the bell, then went back to his newspaper. "M'lady," he mumbled by way of a greeting.

"I have a letter to post to London," she told him, ignoring his inconvenienced tone. "And then I should like to use the telephone."

She half-held her breath as he heaved a sigh and pushed the telephone across the counter to her. "So long as you keep it short."

Ivy rang the operator and after a series of clicks and static, there was a ringing on the other end.

"Hello?" barked a familiar, if not unwelcome voice.

"Hello, Mrs. Beeton. This is Ivy Radcliffe calling for Susan."

Her old landlady grumbled something. "Susan!" she yelled. "Susan, I can hear you up there with that infernal music. Come down this instant and relieve me of this bloody chore!"

Clattering, a muttered curse, and then the sound of footsteps and a muffled exchange ensued on the other end. "Hello?"

Ivy closed her eyes, the silky sound of Susan's voice wrapping around her like a warm blanket, even through the tinny connection. "Susan? I can't believe I'm finally talking to you."

"No thanks to Mrs. Beeton. That old bag is standing around the corner of the hall staring daggers at me—I can see you, Mrs. B!"

Ivy could just see the old boardinghouse's hall in her mind's eye, the dusty carpet and cracked plaster walls. The inexplicable presence of a three-legged tabby cat that no one seemed to feed, yet was always lounging in the doorway. "I miss you. I miss London," she told her friend.

"I miss you too. But don't be silly—you don't really miss it here. You're a grand lady with a grand house now. You have to tell me everything."

Ivy glanced around at the nearly empty post office, then lowered her voice. "I met someone."

Silence on the other end, then: "Someone, as in, a man?"

The bell over the door tinkled, and a woman came in,

a parcel in her arms. "Look, I'll have to ring you back. I'm going to see if I can't have a telephone installed at the abbey."

"How is it that Vera Beeton of Bethnal Green has a telephone, but Lady Hayworth doesn't?"

"Mysteries of the universe abound."

"All right," Susan said with a laugh. "Take care of yourself, will you?"

"I will. And write me back. You have no idea how much I need news of the outside world."

"Goodbye, darling."

Ivy stood a little longer with the receiver still in her hand, until the operator's voice came on and she handed it back to the postman.

One peek through the car window told her Ralph was still sleeping in his seat, so she took a walk around the town green and the old stone church. The cemeteries and churchyards of the East End were higgledy-piggledy affairs, her mother's burial place overrun with ivy and rats, and the occasional vagrant. The rich, of course, had marble residences in burial grounds almost as grand as the streets of Mayfair. But the small churchyard in Blackwood was neat and well tended, with potted red geraniums dotting the tidy graves.

So this was where all the Hayworths were buried. Walking along the crosses and old headstones, Ivy let her fingers trace the inscriptions. Autumn leaves lay scattered on the grass and shafts of warm afternoon light fell across the marble stones. Birds sang, dipping on the breeze. It was peaceful, calm. Cemeteries held no discomfort or fear for Ivy. They were a luxury, something her brother and father had been denied. It was as Arthur had said: everyone deserved to have their name remembered, a prayer recited for them. She stopped at a gleaming marble cenotaph, the engraved name jumping out at her. The late Lord Hayworth, Richard Barry.

Her predecessor. Ivy was surprised to see that he had only been forty-eight when he had died. She had envisioned an old, gray man enfeebled from age. Mrs. Hewitt had said that he had suffered from dementia, but he seemed far too young to have succumbed to such a disease. The portrait Ivy had seen of him had been of a man of middling years, and she had assumed that it had been painted years before his death. But perhaps it was done toward the end of his life, or even posthumously.

What would Lord Hayworth have thought about a young, single woman inheriting his title and his home? Was he spinning in his grave beneath her feet? Or had he been forward-thinking, a progressive like her father, who would have applauded her unconventional ascent?

"Paying your respects?"

Ivy spun around to find Ralph leaning against a stone, his coat slung over his shoulder. He was still tall and broad of shoulder, but in the afternoon sunlight, he didn't look quite as unapproachable as he did in the misty gloom of the abbey grounds. She gave a shrug, trying to appear indifferent despite the sudden racing of her heart. "I thought Lord Hayworth was old when he died," she said, nodding at the stone.

Ralph came to stand beside her, just close enough that his scent of leather and woodsmoke mingled with the warm autumn air. "He wasn't young," he said.

"Still, the way everyone talked, I just assumed."

They stood in silence. He must have known Lord Hayworth, but like any good servant, he kept his opinions about his employer to himself.

"The car is ready, my lady," Ralph finally said. A light touch on her elbow and she looked down to find his hand on her sleeve, as if he would escort her away. Her gaze snapped up to Ralph's face and he quickly dropped his hand. "Excuse me," he murmured in gruff tones, and stalked off ahead of her.

Her arm still warm from his touch, Ivy watched his long, uneven strides, an unexpected twinge of compassion running through her. What had that all been about? She threw one last glance at the gravestone glowing in the afternoon light, then hurried to follow Ralph out of the churchyard.

9

She awoke to a skull in the wood beam above her bed, with two vacant eye sockets and a macabre grin staring down at her.

As her eyes adjusted to the weak morning light, the skull receded back into the grain of the wood, nothing more than three knots in the shape of a face. Ivy lay in bed for what might have been hours or minutes, listening to the comforting tattoo of rain before finally dragging herself out of bed and dressing. She had hoped that her old ghosts would not follow her to Yorkshire, but with nothing but time and an empty house, it was easier than ever to slip into melancholy. Even reading late into the evening until she had a headache could not stave off old memories. Inevitably night would fall and she would be left alone with the moans and screams of a London infirmary, and the scrape of a shovel in the dirt of a communal grave playing endlessly in her mind.

The only thing that kept the loneliness at bay was the library. Cataloging, cleaning, exploring, and reading consumed Ivy's days. Wandering the book stacks at the British Library had always been a favorite pastime, not just because of the books themselves, but because of the stories they held, the hands they had passed through. Dog-ears, unexpected bookmarks, even forgotten love letters tucked into pages made it feel like a treasure hunt. Ivy's father would set her loose among the shelves, and when it was time for tea, she would proudly show him all of her prizes. Once she had found a funeral announcement tucked into a copy of *Crime and Punishment*, and another time a pressed flower in a book of poetry. She wondered if the people who used these little mementos as bookmarks remembered them later, or if they simply forgot about them.

Today she was nestled in the far end of the library, going through a set of drawers that lined the bottom of the shelves. Gray light spilled in from the windows, rain pattering light and comfortably against the glass. With her tea forgotten and cold, Ivy carefully pulled a drawer open, releasing dust that smelled of old paper and cigars. Inside there were a few empty notebooks, loose papers, and old pen nibs. The next two drawers yielded similar results. She was just about to close the last drawer, when a thick ledger caught her eye. Unlike the other books, this was bound in simple paper, and lacked so much as even a title. Lifting it out, she took it by the window where softly diffused light from the rainy day illuminated the browning pages.

Lists of numbers filled the first few pages and her heart skipped a beat. This was the library's record of book acquisitions. Titles were listed in the left column, with the prices paid and dates shelved listed on the right.

When she reached the end of the acquisitions list, another began. This list was written in a shaky hand, words started and then scratched out. Names, it was names of people, and they almost all shared one thing in common: the title of Hayworth. A genealogical record. There were a few other names here and there, but those were few and far between. Spouses, perhaps, or illegitimate children. Reverently, Ivy traced her finger down the list. These were her ancestors, distant though they may have been. But there was something strange about the list, something that made her hands go clammy and cold. Whoever had written it had scrawled it as if in a hurry, the names growing progressively more slanted and unreadable. And while they hadn't included birth dates or any other details about the individuals, they'd thought it important enough to include the death dates and age of each viscount.

As expected, the men in the sixteenth and seventeenth centuries had mostly died in their forties and early fifties, a few outliers younger and older. But even as Ivy progressed through the centuries, the life spans did not increase. Not a single viscount had lived past the age of sixty. She thought of the late Lord Hayworth's gravestone, and his early death supposedly due to dementia. It seemed that the Hayworth family was more than a bit unlucky when it came to life expectancy— some might have even called them cursed.

A headache was forming behind her eyes, and Ivy rubbed at her temples. She felt dizzy and unsettled. The shelves seemed to spin around her, the faint scent of incense filling her nostrils. Suddenly she didn't want to be in the library anymore. She'd had enough of death, and even though the men in the ledger had lived and died long ago, there was something unnerving about the list of names, the abbreviated lives, and all the heartache and grief that must have filled the space between the lines.

Ivy watched as Arthur paced about her parlor, making a show of inspecting the paintings on the wall. He took out a cigarette as if he would light it, then pocketed it again before resuming his pacing.

She had forgotten that she had invited Arthur until Hewitt had arrived in the library with his calling card on a tray. But now that he was here, she was glad for the respite and a chance to clear her head.

But conversation, which had flowed so easily between them at the pub, now stalled after the usual pleasantries. Arthur continued to aimlessly stalk about the room, propelled by a nervous energy anathema to his usual laidback demeanor.

"You seem...nervous?" Ivy finally asked.

"Do I?" He set down the paperweight he had been absently palming. "I suppose I'm just anxious to see the library."

She didn't exactly relish going back to the library with the specter of the dead lords still fresh in her mind. But perhaps with Arthur by her side it would be tolerable though.

"Well, I can hardly blame you. I was the same way when I first laid eyes on it. Why don't we take our tea in with us?"

The tray was brought in, and as they made their way across the hall and into the corridor, Ivy stole a sidelong glance at her companion. For all that Blackwood was a lonely and strange place, what luck that she should find such a kindred spirit who loved books and learning almost as much as she. And what's more, he didn't seem threatened by her knowledge; rather he welcomed it. She wasn't so naïve as to think that many men were comfortable with a learned woman, let alone that they might deign to discuss such topics as literature which were considered unsuitable for the female mind.

Ivy put her hand to the door, then paused. "I should warn you, it was in somewhat of a state when I came here. I'm working my way through it, but there's still a lot to be done."

Arthur hardly seemed to hear her. He craned his neck as

if he would be able to see through the wood door. "Yes, yes. I'm sure it's fine."

Pushing open the door, Ivy switched on the lights, and stood back to let Arthur inside. Two steps in and he came to a halt, awestruck as he craned his neck up toward the vaulted ceiling.

"It's magnificent," he murmured. "More than I could have imagined."

Rather pleased with his reaction, Ivy hurried to give him a tour. "The bulk of the novels and fiction are here, but I'm thinking of moving them to the upper level. As you can see, some of the railings need to be replaced along the gallery, and at some point I'd like to expand the electrical lighting to help reach the higher parts of the library." She looked to Arthur to gauge his thoughts, but he seemed to be in another world, rapturous and lost.

She trailed him, enjoying seeing the library for the first time again through his eyes: the never-ending shelves, the marble busts, the carved balusters and spiral staircase growing like a beanstalk to the second gallery. If his eyes blurred or head swam from the effects of mildew, he was too much of a gentleman to mention anything.

"What is the oldest book in the collection?" he asked, his fingers lingering on an exquisitely gilded set of encyclopedias before moving on.

Ivy thought. "There is a second edition of *The Generall Historie of Plantes* by John Gerarde," she said proudly. "And a great number of treatises from the seventeenth century. There might be others, but I haven't gone through everything yet."

He nodded absently, as if he hadn't really expected an answer. "It's a shame this has been kept closed up so many years. Just think of the knowledge that this room contains."

"Well, now that I'm here, I plan on rectifying that."

Suddenly turning to face her, Arthur took Ivy by the shoulders, peering at her with unnaturally bright eyes. "Ivy," he said, "what you have here is a treasure. A real treasure. You must open it up, make it available to academics. My club, for example, they would benefit so much from even just one afternoon spent here. It's a crime to keep all of this hidden away."

"I... I hadn't thought about it," she managed to say, taken aback by his fervor. But as she watched him wander around the shelves, occasionally pulling a volume out and inspecting it, the idea grew on her. "You're right," she said, musing. "It's a shame the closest bookshop is in Munson, and there's no lending library in town."

Arthur set aside the book he was looking at. "A lending library? That's not quite what I meant."

"But it would be wonderful, wouldn't it?" The idea grew on her. Here was her chance to really become part of the village, to make her mark. She envisioned a mobile cart that could travel to the outer reaches of the village, delivering books to those who normally wouldn't be able to access them. Perhaps there was even a corner of the village hall that could be dedicated to a bookshelf or two. Her dream was building itself faster than she could keep up.

Arthur looked uneasy, and she wondered if she had somehow offended his aristocratic sense of propriety. "Of course, your club must come and visit in either case," she hurried to add.

They spent another half hour in the library, though she got the sense that Arthur wasn't really with her. She hadn't realized that the library would prove so inebriating to someone other than herself; after all, it was her library and while she was enamored with it, it was probably not so different from most libraries held by the aristocracy. It was growing dark outside by the time Arthur ruefully replaced the book he had been leafing through and turned toward her.

"Ivy," he said, taking her hands in his, "this has been sublime. You have no idea what this library means to me, to my family."

She gave him a puzzled smile. "I'm sure I don't, but I'm glad you enjoyed your visit all the same." Her excitement at sharing her library with him had gradually dimmed as it became clear that his visit was more for the books than for her.

He must have sensed her disappointment, because his eyes softened. "I did, but I wouldn't be a gentleman if I didn't mention that it was your company which made it so delightful. How about this. Next sunny day, I'm taking you for a lark in the countryside. No books, no dust, just you and I and the fresh air."

"I'd like that," she told him, unable to help the smile that touched her lips. She knew that she was treading into dangerous territory with this young man, but she couldn't seem to help herself. He *wanted* to spend time with her, to get to know her. He was bright and pleasant and well-read, not to mention handsome. Her mother would have warned her that young men were best approached with caution, especially those who were used to getting what they wanted. Never mind her mother, Susan would have her head if she knew that things were progressing as quickly as they were. But meeting Arthur was like the sun breaking free of the clouds that had shrouded her for the past few years, and she would not turn her face from the light, not after all the storms she had endured.

10

A hesitant sun was peeking through the clouds and a warm autumn breeze stirred the old house to life. Ivy had convinced a reluctant Mrs. Hewitt to open some windows and invite the fresh air inside, and now she moved along the library shelves as dust motes floated in the buttery shafts of light.

Despite Arthur's reservations about starting a lending library, the idea had taken root in Ivy's mind, and, working through the headaches, Ivy threw herself into curating a selection of books, determined to bring them into the village for her first round of lending.

Arms full of books and more in a bag hefted over her shoulder, Ivy practically tripped down the stairs in her excitement to go into the village and see her plan in action.

"Mrs. Hewitt, have you seen Ralph?"

The housekeeper gave her a wary glance from behind the silver urn she was polishing. "I believe he's outside working on the auto. Wait, my lady." She stepped out from behind the urn, hands on hips. "Where are you going with those books?"

Ivy glanced down at the unruly stack of books in her arms. Nothing too valuable, and ranging in a wide variety of interests and reading abilities. Novels and adventure stories, and some history and special interests thrown in for good measure. "I was going to take them to town. I'm starting a lending program."

Mrs. Hewitt dropped the polishing cloth, her mouth twitching. "A *what*?"

"A lending program. There's no library and no bookshop in Blackwood and I thought that the community could benefit from it," she said, some of her excitement draining in the face of Mrs. Hewitt's less than enthusiastic reaction.

"I don't think that's a good idea."

"Why ever not?"

The housekeeper's lips pressed tight. "It isn't the done thing."

"Well, the world is changing, and as I'm lady of this house, I decide what the 'done thing' is." Tightening her grasp on the books, Ivy moved to go find Ralph outside.

But Mrs. Hewitt shot out an arm, blocking the doorway. Ivy took a teetering step back in surprise.

The housekeeper's sharp eyes flashed a warning, and suddenly she seemed taller, dangerous, even. "Do you know what it means to be lady of a house such as this? You are not just a resident, you are steward of all those who have gone before you, of a legacy. This house will stand long after you have come and gone and been forgotten. These books are not simply books, they are part of the house, and they belong here."

If an outsider had been watching the exchange, they might have mistaken Mrs. Hewitt as the lady, dignified and stately in her immaculately tailored navy dress, and Ivy the meek and cowering servant.

"You cannot think to remove a book from the library," she continued, taking a step closer. "It would be like prying a bone from a skeleton, or a painting from a frame. You may be one lady of many, but there is only one Blackwood Abbey."

Blinking, Ivy clutched the books tighter, her shoulder aching from the weight of the bag. It was unthinkable that a housekeeper speak to a lady in such a way, but then, Ivy wasn't a true lady, and Mrs. Hewitt knew it. But she had been looking out for herself for a long time, and she wasn't about to let a sour old woman stand her down.

"It's a lending program, Mrs. Hewitt. The books will come back. Now if you would be so kind as to let me pass."

Short of locking Ivy up, there was nothing Mrs. Hewitt could do to stop her, and they both knew it. Mrs. Hewitt dropped her arm, allowing Ivy to pass but not without a cutting glare. Long after Ivy had emerged into the mild afternoon, she could feel Mrs. Hewitt's disapproving gaze.

Dressed in grease-stained coveralls, Ralph was half under the automobile, clanking away and occasionally muttering a curse. The man seemed to be everywhere around the grounds all at once, whether it was chopping wood, taking out the ponies, or fixing the car. Without Ralph, Blackwood would have been a house out of a fairy tale under some sort of silent enchantment; he brought it to life, even if it was with coarse language and the energy of a restless wolf on the prowl.

"I need a ride into the village," Ivy informed his feet. Being polite had gotten her nowhere with Ralph, and she wasn't in the mood for a drawn-out song and dance of manners.

"Axel is broken," came the muffled reply from under the car.

"Well, when will it be fixed?"

"When it starts working again."

Gritting her teeth, Ivy stalked off.

The gravel crunched behind her, and Ralph emerged from

beneath the car, wiping greasy hands on his coveralls. "Where are you going?" he called after her.

"To get my bicycle." If no one would help her, she would do it herself. She wasn't keen on repeating her disastrous ride in the storm, but she was ready to walk the whole way if it meant putting her newly-found dream into action.

Even fitted out with a big basket on the front, taking the bicycle meant sacrificing some of the books. As Ivy pedaled down the long drive and out onto the winding country road, she could feel the abbey's dark gaze boring into her back, a lazy cat watching a mouse scurrying away. It was only when she crested the hill and was finally out amongst the moors that her shoulders finally relaxed, her heart finally lightened.

Ivy arrived in town damp with perspiration and legs aching. Leaning her bicycle against the stone wall edging the green, she began taking out the books and arranging them on a blanket she'd brought. Sunlight filtered in from the golden leaves of the oak trees, and already her headache was dulling away to nothing. This was the bucolic Yorkshire that Ivy had envisioned, and as she unloaded her books, she felt better and better about her decision to stand up to Mrs. Hewitt and see her plan through.

Standing back, she surveyed her work. Having a table or a display shelf would have been more impressive, but laid out on the blanket, they looked nothing so much like jewels, their gilded titles winking in the sun. People doing shopping and taking afternoon strolls threw her curious looks, and soon onlookers began approaching her, eyeing Ivy warily and whispering amongst themselves.

"Hello, welcome," she greeted them. "All the books you see here are from Blackwood Abbey's library and are available for borrowing."

"You mean to say you're the new Lady Hayworth?" asked

one woman, braver than the rest. She had bright copper hair and was dressed in a smart, if not worn, housedress and looked not much older than Ivy. She jiggled a chubby baby on her hip, the child wide-eyed and drooling. Her companion, a short woman in her thirties with blond hair and sharp features, elbowed her in the ribs. "I mean, my lady," the red-haired woman quickly amended.

Ivy smiled at the women. "Yes, I suppose I am. You'll have to forgive me if I don't speak much like a lady or know all the proper etiquette."

The first woman grinned. "Oh, I like her. You just watch out for some of the old-timers—there are those who still expect a lady to be a lady and act the part. Me, I don't care a tuppence for all that rot," she continued, switching the fussing babe to the other hip. "My Jack fought alongside lords and gentlemen, and I don't see why we have to go back to scraping and bowing now that we're all home again."

"Edith! You can't talk like that!" her companion chided her.

"She just said she wasn't really a lady!"

Ivy cleared her throat and directed their attention to the blanket on the ground. "Would you like a book? They're all from my library, and I'm starting a program to lend them out."

Edith's green eyes lit up. "Have you any novels? Something with some adventure to it."

Ivy selected *The Swiss Family Robinson*. "This has plenty of adventure—I think you'll like it." It had always been James's favorite as a child, and she and her brother had spent many afternoons pretending to be shipwrecked in the local park, until their mother had come to collect them at dusk.

"Oh, thank you," Edith responded, reverently holding out her free hand for the book. "You don't know what a blessing this is. There isn't any money for books, but I do so love to read. It's like going somewhere far away, but you don't even have to leave your kitchen."

A young man chose a book on the monsoons of India, and a local farmer a book on beekeeping. The small stack quickly dwindled. For every book that she lent, Ivy made a note of the borrower's name, the book title, and the author. Even though she had assured Mrs. Hewitt that all the books would come back, she was taking a risk by letting them out of the library and into the hands of strangers.

There was still a queue when the last book had been selected, and she promised the remaining villagers that she would bring more next time. Ralph would have to drive her if she wanted to fulfill her promise; she couldn't fit that many books into her basket, and the weather would not be so accommodating every week as it had been today.

Wheeling her bicycle out to the lane, Ivy rode back to Blackwood. For the first time since coming to Yorkshire, the horizon held something more than just a vague sense of foreboding, her chest more than just a knot of apprehension. She belonged here, and after years adrift, it felt good to know that she was more than just a ghost, that she truly existed.

11

She made it back just in time.

Leaden clouds had quickly gathered, and the first raindrops were starting to fall when Ivy let herself into the library and collapsed on her favorite chair. Though her body was aching from the ride and her head was pounding, she still had work to do. Making little slips of paper, she tucked them into the empty slots where the books had been to make shelving them upon their return simpler.

Her scissors were skimming through the paper, when a sudden wave of nausea washed over her, and she shot out her hand to steady herself against a shelf. The scissors clattered to the floor. Perhaps bicycling to and from the village had been too much after all. She tried to push through the light-headedness, but soon a ringing in her ears joined the nausea and it was all she could do to stagger out of the library without fainting.

Back in her room, the headache eased and she poured herself a glass of water. Sipping it slowly as she watched the rain smear down the window, Ivy made a note to ask Ralph about the possibility of mildew or rot in the library. The mold in her old boardinghouse had always given her terrible nosebleeds and the occasional headache. If she was going to be spending so much time in the library, she couldn't be subjecting herself to a constant barrage of maladies.

Eager to share her success in the village with someone, Ivy sat at her desk and drafted an invitation to Arthur to come call on her the next day. As she folded and sealed the letter, a cold draft raced across the room, lifting the curtains and extinguishing the fire in the grate. Ivy went still, remembering the incident in the bath. Whatever she had experienced that day had been passive, harmless. If it had indeed been a spirit, then it had been content to pass her by, perhaps completely unaware of her existence.

But this...this was different. There was an almost painful awareness between her and this entity. Her hand went slack, the letter falling to the desk as it grew closer. Hot breath touched her neck, like a hungry dog was stalking her, ready to pounce. The malevolent force seemed to press in around her as if it wanted to steal the air right out of her lungs. Ivy's muscles tightened until they ached, and the sensation of being watched intensified until she expected to see a horned devil or a ghost in chains materialize, glaring at her from yellow eyes.

Grabbing her cardigan, Ivy made a dash to the door, pounded down the stairs and out into the afternoon drizzle. She ran through the garden, past the stables and old tenant cottages before she found herself outside the grounds and on the edge of the moors. Lungs burning and legs on fire, she finally stopped running, doubled over as she fought to catch her breath.

A corncrake scurried by and the breeze teased the brown heather, but otherwise it was still. Soggy, colorless moors stretched for miles, their boundaries smudged with fog. A fine mist clung to the wool of Ivy's cardigan, and her shoes were quickly soaking through. But there was an eerie beauty to the vastness, and her own smallness in the landscape was grounding, reassuring.

The uneven fall of footsteps in the mud pulled Ivy from her reverie and her chest went tight. Whatever it was had followed her. She had no breath left to run; she would have to face it head-on.

Spinning around, she let out a choke of relief. "Oh, it's only you."

Ralph emerged from the mist, coatless, hands jammed into his trouser pockets. "Only me."

The pounding of her heart steadied, but did not slow, her mouth suddenly dry. "Were you following me?"

He didn't say anything, but his lack of surprise at seeing her was all the answer she needed. She shivered as the wind kicked up, and Ralph moved a step closer. "You look scared," he said, searching her face.

A chill ran through her, though it wasn't from the damp air. Ivy felt naked under his gaze, as if he could see the silly things that were slowly making her question her own sanity. Ralph looked warm and solid against the craggy patchwork of moors. It would be so easy to unburden herself to him, to let all her fears and misgivings spill out into the space between them. But he had told her explicitly she was not to trust him, and in any case, she doubted he would believe her. "Do I? Just thought I would do a little exploring around the grounds and a bird startled me."

Ralph didn't say anything, but he didn't look like he believed her. He took another step closer, as if he would reach out and touch her. She held her breath, but he stopped short, close enough that she could see a small scar running under his left ear and down his neck and disappearing under his loosely draped muffler. He belonged out here in the wilderness, all rugged angles and unpolished manners, as intensely brooding as the bleak and unforgiving moors.

She felt her tongue loosen under his unnervingly clear gray eyes. "I heard—felt—something, in my room," she said in a rush. "I've heard footsteps and felt drafts around the house, but this was different. This was…" She fell silent, the hot, sour breath on her neck still vivid in her mind. "This was evil," she finished in a murmur.

Ralph's brows drew together in concern. Not disbelief. He opened his mouth, but must have thought better of whatever he was about to say, because he soundlessly closed it again.

Shivering, Ivy wrapped her arms around herself. The cold air was a welcome dose of reality, but the gray clouds were giving way to the gathering dark of evening.

"You're cold," Ralph said, and before she could stop him, he was unlooping his muffler and putting it around her neck.

The intimacy of the gesture brought her up short, and she flushed despite herself. The muffler still held lingering warmth, and smelled like him—woodsmoke, leather, and rain. "Don't you need it?" It looked hand-knit, lovingly made. She wondered if a sweetheart had made it for him, though the idea left an unpleasant taste in her mouth.

"I can't even remember where I got it," he told her. "You keep it."

"Oh, well then. Thank you. I should be going back though," she said, aware that she should give the muffler back, but unable to bring herself to take it off.

"Wait."

Ivy stayed her step, relieved that she had a reason to delay going back inside. She looked at him expectantly, but he was gazing off into the mist, jaw muscles working in thought.

"I'm in the stables," he said finally. "That's where I stay."

Uncertain what she was supposed to do with this information, she waited for him to go on. His gaze returned to her, her breath hitching at the swirling storm in his gray eyes. "If you're ever in danger, you come to the stables. You don't need to stay in the abbey if you feel unsafe. There's an extra cot, and I won't let anything happen to you."

Twining her numb fingers in the hole of her cardigan sleeve, Ivy quickly looked away so he wouldn't see the color blooming on her cheeks. "I don't think that would be appropriate," she murmured.

Kicking at a loose pebble, hands in his pockets, he gave a snort that stopped just short of a laugh. "Not appropriate, eh? All right."

"Why do you talk to me like that?" she couldn't help herself from asking. "Why can you barely look me in the eye sometimes, and then speak to me so familiarly other times? Why do you act as if there is some big secret that I ought to know, but then never bother telling me what it is?"

"Ivy." There was an indulgence in his tone, his broad Yorkshire accent drawing out the cadence of her name. "You know why."

"No, I do not, and it's infuriating. I wish you would either tell me or leave me be." Nothing exasperated her more than a code she couldn't crack, and Ralph was proving to be a cipher without a key.

A crow took wing into the evening, its raspy call echoing in the chasm between them. "Very well, m'lady," he said finally. "Have it your way."

"That's it?" The rain was turning icy, and her whole reason for fleeing outside was beginning to fade from her mind. There was nothing to be gained from standing out here in some sort of stalemate with a man who clearly took pleasure in tormenting her. She turned to leave.

It was funny; as she blazed a trail back to the abbey through the ankle-deep heather, Ivy could almost taste a fiery whiskey kiss on her lips, feel the lingering warmth of a hand on the small of her back. She felt like Catherine Earnshaw, returning from a forbidden assignation on the moors with her Heathcliff, not a London girl who felt terribly out of place here in the North. Addled, that's what she was. Her mind was overtaxed, her stomach underfed. She would go back to the abbey, have a proper meal and lose herself in a familiar book where nothing could disturb her.

The walk back was long, longer than Ivy had remembered it being. Time moved in a strange way here, and she wondered how long exactly she had spent standing out on the gusty moors with Ralph. She was almost to the garden door when she turned around. Ralph was still out there, a dark smudge against the creeping mist. It was much too far to see his eyes, but something told her he was watching her, would still be watching her long after she had returned inside.

12

In her room, she tidied the already tidy vanity, lining up the brushes, combs, and powder jars. She'd already written a letter to Susan, and she'd organized her books several times over. What did ladies *do* all day? This lady certainly didn't feel like spending time alone in a room where only an hour before something evil had lingered with her.

Perhaps the parlor would have been a better choice, with its easy access to the front hall, but she wanted to be surrounded by old friends, so Ivy made her way to the library. The simple act of running her fingers over book spines and breathing in the familiar scent of paper eased some of the tightness in her chest. She settled on *The Importance of Being Earnest*, and lowered herself into her favorite chair.

Somewhere in the house a clock struck the hour, and from the window came the comforting sound of Ralph pulling the auto around in the drive. Then something softer, closer. At first she thought it must have been Mrs. Hewitt, her feather duster softly skimming over books nearby, come to spy on her.

"Mrs. Hewitt? Are you in here?"

There was no answer. The swishing grew louder, until it was right behind the closest bookshelf. Glittering clouds of dust puffed up with every sweep of the sound, as if someone was taking long, deliberate steps in full skirts. The faint smell of incense curled around Ivy.

Setting aside the book, she slowly rose. The gooseflesh which had only just settled on her skin sprang to life again, her heart beating hard and painful. She had to see what was behind the shelf for herself. She couldn't keep running in her own home.

As soon as she stood, the dust settled, the footsteps stopped. Gathering a deep breath, Ivy closed her eyes, then peeked around the shelf.

There was no one there.

She looked down. The polished wooden floor gleamed, but there, so faint that she might have missed them, was a single set of dusty footprints. Slender and petite, they looked as if they had been made with a woman's slipper. It must have been Agnes, playing some sort of trick on her. Then, before she even had a chance to sigh a breath of relief, the footprints began again. Ivy's throat tightened, trapping a scream as disembodied tracks formed right in front of her eyes.

It was still here, and it was moving.

Whatever it was, was leading her somewhere. Ivy swayed, her feet rooted to the spot. Maybe if she followed it, saw what it wanted to show her, then it would stop. That was why spirits visited, wasn't it? To extend a message to the living? To settle unfinished business?

"I—I'm coming," she choked out in a dry whisper. Forcing her heavy feet to move, Ivy followed the swirling dust in the wake of the footsteps. The smell of incense grew thick and heavy, though under it she thought she could make out the sweet scent of flowers. From somewhere faraway yet disconcertingly close, a woman's low voice hummed a song in a minor key. The electricity flickered, throwing the marble busts into sinister shadows. It was so quiet that she could hear the rasp of her own uncertain breath, the tremble of her fingers against her wool skirt.

When the dust cloud had settled, Ivy found herself in front of an unremarkable shelf. This was what it had wanted to show her? Nothing looked out of place, the books the same as those on any other shelf. What if it was some sort of trap? Would the spirit materialize, pouncing on her and—

"There you are, my lady."

At the sound of the voice, Ivy jumped, her heart still furiously pounding. The electricity had restored itself, the smell of incense gone.

Mrs. Hewitt peered around her. "I thought I heard voices."

Ivy followed Mrs. Hewitt's gaze, expecting the housekeeper to recoil in surprise, but the footprints were gone, and the shimmering dust as well. "I must have been talking to myself."

"I'm sorry to have disturbed you. Will you take dinner in your room tonight or—"

"*No*," Ivy said, rather too sharply. "That is, I suppose I'll take it..." She trailed off. What she wanted to say was that she would eat in the kitchen downstairs with the staff, where there were other people and nice, cheery lights. But that wasn't the done thing, and she doubted Mrs. Hewitt would have allowed it. "Here is fine, I suppose."

Mrs. Hewitt was studying the shelf, and Ivy wondered if she could somehow sense that up until a moment ago there had been an otherworldly presence among them. But then the housekeeper turned her attention back to her. "Of course. If I may, my lady, are you quite all right?"

"Yes, quite all right," Ivy lied.

Mrs. Hewitt gave her one last assessing look, then clipped her way out of the library in a swish of skirts and jingle of key rings.

Returning to her chair, Ivy plopped down. No more clouds of shimmering dust, no more creaking floor, and no more cold drafts. She stared at the book in her hands until the words swam, her thoughts simultaneously cloudy and racing, her body fatigued with fear.

Agnes arrived with her dinner tray and set it down on one of the cluttered reading desks. "You're here late, aren't you?" Ivy asked.

"Yes, m'lady. Road is washed out on account of all the rain, so I'm staying here tonight."

Frowning, Ivy drew back the curtain and peeked outside at the driving rain. "Goodness. I didn't realize it was supposed to be so heavy."

"Ralph says he's never seen the likes of it before. Offered to drive me, but he didn't think even the auto could handle the mud."

"Well, I'm glad you'll be safe and snug here tonight. Tomorrow we'll figure out a way to get you home."

"Yes, m'lady," Agnes said, dropping a curtsy. No matter how many times Ivy insisted she call her by her name, her request seemed to go ignored.

"Before you go, may I ask you a question?" Agnes had at least learned by now to tolerate if not expect her employer's attempts at conversation, and she nodded.

"Will you have a seat? You shouldn't be working anyway," Ivy told her, nodding toward the dinner tray. "It's past your hours. So why not sit and have a chat? I'm curious about something, and thought you might be just the one to help me."

Agnes hesitated, then lowered herself onto the edge of a chair, careful not to wrinkle her dress. "What do you want to know?"

"I was curious about the ghost stories. You mentioned there being some rumor that the abbey was haunted." Ivy was spreading rarebit on a piece of toast. She was grateful that her meals were always prepared with familiar ingredients, not the rich, fancy foods she had anticipated she would have to endure as a lady. When Ivy realized it had been some moments and Agnes hadn't said anything, she looked up.

The maid was staring at her, mouth ajar. Ivy automatically dabbed at her lips. "Do I have something on my face? What? What is it?"

"You…you really don't remember, m'lady?"

"Remember what?" There was something unnerving about the way Agnes was watching her, as if the maid couldn't quite believe what she was seeing. "What, Agnes?"

Agnes looked down at her tangled fingers in her lap. "You already asked me to tell you about the ghost stories here. Twice."

Ivy frowned. Had she? Agnes had mentioned the rumors the first time they met, but she was certain she would have remembered actually hearing the stories for herself; she loved ghost stories.

"That can't be true. I would have remembered."

"That's what you said last time. Said you would have remembered if I told thee, but when I did, it was like you were hearing it all for the first time."

A sudden slant in the room, and Ivy put her fingers to her forehead. Something tickled at the back of her mind, but it was slippery and she couldn't quite grasp it. Swallowing back a dry lump in her throat she forced a smile. "Well, tell me again," she said. "Maybe it will come back to me."

Agnes drummed her fingers on her knees, looking torn. But then she nodded, and said, "Well, I was telling thee the story of the Mad Monk. Everyone in Blackwood has grown up hearing it."

The familiar feeling grew stronger, but it was still fuzzy, and indistinct. Ivy nodded that Agnes should go on.

Outside the rain pelted against the windows in unforgiving sheets, the wind groaning. "It was in the days when Blackwood Abbey was a real abbey, a monastery, with monks and priests and the like living here. There was a monk—no one knows what his name was—that was obsessed with...what is it called? When metal turns into gold?"

"Alchemy," Ivy murmured.

"—that's it. Anyway, he began to take up darker interests. Things like life and death, and how it was that dead things could come back again. Said there was a fountain of youth, but instead of water springing from it, it was the blood of virgins. He did experiments, terrible experiments, and recorded everything in a great big book. There was girls that went missing from the town, and even though there was lots of accusations brought against him, nothing was ever proved. Some of the things that were said of him, well, I don't like to repeat."

Her imagination filled in the blank spaces in the story. Ivy could almost see the book, graphic illustrations documenting every horrible thing he had done, full of hellmouths and writhing piles of bodies. Flesh torn from bones, bodies drained of blood.

"When King Henry came 'round to burn all the monasteries, the monk disappeared. Some people say he was bricked up alive in the walls somewhere, but most people think that he ran off to Italy. The one thing everyone agrees on is that he hid the book somewhere in the abbey, and that his spirit haunts Blackwood, guarding his book and its power, hoping for someone to find it and release him from the bonds of death."

Ivy digested this. Agnes was a good storyteller, and the vivid details made it feel familiar. But it would have been quite a stretch to say that she'd heard this story before—twice.

"You really don't remember?" Agnes asked, looking at her askance.

Ivy shook her head. "Not a word of it."

Agnes was fidgeting in her seat, and Ivy realized she'd kept the girl there for some time. "Well, it's getting late. I suppose we both ought to be getting to bed. Do you have somewhere to sleep? All the things you need?"

"Yes, m'lady. Mrs. Hewitt prepared one of the old servants' rooms for me."

Nodding absently, Ivy bid her good-night. Back in her room, she scrounged about in her desk for a notebook. Hastily, she recorded everything Agnes had told her. The girl was unassuming and eager to please, yet was it possible she was playing some malicious trick on Ivy? Convincing her that her mind was slipping? But what had Agnes to gain from that? Worse than that would be that Ivy's memory really was sliding into decline, and if that were the case, then what else might she be forgetting? The late lord Hayworth had died from dementia—what if it was hereditary? But something told her that there was something else at play here, something darker and unexplainable by a simple diagnosis.

13

Ivy watched as the first crimson blood drop forged a slow, steady path down the white porcelain sink.

Soon it was followed by a second, then a third, all converging like crooked streets on a London city map. It was the first nosebleed she'd had since coming here, yet she hadn't been surprised when she'd woken up to the metallic smell and the warm trickle of liquid. The air was cold here, sharp, and if there was indeed mold in the library, then it was little wonder nosebleeds would accompany the headaches. Pressing a cloth against her nose, she let the water run until the blood turned pink and thin, then disappeared down the drain completely.

It was still raining when Ivy ventured downstairs, and from the look of the soggy fields and battered trees, it had rained all night. What was there to do on a stormy day such as this with no company and nowhere to go? She had explored the house several times over, but some of the darker hallways and more remote rooms left her with an uneasy feeling, imagining footsteps following and eyes watching her.

She puttered about the house, inventorying previously unexplored rooms and marveling at the art tucked into every corner. As the home of generations of Hayworths, she kept expecting to find something, well, homey. But the abbey was more museum than anything else, everything more for display than for function.

Wind howled outside, rain smattering against the great arched windows. If ever there was a day meant to be spent in losing oneself in books, this was it. She made her way to the library and leisurely perused the shelves until she found something familiar and comforting to read. There was an edge of uneasiness in the air, but she couldn't think why, so with a contented sigh, she settled into her favorite plush upholstered chair with a beautifully illustrated edition of *Oliver Twist*.

She must have drifted off to sleep at some point, because she was awakened by the sound of voices and activity in the hall. Setting aside her book, Ivy cautiously padded out to see what was happening.

Ralph was stomping out his boots as Mrs. Hewitt hurried to take his wet coat and hat.

"How are the roads?" Mrs. Hewitt was asking.

"Terrible, as you might expect," he said, with a grunt. Water dripped from his dark hair, plastering it to his forehead. Another man might have looked like a drowned cat, but Ralph was irritatingly captivating with his shirt stuck to his chest, a rain droplet blazing a trail down the strong angle of his jaw. He caught Ivy's eye and quickly looked away.

Mrs. Hewitt clucked, shaking her head. "I told you we could fare without coal for a little longer until our delivery. You shouldn't have risked going into town."

"It's not just the rain and wind, it's unlike any storm I've ever seen. I…" Ralph looked lost for words, and a chill ran down Ivy's spine. Ralph didn't strike her as someone who feared much in the world, or had time for hyperbole of any kind. But he looked genuinely unsettled.

Mrs. Hewitt must have been thinking the same thing, because she paused in her fussing. "What is it?"

He shook his head, as if he could hardly believe what he was saying. "Bees."

Ivy and Mrs. Hewitt shared a puzzled look. "Bees? What do you mean?" Ivy asked.

"Mr. Bryson was stung, all over. Said that a swarm of bees chased him all the way from the barn to his front door. Big bees, the size of a half crown each."

Another look passed between Ivy and the housekeeper. "Surely not in this weather?" Mrs. Hewitt asked.

Ralph shrugged. "That's what he said, and he had the welts to prove it."

"Mr. Bryson," Ivy mused. "That name is familiar." She searched her memory, but couldn't place where she might have heard it before.

"Nasty business all around," Mrs. Hewitt said, but the worry in her eyes belied her easy tone. "Come, let's get you some hot tea." She led Ralph to the back stairs.

"Wait," Ivy said, suddenly. "Mrs. Hewitt, may I have a word with you first?"

Ralph shared a glance with the housekeeper before heading downstairs alone. Mrs. Hewitt looked at her expectantly, hands folded. "Yes, my lady? Is something not to your satisfaction?"

"No, it's not that. I was just wondering…" Ivy bit her lip, trying to find the right words. "Do I seem forgetful to you?"

She'd been working up the courage to ask, trying to find a way to come at the question without showing her hand. She didn't want Mrs. Hewitt to sense the alarm that was slowly building within her, but how else would Ivy be able to know if something truly was amiss with her memory?

There was a flicker in Mrs. Hewitt's eyes of something like surprise, or unease, but then she was shaking her head. "Forgetful? I don't believe so, my lady. Why do you ask?"

How much should she divulge to her housekeeper? How much did Ivy even know herself? All she had was Agnes's word, and even that was only in the form of a story. The last thing she needed was Mrs. Hewitt thinking she was mad. It hadn't been so long ago that women could simply be carted off to the workhouse or Bedlam on little more than the mere suggestion of madness.

"Have I ever had the same conversation with you multiple times? Or forgotten something I asked you, only to ask you again?"

"Of course not."

"It's only that Agnes told me that we've had the same conversation over and over again, and apparently I never remember it."

Mrs. Hewitt seemed to study a smudge on the banister before carefully erasing it with the pad of her thumb. "I'm sure that you're just overtaxed. There is much more that goes into running a great house such as this one than many people realize. I hope that I am able to ease some of the burden for you, but you must do your part too by attending to your ladyship's duties, and not wasting so much time in the library. I've never once seen you at church services in the village, nor, well, doing anything besides reading. Now if you'll excuse me, I must make Ralph his tea."

It was only when she'd returned to the library that Ivy remembered where she'd heard the name Bryson before: he was one of the men who had come to the lending library. With a niggling feeling in the back of her mind, Ivy took out her record book. Tracing her finger down the list, she stopped at *Henry Bryson,* then sucked in her breath.

The grandfather clock by the door ticked away. She read the entry over, and then over again. It had to be a coincidence. What else could it be? The title *The Art and Adventure of Bee-keeping* stared back at her, stark in black and white.

Quickly continuing down the list, a knot of cold spread through her stomach. A Mr. Geoffrey Miller had borrowed *The Monsoons of India.*

Outside the wind howled and rain pelted against the windows. Blackwood was no stranger to rain and wind, but Ralph was right—this was no ordinary storm. It had all the force of a hurricane, and had hardly abated for two days. Snapping shut the ledger, Ivy jumped to her feet. Her head was throbbing. She had lent out dozens of books, ranging in subjects from agriculture to the history of the Russian empire. Edith had borrowed *Swiss Family Robinson*; was the village overrun with pirates? Of course not. It was just a coincidence, but all the same, she couldn't help the dark, foreboding feeling that had taken up residence in her chest, like the pressure building before a storm.

14

It was another two days before the wind and rain finally spent themselves, and Ralph deemed the roads passable. As soon as could possibly be managed, Ivy convinced him to drive her into the village. Arms loaded with books and her ledger, Ivy sat in the back seat, lost in thought as the car puttered along.

The unnerving coincidences between the books and events of the last few days weighed on her. Her head felt jumbled, and when she woke in the mornings, it was impossible to parse the night's dreams from the events of the previous day. Her nightmares of London hospitals and bloody battlefields morphed into dark corridors, hooded figures and ominously tolling bells. The sooner she could get out into the fresh air and out of the stifling walls of the abbey, the better.

She caught Ralph watching her in the mirror. "Bringing any interesting books today?"

The question caught her off guard. "Mostly novels."

"Good," came his curt response.

"I didn't realize you read novels, or anything for that matter."

"I don't."

"What do you like?"

"What do I like?"

"You said you don't like books, so what *do* you enjoy?"

She couldn't see his face, but she sensed his surprise at being asked.

"Never mind," she said when it became clear he wasn't going to answer. "Forget I—"

"I like to drive," he said, his words quiet but decisive. "I like driving fast and far and not having a single thought in my mind while I do it. I like that it's silent and loud all at once, and that I can forget about everything except the road in front of me."

He so rarely let his guard down, showed her anything besides his prickly exterior. She weighed her next words carefully, aware that whatever she said could serve to either nudge open the door between them, even just a bit, or close it more firmly. "I feel the same about bicycling," she told him finally. "There's a freedom to it."

He made a soft noise of agreement, his eyes still trained on the road. "Freedom," he said. "That's it."

This time, when they lapsed into silence, it felt a little warmer between them.

"Ralph," she said suddenly, "do I strike you as a forgetful person? Or prone to flightiness?"

The pause was so long that she almost thought he hadn't heard her, but then his answer came out low and soft. "No, you don't."

He didn't press why she had asked, but Ivy found herself explaining anyway. "It's just that apparently I've had the same conversation several times with Agnes, and I never remember it. And my head, sometimes it just feels so...so fuzzy, especially when I work in the library."

Another heavy pause. "You must have remembered the conversation the last time though," he said. "Otherwise you wouldn't be telling me about it."

"I don't know why I remember it now. Maybe because I wrote it down right after it happened so I wouldn't forget." After that night, she'd gotten into the habit of recording everything that happened to her every day, no matter how mundane or trivial. As long as she remembered to write in the journal and read it, then nothing should fall through the cracks.

Ralph didn't say anything else, and she let her head fall back against the seat, watching the fields and farms pass. She wasn't certain what she was looking for from him. Reassurance? He was hardly the person to give her that, given his clear dislike for her. If anyone had reason to play tricks on her, it would have been more likely to be Ralph than Agnes. Even Mrs. Hewitt took her position too seriously to engage in deceit and subterfuge. But serious, mercurial Ralph hardly seemed the type to spare time for playing tricks either.

In town, the ground was saturated from all the recent rain, but there was a crispness in the air that promised better weather ahead, and the sun was making a valiant effort at burning through the clouds. She laid out her blanket with a tarpaulin she had found in the stables under it to protect the books from the wetness.

The traffic was slower today, with fewer people out and about looking for books. Her first patron was an older man with thick gray hair and ruddy cheeks in a green jacket, a pipe hanging from the side of his mouth. "I've come to return a book," he said.

Ivy took out her ledger and ran her finger down the columns, trying to place him. She was usually good with names, but for some reason she couldn't for the life of her remember his.

"Henry Bryson," he told her, when it became obvious she couldn't remember.

"Of course. How are you?"

"Well enough. Turned out useful to have that book," the older man told her with a good-natured grin as he handed it back to her. Angry red welts peppered one side of his face, and his left eye was caught in a permanent squint. "Never thought I'd be learning firsthand about bee swarms."

Ivy winced. "I was sorry to hear about what happened. Do you keep bees?"

"That's the thing though, innit? I don't keep 'em, but was thinking of starting a hive. Sell some honey for a little extra pocket change. But after what happened, don't think I'll be bothering with the nasty little buggers."

She wanted to ask him where he had been that an angry swarm of bees had found him, but there was a commotion at the periphery of her vision, and a ripple of movement as her patrons were jostled and pushed aside from the queue.

Where there had only been a handful of people, it now seemed that a crowd had appeared out of nowhere, and everyone was talking on top of each other, shouts of excitement cutting through the rabble.

Mr. Bryson's pipe fell from his mouth, ash spilling on the books. "Lord almighty, it's Harry Oliver and he looks like the devil himself."

Ivy vaguely recognized the name as one of her patrons, but the man who was staggering through the crowd hardly looked human. His neck was grotesquely swollen, pustules the size and color of overripe plums protruding from his collar. A woman shrieked as he grabbed at her coat in a desperate attempt to right himself.

Unable to tear her gaze away from the unfolding horror, Ivy stood rooted as he sank to the ground, his hands at his throat as if he were choking for air.

The hospital where her mother had died had been full of the foulest illnesses and injuries imaginable, but at least those were expected at a hospital, and there was a sort of dark comfort that such things were dealt with in the correct place. This was the middle of a village, with birds singing in the trees, and people going about their daily shopping. Whatever was happening, did not belong here.

"For Christ's sake, someone call a doctor!" The commanding voice cut through the chaos, and soon Ralph's tall frame was pushing through the crowd. "Bunch a' ninnies, standin' about," he muttered as he dropped to his knees beside the convulsing man. "Hand me that blanket, will you?"

Snapped out of her stupor, Ivy snatched the blanket out from under the books and thrust it at Ralph. The man's breaths were coming fast and shallow, and his lips had taken on the putrid shade of bruised meat.

The man's chest rose and fell as Ralph cushioned his head on the blanket, and for a moment, she caught a glimpse of what Ralph must have been like in the field, decisive and imposing, making lightning-fast life-or-death decisions.

It might have been hours or minutes before an ambulance came careening through the village, sending the gawkers and bystanders scattering. Ivy watched in stunned silence as Ralph conferred with the medics and the man was lifted onto a stretcher and then whisked away.

Birdsong gradually returned and the rest of the crowd dispersed, whatever horror they had witnessed relegated to an unpleasantness best left in the past. Hearing a soft sound from beside her, she glanced down to see Ralph's hand at her elbow. His sleeves were still pushed up, a smear of blood smudging his cheek. He looked tired. "My lady," he said. "I'll take you home."

Nodding, she allowed him to lead her to the car. "What—what was that? Will he be all right?"

Ralph was grim-faced as they made their way back across the green, his silence only compounding her fears.

"Wait a moment." Something had caught her eye, and Ivy bent down to find a tented book in the grass. Someone must have dropped it in the commotion. Picking it up, her heart went cold in her chest as she slowly turned it to the title page.

"What is it?" Ralph asked.

She wetted her lips before answering, wishing very much that she hadn't stopped to look. That morning, when she had chosen books for the lending program, she had thought it would make an interesting, if not slightly gruesome addition. Now she saw it through new eyes, and wished she had left it on the shelf.

"It—it's called *The Black Plague*."

15

"You can't possibly be considering continuing this program."

Ivy was crouched in front of a shelf, replacing the returned books from the previous week and looking for new ones to bring. Behind her loomed the severe presence of Mrs. Hewitt.

"I'm not considering it," Ivy informed her. "I'm doing it." She examined the cover of a book of American poetry, then added it to her pile. Despite her determined tone, images of Harry Oliver and his swollen neck and panicked eyes the previous week spun through her head, the title of the dropped book an incessant ringing in her ears. But if she didn't throw herself back into the lending program, she would lose her nerve, and she couldn't let a ghastly coincidence put a stop to what was quickly becoming an institution in the village.

"I suppose you heard what happened to Mr. Oliver?" Mrs. Hewitt asked, though it was really not a question so much as a thinly veiled attempt to bait her.

"I was there," Ivy reminded her. "It was awful, but if you think to frighten me, you're mistaken."

"No, my lady. I mean, what happened to him afterward."

Ivy had been so preoccupied with the horror of the spectacle, she hadn't considered what had happened after the unfortunate man had been whisked away. Wondering if her guilt showed on her face, she paused in her work and rocked back on her heels. "Did he...did he die?"

"He is in quarantine," Mrs. Hewitt continued. "His diagnosis was such that it would be quite dangerous for him to be treated around other patients. I could tell you what it was, but something tells me you already know."

Ivy swallowed down the bile churning in her throat. "It was bubonic plague," she said from dry lips. She stood up, facing the housekeeper. "How did you know that I would know?" she asked.

Mrs. Hewitt's flinty eyes betrayed nothing.

"There's some connection between the books and what happened, isn't there?" Ivy asked. "That's why you don't want me to lend them out."

"You have an overactive imagination, my lady. I simply saw you had the book out," she said, gesturing to where the book in question lay. "But I cannot deny that the experiment of the lending program has failed. This is a village that thrives on normalcy. Do you know how many young men from Blackwood perished in the war? Near on fifty, and that from a village hardly big enough to boast a cricket club. People here crave familiarity, tradition. Then you come in, telling them that up is down and down is up, and disseminating who knows what sort of nonsense. Is it any wonder that trouble seems to follow you around? I daresay that—"

"Mrs. Hewitt!" Ivy's voice echoed off the ceiling beams. Pressure was building behind her eyes, and Mrs. Hewitt's demanding voice was grating her nerves. "Stop! I am going to continue, and that is the final word on that." Brushing past her stunned housekeeper, Ivy headed outside. Mrs. Hewitt might have been cold and aloof and even borderline rude on occasion, but to openly demand anything of Ivy was a bridge too far.

Once out in the cool, damp air, the headache subsided and Ivy was able to regain her bearings while Ralph silently helped her load the books into the car. He had brushed off any praise for his role in saving Mr. Oliver and he seemed unwilling to speak of the incident at all.

The crowd was more subdued this week—if the handful of people who came by could even be considered a crowd, but Ivy still made sure that each left with a book. She was just finishing updating her ledger, when a sleek sport coupe pulled up, and out hopped Arthur.

"Lady Hayworth," he said, doffing his driving cap. "Educating the masses?" Judging by the sardonic edge in his tone, he certainly hadn't warmed to the notion of her lending books to the townspeople since she'd first broached the idea to him.

She gave him a tight smile, still a little cross from her encounter with Mrs. Hewitt earlier. "What brings you to town today?"

"Why, you, of course," he said. "I stopped by the abbey but was told that you were out here with your books." He shot a glance at the blanket and the remaining books lying on them, his eyes momentarily darkening. "I thought I would make good on my promise and take you for a drive in the countryside," he said, all smiles again.

She *was* desperate for an excursion. Now that she was away from the abbey in the fresh air, some of the strangeness around the headaches and forgetfulness had fallen away, and she was eager to put them even further behind her. If only it was as easy to forget the image of Mr. Oliver's wild eyes, the weeping pustules on his neck, and his extraordinary diagnosis.

"I'll let Ralph know."

Ralph still insisted on waiting in the car during her trips to town, and he was parked across the road, resting with his cap pulled down. Ivy tapped on the glass and he startled, rolling down the window and looking at her expectantly.

"Sir Arthur is going to take me for a drive. He'll see I get home."

Ralph's hands tightened around the wheel. "If you say so, my lady."

Ralph certainly hadn't tried any harder to hide his feelings about Arthur. She gathered up the few unborrowed books, jotted down some notes in her ledger, and had Ralph load them into the car.

Across the road, Arthur was leaning against the coupe, arms crossed as he waited for her, watching closely. Someone was always watching her. Whether it was the house staff, or the walls of the abbey. At least when she was on her bicycle, there was nothing but the indifferent moors and the endless winding road. She gave Arthur a smile; it wasn't his fault that she was on edge. He was doing something kind for her, something that she sorely needed.

"Ready?" He opened the door for her, and she climbed into the low seat, gathering her skirt around her knees.

"I've never been in one of these before," she said, her heart suddenly beating a little faster. The coupe was painted a splashy shade of red, and sat low down to the ground. It looked like the sort of contraption that required one to don goggles and an aviator scarf.

Arthur grinned as he tugged on his cap. "As long as you don't mind a little wind in your hair, you'll be fine."

Before she had a chance to respond, he was cranking the auto into gear and then they were off.

The countryside whizzed by in a dizzying blur of fields dotted with cows and stone cottages. Wind snapped through her hair and stung her eyes with tears. It was intoxicating; she'd never traveled so fast, felt so close to flying. Occasionally Arthur would point out some feature of the landscape, but his words were lost to the wind.

They pulled off onto a dirt overlook, the wind almost as brisk as it had been in the auto, and Arthur produced a basket from the back. "I thought we might have a little rest here. This is the best view in Yorkshire."

A patchwork of brown and green fields rolled into the distance, quiet except for the occasional bleating of a sheep. Clouds scudded across the sky, allowing for brief rays of sun to filter through. Even the dead heather had a dramatic sweep to it. It was vast and wild and full of possibilities, a landscape worthy of the Brontës and poets of yore.

Arthur took Ivy's hand and led her to an outcrop of grass protected by a stone wall, where he spread a checkered blanket and laid out plates of cut meats and cheese, bread and cold sausages. Without the wind in her ears, it was peaceful and cozy, and felt like they were the only two people in the world. "You certainly came prepared," she said, eyeing the elaborate spread.

"A military man is always prepared." He uncorked a bottle. "Learned that from my father."

He poured her a glass of something cool and bubbly, which she wordlessly sipped as he assembled a plate for her. So, this was the life of leisure that the upper class enjoyed: impromptu picnics in the countryside, fast cars and expensive wines. It was certainly novel for someone like her, but what happened when the first thrill wore off? Was it a continual search for the next flush of excitement? Maybe if she threw herself into this lifestyle, she could rise above the strange happenings of her brief tenure at Blackwood Abbey. She had a new world laid at her feet, but all she could think about was her books, and the strange thread of coincidence between them and what had happened in Blackwood. When Ivy put down her glass, she realized Arthur had been studying her for some time.

"Something eating you?" he asked.

"I don't know. It's probably nothing."

Reclining on his elbow, he leveled his warm, dark gaze on her. "You can tell me. I promise to be impartial."

Against her better judgment, Ivy told Arthur about the books she had lent out, the rainstorm, bee attack, and Harry Oliver's gruesome display on the green. She even told him about the ghostly encounters and how she felt as if she was sharing the old house with someone—or something—that didn't want her there.

Arthur held her gaze while she spoke, but his expression was a blank mask, and she couldn't gauge how much he believed.

"Well, that's easy to explain," he said when she was done. "It only makes sense that strange weather or a brush with bees would lead people to seek more information from books."

She frowned. "But they took the books before those things happened."

"But their interests must have stemmed from somewhere, don't you see? The man with the bee book—"

"Mr. Bryson," she put in.

"Yes, him. He must have been interested in bees, perhaps had even started a hive and wanted more information."

She didn't bother telling him that Mr. Bryson had said he didn't have a hive. "And the storms?"

He gave her an indulgent look. "It's Yorkshire, darling, it rains. As for the unfortunate man with the boils, well, it only stands to reason that he contracted some concerning symptoms and thought to diagnose himself from a book. How do you know that he truly had the plague, and not just an unfortunate case of measles?"

"Mrs. Hewitt told me."

"Well, there you have it. I would not take the word of a gossipy servant, let alone one who clearly takes issue with her mistress."

Fiddling with a stem of heather, she gave a distracted nod. She wasn't wholly convinced, but then, what was the alternative? Mrs. Hewitt would have her believe that she was nothing more than a flighty girl with an overactive imagination, but perhaps there was a grain of truth to the idea, no matter how distasteful. Ivy *was* prone to take a rather romantic view of things. What else had she to do in the old house beside drown in her anxieties and read too much?

"Do you know what I think?" Arthur asked, breaking into her thoughts. "I think you're a clever woman stuck in a house by herself, with not enough to occupy her mind."

Just because she had been thinking as much, didn't mean that she appreciated the implication coming from him. Ivy opened her mouth but he stopped her before she could say anything. "This is why education for women is dangerous— you have all this knowledge and nothing to do with it. Come to the club. You'll meet some interesting people, have some lively discussions."

Ivy bit down on her tongue, hard. "I'm not sure I would fit in with that set."

"Oh, come now," he said, oblivious to her annoyance. "They will be utterly charmed by you, and I can show you off by my side."

She stared out at a kestrel hovering on the wing in the distance. How little it cared for the world around it, content to drift and let the wind take it where it may. "What is this club exactly?"

"Oh," Arthur said, gesturing vaguely, "a group of learned individuals committed to preserving the Blackwood library. We've been meeting for years. Never thought to come up with a name or anything like that, but my father has always referred to us as 'the Sphinxes.'"

"Surely there are other libraries that warrant preservation?" It was strange to think of these people devoting their time to a library which, as far as she could tell, most of them had never stepped foot in.

"Well, yes, of course. But as I've told you Blackwood is special, and you yourself saw the state it was in."

The kestrel dove and disappeared from view. "What's so special about it?" she asked.

Giving a deep sigh, Arthur looked about as if they might be overheard by the sheep and the gathering clouds. "Can I trust you?" he asked, leaning in.

"Of course."

He regarded her for a long moment and then nodded. "I believe I can, and what's more, I like you, Ivy Radcliffe." Sitting up, he draped his arms across his knees. "What you don't realize about the Blackwood library, is that it's not an ordinary library. It's special, more special than you can possibly understand. It contains some of the most valuable and rare manuscripts on esoteric and occult subjects. Before the Dissolution, Blackwood was a center of monastic learning. Its collection was the destination for countless pilgrims and wise men, all seeking the answers to some of life's most unknowable truths. The sheer amount of knowledge in that library..." He broke off, shaking his head. "It's unfathomable."

He didn't mention that there was a curse, or some sort of spirit haunting it—Ivy almost wished he had so she had an explanation for the dust and footsteps she had seen. It was an important library, full of real history and rare books. Solid things, real things.

"If it's as simple as that, then why has no one told me that before? Mrs. Hewitt didn't even want me to go into the library."

Arthur gave her a sad smile. "That's just it, isn't it? There are those who would see it locked up. Not all of the Hayworth family has been happy to share their gem. That is where my club comes in…we exist with the mission to catalog and share the rare works found in Blackwood with the world."

Doubt still needled her, but it was gradually fading, secondary to her curiosity. Never had Ivy imagined that she was steward of such a diamond, one coveted by so many important people, no less. Suddenly Mrs. Hewitt's reticence began to make sense; if Blackwood was indeed as singular and important as Arthur claimed, then no wonder the housekeeper was nervous to see Ivy lending out the books. She had served the Hayworth family for decades, and probably saw the library as an extension of her service. Perhaps the housekeeper was planting seeds of doubt in Ivy's mind about the strange occurrences as a way to scare her off from her lending program.

"Do you see now?" Arthur's eyes were bright as he leaned forward and took her cold hands in his. "Let us help you, Ivy. We can restore the library to its former glory. Universities would send their faculty to study there. You could charge admission or reading fees. I know how expensive these old estates can be, and you wouldn't have to worry about selling any of your land or taking on tenants."

Ivy's heart quickened. It would be like her lending program, but with so much more reach. And as much as she didn't want to admit it, she needed the help. Simply keeping the library dusted was a Herculean task unto itself, never mind cataloging. While she didn't truly understand the finances of Blackwood, judging by the skeleton crew of staff she knew that they were nowhere what they used to be. Eventually she would have to make some hard decisions about the future of the estate.

"Have us over," he said, watching her emotions flicker across her face. "That's all I ask. If after meeting everyone you decide to decline our offer, that's your prerogative. But I truly think you will see how much good we could help you do."

A raindrop fell on Ivy's cheek, startling her from her visions of a restored library, humming with the activity of hungry readers. "I'll think about it," she told him as she shrugged further into her coat. She could only imagine the look on Mrs. Hewitt's face when she broached Arthur's proposal to her.

As Arthur hurriedly packed up their picnic and threw everything in the auto, Ivy turned his offer over and over in her head. Was it all true? Could she really be sitting on the eighth wonder of the world? After all, if his society was so concerned with the library, why hadn't the late Lord Hayworth taken them up on their offer?

16

Someone had been in her room while she was gone.

The door was closed. Ivy never closed her door, mostly because after her first few days at the abbey she'd learned that there was no use in keeping it closed; Agnes came in the late mornings to turn down her bed and then several more times over the course of the day to tend to various tasks, so Ivy had gotten in the habit of simply leaving it open. This wasn't Bethnal Green where one needed to worry about locking and bolting the door against thieves and other unsavory characters.

The first thing she noticed when she peeked inside was the cold. The abbey was drafty and prone to dampness, but this was like a wall of ice. Crossing to the windows, she tested each of them in turn. They were all closed tight, just as always.

The second thing she noticed was the paper scraps strewn about the furniture and carpet, like a flurry of snowflakes. It looked as if someone had shredded an entire book and left the evidence in plain sight. Crouching, Ivy scooped up some of the paper scraps. Phrases like *Mad Monk* and *Agnes in the library*, all written in her own hand, jumped out at her.

Rocking back on her heels, she let the paper slip from her fingers. Someone had come into her room, found her journal, and then destroyed it. Not just destroyed it, but made a violent mess of it. It felt like a message, a warning. Hastily sweeping up the scraps, Ivy opened the grate and fed them to the fire.

The solitary clink of silver on china and the occasional gust of wind rattling the window were the only sounds as she ate her dinner alone in her room that night. A deep sense of wrongness had settled in the pit of her stomach after finding the destroyed journal. Someone had come into her space, violated her most private possession. This might have been her house, but with rooms always being opened for cleaning and furnishings and decorations already established generations before her arrival, it hardly felt like hers. The journal had been a place to keep her secrets, document her fears and the events of her day-to-day life.

Ivy pushed her plate away, having no appetite for even the soft white bread and delicately seasoned ham. Who could she trust? Who would do such a thing? Although Mrs. Hewitt and the rest of the staff were protective of Blackwood and its library, there was also something they weren't telling Ivy. Otherwise, why hadn't they simply explained everything to her the way Arthur had? Why did they go to such trouble to dissuade her from taking an interest in it? Ivy would have understood, and it would have made her job of cleaning and cataloging that much easier. The more she mused on the whole situation, the more she was inclined to accept Arthur's offer of help. She was only one person, and the library *was* special and warranted the best care that could be had.

Determined to make her mark on Blackwood and refusing to be intimidated, Ivy braved a headache the next day and headed for the library. Arthur had asked her what the oldest book was in the collection, and now that she knew there were monastic texts dating back centuries, she was eager to find out. If nothing else, she was sorely in need of a distraction.

There were countless shelves and corners that she hadn't yet inventoried, but today she started with the end furthest from the great windows. The dust was thicker here, the book spines faded and soft-edged from wear. Each shelf was fitted with a reading desk, though most of the chairs had long since gone missing. It truly was a magnificent library. She had been to countless libraries and reading rooms with her father, but none of them had possessed such character, such a sense of arms opening wide to embrace her. Someday she would polish the mahogany rails that lined the gallery, buy chairs to replace the missing ones, and polish the grimy marble busts until they glowed white. But even now, in its decaying glory, it was the most beautiful sight in the world. Something told her that if there were to be a true treasure in the collection, it would be lurking here, in this forgotten corner. Heaven truly was an untouched stash of books, just waiting to be opened and read.

The carpet whispered under Ivy's feet as she made her way along the shelf, eventually giving way to bare wood. It was so quiet when it wasn't raining, every sigh of the wind, every turn of a page amplified in the cavernous room. Stopping in front of one of the shelves lining the wall, Ivy traced her finger down a gilded spine. She had all but forgotten that this was the spot where the ghostly footsteps had led her. It had been dark that evening, but now with the gray light filtering in through the window, she could see that it looked as innocuous as any other shelf. She stayed her finger. There was one book that was wrong though, somehow out of place. It wasn't leather-bound as were most of the other books, and the texture beneath the fabric binding was soft and worn, as if many fingers had touched it over the years, but just in one spot—the top of the spine. Tentatively, Ivy grasped the spine to pull it down, when suddenly the entire shelf groaned and simply disappeared. She stumbled backward as a secret passage revealed itself.

The light from the window seemed to dim, and the rest of the library faded away as she stared at the dark recess where but a moment ago a shelf had been. Her heart pounded in her ears, the weight of her discovery slowly sinking in. This happened in Sherlock Holmes novels, not real life. Curiosity quickly overtook her, and before she could think better of it, she was squeezing through the opening and into the dark passage.

Ivy was only three steps in when she realized she would need some sort of light to help her see. Pushing cobwebs aside, she hurried back out to the library, grabbed the torch that Mrs. Hewitt kept by the door in case of the electricity going out, and plunged back in. The torchlight bounced off roughly hewn stone walls, a musty heaviness settling around her. The passageway was short, and in no more than five steps she was through it, and expelled into a small, dark room with a surprisingly high ceiling. Stringy cobwebs hung from every corner, and the air was thick and warm, old. The only furnishing was a heavy wood table which stood against the far wall, and next to it a lectern draped in brittle velvet. As Ivy slowly made her way to the table, the air turned cold, her arms prickling with gooseflesh. At any moment the hidden door could swing closed behind her, and she would be trapped. No one knew where she was, and she doubted that anyone would be able to hear her yell for help. But she moved forward all the same, pulled to the table by some unseen force.

Brushing aside the dust, Ivy studied the empty table. It was old, simple, devoid of decoration save for the turned wooden legs and empty cubbyholes that lined the back. Perhaps it had belonged to one of the monks when Blackwood had been a proper abbey. She ran her fingers gently along the top of the lectern. The cloth draped over it was insubstantial to the touch, and it was a wonder that it didn't simply fall away to dust as she lifted it. Whatever lay under that cloth, she was probably the first one in decades—if not centuries—to gaze upon it. Perhaps she should leave it be, come back another time with gloves and a better light. But something drew her to it, and she couldn't help herself.

With the cloth lifted, she stilled her hands, her heart beating hard. Mounted to the lectern was a single manuscript, older than any Ivy had ever seen. Its creamy vellum pages had turned brown at the edges long ago, and a frayed red ribbon lay disintegrating on the open page.

Even the most elaborate manuscripts that she had spent nights poring over with her father paled in comparison to the book that lay before her. Strange figures danced in the margins, bathing in pools of turquoise water with exotic flowers. The language was unfamiliar. Not Latin, and not some older form of German or Italian. Not having been exposed to centuries of light and pollution, the images were as brilliantly colored as the day they had been painted. Leaning closer, Ivy was just about to risk turning the page when a noise stopped her. The hairs on her neck lifted, and her fingers fell away from the manuscript. The room was still and silent as a tomb. Then another creak, deliberate, this one closer.

Why had she thought exploring this remote and hidden chamber was a good idea? Mrs. Hewitt would find her decomposing body months later, clucking her tongue that her young mistress could have been so stupid. Spinning around, Ivy half expected to come face-to-face with some ghastly apparition. But the torchlight fell upon a man of flesh and blood. A man she knew.

Ralph filled the doorway, a dark silhouette, before he moved all the way into the room and the torchlight threw his face into shadows. "What are you doing here?" His voice cut through the stifling silence, and despite it being Ralph of all people, she had never been so glad to see another human being in her life.

But her relief was short-lived. Her breath steadying and heart rate slowing, she drew herself up. "I could ask the same of you."

The room grew even smaller with Ralph in it, his energy dark and dangerous. Was he angry that she had stumbled upon this place? Had he followed her to make sure that she never spoke of it again? He was like a shadow, always at her heels, and she wondered how often he was just out of sight, watching her.

His jaw worked, but he didn't say anything, just took a step closer to her. Instinctively, she moved away, backing into the table.

"For Christ's sake, Ivy, I'm not going to hurt you."

He had never used her Christian name before, and there was something vulnerable, hurt, in his tone that stopped her. A wave of déjà vu washed over her. No, he *had* used her name before, but when? She had faced Ralph before, outside, on the moors with the wind and rain at her back. But why would she have been alone with him, in the moors of all places? Her mind desperately fought to gain purchase on the memory, like waking from a beautiful dream with only the faintest notion of what it had been about. But no details crystallized, only a deep, unnervingly familiar ache of longing that settled in her chest. She shook the half-formed memory from her head. That wasn't what was important right now.

"Did you follow me here?" Ivy asked in a whisper.

Ralph didn't say anything, he didn't need to; his silence was answer enough.

"What do you want from me?" Her heart had started racing again, Ralph's closeness robbing her of any clarity of thought. The little room filled with the scent of woodsmoke and the outdoors. This was madness, yet she couldn't help the hopeful expectation that he come closer to her, touch her. She could practically feel the warmth of his hands on her skin, his breath on the tender spot behind her ear. Why did this all feel so familiar? Why did she want Ralph of all people to step into her space, to wrap his arms around her and pull her to his chest and never let her go?

But Ralph didn't move. "You shouldn't be here," he said in a low voice that sent shivers down her spine.

The gravity of his tone snapped her out of whatever silly fancy she had been indulging in. "What do you mean? What is this place?"

Sighing, Ralph ran a hand through his hair, standing the short, golden-brown strands on end. He looked as if he had been working in the stables, his shirt collar loose, his sleeves rolled. "You're too curious for your own good," he said on the back of a heavy sigh. "Too stubborn."

The way he said it, it was with a familiarity, an *intimacy*. This was more than a breach of conduct between an employer and employee. He spoke with the confidence of a friend, or even a lover. "You've been spending time with Arthur Mabry," he continued before she had a chance to respond.

"What does that have to do with anything?"

"What has he told you about the library?"

Ivy's tongue darted over her dry lips, Arthur's strange plea coming back to her. Something told her to tread carefully, that there was more to the mutual distrust between Ralph and Arthur. "He told me that the Blackwood library is special, that it holds a lot of rare books on occult subjects."

Ralph's gaze sharpened. "Did he ask to come to the library?"

She knew he wasn't going to like her answer, though she wasn't sure why. "He—he already has come. He asked if he could bring his club next time."

"Christ," Ralph muttered to himself, confirming her suspicion.

"It's my home," Ivy countered. "I may invite who I wish."

Ralph drew his hands down his face, looking unbearably tired. "You have no idea," he said. "No idea. Don't let them come."

Something in the weariness, the hollowness of his tone brought her up short. "What do you mean?"

He shook his head. "You should go." He stood aside, waiting for her to pass.

But she stood her ground. "There is something strange about this library, something more than what Arthur told me." Her words came out in a rush. "I get headaches here, but I went to see the eye doctor and he said my vision is perfect. The books I lent out unleashed...something. There's a reason Mrs. Hewitt and everyone else doesn't want me to spend time in here." She drew herself up to her full height which was only to his shoulders. "I am your mistress and I demand you tell me what is going on."

There was a hint of amusement in his eye as he raised a brow at this, but it quickly dissipated. "You're right," he said, taking her by the shoulders. "I am going to tell you something, and I need you to listen. To really listen. No questions, no interrupting."

She opened her mouth but he stopped her. "I mean it, Ivy."

The use of her name again, the gravity of his tone, and she

clamped her mouth back shut. Her nerves were alive, dancing in anticipation.

"Leave. Go now, today. Pack up your things and go back to London. Don't listen to anything Mrs. Hewitt says, or Sir Arthur for that matter. Just leave, as soon as you can."

Ivy stared at him, the muscle working in his jaw, his anxious eyes searching hers. That was it? Was she going mad? She had braced herself for…well, she didn't know for what. But something more than *that*. She wrenched herself free of his grasp, and his hands fell away. It was getting harder to breathe in the small room.

"What on earth are you talking about? Why would I leave?"

Ralph cut his gaze away, a lump rising and falling in his throat before he spoke again. "I told you already, but you forgot."

Clutching at his arm, she forced him to meet her eye. "So there *is* something to do with my mind, with the forgetting. What does it have to do with the library? Why can't you just tell me?"

"I—I don't want to frighten you," he said, his voice suddenly unsure, as if he were a shy suitor at a dance.

"But I'm already frightened! Terrified, even. My mind is starting to slip and I don't even know what's real anymore or who I can trust. I wake up in fogs, and my mind…it feels like a book with missing pages, like I'm constantly trying to piece an incomplete story together. There's something wrong, I don't know how I know, but there is."

His eyes dropped to her hand on his sleeve, as if he was momentarily entranced by her fingers. "It's no use. You'll forget I said anything about it in any case. It's for the best."

Openmouthed, Ivy stared at the man who only moments ago she had thought was going to kiss her. Then realization dawned on her. "This is about Sir Arthur, isn't it? Someone told me there was a history between his family and the Hay-worths, and you don't want me to associate with him. Though why a brooding chauffeur would care about my personal life is beyond me."

Ralph drew back, a flash of hurt deep within his eyes that almost knocked the breath out of her. She expected him to put up some pretense of denial, but all he said was, "There you have it."

His words fell flat between them.

"So I should leave my home because of some bad blood between a distant relation and the man with whom I choose to spend my time?"

It was a small room, but it felt downright claustrophobic now. Ralph had a controlled sort of energy, like a hound waiting for a command before the attack. She shivered with anticipation. "He's only interested in the library, Ivy," he said. "It's no secret that his father is insolvent, that they're holding on to their estate by a thread. The Mabrys will bleed you dry in more ways than one. He doesn't care about you. Not like I—"

Ralph broke off, but her retort was already pouring out of her, fast and desperate. "You think that Arthur is only spending time with me because he's using me to get to the library?" Heat climbed her body. The idea was insulting beyond belief, yet she couldn't help remember the look on Arthur's face when he first set foot in the library, how entranced he had been, as if he had finally found Elysium. "Isn't it possible that he finds my company enjoyable? That he wants to be with me for me?"

Arthur had been her one friend here, someone who had sought her out. But then the doubts came crawling out of the wall like hungry little rats. Why *would* someone like Arthur Mabry be interested in her? She was attractive enough, and she was clever and possessed a title and estate. But she didn't speak the right way, carry herself the right way, and she hadn't come by her money in the right way either. Hadn't her mother faced the same predicament when she'd set out from America, a rich heiress looking to pair her wealth with the title of an Englishman? And hadn't her mother told her a thousand times that such matches were sure to flounder and result in misery?

"Ivy, please, listen to me. I'll drive you to the train station, today."

Crossing her arms, Ivy stared past Ralph's shoulder. "I'm not leaving." Even if she wanted to, where would she go? Back to barely scraping by in London? Back to living a half life? Blackwood might have been a strange, dreary place, but it was her birthright. It was the only place she made sense, and she would not admit defeat and go running.

"Ivy—" he started.

"And that's another thing—you can't keep calling me that. It's Lady Hayworth. Think me a snob if you will, but this is my home, my birthright, and I'm staying."

The pause that followed was only heightened by their closeness, the stillness of the room. When Ivy chanced a look at Ralph, he didn't just look upset or disappointed, he looked… heartbroken. His large body seemed to shrink in on itself, a little of the quicksilver light in his eyes dimming. It did something to her, an uncomfortable fissure opening deep within her chest, and she wished it were as simple as going to him, putting her head on his shoulder and telling him that she didn't mean it. But there was nothing simple about their situation, and the threads of her feelings for Ralph and Arthur were getting all tangled up. She needed space, needed to get out.

Ralph shook his head, his soulful gray eyes awash in sadness. "You're making a terrible mistake."

"But it's my mistake to make," Ivy said, shouldering past him, leaving him to the cobwebs and forgotten manuscript.

17

Breathe, Ivy, breathe.

Cocky, arrogant, insufferable man! She paced her room, came up with several more epithets, and then threw herself on her bed. She'd left Ralph in the secret chamber, and she'd had half a mind to shut him in there. Who did he think he was, demanding that she leave her own home, just because *he* didn't approve of her friendship with Arthur? It was unbelievable that he thought he had the right to demand such a thing from her. Besides, he was wrong about Arthur's motives. Arthur had approached *her* before he knew who she was, and they'd struck up a conversation. He knew her background, and wasn't deterred by it. And wasn't this all beside the point? Arthur hadn't made any declarations or asked her any life-altering questions.

But for all her disbelief of what Ralph had told her, there was one thing that she kept coming back to like a scab that begged to be picked. He'd said something about how she would soon forget. There was something familiar about his warning, and again the strongest sense of déjà vu came over her. *I don't want to frighten you.* Well, Ivy was already frightened by the increasing gaps in her memory, the way she could no longer rely on herself to keep the strands of her life from fraying. Or did he think she was going to forget where she'd come from, turn into some autocratic mistress of the house? She winced as she remembered how she'd reprimanded Ralph for using her given name. Maybe he was right, in that one thing at least.

She let her gaze ramble out the window. After the last few weeks, the view was becoming familiar, ordinary, to the point that she hardly noticed the breathtaking beauty of the rugged moors and hidden valleys anymore. Ivy sent for tea and drew herself a bath. Already her conversation with Ralph was growing fuzzy and distant, like a strange dream. She would be fine. She had taken care of herself for this long, and it would take more than a disgruntled servant to make her leave her home.

When she had eaten her fill of biscuits and sandwiches and was finally able to breathe again without shaking with anger, Ivy ventured back downstairs where she was relieved to see no sign of Ralph. The secret door had been closed back up and the library books stared innocently back at her. Had he seen the manuscript? If he had, he probably wouldn't have been curious enough to try to read or take it since he was so disdainful of books. She would go back another day, take it out and really examine it. Something told her it could be an important find, monumental, even. After all, it wasn't every day that a medieval manuscript was discovered in a secret chamber, let alone one with such singular artwork and in a strange language. If the library's collection was as prolific as Arthur claimed, then it was probable that the manuscript could be quite old.

Satisfied that no one would be going into the secret room again now that the door was once more hidden, Ivy drifted to the parlor to listen to the news program on the wireless. Rumblings of food shortages and labor marches seemed far away and inconsequential here in the wild Yorkshire moors. Her entire life seemed far away and inconsequential. At least in London she had been part of the moving machine of the city, the throngs of people, the art and culture that grew like weeds out of cracks in the sidewalk. She had thought that becoming a lady would give her a better view of all the world had to offer, but instead she felt like a doll put on a shelf to collect dust.

She had hardly sat down when Hewitt appeared in the doorway, a pained look on his face. "My lady, Sir Arthur is here to see you."

Ivy didn't remember sending Arthur an invitation, but she was glad nonetheless that he was here. He, at least, made her feel important, like she was someone worth being remembered. A moment later Arthur strode in, self-assured, and achingly handsome in a dark tweed suit and driving coat. Ivy's worries instantly melted away as he crossed to her and kissed her cheeks, his clean, sharp scent of shaving soap cutting through the musty fug of the abbey.

"I've come to whisk you away, no arguments."

"Oh? To where?"

"Does it matter? I received a vision of you, bored and lonely and came straightaway to collect you."

As Ivy accepted his elbow and he led her out to his waiting auto—*not* the roofless sport coupe this time—Ralph's warning came back to her. She couldn't deny that Arthur's interest in the library was borderline obsessive, but then, that was part of what she liked about him. He made her feel safe, taken care of, and he shared her passion for the written word.

"Where are we going today?"

Arthur grinned at her as he shifted gears. "It's a surprise."

Ivy relaxed a little more into the seat and let her weary eyes drink in the earthy greens and browns of the passing landscape. She was tempted to tell Arthur about the hidden room and the strange manuscript she had discovered in it. But every time she started to, she stopped herself. As much as she was loath to admit it, some of Ralph's words about Arthur had found their mark. Besides, what was there really to tell? She hadn't gotten a good enough look at the manuscript to even accurately date it.

Swinging the car off the road, Arthur drove them under a grand iron archway and down a winding drive lined with privet hedges. Anticipating the question on her lips, he flashed her a grin. "Don't bother asking me again where we are—I won't tell you until we're there."

A sprawling Georgian house loomed into view, maybe not quite so large as Blackwood, but with well-maintained grounds and gurgling fountains. Pulling up in the front, Arthur hopped out and got Ivy's door for her. She was wearing a simple knit day dress, and while it had been fine for lounging about at the abbey, she was nowhere remotely close to being passably dressed to mix with the upper echelons of society that no doubt lived here.

Ivy gave him a quizzical look as he took her hand.

"Not yet," he told her, dark eyes glinting with merriment.

They made their way up the broad marble steps, and a tall, middle-aged man with peppered hair and wire-rimmed spectacles greeted them. "Sir Arthur," he said, his long face cracking into a smile. "How good to see you. And you've brought a friend!"

"Indeed I have, Martins. May the lady and I have a look inside?"

"Of course. You know you need not ask. Your family is always welcome."

The man gave a deep bow and stepped aside as Arthur led Ivy inside. Their footsteps echoed on the black-and-white tiles, chandeliers throwing shards of light on the airy walls. On every surface paintings hung, frames so ornate that they were works of art in their own right.

Ivy rubbed a crick out of her neck from staring up at the light pouring in from a glass atrium above them. "I think you really have to tell me where we are now."

"This," Arthur said, sweeping an arm to encompass the grand hall, "is Watson Castle. It was built in the last century by the 10th Duke of Montrose for his wife as a museum for their collection. He was viceroy of India, and they traveled extensively throughout the continent and Asia. It houses over ten thousand paintings, decorative pieces, and a fine collection of silver. But this is what I really brought you to see."

He took her hand and led her out of the airy atrium and into a cavernous, wood-paneled room. Books lined every wall, soaring up to a third-story gallery. Iron staircases spiraled up into the heavens, and brilliant glass lamps illuminated everything in soft, yellow hues. A handful of gentlemen sat at reading stations, heads buried in books. A reverent hush ran through the magnificent library, the only sounds the occasional cough or crisp turning of a page.

"It's beautiful," Ivy murmured as she craned her neck to get a better look at the gilded mosaics that sprawled across the ceiling.

Turning to face her, Arthur took both her hands in his, bringing her attention back to him. "This could be Blackwood. This could be a fraction of Blackwood."

"What do you mean?"

"Together, we could transform Blackwood's library into a

place like this. A place of learning and research. You know how important the library is, it's a crime to keep it behind lock and key. Scholars would come from every corner of England, from the world, just for the chance to sit among the knowledge housed there."

The gilded allegories of the four winds winked down at Ivy from the ceiling. Everything was glittering, clean. "I don't know," she said.

The idea of sharing her treasure with the world was appealing, but this place wasn't a resource for the world; it was a resource for the few. The rich few. Would a place like Watson Castle ever have admitted a woman through its doors, and a poor woman at that? It was one thing to lend out books, but another entirely to invite the world into her home, and a feeling of protectiveness washed through her.

"It…it would be a great deal of work," Ivy said weakly. Already cataloging and trying to keep everything clean was taking its toll on her. How could she possibly bring the library up to this standard? It would be like turning her old boardinghouse into Buckingham Palace.

He drew her closer, his warmth and decadent scent wrapping around her. "We'll take it on together. There's no need for you to be struggling alone anymore. I want what's best for the library, but also for you. You must know that I care for you. Let me help you." His voice was smooth and comforting, a whisper so that they didn't disturb the other patrons. "Let me into your life, Ivy. I swear that you will not regret it."

Her eyes drifted closed, and she tipped into him, the movement involuntary but so good and right. "What are you suggesting, exactly?" she asked in a whisper.

Taking her chin, he gave her a knowing look, his dark eyes all velvet fire. "I think you know what I'm suggesting, darling."

The hush in the library intensified, and she became aware of the charged air between them, the way he was studying her.

"Are…are you proposing to me?" Ivy asked with a suddenly dry throat.

Dropping to one knee, Arthur produced a gold ring, holding it up between his fingers. "Marry me, Ivy. Together we could be unstoppable, and Blackwood could take its rightful place in England, in the world."

Her heart beat faster, the implications of his proposal racing through her head. But the memory of Ralph's pleading eyes and warnings came back to her. "Are you asking to marry me, or the library?"

Arthur stood, cupping her cheek in his hand and drawing her closer. The other patrons and silent stacks of books faded and dimmed, leaving only the two of them locked together. "You, only you. I know you, Ivy, and I know what books mean to you, because they mean the same thing to me. If I seem eager about the library, it's only because I know it's the way to your heart. And I very much want to be let inside that heart."

Ivy felt light and deliciously dizzy with Arthur's hands warm on her face, as if she might float up to the ceiling and join the trumpeting figures in the mosaic. She wouldn't be alone anymore; the hole that had only grown larger since her family's deaths could start to heal around the edges, maybe even shrink. Her dreams of having a family of her own were within reach. Arthur was a good, honorable man, and he valued the same things as her. Arthur knew this strange new world to which she had been elevated, could help her navigate it, find a home in it. But most of all, he would help her, with the library, with Blackwood, all of it. She didn't have to bear the headaches, the dreams, and the ghosts alone anymore.

"Ralph—that is, my chauffeur—told me something about you. About the club you're a member of."

Arthur raised a brow. "Your chauffeur? Do tell."

Forced to recount his warning out loud she realized how ridiculous it sounded. "He said that you're only interested in me because you want your club to be able to use the library."

Laughing, Arthur drew her closer into his embrace. "It's no secret that my father and Lord Hayworth had differing ideas when it came to the library and the dissemination of information. If the staff at Blackwood overheard one of their heated discussions, I could see how they might have thought that the old fellows might come to blows. Though in general, I would not trust the gossip of servants. Especially young male servants who may have a passing fancy for their mistress."

All of Arthur's explanations were so simple, so logical. It felt good to let him explain everything away and to forget all the unknowns and cling to something real.

"Yes," Ivy said against his chest. She hadn't realized that she had been drowning since she arrived, but now that the surface was near, she couldn't break through and get air fast enough. The niggling sense of wrongness that had haunted her since coming to Blackwood suddenly faded away. It was like falling into a soft, warm bed after miles of travel, her weary body finally given permission to rest.

"Yes, I'll marry you."

Breaking into a grin, Arthur lifted her up and swung her around, startling the men from their reading and drawing censorious looks. "Oh, my darling." He placed her back down, but not without a big, smacking kiss to the cheek. "You've made me so happy, happier than you can ever know."

18

"My lady, where have you been?"

It was a good question. Mrs. Hewitt watched as Ivy stopped at the bottom of the staircase and looked about, trying to remember what she had just been doing. There was mud on her boots, so she must have been bicycling or out walking, but she couldn't recall why or where. It had been what—a week? two?—since Arthur had swept her off her feet with his proposal, and her days were becoming progressively blurrier, moments strung together on a tangled string.

"I was… I believe I was bicycling."

"Well, there was a message from Sir Arthur," Mrs. Hewitt said. "I told him you were indisposed."

"Thank you, Mrs. Hewitt," Ivy said crisply as she peeled off her gloves. But Mrs. Hewitt made no movement to leave. "Yes?"

Mrs. Hewitt pursed her lips, her long face stamped with

disapproval and an edge of worry. "Is there…is it true, that there's an understanding between you and Sir Arthur?"

Ivy paused before taking the first stair. Word certainly traveled fast. "I don't see how it's any of your business, but in fact, yes. We are engaged to be married."

The color drained from Mrs. Hewitt's face. "Oh, my lady, you can't," she said.

A movement out of the corner of her eye, and Ivy caught sight of Ralph, hovering just outside the doorway. She found herself unaccountably irritable that he was once again looming about watching her, as if he had some claim on her. At her words, he threw down the tool belt he had been carrying, the clatter echoing through the hall. There was a wild glimmer in his eyes as he stalked away that sent her stomach into a free fall.

"I can, and I will," Ivy snapped, dragging her gaze from where it lingered at the doorway. "Now please, I don't want to hear any more about Sir Arthur or what I may or may not do. I am an adult woman, and lady of this house. I will marry whom I please."

A headache was coming on, and the pain was building hot and fast behind her eyes, almost to the point of blinding her. She reached for the marble banister to steady herself, and was vaguely aware of Mrs. Hewitt's brows drawing together in concern.

"Excuse me," Ivy mumbled. She turned and hurried upstairs, collapsing into her bed.

Something was pressing down on her eyes, as if someone had tied a blindfold tightly about her head. When she raised a shaking hand to her temples, her fingers met a damp towel. She was groggy, and it felt as if she'd been sleeping for years under some sort of enchantment. Dried blood caked her nose, and her mouth was dry as cotton.

A shift in the air and faint rustle of movement told her that she wasn't alone. With the effort of what felt like rolling a boulder up a mountain, Ivy cracked open her eyes. Blue wallpaper and the familiar pattern of crenelations on her bedroom window greeted her. Then a blurry face leaned over her, slowly coming into focus.

She squinted against the gray window light. "Arthur, what are you doing here?" Her voice came out cracked, as if she had not spoken in many days.

"You're awake." Relief flooded his face. He perched on the edge of the bed, the mattress dipping toward him. "You never returned my message, and I was beginning to worry. Then you missed the charity auction, and I knew that something must be wrong."

"What are you talking about? What auction?"

"Why, for the war orphans. When I told you that the Ladies' Auxiliary was holding one, you insisted on helping coordinate it." He paused, looking at her with concern anew. "Don't tell me that you forgot about it?"

"I..." Ivy trailed off. "I helped plan an event?" It sounded plausibly like something she would do, but she hadn't the faintest recollection of it.

Arthur's expression softened from incredulity into something like pity, and Ivy felt like a small child being comforted after a tantrum. "Yes, you were very keen to help the cause. Of course, I cautioned against it. But you *would* stay up planning it all night and oversee all the little details yourself. That's why I was so alarmed when I arrived and you were nowhere to be seen."

"Oh, dear," Ivy said. She could bear her forgetfulness if it was only her that it affected, but now it seemed that others were suffering for it. "Were the children very upset?"

"There were some tears, yes. But not to worry, it went off otherwise without a hitch, and the ladies were able to raise a good sum of money, I was told."

"When…when was that?" Patches of memories came back to her: the engagement, riding her bicycle, confronting Mrs. Hewitt, a terrible headache. But she couldn't for the life of her remember anything about a charity event.

In the doorway, Agnes was hovering, her fingers twining around each other at her waist. She shared a concerned look with Arthur.

"Almost a day ago," he told Ivy.

No, that couldn't be right. She closed her eyes and swallowed. "It's nothing, just a headache." But even as she struggled to her elbows, a wave of fatigue washed over her. This wasn't just a headache and a bloody nose. Desperately, she tried to remember what had led her to this moment, but it was like water running over smooth pebbles, and no memories stuck.

Arthur gently pressed her back into the pillows. "I've already sent for a doctor—my personal physician."

"That's not—that's not necessary," Ivy protested.

Bringing a glass of water to her dry lips, Arthur tipped her head back to help her drink. "I'm afraid it is, darling."

The water blazed a deliciously cold trail through her body. She could have drunk an entire bucket's worth, but Arthur drew the glass away after a few sips. "Easy now," he said gently. "Won't do to make yourself sick on your empty stomach."

At some point Agnes had gone to fetch Mrs. Hewitt, who had insisted on joining them in the room, as apparently it wasn't proper for her to be in bed with a man beside her. Ivy hadn't the energy to dismiss the housekeeper, so she lay there with Arthur tenderly holding her hand, and Mrs. Hewitt hawk-eyed and disapproving in the corner. At last the physician arrived. Middle-aged with silver-gray hair, piercing blue eyes, and neatly dressed in an expensive-looking dark tweed suit, he was a far cry from the neighborhood pharmacists from whom her mother used to purchase two-penny bottles of cures.

"Lady Hayworth," he said, giving her a short bow at the neck. "My name is Dr. Prescott. I hear you are in some discomfort."

Ivy opened her mouth to respond, but Arthur swooped in. "Headaches," he told the doctor. "My fiancée is suffering from terrible headaches, perhaps brought on by eye strain from reading. As you can see, it's gotten so bad that she became incapacitated."

The doctor gave a knowing nod. "All too common, I'm afraid." He opened his black bag and pulled out a stethoscope which he placed modestly on Ivy's chest over her blouse. Apparently satisfied with whatever he heard, he removed the tool, and proceeded to rifle about in his bag for something.

"This is absurd," she was able to mumble.

Dr. Prescott ignored her protest. "My lady, may I ask what you have been doing in addition to reading lately? Anything that might have overexerted you?"

Doing her best to keep a level voice despite his patronizing tone, she said, "I've done nothing out of the ordinary. I—"

"My fiancée has started a book lending program in the village," Arthur cut in. "She spends hours selecting books in the library, then bicycles all the way into town and back by herself. She helped organize a charity auction for war orphans, and this is in addition to her duties at the abbey. She's unstoppable, I'm afraid."

The doctor shared a look with Arthur as if they were both in on some big secret, one which her feminine mind was incapable of understanding, then gave her a wan smile. "My lady, I believe what we have here is a case of nerves coupled with fatigue. And is it any wonder? A young woman thrust into a new social position, running a large household by herself, and taking on extra projects which involve long bicycle rides. It's a well-studied phenomenon that bicycling for women can upset the flow of blood, causing it to rush from the head to the uterus. I'm prescribing you something to take in the evening to help you sleep, and lots of rest besides that. Absolutely no more bicycling. I saw you have a lovely Austin motorcar in the drive, and I should think that would be a preferable mode of transportation." He paused, thoughtfully stroking his little beard. "You're lucky your fiancé will be helping you, and relieving you of some of your burdens—not all ladies would be so lucky. Now, I don't want to hear about any more bicycle rides or long nights spent in the library." Standing, Dr. Prescott shook hands with Arthur, who showed him out.

When the men were gone, Ivy's gaze slid over to Mrs. Hewitt who was sitting still as a statue in the corner, eyes trained at the foot of the bed. Though her back was straight and jaw set, she looked less severe today, her graying hair more loosely styled, a fine mist in her dark eyes. "I told you to stay out of that library." Her voice held no reproach, only a weary sort of resignation.

"I hardly think reading is the cause of this."

Mrs. Hewitt sighed, looking tired, older than her already advanced years. "I should have sent you packing the moment you stepped foot here. Imagine, them sending a young woman!"

"What do you mean, 'they' sent me? I'm the heir to Blackwood, and I've the paperwork to prove it. I came of my own volition. No one sent me." Closing her eyes, Ivy sank back onto the pillows. The staff were all bitter. It was the only explanation. Alone in the house with naught but the lonely moors about them, and they turned to cruel tricks and stories to torment her, to see how long it would take them to drive Ivy out. They were used to having the house to themselves, and resented a new young mistress coming in and stirring the pot with modern ideas. Ivy gave a huff, turning her attention to the window where gray clouds were scudding low across the sky.

Mrs. Hewitt ignored the question. "The others, well, they were all men, and all had a sense of entitlement about them, which is to be expected. But it seems you've made your mind up. You've seen it for yourself," Mrs. Hewitt continued. "Why do you think we tried to stop you from lending the books out? Don't you see what happens? It's not my place to interfere— quite the opposite. But it's untenable that things carry on in this way."

Ivy sat up as straight as her aching body would allow, the coverlet falling away. "You're talking about the books," she said. There was a connection to be made, but her groggy head was struggling to make it, like a flint not quite catching the flame. "Something happens when they leave the library. Is that it?"

Mrs. Hewitt worried at the ring of keys at her belt, before quickly catching herself and returning to her usual composure. When she didn't offer any more information, Ivy rubbed a frustrated hand across her bleary eyes. "But Arthur said it was all coincidence."

"And you would believe him?"

"Seeing as he's the only one who's offered so much as one word of explanation, then yes, what choice do I have but to believe him? You sit there and hem and haw and beat about the bush, dropping crumbs of hints, but you won't tell me a thing."

Mrs. Hewitt drummed her fingers on the arm of the chair,

her lips sealed as tight as a tomb. "I'll leave you to your rest," she said, standing abruptly.

"Wait," Ivy said, sensing her chance to learn more slipping away. "Wait, please stay. I'm sorry I—"

But the door had already clicked shut, and with it, the closest chance she had to any answers from Mrs. Hewitt disappeared.

Ivy let out a curse. Fumbling on the bedstand for the bottle the doctor had left, she read the label and gave a weak laugh. Morphine. It would help with the headaches and then some. With shaking hands, she administered three drops of the clear liquid into the glass of water beside her, and gulped it down.

Closing her eyes, she let the room swirl around her, the morphine taking the hard edges off reality. How had it come to this? Only weeks ago she had boarded a train, full of hope and excitement. And why not? She now had a home, food in her belly, and a fiancé who adored her more than anything. But what was real was starting to grow fuzzy and soft, like an old daguerreotype. The strange conversations, the books that seemed to foreshadow, if not cause, the contents of their pages to spill over into the world. How did she know if any of that was real?

Once, in the early days of the war, one of James's friends had joined them for dinner. He had already seen action, and been sent home on leave on account of a shrapnel wound in his shoulder. Mother had uncorked a bottle of wine to celebrate, the loud *pop* reverberating through the small flat. James's friend had fallen to the floor, and for a moment Ivy had been afraid that the cork had hit him. But he was unharmed—physically at least. It took them at least half an hour to coax him out from under the table, and when he sat in his seat again, his eyes were far away, haunted, his body shaking. Afterward, her father had told her that some soldiers were coming home changed by what they had seen in the trenches, doomed to be haunted by their war memories for the rest of their lives. Shell shock, he had called it. Was that what was happening to her? She had never been in a war, but perhaps it was the same principle. Perhaps the shock of receiving the bequest and moving into Blackwood after everything she had been through had taken a toll on her mind that was only now coming to light.

Ivy's dreams were vivid and feverish that night. An older woman in a medieval gown and white headdress floated through her room, pausing at the foot of her bed to turn all-seeing eyes on Ivy. Something in the woman's placid demeanor was kind and warm, and made Ivy feel safe, like a guardian angel. But then she was gone, and in her place, a hooded monk. His face was obscured, but all the same, something cold gripped Ivy by the spine, telling her that she did not want to know what lay in the depths of that crimson hood. She tried squeezing her eyes shut, but her dream mind would not let her, and she was forced to watch as the hood fell away. A scream stuck in her throat as it revealed a hideous skull, bits of crusty flesh and skin hanging from the bone, and eye sockets crawling with maggots. One fell on the bed, and she kicked at the blankets, desperate to get the wriggling thing off.

She awoke the next morning to sheets bunched and tangled, damp with sweat. Her mouth tasted of chemicals, and the fatigue that weighed her down felt artificial, as if she had been pushed deeper and deeper into her mattress by heavy hands. Bolting up, she clawed at the covers, looking for any sign of the maggots, but of course there were none. It had been a dream. A terrible dream, but a dream nonetheless. At that moment she pledged she would not touch that horrid morphine again, no matter how bad the headaches became. She didn't trust that doctor and how quick he had been to diagnose her. In fact, she didn't trust anyone. Not Ralph, not Mrs. Hewitt, and as much as it pained her to admit it, not even her fiancé.

19

Ivy had never been particularly fond of opera, but the singer on the wireless was entrancing, her notes soaring clear and high to fill the parlor. Leaning back into her chair, Ivy closed her eyes, and let the aria carry her to exquisite heights. The music was a balm, easing her jumbled mind the way a warm bath would ease the body. And after a week spent in bed plagued by nightmares, Ivy had been in need of warm, comforting things.

With light streaming in the windows from a rare sunny day, more and more the strange events of the past weeks began to seem like nothing more than the lingering memories of a morphine-induced stupor. Mrs. Hewitt's cryptic words gradually faded from Ivy's mind, and if the staff were indeed trying to drive her mad, they seemed to have been content to give her a reprieve.

The aria ended, the last note quavering over the static until the announcer came on and the program changed to a news segment.

"Darling, I'm so glad to see you up and about," Arthur said, breezing into the room. "You look surprised to see me. Did you forget I said I would call on you today?"

"Of course not," Ivy said, though in truth she had no memory of it.

He kissed her cheeks, and held her back to inspect her. "No more headaches, I take it?"

"No, rest was just what I needed. You were right."

"The words every man loves to hear." Hands in pockets, he looked even more relaxed than usual, handsome in an un-bothered way.

"But there is something that I wanted to talk to you about," she told him, gesturing for him to sit. She chose her words carefully, aware that her gender put her at a disadvantage when it came to advocating for herself. "There was no need for you to speak to your personal physician on my behalf. I've been looking after myself for a long time, and am very capable of describing my own symptoms and health."

Arthur lowered himself beside her; the sofa cushion dipped slightly, bringing their knees together. He gave her an indulgent look. "You forget that you're my fiancée, and that even though we aren't married yet, I feel obliged to look after you and your well-being. If I seemed overbearing, it was only because I was worried about you. Desperately worried."

Ivy ran her finger along the swirls of the carved wooden sofa arm. She supposed he was right, yet she still bristled that in exchange for security and companionship, she would be giving up some of her hard-won freedoms.

Arthur shifted toward her, lifting her hand and grazing the sensitive skin of her wrist with his lips. The tenderness of the gesture startled her, and she stiffened for a moment before giving in to his touch. It had been so long since someone had touched her like that, and she hadn't realized how hungry she was for affection.

"There now," he said, gently brushing aside the tear that was welling under her eye. "This is why I rang for the physician. Not because I thought to pull rank, but because I can't stand to see my darling girl so upset. You don't need to take care of yourself anymore, I'm here."

It felt so good to lean into him and smell his now-familiar cologne. He was steady, real. Why had she thought she couldn't trust him? There had been some business about the library, and she could recall Mrs. Hewitt's face drawn tight with worry in her room. But beyond that, Arthur had proved himself loyal and good. If only they were already married. She didn't want to spend any more time alone in Blackwood. When Arthur was here there was laughter and brightness and Ivy could put her worries aside.

Sniffing back her tears, she nodded. "Shall I ring for tea?"

"No need, I can't stay long. I came because I wanted to propose something."

"Goodness, I already said yes," she said, mustering a smile.

"Yes, and thank God for that. I was thinking that we should host an engagement party. Here, at Blackwood. It would be a marvelous way to introduce you to Yorkshire society, and besides, I want to celebrate my bride-to-be. What do you say?"

Ivy worried at her lip. Although things had calmed down, there was still a niggling sense of wrongness about everything. She had thought that by now she would have found her footing among the local gentry, but she had largely been able to avoid social gatherings. How would she navigate a big party? Never mind navigate, how would she host one? But maybe a party was just the thing to force her to face her fears. She could invite Susan, and Arthur would be by her side to help her.

"Yes, why not?"

"Excellent." Arthur drew her face to his, brushed her lips with a kiss, just as Ivy caught a disapproving Mrs. Hewitt passing by the door out of the corner of her eyes.

"It will be a lot of work for the staff," she mused. "I wonder if we should hire on more help, for the preparations and the party itself."

"No need," Arthur assured her. "I'll send over our cook and some footmen and housemaids. You won't have to lift a finger."

The house was colder, emptier, the moment Arthur said his goodbyes and left. Ivy watched his car disappear in a cloud of exhaust and gravel, then, with a sigh, turned and headed for the kitchen to inform Mrs. Hewitt of the plan.

Downstairs, the sound of voices arguing in hushed whispers spilled out into the servants' hall. Staying her step, Ivy pressed her ear against the half-opened door, straining to make out the words.

A masculine voice. "…need to tell her…"

"Absolutely not," came the sharp counter of a woman's voice.

The man's voice again, but it was too low for Ivy to make out.

Carefully shifting her weight, she placed her palms against the door, trying to get just a little bit closer. "…she'll have forgotten by now in any case," the woman said.

She edged closer, but her hand pressed too hard against the wood, and the door creaked open. She stood frozen, meek as a dog caught with the Christmas goose, before stepping the rest of the way into the kitchen.

"My lady." Mrs. Hewitt slowly rose to her feet. "I trust you are feeling better if you were able to venture down here?"

Ralph gave the smallest nod of his head to acknowledge her, but did not meet her eye. His jaw was set, whatever the argument had been about clearly still weighing on him.

"Thank you. I am feeling much better." The air hung heavy

with tension, perhaps from the fight she had just interrupted, or perhaps because of what she was about to ask of her staff. "I came to see you because Sir Arthur and I are planning an engagement party. Here, at Blackwood."

She tried not to notice the way that Ralph stiffened in his seat, the way his fist was clenched around the handle of his cup, but her traitorous eyes kept darting to gauge his reaction.

"I see," the housekeeper said.

Ivy soldiered on. "I know it's a lot to ask of you to prepare a party and serve so many people, so Sir Arthur has kindly offered to send his cook and some house servants to help."

A blanket of silence settled over the kitchen until Mrs. Hewitt finally spoke. "You cannot be serious. My lady."

"I am quite serious. This is my home, my life. I am not asking for anything besides a little respect. If there is some reason why you find that so difficult, then I would be very glad for you to just be out with it for once and for all."

Ralph opened his mouth as if to interject, but Mrs. Hewitt shot him a caustic look. "Very well, my lady," she said, folding her hands and leveling an infuriatingly bland expression at Ivy.

She hadn't expected that Mrs. Hewitt would actually capitulate. "Very well, you'll help with the party? Or very well, you'll tell me what's going on?"

"Very well, we will have your party. But I warn you, my lady, the Mabrys are a bad lot, and I shouldn't trust them for one moment in this house."

"I happen to be marrying into that 'bad lot,' as you say, so I would appreciate it if you showed both Sir Arthur and me the respect that we deserve!" Ivy's voice rose to a shrill pitch that she didn't recognize and the kitchen fell silent. Was this who she had become? Someone who shouted and demanded the groveling respect of her servants? She more than anyone understood what it was to belong to an invisible class, living at the mercy of the rich and powerful. But she was also angry, at Mrs. Hewitt and the rest, that they had driven her to this. Not once had they been welcoming, or treated her like a long-lost family member come home. Not once had they made anything at Blackwood easy for her.

Ivy turned on her heel. "If you need me, I'll be in the library."

"Wait, my lady." Mrs. Hewitt stopped her with a hand on her arm. There was a gentling of her voice, the lines around her mouth smoothing out. "You have no one to watch out for you. If I appear strict or uncaring, it is only because I am concerned and feel it my duty to look out for you, whatever that may entail."

"I have been looking out for myself for quite some time," Ivy told her, pulling away. "I don't need your concern." Mrs. Hewitt's hand fell away, her lips pressed tight, as Ivy beat a hasty retreat back to the library.

20

Cold air wrapped itself around Ivy, her bare arms prickling with excitement. She felt small standing at the bottom of the stairs in the great hall, anxious. The slinky, beaded gown had appeared in her room that morning with a note from Arthur. And with it, the daintiest little black slippers with matching beading appliqued into rosettes. Agnes had styled her hair into loose waves secured with a black feather fascinator, and when Ivy had looked in the mirror, a real lady had gazed back at her; she couldn't have asked for better armor for a battle against her nerves that night.

Despite Mrs. Hewitt's reservations, the party had come together beautifully. Fires roared in the grates, empty bedchambers had been cleaned and aired in anticipation of overnight guests, and everywhere the glitter of chandeliers sparkled in the candlelight. Servants Ivy didn't recognize scurried to make last-minute preparations, and Hewitt appeared with a tray of champagne flutes. She commandeered one in passing, draining it quickly and letting the bubbles float to her head. As long as Arthur was beside her, she would survive—no, conquer—the night.

Ralph was conferring with Hewitt near the door. Shaved and dressed in his sharp navy chauffeur uniform for once, Ivy felt as if she was seeing him for the first time, and her stomach gave a little flutter. He looked strong and handsome and reassuring, a solid figure against the unknowns of the night. He caught her eye, but did not return her anxious smile. Then he was gone again and the crunch of gravel outside drew her back to the present moment.

A footman materialized and announced Sir Arthur Mabry. Ivy all but ran to him; her anchor had arrived, and she need not fear being adrift in a sea of foreign social mores and obligations.

"Darling." He embraced her, then held her at arm's length, his dark eyes roaming over her. "You look…you're stunning, Ivy." There was a choke in his voice, and she shivered under his heated gaze.

"I'm so glad you're here," was all she could say. Dressed in white-tie with his black hair neatly slicked and parted, he looked like Rudolph Valentino, sparkling and handsome. And tonight, the world would see that he was hers, all hers. There were no ghosts or headaches or an intangible sense of dread; there was only the present moment, and it glittered and shone like a golden coin for the taking.

She'd barely had time to finish her champagne and reapply her lipstick when the first guests began to arrive. Every time the footman announced a new arrival, Arthur would quickly whisper in her ear who they were and how they should be greeted. Soon she found that her pasted-on smile was becoming genuine, and that she was actually enjoying herself. Everyone who came down the line was lovely, shaking her hand or kissing her cheek, treating her like an old friend. Why had she been so afraid of these people? She was one of them now.

A tall, serious man was the next down the line, and Ivy felt Arthur stiffen beside her. "My father," he murmured, as the man came to a stop in front of them.

"Father, may I present Ivy Radcliffe, the Lady Hayworth? Lady Hayworth, this is my father, the Honorable General Mabry, Earl of Norbrook."

He wore a full white-tie suit with starched shirt and tail-coat, looking altogether like a relic of a different era. Deep lines creased his long, jowly face, his stark white hair severely parted.

"How do you do, my lord?" Ivy greeted him, dipping a small curtsy.

"A pleasure, Lady Hayworth," he said, his voice all clipped vowels and upper-class nasal tones. "I couldn't have been prouder of my son when he told me the good news," he said. "The joining of two great families. Just think of the line your children will be starting."

"Father, you'll scare her off," Arthur said with a smile, though his eyes were hard, his body tense.

Ivy held her breath, sensing the tension and waiting for an argument between father and son to break out. But despite the skirmish, it seemed that they were not at war tonight.

By the time the line had ended, Ivy's feet were starting to pinch in her shoes. Her stomach rumbled, but before dinner there were to be cocktails in the parlor. Opulent bouquets of roses and lilies filled the vases, their sweetly cloying scent making her light-headed. It was strange to see the usually empty room filled with guests, the mingling scents of lady's perfumes and the autumn winds brought indoors. It felt as if the strings on a limp puppet had suddenly been picked up, setting it dancing and spinning. Maybe there was hope for Blackwood to be a real home yet.

"Lady Hayworth, so good of you to invite us," a gentleman with prolific side-whiskers told her as he grasped her hand in his clammy grip. "You must know how very eager we are to see the library. I've been waiting these twenty years to find myself in Blackwood, and now I'm afraid even another twenty minutes will be too much for me to bear."

"Easy, Sir Alfred," Arthur said, cutting in with a smooth smile. "There will be a viewing after dinner. No need to accost the lady while we are all simply enjoying good drinks and conversation."

"Of course, of course," Sir Alfred blustered. He murmured his apologies and blended back into the crowd.

"I wonder if some of them are here simply to see the library and the engagement was just an excuse to come," Ivy said.

"You mustn't mind some of our more enthusiastic members," Arthur told her around sipping his drink. "They're well-meaning, but unfortunately lacking manners."

Ivy watched the man snatch another drink off the tray of a passing servant. "I suppose you're right," she murmured. A headache was building at the base of her neck, tension blossoming upward to her head. The endless platitudes and introductions were beginning to wear on her, and the only thing filling her empty stomach was alcohol.

At last dinner was announced, and the party moved into the dining room. It was the first time Ivy would eat in the room since she lived at Blackwood. The dust sheets and spare furniture had been banished, and in their place were glittering crystal goblets, silver flatware, and hothouse flowers arranged in oversized urns. She ran a gloved finger along the back of a gilded chair. For every plate there were a dozen forks and spoons. Did all this finery belong to Blackwood? Was it hers?

She would never understand the rich decrying their dwindling means, when so much wealth sat right under their very roofs in the form of fine furniture and silver collections. Was it really such a hardship to them to part with a few candlesticks and paintings?

Arthur helped Ivy to her seat, and at long last the food was served. As she sipped a dainty spoonful of broth, Ivy discreetly let her gaze roam over the dinner guests. There was an undercurrent of restless energy flowing around the table; men checked their pocket watches, and ladies whispered to one another. They all wanted to see the library, and were just muddling through the meal until it was time. Ivy's heart sank. This was supposed to be a celebration of her and Arthur's engagement, an introduction for her into society. Ivy dutifully made small talk with the gentleman on her left, but the luster of the evening was quickly wearing off. She couldn't shake the feeling that there was someone else who was supposed to be here, a friendly face who she had been looking forward to seeing. But she couldn't for the life of her remember who.

"Tell me, how do you find Blackwood Abbey?" Lord Mabry asked as he viciously stirred at his soup. "I knew the late Lord Hayworth and he wasn't terribly keen when it came to improvements and upkeep. Dreary old place, but not without its charm."

"It's far grander than I ever imagined," Ivy said, trying not to sound too much like the starry-eyed girl from Bethnal Green she was. "The library in particular is divine."

The older man's gaze lifted from his bowl and a nostalgic smile touched his thin lips. "Ah yes, the library. The jewel of Blackwood. I am very much looking forward to the viewing after dinner. I do hope that it hasn't turned to dust after it was commandeered as an infirmary during the war."

Here, at least, Ivy could find her footing. "In truth, the staff seemed reluctant to open it. But I've had the wiring redone and am in the process of cataloging the collection and cleaning it up. I hope to bring it back up to snuff."

"Admirable, my lady. I am glad to hear it. Servants have no business dictating anything," Lord Mabry said, stabbing his spoon in the air to punctuate his words. "That is the one piece of advice I will give you as you embark on this venture. Don't let them forget who pays their wages and provides the roof over their heads. It's the only thing that separates us from anarchy, and it's the prerogative of our bloodline to keep the order."

He sounded like one of those eugenicists, always concerned about the purity of English blood and keeping the classes and races separate. She briefly considered pouring the contents of her soup on his head, but thought better of it. Taking her smile as encouragement, he continued.

"When I came back from the front, I found my butler had been making himself familiar with the wine cellar, and all but two footmen absconded off to the city to find factory work," he said. "Can you imagine? Off fighting for Crown and country, and the mice are at play." He gave a heavy sigh and took a long draught of his wine. A stone-faced servant refilled his glass. "Ah well. We all had to do our bit, didn't we?"

Ivy gave a minuscule nod, focusing on lifting the spoon of broth to her mouth without spilling it.

"Arthur couldn't fight," Lord Mabry said, oblivious to her discomfort.

Until now Arthur had remained silent. "Father—" he started, putting down his spoon.

"Bad lungs when he was a boy," his father continued. "Can you imagine how that looked? A general asking his men to give their lives, while his own son sat at home and played tennis and read books?"

A muscle worked in Arthur's jaw.

"I'm sure your son has made you proud in other ways," Ivy hurried to put in, hoping to defuse what looked to be an explosive—if not common—matter of contention between the father and son.

"Your idealism is a credit to you, Lady Hayworth," the old general said, "but I am well acquainted with my son and his flaws."

"What my father won't tell you, is that I was active in the local Home Guard, and visited the infirmaries to offer my services."

"Bah." Lord Mabry gave a dismissive wave of his hand. "Women's work, is what that is."

Arthur motioned for a servant to refill his glass, and quickly drained it before having another poured.

By the time the fish course was served, Ivy could hardly stomach another bite, her head swimming and her stomach churning with rich foods. Arthur had her glass refilled, and leaned over to whisper in her ear, "You're doing brilliantly, darling. I know this must be so tiring."

Her hand found his under the table and gave it a squeeze. A not unpleasant buzz was overtaking her headache, making her feel light and giddy. Too much wine, but it was the only thing that helped soften the hard edges of her duties as hostess, and dispel the heavy cloud that had settled over her since meeting her future father-in-law.

The tinkling of silver against crystal, and then Arthur was standing, glass in hand, clearing his throat. "I know we are all eager to move into the library, but I would be remiss if I did not raise a glass to the real reason we are here tonight." Here, he turned to Ivy and graced her with a brilliant smile. "My lovely fiancée, Ivy. I knew as soon as I saw her in the bookshop that I had found a rare treasure indeed, a woman who not only bore my bookish habits with grace, but encouraged and matched them as well."

A ripple of polite laughter and round of *Hear! Hear!*

Ivy focused on the glass in Arthur's hand, concentrating on the moving glints of light as he gestured. Sitting upright was becoming more and more difficult, the faces around the table starting to blur together. She caught the eye of one of the servers, and could have sworn it was Ralph. But what would he be doing up here serving dinner? She rubbed her eyes, made an effort to appear interested. She just had to make it through Arthur's toast, and then she could beg off and go to her room. Why had she allowed herself to drink so much wine? She was going to be too drunk to even enjoy her own engagement party.

"So, a toast, if you please. To the most enchanting and gracious of women, the Lady Hayworth."

Ivy managed what was probably a terrible smile, half standing from her seat to accept his praise. But she stumbled, and Arthur had to catch her by the elbow.

"You'll have to forgive my fiancée," he said with a laugh. "I'm afraid she's enjoyed the evening a bit too much."

Embarrassment burned her cheeks. Couldn't he have handled that with a bit more tact, in a way that didn't leave her feeling exposed and ashamed in front of all these important people? But she found that she was too far gone to object, and besides, she was tired. So tired.

"I think... I think I need togoliedown," she managed to slur.

"Of course, darling," Arthur whispered in her ear. "You're not needed for this next bit anyway."

Before she could ask him what he meant, the room was spinning away under her feet, the blur of smiling faces fading until all that was left was black.

21

"Ivy, wake up!"

Someone was calling her name, but Ivy was floating through the most exquisite dream, her headaches gone, her worries nothing but a distant memory. She was standing on a verdant hill overlooking an expanse of clear, gurgling water. Everything here was in bloom, the most extraordinary flowers and trees in colors that could never exist in nature. The wind was soft and warm—a far cry from the damp chill of Yorkshire—and caressed her as gently as a silk scarf. It had to be paradise, with exotic birds drinking deeply from trumpet-shaped flowers, and women bathing in aqua pools, their long hair streaming out around them like Botticelli's Venus. Why would anyone try to wake her up? Inside this luminescent and heavenly dream it was safe. Out there dwelled chaos, horror. Parents died, leaving children to fend for themselves, and adored older brothers were sent off to perish in the trenches. Out there, a young woman had to survive by her wits alone, and even then, nothing was guaranteed. No, she did not think she wanted to return to all that.

Cold water hit her face and she bolted upright with a gasp. The birds took flight, the flowers faded. As she rubbed her wet eyes, the world began to take shape around her. A bed, not her own. Heavy velvet curtains blocked the windows and any light, but there was a stillness that told her it was night-time. A sickly arsenic-green wallpaper swirled and danced in the dim candlelight. She looked down, and saw she was still wearing her black evening gown, the delicate silk clinging to her chest from the dousing of water. When she glanced back up, the dark outline of a man crouching in front of her be-came visible, his silver eyes piercing through her as if his next breath depended on hers. He wore the bottle-green livery of a footman, but something in the way he held himself told her he was no servant. Scuttling back up against the pillows, Ivy grabbed at the covers and pulled them over her chest in a flimsy display of modesty. The man's dark brows drew to-gether, and he scowled.

"Trust me, m'lady, I've no interest in what's under that blanket."

She blinked at the rough yet familiar voice. "Ralph?"

"The very same. We need to leave. Now."

"What?"

"Oh for Christ's—" He ripped the blanket away from her, and in a surprisingly gentle yet self-assured movement, scooped her up into his arms.

"What are you doing? Put me down!"

"There's no time," he said as he carried her toward the door.

Her legs felt like jelly but she was able to land a good kick between his thighs, and Ralph instantly dropped her, cursing.

"I'm not going anywhere until you tell me what's going on." Ivy's head was swimming and her mouth tasted like chemicals. The last thing she remembered was sitting at the dining room table, listening as Arthur gave his toast. "Where's Arthur? What have you done with him?"

Through the darkness, she could see Ralph quickly cut his gaze away, still kneeling from the blow. It all became clear in an instant. Ralph *was* jealous of Arthur. How many cryptic warnings had he given her about Arthur Mabry? How many times had he had murder in his eyes when Ivy mentioned him? There was no ancient family feud, no dispute over the library. It was a simple case of jealousy. Though why Ralph cared about Arthur was beyond her.

"I didn't do anything to your bloody fiancé," Ralph gasped as he stood with a grunt. "Though I'd like to."

Ivy crossed her arms over her chest. The room was cold and her dress was still wet from her rude awakening. "I don't believe you."

"You don't have to, but you need to come with me. Now." Ralph kept glancing over his shoulder at the door.

As if on cue, the door swung open, and Ralph raised his fist, preparing for an attack.

"Is she awake?" Mrs. Hewitt asked as she peered into the dim room, a thick shaft of lamplight from the hall spilling inside.

Ralph dropped his fist. "Yes, and she's stubborn as a bloody mule."

Mrs. Hewitt would help her, wouldn't she? Even if she had no personal liking for Ivy, she was a woman and would surely not just stand by while Ralph abducted her. But the housekeeper quickly extinguished Ivy's hope. "Come with us, my lady. None of this dawdling now."

Still on the floor near the fireplace where Ralph had dropped her, Ivy groped behind her until her hand closed around something long and cool to the touch. Scrambling to her feet, she brandished the fire poker wildly in front of her. Ralph had the audacity to actually roll his eyes at her.

"Just tell her," he growled at Mrs. Hewitt. "She won't cooperate unless she understands."

"Understand what?" Ivy swayed on her feet, still very much under the effects of the alcohol.

"She won't believe it unless she sees it for herself," Mrs. Hewitt said quietly.

"Believe *what*?" They were speaking around her as if she wasn't even there.

Both turned to her, and there was something in their looks that made Ivy wish maybe she didn't have to see whatever it was to believe it.

"My lady, please, come with us. I promise you will come to no harm if you do, but I cannot guarantee the same if you stay here. They'll be coming to check on you any time now."

Ivy tightened her grip on the poker. "This doesn't make any sense. You don't make any sense." She closed her eyes, trying to remember how she had gotten here. "I had too much to drink at dinner, and Arthur must have shown me to the wrong room. If I'm not here when he comes back, he'll be worried. I must change and get back to the party."

Carefully, as if he was corralling a skittish horse, Ralph approached her, palms up. "You aren't drunk, Ivy," he said, his rough voice the gentlest she'd ever heard. "There was something in your drink. I tried to stop it, but they got it to you anyhow."

Ivy rubbed her eyes with her free hand, shards of memories flashing through her mind: Arthur continually having her glass refilled, Ralph dressed as a servant, hovering at the edge of the room. A room full of strange faces watching her with detached interest, no one coming to her aid as she fainted.

"No," she said, though it was a weak protest. "No, I had too much wine. Arthur would never do that to me."

Ralph didn't say anything, but the pity in his eyes was somehow worse. "Please, Ivy," he said, extending his hand. "Please, just come with us."

She was so tired, and something deep within her responded to the gesture. She had pledged that she wouldn't trust anyone, but there was a bone-deep exhaustion that was forcing her to let her guard down. Before she could stop herself, Ivy was placing her hand in Ralph's, allowing him to take some of her weight. His fingers closed around hers, gentle and firm.

"I'm taking this though," she demanded, clutching the fire poker to her chest.

There was a quirk at Ralph's lips, though it was gone so fast that she wasn't sure it had been there at all. "Of course."

Mrs. Hewitt was in the hall, craning her neck in both directions. "It's empty. This way," she said, motioning them to follow her.

Mrs. Hewitt set a brisk pace, but Ralph lagged behind, helping Ivy when she realized just how unsteady her legs were. Judging from the musty carpets and closed-up rooms they passed, they were in the rarely used north wing of the house. Why had Arthur brought her here instead of to her room?

Ivy chanced a sidelong glance at Ralph, though he was so close to her that she could only see the green wool of his coat, the brass livery buttons glinting in the dim light. His arm was looped gingerly around her waist, almost as if he was afraid to touch her. Was Ralph right, had there really been something in her drink? She'd heard the stories whispered between women in powder rooms, about girls who'd had their drinks tampered with in the dance halls. But Arthur was her fiancé, he loved her, or at the very least, cared about her. He wasn't some anonymous cad in a club. He was a gentleman.

Ivy had only been in this part of the house a handful of times, but Mrs. Hewitt was taking them somewhere that she was sure she'd never seen before. They abruptly stopped at the end of the hall, moonlight pouring in from a window and casting the wood-paneled walls in deep shadows. Mrs. Hewitt put her finger to her lips, and then pushed on the wall next to the window alcove with both hands. The panel swung away, revealing a hidden door.

Ralph's arm tightened around Ivy as he guided her through the dark passageway. It was musty and narrow, but the assurance with which they moved told her that both Mrs. Hewitt and Ralph had been this way before. They emerged onto a gallery so low that they had to crouch, and Ivy caught her breath as it dawned on her where they were. She'd never been on this level before, hadn't even realized there *was* a third gallery in the library. They were well hidden by a heavy wood guardrail and thick shadows cast from the dim lamplight below. Chancing a peek over the side, Ivy's head swam at just how far up they were. She leaned into Ralph, glad that his strong arm was there to support her.

Below them, the various members of the party chatted in groups, some browsing the shelves. Their voices carried up even to the third gallery, the acoustics as clear as if Ivy was standing among them below.

Arthur was in conversation with his father, a drink in hand. "Should we go have a look, just to make sure she's all right?"

Lord Mabry scoffed. "Dr. Prescott said that the dose was enough to put her out for hours yet. In the meantime, I say we find the manuscript and begin."

Coldness shot through Ivy's veins. Arthur *had* drugged her, and they were down there talking about it as if it was just another item on the evening's itinerary. Ralph must have sensed that Ivy's body was coiled and ready for an outburst, because he placed heavy hands on her shoulders with a squeeze, ensuring that she couldn't move. Biting her tongue, Ivy felt her eyes water as the betrayal washed over her in waves.

Lord Mabry cleared his throat and raised his glass. Immediately the crowd fell silent. "Esteemed friends and colleagues, Sphinxes, your attention for a moment, please." His commanding voice carried through the library—*her* library. "We find ourselves in an extraordinary position, one never before achieved by our society. The library is not only within our grasp, but we are poised to seize the manuscript for ourselves. Arthur will be married to the Lady Hayworth, and the library will be de facto in our control."

A murmur rippled through the small crowd. One man was helping himself to a cigar, waving his match perilously close to the books, and another had made himself comfortable in Ivy's favorite chair, his boots propped up on the velvet ottoman. It was like watching a horde of soldiers desecrating a temple.

"Will she allow it?" the man with the boots asked.

"She is a woman and will be a wife—she has little choice in the matter. Besides, the library needs her, needs her to feed. I will not risk my son to its appetites by removing the lady from the picture."

What were they talking about? Why did the library need her? Ivy shot a look at Ralph, but he just gave her a slow shake of his head.

"But we still need the manuscript," said a man Ivy recognized as Sir Alfred from the parlor.

"And what do you think we're doing here?" Lord Mabry snapped. "We have tonight to find it, and then everything else will fall into place. Once the wedding takes place, both library and manuscript will be ours completely. But I don't want to take any chances until then. We find it tonight, then ensure that we have it well and firmly under our control."

There was a ripple of agreement in the crowd. Through-out all of this, Arthur had been hanging back, his face horri-bly blank. Never once did he step in and defend Ivy or refute what the others were saying. He was not only party to what-ever was happening, he was instrumental in it. Tears stung her eyes. He had used her, betrayed her in the very worst way.

A light touch on her arm brought her back to the mo-ment, and she looked up to see Mrs. Hewitt motioning them to follow her. Ivy didn't want to watch the man who she had thought loved her stand by while others devised her downfall, yet she couldn't bear to tear herself away. Gently, Ralph laced his arm under hers, and half carried her out. Once they were back through the hidden passage and in the hall, Ivy allowed herself to finally crumple against the wall. Her stomach was churning, but it was not from the food or whatever they had put into her drink; it was the sickening, acidic compound of heartbreak and betrayal.

22

"What...what was that?" Ivy forced herself to ask.

"Come, let's go to the kitchen. I'll make some tea," Mrs. Hewitt said quietly.

Ivy didn't want tea. There was something sinister transpiring in the library, and as hard as it was to watch, she was desperate for the answers. But Mrs. Hewitt was already sweeping down the hall, and Ralph was taking Ivy by the arm, helping her as much as his limp would allow. She let herself be borne along like a leaf in a stream, too stunned to protest.

In the kitchen, they were met by Hewitt, who raised his head from a newspaper when they came in, a question in his eyes. Mrs. Hewitt nodded. "She knows."

"Knows what? I don't know anything," Ivy protested as Ralph helped her into a wooden chair. "Why were they talking about a manuscript? Why did they want the library? I would have given them access to it anyway if—"

Mrs. Hewitt stopped her. "Tea first, then questions."

"Do you really think we have time for tea?" Ralph said, eyeing the door. "They're already looking for the manuscript."

"There is always time for tea," Mrs. Hewitt said firmly, putting the issue to rest.

Ivy waited in miserable silence as Mrs. Hewitt bustled about the kitchen and prepared a plate of biscuits for which Ivy had no appetite. Traces of the engagement dinner were still evident in a scattering of pots and pans on the counters, and the lingering scent of roasted meat. It looked as if the kitchen staff had abruptly left after the last course, simply getting up and walking away.

When a steaming cup had been placed before her, Ivy's hands automatically went around it, the warmth seeping into her. At some point someone had draped a warm flannel blanket over her shoulders, and little by little some of the coldness that had overtaken her body began to thaw.

Settling into a chair across the table, Mrs. Hewitt took a sip from her own cup. "My lady, I wish that I did not have to impart this information to you, but it seems that I have no choice. I need you to listen to me, and listen carefully. What I am going to tell you will sound improbable, impossible even. But you must believe me and then be ready to act quickly."

Ivy had no choice but to nod. After what she had experienced and seen, any answers were preferable to the wild conjecture that was churning through her mind.

Hewitt cleared his throat and went to lock the kitchen door. "I suggest that whatever you tell her, you tell her quickly. We haven't much time."

Mrs. Hewitt gave a tight nod, then turned back to Ivy. "My lady, Blackwood is no ordinary library, and you are no ordinary heir to it."

"What do you mean?"

"There is a power, a dark power, that runs through the library, and at its heart, is a very old, very important manuscript. Ralph told me that you found it, saw it for yourself."

Ivy shot a look at Ralph, who was absorbed in scratching at a stain on the table with his fingernail. "I did?" she asked. There were many manuscripts in the library, but Ivy didn't remember finding anything particularly noteworthy.

"Yes, you did." Mrs. Hewitt confirmed. "For four hundred years, the Hayworth family have held the viscountcy of Blackwood, and their stewardship of the library has carried with it a curse." Mrs. Hewitt drew in a deep breath. "The library, it demands memories, dreams, from each and every heir. It adds them to its ever-growing collection, imbues the books with a dangerous kind of power that brings the words to life. Once the heir is drained and no longer of use, the next heir is sent for and the cycle begins again. You are the latest, and unfortunately the youngest, in a long line of Hayworth descendants."

There was a chip in the rim of Ivy's teacup, the dainty floral pattern interrupted by the chiseled clay beneath. Words were coming out of Mrs. Hewitt's mouth, but they held no meaning, made no sense. Ivy was still in her dream, that was it. The beautiful birds and flowers might be gone, but it was a dream nonetheless, surreal and nonsensical.

"The library is a living thing, hungry for new books, new stories," Mrs. Hewitt continued, "and the manuscript is the heart that circulates them. Every Hayworth heir has contributed a book, but they do not sate the library for long."

Ivy had to tamp down the urge to laugh; it was all so ridiculous. "Are you telling me that all my memories are in a book somewhere?"

"Your memories, your dreams, your every movement and thought," Mrs. Hewitt confirmed.

She swallowed, once and then twice before forcing herself to ask, "How do you know all this?"

"Because the Hewitts likewise are tied to the library. Our family has stood guard for those same four hundred years, ensuring that the library gets what it needs from the Hayworths, but never escapes beyond the confines of the abbey. We are immune to its powers, the result of an ancient pact made between our families."

When she was younger, Ivy's father had taught her about Occam's Razor—the simpler the theory, the more likely it was to be true, but the more complicated it was, the more likely it was to be false. What Mrs. Hewitt was telling her wasn't simply complex, it was full of downright fantastical details that simply could not be real. Ghosts and spirits were one thing, but magical libraries with sentient desires and hungers were simply a bridge too far.

"I don't believe you."

"I'm afraid that you don't have the luxury of disbelief," Mrs. Hewitt said with a grimace. She paused. "What, exactly, has Arthur told you about his family and the Sphinxes?"

Ivy pushed the cup away, crossed her arms as if that would offer some sort of protection from this new reality. "He said the library is special because it contains rare manuscripts, and that his club is committed to opening up the library for research and academic pursuits. They think it's a shame that it's hidden away and inaccessible to scholars."

Mrs. Hewitt nodded. "The Mabrys have long coveted Blackwood and its powers," she continued. "You see, the manuscript isn't just valuable, it contains secrets that have driven men to madness for centuries. How to bring back the dead and attain immortality. How to achieve eternal youth. They see it as a powerful tool that should be in the hands of the military. But they don't understand how dangerous it would be, how impossible to harness its powers for such a specific use. You saw for yourself what happened when you lent out the books. Now imagine that, but in the hands of men hungry for power and mass destruction."

"It's the Mad Monk's manuscript," Ivy whispered, as memories surfaced and pieces began to fall into place. She had forgotten about the ghost story, but now it tangled with memories of a hooded skull at the end of her bed, a hot, sour breath on her neck. And the manuscript, she could vaguely see the illustrations in her mind's eye, fantastical flora and fauna, and more disturbing tableaus of women in pools of blood. But the images remained indistinct and it was impossible to parse what was a memory and what was a dream.

"A fanciful name, but yes, the tale does have some truth to it. We don't know much about him, except that he lived here during Henry VIII's reign, and was fascinated with alchemy and the fabled fountain of youth. He was the author of the manuscript, and put all the dark magic that he studied into it. Whatever was in the manuscript is what imbues the library with its power. They feed off each other and hold the monk in half death."

Ivy took a sip of cold tea. Pushed it away again. The only sound in the kitchen was the clock ticking in the corner, yet her head throbbed as if a symphony had taken up residence in it.

"Arthur is only marrying you so that he can have complete control of the library." Ralph's low voice cut through her racing thoughts. "Do you see it now? I told you, you should have left."

Ivy bit her lip, unwilling to meet his piercing stare. She hated that he was right, but more than that, she hated that she felt as if she had somehow disappointed him.

"No, she shouldn't have," Mrs. Hewitt countered sharply. "You know what would happen if she were to leave."

Ivy barely heard them. Everything was falling apart faster than she could piece it together. Arthur didn't care for her, had never cared for her. Worse than that, he had used her for some dark and terrible purpose. She couldn't deny what she had seen with her own eyes in the library only an hour before.

"I can't marry Arthur," Ivy whispered, staring at the scarred and stained oak table.

Mrs. Hewitt grimaced. "I would not recommend it, no."

Ralph stood up abruptly, pushing back his chair. "She can't stay here."

"Why? What will happen to me if I stay?"

An indecipherable look passed between Ralph and the Hewitts. But Ivy already knew. She had seen the list of the Hayworths, had seen how they all died far too early.

"It has to do with what you said about the library taking memories, doesn't it?" A foggy recollection of her conversation with Ralph resurfaced, something about how she would start forgetting. "Is that what will become of me? I'll lose all my memories, and then die?"

"If you stay here, yes," Mrs. Hewitt confirmed. "As soon as you stepped foot in Blackwood, you bound yourself to the library."

"And if I leave?"

Mrs. Hewitt's lips compressed into a tight line. "You would need to find a replacement, a librarian who would live here, tend to the library. A small number of the lords in the past realized this, and brought on librarians to take their place. The library fed off of them instead, sparing the current holder of the title."

"For some time, anyway," Hewitt amended. "There's no escaping the library for good."

"So I would be condemning someone else to die." Ivy's shoulders slumped. It was hopeless.

Hewitt stood, clearing his throat. "We need to go make certain that they haven't found the manuscript. It's well hidden, but I don't want to leave anything to chance."

His wife nodded and began gathering up the tea things. "Most of the Mabry servants have returned but I don't trust Lord Mabry not to have left any spies or sentries."

Ivy moved to stand, but Mrs. Hewitt stopped her with a firm hand to her shoulder. "It would be best if you stayed here, my lady."

She didn't want to be in the kitchen by herself. The world was spinning away from her, the basic truths of her existence and what was real called into question. Now was not the time to sit with oneself and reflect on immortality and the vengeful nature of ghosts. She desperately wanted to be back in London, with bright city lights and the sound of motorcars around her, people going about their shopping and everyday errands.

"Ralph will stay with you. You'll be safe here." Mrs. Hewitt offered Ivy a rare smile, but it did little to assuage the feeling of dread which had taken root in her gut.

After the butler and housekeeper had gone, Ivy chanced a look at Ralph brooding across the table, arms crossed and jaw stubbornly set. His hair had grown just long enough to fall over his eyes, giving him the look of a moody schoolboy.

"You should have told me," Ivy said finally.

Ralph gave a grunt. "You wouldn't have believed me, and even if you had, you would have forgotten."

"You did though, that day I found the manuscript. You told me that I should leave. I remember that much now. What would have happened if I had left? Because it sounds as if someone else would suffer in my place."

He finally looked up, the flashing anger in his eyes almost

enough to make her wish she hadn't said anything. "Does it matter? You would have been safe."

Her face heated. "It does matter, to me. I don't want people to die, and I certainly don't want to be the one to send them to their death."

Ralph tipped back in his chair, eyes trained on the ceiling as if searching for the right words. "That's the problem. You're too—"

"Too what? Too stubborn? Too independent? I assure you, I've heard it all before."

Tipping the chair back down with a *thud*, Ralph gave a long exhale. "Too good," he muttered. "The problem is you're too good, Ivy."

There were a thousand pressing matters that should have taken precedence, but somehow her name from his lips utterly undid her. It was resigned and angry all at once, and so, so tender. Every look at him tore her heart further, threw her already muddled mind into delicious chaos. She took a long sip of her cooling tea as the silence deepened around them.

"What will Mr. and Mrs. Hewitt do?" she forced herself to ask, desperate to steer the conversation in another direction, one that wouldn't leave her feeling strangely unsettled and stormy inside.

"Make sure that the Mabrys don't find the manuscript." He paused, darting a glance at her from under dark gold lashes. "In however many years, you're the only one to have found it."

"And then what?" she asked. Would there be a tug-o-war between the Hewitts and the Mabrys over the manuscript? Would military lorries come rolling in and confiscate it?

"You ask a lot of questions."

"You're right. I suppose I should just sit back and drink my tea while a convoluted plot to secure an old manuscript and let it destroy everything unravels around me."

Ralph tapped on the table, distracted. "Then they'll probably either move it, or stand guard with it," he offered with a shrug. "I don't really know."

Ivy considered this. "How come you aren't affected?" At his raised brows, she pressed on. "The Hewitts are supposedly immune to the library or the manuscript's powers, whatever it is. But you, you work here too and you don't seem to be affected. Same with Agnes. Why not?"

Draining his cup of tea, he set it down with a rattle and pushed it away. "I'm not in the house much. Try to stay out of the library. Same for Agnes, I guess."

Trying to tease out more information from Ralph was like asking a stone to spill its secrets. Eventually Ivy gave up and settled back into her seat, eyeing the door and trying to decide if it was worth simply making a dash for it and finding answers for herself. As she raised her cup to her lips, a tremor in her hand flared up out of nowhere, tea splashing onto her dress. It seemed her nerves were finally catching up with her. She reached for a cloth to wipe it up, when there was a violent shaking. This time there was no mistaking it for a tremor in her own body; it came from the very house itself. The floors rumbled as if they might open up, and the walls swayed, dishes clattering to the ground. Nearly toppled from her chair, she grabbed ahold of the table.

Ivy had read about the great earthquake in California in the newspapers, but England didn't have those, did it? "What was—"

She didn't have a chance to finish. "Ivy, come here," Ralph said in a low voice, eyes trained on the door.

There were no second thoughts, no hesitation. As quick as she could she slid from her chair and bolted around the table, taking Ralph's arm. "What is it?"

His mouth was set in a grim line, the muscles in his arm tensed and coiled. "The Mabrys found it. And they've released it."

23

A frigid sense of dread laced its way through Ivy's veins at Ralph's ominous words. How exactly did one "release" a manuscript? Or was it something darker, whatever it was that lurked in the pages of the library? She looked down at the floor, half expecting snakes to come slithering in, or the ground to open up, the flames of Hell licking at her ankles.

But the tiles remained as they were, and before she could bombard Ralph with questions, there was a noise outside the door. The knob rattled, and Ivy tightened her grasp around Ralph's arm.

"The door is locked, isn't it?" she asked in a whisper.

Ralph didn't answer, just firmly pushed her behind him. "Get back."

The sound of someone throwing their weight into the door reverberated through the kitchen, and then it was flying open in a shower of splinters.

Ivy should have run—though who knew where—but her

feet were frozen to the ground. A tall man with an athletic build stood breathing heavily in the doorway, fair hair falling into his eyes, his dinner coat torn at the shoulder. Ivy vaguely recognized him as being one of the many guests from the party.

"In here! She's in here!" he yelled back into the hall.

Almost instantly, a handful of men still dressed in their party attire appeared behind him. Ralph moved with lightning speed, putting himself between Ivy and the men at the doorway. She stood planted behind the table, gripped by something between fear and fascination as she watched Ralph take a swing at the first man.

He was a good fighter, graceful and economical in his blows. But it wasn't a fair fight. A moment later one of the Mabry servants joined and there was a flash of bronze, and then a candelabra connected with Ralph's head from behind. He sagged to the floor like a marionette with cut strings before Ivy even had a chance to warn him.

Heedless of the men standing around them, she fell to the floor beside him. "Ralph," she whispered urgently, shaking his limp body. "Ralph, wake up!"

Blood pooled from his head, racing across the white tiles. How could anyone lose that much blood and be all right? Jerking her gaze up, Ivy frantically searched about her for some way to protect herself. The fire poker she had been so insistent on bringing lay uselessly across the room, behind the table. Cold sweat beaded across her temples. This wasn't a sneaking suspicion or a story told round a table while drinking a cup of tea anymore; these were dangerous men with a deadly agenda.

The man in servant's garb took Ivy by the arm and sharply hauled her up. "Leave him," he said, before adding with a sneer, "my lady."

But Ivy hadn't come of age on a rough street for nothing,

and she was able to land a good kick where it hurt, the man letting out a gratifyingly shrill yelp and going down like a rock. His companion made a grab for her and she jumped back, but her leg went out from under her in the slick blood, and she fell, slamming into the floor.

Ivy winced at the sharp pain in her shoulder as she was yanked back up.

"You're not to lay a finger on her," the man with the torn coat reminded the servant as he struggled back to his feet. "Sir Arthur specifically said that she's not to come to any harm."

Ivy's gaze ricocheted between the men. "What about him?" she asked, her breath coming fast and jagged. Blood was still pooling around Ralph's head, but it was turning brown, thick. "What will you do with him?"

The big man in the livery shrugged. "Not my job, and not your place to ask," he said.

"If we leave him here, he'll bleed out." She nearly choked on the horrible words. "We can't leave him here."

"Sir Arthur's charity only extends so far as you," the man said. "And I've something of a temper, so I can't promise what'll happen if it's tested."

"I'm not leaving him."

The man laughed, a dry, rattling sound, and gave a hard tug on her arm that sent pain spiraling through her shoulder again. "Funny you think you have a say in the matter."

She cast one last look back at Ralph's motionless form as she was pulled away. He would be all right, wouldn't he? Ralph was so strong, so vital. He'd been a soldier. He would wake up a little worse for the wear, but all in one piece. It would take more than a knock to the head to fell him.

Ivy was deposited back in the room with the green wallpaper, the door slamming and locking behind her. She stood in the still room, her breath coming in short gasps, her heart racing. In a matter of hours her whole life, her whole perception of reality had been yanked out from under her, leaving her afloat without a safe horizon in sight.

"Breathe, Ivy, breathe," she muttered to herself as she closed her eyes and leaned against the wall. Ralph's blood still coated her fingers, leaving rusty streaks on the wallpaper.

All she wanted to do was to lie down, but the bedspread was still damp from where Ralph had doused her with water. Had that really only been a few hours ago? She was locked in a room. Ralph was incapacitated, maybe even dead. Wherever Mr. and Mrs. Hewitt were, they hadn't been able to secure the manuscript. Ivy had to assume that Arthur and the Sphinxes had found them and likewise injured them. The library was...alive? She wasn't certain she understood everything Mrs. Hewitt had said, but it didn't matter if it was true or not. What was important was that Arthur clearly believed it was true, and he was willing to lie and even kill to get what he wanted.

As if summoned by her thoughts, there was the scrape of a key in the lock, and then the door swung open, revealing her fiancé.

Arthur's eyes darted about the room before landing on Ivy, something like relief passing over his face. There was a sheen of perspiration on his temples, and his shirt was crumpled, his Rudolph Valentino hair mussed. "Darling," he said in a rush of breath. "Thank God you're safe."

Her body was tired, her mind aching for something familiar. Relief spread through her, and her whole body sagged in on itself. He had come to save her. Everything had been lies, or at the very least a terrible misunderstanding. He would explain it all, and someday they would look back at this night and shake their heads in wonder.

"Arthur." Ivy closed the distance between them, collapsing into his arms. "I thought… I thought that…" Emotion choked in her throat, robbing her of words.

But her relief was short-lived. Arthur didn't say anything, and when he drew back, there was a hard set to his face, and he wouldn't meet her eye.

"You *have* come to get me out of here, haven't you?" she managed to ask.

Raking a hand through his already disheveled hair, he shook his head. "Ivy, I'm so sorry you had to find out this way. It was never my intention to have you witness anything unpleasant."

Ivy took a jerky step back and bumped into the side of the bed. "No," she whispered.

Arthur lowered himself into the chair in the corner and lit a cigarette. When he caught her glancing at the closed door, he gave her a sad smile. "It's locked, with a man on the other side guarding it," he told her. "I'm afraid you're stuck with me for the moment."

"Arthur," she said slowly, "I need you to tell me everything."

He yanked at his tie, loosening the elaborate knot. "God, Ivy, I don't want to be the one to explain this messy business to you. You're a clever girl, aren't you? Certainly you've put the pieces together by now."

She forced her words out from between gritted teeth. "You're the one who drugged me and is holding me hostage, so the very least you could do is explain why I'm here and what's happening."

He gave a deep sigh. "Very well. What do you want to know?"

There were a thousand more important questions, but the only one she could bring herself to ask was, "Why did you ask me to marry you? Was it for me, or for the library?"

Elbows on knees, Arthur leaned over and scrubbed at his bloodshot eyes. "You, of course. Always you, darling."

"I don't believe you. Mrs. Hewitt told me everything. That the library contains a manuscript that has all sorts of knowledge in it. The secret to eternal life, things that men would kill for. You and your family want it, and used me to get it."

"The old hag told you that, did she?" Arthur sat back deeper into the chair, tenting his fingers in thought, cigarette dangling from his lips. "Well, she's not wrong I suppose. This would be best done with a drink," he said, looking about as if he expected one to materialize in his hand. "I wasn't lying when I told you that Blackwood was special. During the Dissolution, a genius monk lived here. He could turn metal into gold, cure all sorts of diseases and ailments. He traveled to the mountains of Italy where he learned the secrets of the friars and ancient orders of monks."

"Yes, I've heard the story," she said.

He looked surprised. "And you remembered it? Well, then I'm not sure what you want me to tell you."

"Mrs. Hewitt said that the library drains memories and somehow adds them into its collection. All the Lords Hayworth died young. Is that what you want? To die for this… this thing?"

"That's why I have you, darling." Arthur took a long pull from the cigarette, an elegant finger tapping the ash into a bowl. "You're a Hayworth, however thin the connection. The library will feed on you before ever turning on me, and by that time, I'll have employed another librarian. It has a taste for you, I think. You've spent so much time there already, are so weakened."

"But it will kill me!"

"Death comes for us all eventually. Every soldier knows that. Just think of the glory, the nobility in it. You're contributing to something bigger than yourself, bigger than all of us. Think of it as a war against ignorance, and you are on the front line, a soldier fighting for progress."

"And after me? Who do you think the library will take next?"

"We'll find someone, don't worry yourself over that. There will always be those who are eager to enlist for a worthy cause."

Standing, Arthur stubbed out his cigarette and clapped his hands together. "Well, as much as I have enjoyed chatting, I had best be going. I just wanted to make certain that you were unharmed. There are preparations to be made and research to be done."

"Arthur." Forcing aside her revulsion, Ivy went to him, placing a hand against his chest. It was warm and hard and had once felt like a refuge. "Let me help. I can make the wedding plans, help with the library and make sure everything goes smoothly."

He looked down at her, pity in his eyes. But it quickly passed. "You're a gem for offering, but I think it best you stay here until the wedding."

She dropped her hand. "You can't keep me prisoner!"

"I would never. But I know you, Ivy. You're much too clever for your own good. I'll have my personal servants attend to you, and I'll even have you moved back to your old room for your comfort. Then when we are married, we can discuss living arrangements."

Mrs. Hewitt would never concede to this madness to be carried out, and Ralph would dislocate Arthur's jaw before he allowed Arthur to sleep under the same roof as him. That was, if Ralph were still alive.

As if reading her thoughts, Arthur chucked Ivy gently under the chin. "See? You are clever. I can see the wheels turning in your mind. Your servants will likewise be sequestered. If it were up to my father, they would be killed. But I suppose he is right in that I am much too soft for my own good sometimes."

As if on cue, Arthur nodded to the big servant who had appeared at the door. "Mercer, please see the lady to her room." Before Ivy could protest, the man had her in a viselike grip, and was dragging her down the hall. Her flailing punches met with unyielding muscle, leaving her with bruised knuckles.

"You can't do this to me!" Ivy screamed as the man bore her away. "Arthur, you have to help me!"

"You'll be fine, Ivy," Arthur called after her. "I swear it."

24

Someone had fitted the windows with bars and emptied her vanity of hairpins and anything else that might have been used to pick a lock. Ivy was a prisoner, and was being treated accordingly.

Soft rain whispered against the window, the sky so uniformly gray that it might have been dawn or dusk. Arthur had provided her with morphine, left at the bedside with a pitcher of water. He thought that she would drug herself into oblivion. Well, he was wrong. It was bad enough that the headaches came and went, hours lost in a fog. She needed to keep her wits about her as much as possible, not let what was left of her mind drift away on a cloud of drugs.

A tray was brought in, but instead of the usually modest spread of cheeses and meat and toast, there was a bowl of murky soup and some sort of stuffed game fowl. Arthur must have let the cook go, and brought on his own servant. It had been a hostile takeover, the abbey infiltrated by the Mabry servants and Sphinxes in a single night. How long had they been planning it all? Since she and Arthur had gotten engaged? Or, good God, what if it had been planned from the start? Her chance meeting with Arthur in the bookshop no accident at all? Guilt nibbled at her conscience; had she been the one to allow the Trojan Horse to breach the walls?

Ivy stirred at the soup. She would need her strength, but couldn't find it in her to eat any of the food. He had drugged her once; what would stop him from doing it again?

After her untouched tray had been whisked away by another unfamiliar servant, Ivy waited until their footsteps could no longer be heard out in the hall. She quickly peeled off the torn gown, sending the delicate beads scattering to the floor. It belonged to a different Ivy, an Ivy who had dared hope that she could find love and happiness in the arms of a man. Then she pried off the pinching shoes, and pulled out an old pair of James's trousers and a cardigan. When the time came, she would be ready to run.

There were secret passages and rooms all over the abbey, so maybe there was one in here. Starting just to the left of the door frame, Ivy began a meticulous survey of the room, running her fingers over every floorboard, every panel in the wall. But after what must have been hours, she collapsed on the bed, no closer to escape than she had been when she started. Of course Arthur would have made certain that the room offered no chance of escape. He was a villain, but he was no fool.

Ivy's eyes were heavy, her head throbbing like a steam engine was running through it. It felt as if she'd been awake for days straight, not only a matter of hours. Somewhere downstairs, Ralph lay bleeding and possibly dead. Were Mr. and Mrs. Hewitt likewise injured? What had happened that the manuscript had fallen so quickly into the wrong hands? As she fought sleep, images of women wading into pools of blood filled her head, exotic flowers with gnashing teeth, and Ralph's body lying on the ground, bloated and green and rotting. *I told you, Ivy*, his corpse whispered over and over. *I told you.*

The hushed sound of voices from outside her door pried her out of her dream. The door stood ajar, a thin shaft of light spilling into the room. Silently swinging her legs over the side of the bed, Ivy tiptoed to the door and pressed her cheek against the cool wood.

"Can you translate it or not?" asked a nasal voice, thick with condescension. Lord Mabry.

Then Arthur's voice. "I—I don't know. It's not in any language I've seen before. I don't even think it *is* a language. It must be some sort of code."

Sir Mabry coughed, a wet rattle that obscured his words.

"I'll try my best. I—"

"Not good enough!" was the booming rejoinder.

"Father, she'll hear you," Arthur pleaded in a whisper.

"And? Do you think I care if she does? Now—" He broke off, erupting in a fit of coughs again.

Arthur murmured an offer of a handkerchief, but the older man rebuffed him with what sounded like an open-palmed slap.

"It's a good thing your mother isn't here to see you. What would she think of her son who couldn't fight, not even being able to read an old book!" Another coughing fit. "Figure it out, boy, and be quick about it."

The sound of retreating footsteps and Arthur letting out a frustrated sigh sent Ivy bolting back to the bed and diving under the covers. She clamped her eyes shut just as Arthur let himself back into the room. She held her breath, certain that he could sense she had been eavesdropping. But there was only the sound of another heavy sigh, and then the chair creaking as he lowered himself down.

Chancing it, Ivy cracked one eye open to watch him. He scrubbed at the fine sheen of bristle that was sprouting along his jaw, looking very much like a man at the end of his rope. He lifted his head, and she quickly clamped her eyes shut, pretending to sleep.

"I'll show him," Arthur muttered. "All of them. The old man will choke on his words when he sees what his son is capable of."

Ivy sensed his presence hovering at the side of the bed, the smell of alcohol on his breath, and she prepared herself for him to shake her awake. But he just stood there breathing heavily for a drawn-out moment, and then his footsteps were retreating, the door closing and locking behind him.

Her eyes opened, and she lay still for what felt like hours. Rain was just starting to fall when the sound of an auto cut through the silence. There was a pounding at the front door, and a flurry of voices. Rushing to the window, Ivy craned her neck, trying to see round to the front drive. But the angle of the windows and the bars made it impossible. She went back to the door, and pressed her ear against the wood. It was a man, or maybe a few men, and a woman. They must have been speaking very loudly for her to be able to hear them all the way from her room.

One rang out louder than the rest. "Ivy? Ivy, are you here?"

The voice was familiar, a woman's voice. It brought to mind smoky dance clubs and mornings spent in robes drinking tea in a cold room with mildewy wallpaper. It didn't matter if it was the queen mother herself; if they could hear her then they could get her out.

"In here!" Ivy banged against the door. "I'm in here!" There was a pause in the commotion, and then footsteps growing closer.

The doorknob rattled. "Ivy? Can you open the door?"

"It's locked!"

A second set of footsteps, heavier and slower, approached and the rattling stopped. "Just what do you think you're doing here?"

"I'm here to find my friend. What have you done with her? Why is she locked up?"

"Ah, yes, the infamous London friend. If you had bothered to ask before you barged in, you would know that Ivy is very ill, and suffering from a nervous collapse. She is being kept safely in her room under strict orders from her doctor, lest she hurt herself or others."

No no no. Ivy wasn't sure who the "London friend" was, but they were clearly on her side. She shook the doorknob again, sending pain lacing up her sore shoulder. "He's lying! Let me out!"

"Ivy would never harm herself, never mind someone else. She also never mentioned being engaged. I'm her best friend, she would have told me."

A deluge of images of a tall woman with light brown skin and an infectious laugh came flooding back to her, causing her to wince with guilt. *Susan.* Her friend. How could she have ever forgotten about her?

"Lady Hayworth is ill. If you require proof of this from her physician, then you are more than welcome to seek him out and ask him yourself. In the meantime, I would thank you to keep your voice down and not inhibit her recovery with your hysterics."

"I will not, you can't keep someone locked away against their will!"

"As Ivy's fiancé, I assure you I have only her best interests at heart," Arthur said with barely constrained impatience. "Now, if you please, I'll show you back out."

"I'm not moving until you prove to me that Ivy is safe. Unlock the door."

Ivy held her breath, but there was no sound of a lock or movement of any kind. "Susan!" she screamed. "Susan, don't leave!"

"Ivy? Are you all right?"

"I must ask that you keep your voice down," Arthur commanded, his own voice crawling with irritation. "Mercer, show the lady to the drawing room, and I will have Ivy sent down presently. There," he said. "Will that satisfy you? Take tea with Ivy and see for yourself that there is nothing untoward afoot."

Susan must have nodded, because it grew quiet save for the sound of a woman's heels clicking down the hall. A moment later Arthur was showing himself in.

Ivy glared at her fiancé. He had changed since she'd seen him last, dressed now in tweeds, his hair foppishly combed. Locking the door behind him, he heaved a sigh and propped an elbow on the mantel. Even now, as he kept her under lock and key, Arthur was so handsome, his face so familiar and comforting amongst a sea of lost memories and unknowns. Ivy pushed the traitorous thoughts from her mind. He was repulsive, and she had been a fool to only see the shiny veneer that protected a rotten core.

"I'm sorry for the disturbance. Your friend was very rude, barging in here and making a scene like that."

"I want to see her. You have no right to keep me from receiving friends."

"I couldn't agree more. Which is why you will be joining her downstairs for tea presently. Well, don't look at me as if I was a monster! I don't appreciate people calling unannounced and then making demands. It's terribly uncouth, and judging from her dress, she is not the sort of person I want my fiancée associating with. But if it would give you peace of mind, then I'm only too happy to oblige."

"Why would you allow that?" she asked.

"Other than the fact that I don't like to see you sad?" Arthur crossed to her, crouching and running a thumb along her jaw. She jerked away. "Ivy, I care about you," he said softly. "I know this isn't how you thought things would go, but you have to trust me. Besides," he said, standing, "it wouldn't do to have the village think that I kidnapped you or something equally macabre. Rumors are nasty things, and they fly fast and plenty around here."

"I'll tell her what you're doing, what your family is doing."

Arthur tutted, searching his breast pocket for a cigarette. "I think it would go very badly for you if you do, but if you insist then, I'll have no choice but to tell my side of things. *Isn't it a shame?*" he said, affecting a shrill, gossipy voice. "*Sir Arthur's pretty new bride went mad, raves like a lunatic. Well, she was from the gutter, you know. It can hardly be surprising that her upbringing won out over her new title.*" His little vignette finished, he lit his cigarette and gave her a meaningful look.

She dug her fingernails into the edge of the bed. Who would ever dare to go against the word of a man, and a lord? If Arthur said Ivy was mad, then she was all but mad in the eyes of the world. She would rot in this room, slowly losing her memories and everything about her that made her Ivy Radcliffe, and marry the man who had put her here. There was no one to save her, and she was rapidly losing the ability to save herself.

"So, you will have a lovely tea with your friend, and assure her that all is well. And if you need another reason to comply, I'll give you one." At this, he came closer, taking her chin in his hand, tilting it up to him with more force than was necessary. "If you so much as *breathe* a word of nonsense about the Sphinxes or the manuscript, I will cut off the ear of that chauffeur that so obviously is in love with you."

"What are you talking about?" Ivy managed to ask from dry lips.

Arthur gave her a patronizing look. "Oh, please. It's obvious the man is obsessed with you. Stares after you long after you've passed by and can hardly keep the hunger out of his eyes. Disgusting, really."

Heat climbed her neck, and she swiftly looked away. "Don't be ridiculous. You must be imagining things."

"If only I was imagining it," he said. He was leaning against the mantel now, making a show of nonchalantly inspecting his fingernails, but there was a tightness in his jaw.

He's jealous. Ivy stared at Arthur, the man who seemingly had everything and was happy with none of it. He shot a sidelong glance at her, as if waiting for her to deny it.

"Does that mean that Ralph is alive? That all the servants are alive and safe?"

"For now," he said, affecting a careless tone. "Though that depends on your conduct."

When she didn't say anything, he gave a sigh. "Knowing you, you would fold if I so much as threatened to harm a dog. So I think all in all, you will be a good girl and cooperate."

He was right, damn him. She had already lost so many people she held dear; Ralph might not have numbered among the few people she loved in her life, but she would not have his blood on her hands. And she had no doubt that Arthur would make good on his threat. He was a soldier without a war, a man hungry to prove himself to his father and peers.

"I'll leave you to dress and then come back to show you down." Arthur threw a glance at the untouched tray of food on the table before unlocking the door. Lingering with his hand on the knob, he gave her a look that almost passed for concern. "Please do eat something, darling. I would hate to see you waste away."

Rain was falling soft and steady, a gentle rhythm that should have been comforting but heralded only a deeper sense of despair. From somewhere on the grounds, a raven crowed into the misty afternoon. If only Ivy possessed wings and fairtrade winds, she would fly away, never to return.

Dressing with lightning speed, she surveyed the tray of kippers and porridge, with toast and marmalade on the side. There would be tea downstairs, but she was hungry. More than hungry—ravenous. She would have to trust that Arthur had not tampered with her food; it wouldn't look very good if Ivy was foaming at the mouth.

No sooner had she finished her food than there was a knock at the door, and one of Arthur's servants came to escort her downstairs.

Susan was pacing in front of a window in the parlor, her fingers flicking her cigarette lighter open and closed over and over. The rain was letting let up, and a weak ray of sun filtered into the room, illuminating her dark hair and the stubborn set of her chin. Relief instantly unfurled in Ivy's chest.

At Ivy's entrance, Susan left off her pacing and spun around. Her face was tight with worry, her finely-drawn brows gathered in a frown. "Ivy, my God." Susan closed the distance between them, throwing her arms around her.

Closing her eyes, Ivy allowed herself to breathe in her friend's familiar scent of rosewater and cigarettes, bringing with it buried memories of their time together in London.

"Ladies," Arthur said from the doorway as they drew apart. "I've arranged for tea to be brought in shortly. I'll give you your privacy, but Mercer here will be on hand if needed. Ivy," he said, turning eyes deep with concern on her, "if you become overwrought or feel at all unwell, just let him know and I'll come at once. There's no need to overexert yourself simply to prove a point to someone." He shot Susan a caustic look.

A table had been set near the fireplace, laid out with dainty china and lace napkins. It was all so ordinary, as if she were a lady receiving morning callers. It was the first time Ivy had been out of her room since the night of the party, and she had expected to see shattered windows and other signs of chaos, figures in black hoods chanting around the manuscript. But the abbey looked much the same except for some wilting flower arrangements and abandoned champagne flutes, remnants of the party.

Arthur pulled out a chair for her, but as she sat down, she momentarily lost her balance, her legs wobbling beneath her. She shot a questioning look at Arthur, and he gave her the ghost of a smile. The bastard had put something in her food after all. Probably a light sedative, but it was enough to make her foggy and a little unsteady. It seemed he was taking no chances.

Susan was watching them with needle-sharp eyes, sitting straight as a board with her hands clenched around her silver lighter. After Arthur had left, an unfamiliar maid scurried in with tea, hastily poured, then curtsied and left.

"Is he going to watch us the entire time?" Susan jutted her chin to the door where the guard was standing with arms crossed.

"Just pretend he's not here," Ivy said, forcing a smile. "It's so good to see you. I'm glad you were able to come for a visit."

Susan pursed her lips, and she fingered her cigarette lighter on the table, *tap tap tap.* There was a drawn-out moment of silence, and then, "Ivy, what on earth is going on? You completely disappear—no telephone calls, no letters, nothing—

and then I come and find out that you're engaged? To this prig Sir Arthur?"

"It all happened so fast. I didn't have time to write or—" Ivy stopped at the incredulous look on Susan's face.

"And what is this rubbish about you being ill? Why were you locked up? Sir Arthur said you had some sort of nervous episode. You may live with your head in the clouds, but you've never showed any signs of hysterics or nerves, or whatever it is the doctors are diagnosing ladies with these days."

"Oh, that." Ivy worked her cup around in her hands, wondering if the tea had been tampered with as well. "I—I've been having some terrible headaches, and disorientation. The medication the doctor gave me makes me foggy, and Arthur was worried that I would hurt myself if I was up and about."

Susan's eyes ran over her, taking careful inventory of her friend and leaving Ivy's cheeks hot. "I don't like this, Ivy. Why don't you come home with me? It's no grand house, but you'll be with someone who actually cares about you, doesn't lock you in a room when you're unwell." She glanced around at the parlor, and Ivy saw it through her friend's eyes: the high ceilings, the overly formal furnishings and dark paintings. "This is no place to be by yourself without friends. Do you know, I couldn't even find a cab willing to take me up here?"

Nothing sounded better than going back to London with Susan. They could make a go of it together again, start fresh. Ivy would be free of this wretched house and the curse of the library. But if she left, people would die. And besides, Arthur would never let her leave.

She shook her head and forced what must have looked like the world's least convincing smile. "I'm in good hands here, truly. You know me, if something was wrong, I would be the first to sound the alarm."

"I *do* know you, and you would carry on as if nothing was

the matter, all the while letting whatever it is chew you up from the inside."

"Please, just leave it."

"Is that supposed to convince me?"

When Ivy didn't respond, Susan gave a resigned sigh and took a long sip of tea.

With nothing left to say on the matter, the rest of the meal was finished in silence. Soon, Susan would leave and Arthur would come to return Ivy to her room. How long was he planning on keeping her hostage? And what was he doing with the manuscript? What sort of horrors might be released at any moment? She wasn't certain what was going to happen, but she knew she had to buy herself time, as much time as she could.

"Would you like to see the library before you leave?" she asked Susan as they stood.

"If it means I can spend a little more time with you, then yes, by all means."

Ivy rang the bell, and Mercer materialized from the doorway. He was a stocky man with little in the way of a neck, and a nose that looked as if it had taken some punches in its day. "Please tell Sir Arthur that I would like to show Susan the library before she leaves."

They waited in awkward silence until Arthur appeared. He cast a wary glance between the two women as he came in.

"Hello, darling," Ivy made herself say with a smile. "We had a lovely tea, and now Susan would like to see the library before she leaves."

"I'm not certain that's a good idea. Some of my father's friends are in there, and I don't think they would appreciate the interruption."

Out of the corner of her eye Ivy could see Susan opening her mouth to argue so she swooped in. "Please? This may be the last time I see Susan before the wedding." *This may be the last time I see her at all,* Ivy thought. But if she could just get Susan into the library, she might be able to slip her a message in a book. Might be able to do *something* to alert her friend that all was not well without raising Arthur's suspicions any further.

"I'll escort you both," Arthur said finally. "But you mustn't disrupt my father or anyone in there."

"It's her house, isn't it?" Susan said, lighting a cigarette and blowing the smoke in his direction.

Arthur's coiled posture said that he was only barely tolerating Susan. But he gave her a tight smile. "Of course, and that's why I am more than happy to escort you."

They made a wordless procession across the house, Ivy forcing her sluggish mind to come up with some sort of plan. She would have written a note before she'd come downstairs, tucked it into a book, but Arthur had taken away all her paper and correspondence in her room. Her only option was to slip Susan a book, let the book speak for itself. She would have to pick something that would let Susan know that there was something amiss. But what? The wrong book could unleash more harm than good.

Now that she knew the dark nature of the library, Ivy felt as if she were seeing it for the first time. Had the air always been so heavy, the windows so sinister and watchful? Sir Mabry and some of the men from the other night were gathered round a table, backs to her. No black robes, no incantations or burning incense. They simply looked like a group of scholars engaged in intense study. They looked up sharply at the sound of the door opening.

"What is she doing in here?" Lord Mabry demanded.

"Father," Arthur said with cool politeness, "this is Ivy's good friend from London. She has come to visit and wanted to see the library before she goes back."

A long look passed between father and son, but finally Sir Mabry gave a tight nod before returning to his work.

Ivy made a show of parading Susan around the library, pointing out coats of arms and architectural features. Arthur trailed them like a shadow, never more than a few feet away. But the other men had gone back to working with hushed whispers, paying no attention to Ivy and Susan. Behind their bowed backs lay the manuscript, she was sure of it. What did they see in it? What secrets might they be prying out at that very moment? Since the house had shaken, there had been little evidence of anything amiss.

Ivy led Susan to the back of the library near the great window. The cushions lining the low casements were warm and inviting, but there was no time to rest. Arthur had just turned his back for a moment to inspect a book that had caught his eye, and if she was going to slip something to Susan, it had to be now. Her movements made clumsy from the sedative, she grabbed at a book, only to have it slide through her fingers and land with a soft *thud* on the floor.

Arthur spun around, his gaze narrowing in on her.

Susan quickly bent down and picked it up, sliding it back onto the shelf. "My fault," she said brightly. "I'm all thumbs."

"These are old books, Miss…"

"Loveday," Susan supplied.

"These are old books, and very valuable, Miss Loveday," Arthur continued. "Please do be careful."

"Arthur!" Lord Mabry's voice rang out from the other end of the library. "Come here a moment."

With a lingering look of misgiving, Arthur made his way to his father, leaving the two women alone.

There wasn't a moment to lose. Ivy opened her mouth, but her words got stuck, the entire ridiculous situation too fantastic to explain. Susan was her dearest friend, but even her capacity for understanding had limits. It had to be a book so that Susan could see the strange power for herself, and it had to be now. Ivy's hands shook, clammy with perspiration, as she grasped at a random shelf.

Arthur turned back just as she slid the book into her cardigan pocket. "It's getting late. Ivy, you need your rest. Perhaps it's time to say goodbye to your friend."

In the hall, Ivy embraced Susan, burying her face in her friend's shoulder as she slipped the book into her purse. She committed to memory the lemony scent of Susan's pomade and her rosewater perfume, the silky texture of her blouse under her fingertips.

"Call me, darling. Or write," Susan said. "And you know that you're always welcome to stay with me as long as you like. I'm staying at the King's Head just outside the village— you can come there and stay with me, no questions asked." She shot a glance at Arthur who was standing with his hands clasped behind his back, endeavoring to look casual while they said their goodbyes.

Ivy reluctantly pulled out of the embrace. "I'm fine, really."

Susan looked as if she wanted to say something, but just nodded and gave her hands one more squeeze before disappearing out the door.

25

Ivy had hardly had time to splash some cold water on her face and kick off her shoes, when the door to her room flew open and Arthur strode in. He wore a stormy expression, a fine red vein standing out on his temples. He looked remarkably like his father when he was angry. Slamming the door behind him, he threw something on the bed. Ivy's heart sank; it was the book.

"Did you really think I wouldn't check your friend's bag before she left? I'm not sure what you thought a book of poetry would accomplish, but for Christ's sake, Ivy, you have no idea the harm you could have done."

That was it, then. Her one chance to get a message to Susan, squandered. A cold hopelessness settled around her like a noose.

"Do you know how delicate the balance of power is? What this place is capable of? I watched as you handed books out like cans of soup in a bread line, but those at least came back. Who knows what would have happened if this one had disappeared out into the world? My father was right—you are proving to be more of a liability than anything else. If it weren't for the library's need to feed…"

Ivy closed her eyes while Arthur droned on. Had he always possessed that cruel edge to his voice? Had she simply been too infatuated to notice? He might not kill her, but there were any number of things he might do to make her life even more miserable.

When she opened her eyes, he was regarding her with a malevolent contempt that made her shift in her seat on the bed despite herself. "I think we ought to see about some sort of restraint, or perhaps moving you somewhere more secure. You might have failed in your little scheme this time, but I don't trust you not to try again." He turned to leave, and with him went her chance to escape.

"Wait!"

Arthur halted, his lip curling as Ivy grasped his hand.

"I can translate the manuscript."

His body went still. "What did you say?"

"The manuscript. It's in a strange language, or code, isn't it? I can translate it. I know I can."

He slowly extricated himself from her grasp. "How did you know that?"

"It doesn't matter how I know. That's the case, isn't it?"

He glanced around as if they might be overheard. "What makes you think you could translate it?"

"I told you before that my father was a great mind in the field of cryptology and esoteric manuscripts, and I assisted him in his work. Let me look at it," she said, sensing that his misgiving was slowly waning. "I am sure that I can at the very least identify the language."

Ivy's father had been brilliant, a genius, really. She had

spent her childhood hanging over his shoulder at his desk, as he taught her everything that he knew about cryptography and ciphers, ancient riddles. But that was before she started to lose her memory, and she had only been a child. Even when she was clearheaded and with all her faculties about her, she still wasn't her father.

Arthur regarded her for a long moment, his expression inscrutable. "And why should I trust you with the manuscript? What assurance do I have that you will not use it for your own ends?"

"I suppose you will just have to risk it," Ivy said, endeavoring to sound indifferent. "I'm losing my memory, and I don't understand the workings of the library such as you do. Even if I wanted to, I wouldn't know what to do with it."

Arthur ran a thoughtful finger along his jaw, then with a sudden exhale, shook his head. "It won't do. I must do it myself, show my father that I'm worthy of inheriting the title as well as the legacy of the Sphinxes. I won't give him the chance to gloat. I must do it myself," he repeated.

"But can you?" she asked, unable to help herself from poking at the irritable beast.

His gaze snapped up to her, sharpened. "You're very bold considering I hold your life in the balance. But I—"

Whatever he was about to say next was lost as a heaving shudder ran through the house. The mirror in the vanity cracked, the floor undulating as if it were a carpet being shaken out by a giant. Wild-eyed, Arthur steadied himself against the wall, and Ivy grabbed at the bedpost, just narrowly avoiding being thrown to the ground. They locked eyes, an unspoken understanding passing between them. The abbey was making Ivy's case better than she could make it herself.

The shuddering stopped, a preternatural stillness following. Arthur cursed, straightening his tie. "Very well, you can try your hand at translating it. But I warn you," he continued, his voice hardening, "if you so much as try to twist the manuscript to your own gains, I'll see to it personally that your tenure at Blackwood is as unpleasant as possible."

"And if I'm successful?"

"You're mad if you think I'd release you."

"Of course not," she said. "But I want assurance that you will at least not make things harder for me. The staff must likewise be treated well. And books. I must be allowed to read if I am to be a prisoner."

Ivy's throat grew dry as she waited for Arthur's response, but he finally nodded. "Very well. I will try to transcribe it tonight after the rest of the house has retired."

Arthur finally left her, the sound of his receding footsteps growing quieter until the house settled back into its prevailing laconism. Slumping against the door, Ivy let her tired eyes close.

The weak sun was dipping low, gray clouds gathering out the window. How long would it take for the library to drain her? And what had it already taken from her? With Susan gone, there was no one else to come looking for Ivy. She would slowly rot here, her mind turning to dust, and the only legacy she would leave behind was a vague impression of a woman who once was. Arthur was all but giving her a key to escape, and all she had to do was fit it to the lock. But if the greatest minds in the country couldn't decipher it, what hope had she?

26

The bed was shaking.

Ivy bolted upright. The whole *room* was shaking; pictures on the walls rattling in their frames, and the cloying scent of incense choking the air.

She had hardly regained her balance when the door opened, and a servant deposited her tray along with an envelope of neatly transcribed papers on the small writing table.

"Did you feel that?" Ivy asked, grabbing at the old woman's hand. "And the incense—can you smell it? Surely you realize that something is wrong, that I must be let out!"

The woman shrank back. "I know nowt 'bout it, m'lady," she said, snatching her hand back. The door slammed shut and locked behind her.

Sighing, Ivy sat down at the table and fingered the thin envelope. Was this the entire thing? Arthur had only had a night to do the transcribing, so he must have just given her part of it. She sat with the envelope in her lap, turning it over and over in her hands. How much of the manuscript's power lay in these pages? If she opened them, would something terrible happen?

She had little choice in the matter. Beyond the walls of her room, the Sphinxes were consolidating power. Dumping the envelope out on the bed, Ivy frowned at the sparse pages of text. Of course Arthur wouldn't have trusted her with the entire manuscript, even if he'd had time to transcribe it all.

As she'd expected, it wasn't Latin. Arthur would have been able to read it if it was, as well as Italian, French, German, and any other number of languages a young man of his station would have studied. The characters were uniform and flowed neatly, though they didn't look like any language Ivy had ever encountered. If there had been illustrations, the text would only be half the story without the accompanying pictures. Maybe Arthur simply hadn't felt up to the challenge of copying the pictures, or else was afraid that they would give her too much information.

Yet the strange text tugged and pulled at her, inviting her to sink into the pages and swim through the unfamiliar characters. The sun rose and sank again, her tray collected and refreshed for dinner. Her room had grown stale, but this manuscript was a portal, not just to the outside world, but to an entirely different plane of knowledge altogether. If only she could read it. Rubbing a crick from her neck, Ivy set the papers down and closed her eyes. Would her father have been able to decipher it?

Though her father's features had grown vague—no more than an impression of a kindly face and gentle brown eyes— their evening lessons still stood out in her mind, as fresh and sharp as the ink on the page before her. Why the library drained her of some memories and left her with others was a mystery. Perhaps some memories were so ingrained in bones and blood that they were beyond the leeching powers of the hungry library.

As she scanned the rows of Arthur's neat cursive, Ivy's resolve began to waver. Even if she was somehow able to decipher it, then what? There would be no sense of elation, no triumph in the hard-won task. At best she might be able to bargain for the servants' freedom, but she wasn't even optimistic about that.

When Arthur came that evening to check on her progress, she was no closer to making sense of the text than when she'd first opened the envelope.

"It's either encrypted, or in a completely dead language," she told Arthur before he had a chance to ask.

Irritation flashed across his face as he stalked over to the little table and bent over the papers. "I knew that much. I thought that you might have at least come across something similar while helping your father."

She shook her head. Why was she frustrated with herself when her success would only help Arthur? She decided to take a gamble. "There are illustrations in the original manuscript, yes?" she asked. "Strange ones. Flowers that don't exist, women performing bizarre rituals."

He put down the papers. "How did you know that?" Then, "Why, you little minx. You've seen it, haven't you?"

"Only once, and very briefly." He didn't need to know that her memories of the manuscript were clouded, indistinguishable from her dreams and what Mrs. Hewitt had told her.

Arthur laughed, though it was a harsh, unpleasant sound. He looked no better than he had the day before. If anything, he was more haggard, with another day's worth of growth on his jaw, darker circles under his eyes. "Oh, my clever darling. Yes, there are illustrations. I'm afraid my transcribing skills end at text though."

She worried her lip. "I think I can crack it, but I need the illustrations. They'll provide context, and they may even contain a cipher needed to unlock it."

Arthur stood. "I'll think about it. In the meantime, get some sleep, and please do eat. We need you healthy and rested if you're to be of use."

27

The world outside Ivy's window was slowly slipping into winter, the trees reluctantly shedding the last of their brittle leaves, the moors fading ever deeper into muted browns and washed-out golds, dismal grays. Frost touched the edges of the window, and in the garden, robins squabbled over flower heads gone to seed. But Ivy noticed none of this quiet drama. She was lying in bed, staring at the ceiling and trying to recall the plot of *Little Women*. Following a hairline crack in the plaster molding, names like *Amy* and *Jo* floated through her mind, but their faces and stories remained elusive. Her empty hands ached to hold a book in them again, and a new kind of loneliness spread through her, a kind that held no reprieve nor secret glimmer of hope.

Ivy's melancholy thoughts were interrupted by a noise in the hall, followed by a key sliding into the door. Sitting up, she watched as Arthur came in cradling something swathed in maroon velvet, a servant behind him carrying a small wooden desk.

Wordlessly pushing aside the table which she took her dinners on, they arranged the desk in front of the window. Arthur produced fresh sheets of paper, pens and ink, and paperweights. "Don't say I never did anything for you," he muttered as he arranged them all. "My father would be apoplectic if he knew that I was giving you all of this. He thinks that I'm off to find the late Lord Hayworth's notes."

Ivy pressed her lips together, too curious as to this new turn of events to muster an argument.

When the desk had been prepared, Arthur took the manuscript from the servant with reverent hands, and placed it down. The servant was dismissed, and Ivy watched as Arthur carefully pulled back the velvet covering.

It was not an impressive book, not in the sense of elaborate binding or gilded embellishments. It was bound in simple leather, worn so soft and light that it might have been butter. But an overpowering sense of awe gripped Ivy all the same. The manuscript radiated potency, something drawing her to it yet repelling her at the same time. Her fingers twitched at her side, her eyes trained on the browned edges of the pages, just begging to be opened.

Arthur caught her staring and gave a smug smile. "It's magnificent, isn't it," he said. "Truly magnificent."

Slowly, Ivy approached the desk, letting her fingers graze the soft vellum pages, a shiver running through her body. The book seemed to sigh a breath of relief as she opened it, releasing the smell of old paper and something almost metallic. "What is it supposed to do?" she asked. "How will I know if it's been...activated?"

Behind her, she could hear Arthur shift his weight, slide his hands into his pockets. "I'm not certain, to be honest. My father seems to think that there will be some sort of celestial event, though dashed if I know where he got that notion.

Even if we could just access the knowledge within its pages, then that would be enough."

But of course, that would not be enough. Arthur was right—it was magnificent. Even Ivy could feel the power in the pages, the promise that they held. The Mabrys and their Sphinxes would want every part of the manuscript, not just its knowledge. They would want to be able to take memories from people, mine their knowledge and secrets. They would want to control and kill and dominate. They were, at their hearts, military men. And that's what men with power did.

Taking a seat at the desk, Ivy straightened her workspace to her liking. Arthur had provided her with pads of scratch paper, a jar of pencils, and even a dictionary. How many times had she dreamed of having her own desk, her own office? Of being a respected professor at a university? And how many times had the world not so gently reminded her that such dreams were impossible for a woman, and a woman of her class, no less? If only she could take some joy in the task that lay before her now, but Ivy's head ached and light was starting to dance behind her eyes.

"I can't work with you looking over my shoulder like that."

"And I can't leave you alone here with it."

Ivy was about to protest, when a tingling at the nape of her neck worked its way down her spine, and the house trembled, the water in her basin sloshing over the sides. The tremors lasted for only a minute, but they felt urgent, like a prelude to something more.

"Do you see what I mean? It's powerful, and highly voluble. I need to know that you won't subvert anything you find for your own gain."

Suddenly, Ivy's stomach was churning with acid and she felt as if she might be sick. She pushed away from the desk. What good was deciphering the manuscript really going to do her?

It could only unleash more power, cause more destruction. She was to be a captive in any case, and Arthur had no reason to honor any agreement they might come to.

"I take it back—I won't do it," she said, her legs shaking. The manuscript which had only moments ago held her in such thrall, now felt like a wicked maelstrom, expanding and threatening to pull her into its depths.

"Oh, I think you will though. I think you will do anything that I ask of you."

Revulsion pulsed through her. The sense of entitlement that she had seen as confidence had worn through, showing the ugly truth beneath. "You can't possibly believe that I would still marry you, not after all of this."

"Darling, we've been over this. Besides, it's in your best interest to help."

"Well, I won't do it." She pushed her chair away and crossed her arms. "You can have your manuscript and the library and all the power that goes with it, but I'll be damned if I'm party to this scheme of yours."

Arthur was staring at her with unnerving interest. "My God," he said softly. "You really don't remember, do you? I thought perhaps you would forget bits and pieces, but not the whole thing."

Ivy shifted despite herself, the sudden earnestness in his tone sending alarm bells ringing through her head. "Remember what? What are you talking about?"

"I'm afraid you haven't much choice, because the fact of the matter is, we're already married."

Ivy sat down, hard, nearly missing the edge of the bed. "What? No, that's not possible. I would remember—" but the words caught in her throat and she faltered. *Would* she remember it? Who knew what had transpired since coming to Blackwood? She might have done any number of things, and forgotten all of them. If some things were etched into the marrow of her bones, then others were as temporary as washing soap out of one's hair.

"How do I know you aren't lying?"

"Look," he said, rising.

She followed him with her eyes as he stood and reached into his vest pocket. "Here."

Ivy automatically outstretched her hands and Arthur placed a thick card into them. The blood stopped in her veins, her dry throat working compulsively to say something that would make sense out of what she was seeing. But there was no arguing with the picture in her hands. The young woman in the white dress with lace headdress was clutching a bouquet of calla lilies, looking, if not altogether happy, then at least content. Next to her stood Arthur, his dark eyes triumphant, his hand resting possessively on her shoulder.

"Our wedding portrait," he said.

She threw the picture to the floor, as if it could erase the image already etched into her mind. "No," she made herself say. "No, I don't believe it."

"I can show you the marriage registry, if that would help," Arthur offered. "But I rather think that you're either inclined to believe me or you're not."

"When? When were we…married?" she forced herself to ask.

"After your friend came to call. We both agreed that there should be no more delays and when I proposed an abbreviated engagement, you were all too happy to oblige."

She never would have said that, not even on her foggiest of days. Ivy was sure of it. Yet the portrait seemed to tell a different story. "Well, it doesn't change anything. I still won't do it."

"Doesn't it?" Arthur looked at his watch and clucked. "I'm terribly sorry, but I must be going. I'll make a bargain with you though—you take as much time as you want with the manuscript, by yourself, and I'll be back tomorrow, and we can go over your notes then. Don't let me down, Ivy," he said, bending to retrieve the portrait and slide it back into his pocket. "I expect great things from my wife."

28

Vibrations quivered through the bedroom air, like the collective wingbeats of starlings taking flight ahead of a storm. Ivy had always cherished books for the stillness they allowed in a world that valued fast, unforgiving progress regardless of the human expense; there was a magical link between words on the page and the vivid images that simultaneously unfolded in her mind. But there was no unspoken pact between the secret manuscript's author and herself, wherein she was given the bricks for building castles in the air. Instead, it felt as if she were on a derailed train, forced to helplessly witness the destruction wrought in its wake. The most unsettling and grotesque images filled her mind, even when she set aside the pages and closed her eyes. The manuscript demanded to be seen, an insistent tune that wormed its way through her head.

And yet, she still made headway with the decryption. She had been right: the illustrations did provide context. Occasionally a set of characters were repeated next to similar images, and Ivy was able to pair them together. Every night she meticulously recorded her progress, and spread her notes over the top of the desk so that she would see them when she awoke, a trail of bread crumbs for Hansel and Gretel wandering through a fog of memory. Some mornings everything came back to her fast and sure in a flash. Other days it felt as if she was starting from scratch, and she would stay up into the small hours of the morning only to fall asleep from exhaustion and lose everything again.

On a dreary day, when the wind mercilessly howled outside, Ivy pored over the pages, her porridge gone cold and gluey, the steam from the teapot long since evaporated. She stifled a yawn as she studied a page filled margin to margin with cramped text. Based on the illustrations alone, the manuscript was clearly someone's life work, a compendium of knowledge on herbs, astrology, fertility, and so much more. But in addition to the fantastical birds and blooming flowers, there were disturbing drawings, hellmouths and figures engaged in bizarre orgies, bloody rituals. And the words still remained elusive; every time she thought she had found purchase with the encryption, the key fell through her fingers, slippery as an eel. Even with her notes laid before her, Ivy's mind wandered, but finding no memories upon which to dwell, it quickly returned, submissive as a broken dog.

She stopped her fingers on a page toward the end, sat back, then leaned forward and squinted at the text again. It was in a different hand, she was sure of it. The hand that had written the rest of the manuscript was tight and neat, but this script was flowing, and in another style entirely, perhaps a different language too.

There had been two authors.

And? What difference does it make? Ivy thought. Many manuscripts had been completed over the course of years, decades even, and were written by more than one scribe. The monk who had illuminated the capital letters on each page might not have been the same one who had penned the text. But this manuscript was different. This was not a manuscript that would have graced the halls of the British Library, open to an illuminated and gilded frontispiece. The drawings were crude, and any embellishments were more utilitarian than decorative. It hadn't been made for a wealthy patron, or even for the glory of a monastery, so why had there been more than one author?

Ivy's eyes were burning, and the light was growing low. Someone had taken her tray away, replaced it with another that also sat untouched. Soon she would have to succumb to sleep, and her revelations would be subjected to a perilous waiting period while she rested. Scrawling out her thoughts and questions, she climbed bone-weary into bed. Tomorrow, she would find her answers.

The monk arrived on a gust of frigid air, sour breath, and half-buried memories.

The sound of a thousand writhing maggots crawling over each other filled the air, the clicking of bodies on bodies. Ivy clamped her eyes shut, willing it to be a dream, to be a trick of her overtired mind. But dream or not, when she opened her eyes, the monk stood before her as real as the manuscript that lay open on her desk. He brought with him blood-curdling screams, knives on bone, flesh ripping. The calm, removed voice of a man documenting his experiments as he conducted them, searching for the answer to eternal life and death and everything in between. Ivy clamped her hands over her ears, but it was no use; the voices were inside her head, echoing relentlessly through the chamber of her mind.

Flying to the door, Ivy began pounding furiously against

the unforgiving wood. "Let me out! Arthur, goddamn you, let me out!"

The screams drilled through her head, her chest tightening until it felt like her heart would implode from the pressure. Her palms were red and smarting, but it was no use. No one could hear her here; she was simply another forgotten memory in the abbey.

With the blanket over her head like a child hiding from the monsters in her room, Ivy curled herself into a tight ball, waiting for exhaustion or death to take her, whichever came first.

Rain was drumming on the windows when she awoke, the pleasant smell of woodsmoke distantly drifting in from outside. Ivy had fallen asleep propped up against the door, and her body was restless, as if she had not used her legs in a long time. Perhaps she would find a pair of wellies and take a walk on the grounds today, really explore the gardens. There was so much she still didn't know about her new home in Blackwood. But then the bars on the windows came into focus, and she remembered that she was a prisoner, trapped. There would be no walks, no exploring, no freedom.

Her head was pounding as she slowly got up, and she had the vague notion that she'd had an unpleasant dream, but nothing lingered more than a hazy feeling of disquiet.

Wandering to her desk, Ivy idly sorted through the neat stack of papers. She frowned. The manuscript was open, and notes in her handwriting directed her to the last page. There, amongst the strange language were two sentences written in the Latin alphabet, as clear as day. The words were scrambled though, with extra characters. All she had to do was remove the nulls, and she would have something readable. Why hadn't she seen it before? It looked simple enough. Pulling out her chair, she sat down and set to work, mindless of her night-gown and growling stomach.

The code was complex, and this was only the first step. With the null characters removed and letters unscrambled, she had a legible sentence:

LIGHT SHAFTS AGLOW, COMET, SUN REBORN

It was nonsensical, but then, it didn't need to have any meaning on its own; the letters had to be rearranged in an anagram, the simplest of encrypting techniques. In theory, once they were, they would provide the first key for trans-lating the rest of the text. Squaring her shoulders, she indi-vidually wrote out all the letters in the phrase and began the painstaking process of rearranging them.

She quickly fell into a comforting pattern. Try a word, scratch it out. Try a word, scratch it out. Some of the phrases she produced were just as nonsensical as the original sen-tences. But unlike the cipher clue, she was looking for some semblance of meaning. When she found it, it would be like a key fitting into a slot.

ALCHEMIST'S STONE ORB FUNGAL GROWTH
HOW BURGS GET CONSTELLATION FARMS
SUCH STRANGE FLOWERS BLOOM AT NIGHT

Sitting back, she reread the last phrase in her list. The prob-lem with anagrams was that there could be multiple correct answers, and the more letters one contained, the more pos-sibilities there were.

Her gaze wandered to the window, where a sparrow sat preening its damp feathers. It cocked its head, regarding her for a moment before returning to its bathing ritual. Then, when some mysterious threshold had been reached, took wing into the misty garden, landing on a skeletal rosebush.

Such strange flowers bloom at night. The flowers. Hastily thumbing through the pages, Ivy stopped at a colorful illustration of a monstrous flower with thorny leaves and red, dagger-like petals. The key was right there in the strange flora in the margins. It was easy to be distracted by the bizarre figures and their baths of blood, but the flowers were equally enigmatic if one studied them long enough. And there, in the space above them, pinpricks, dots. Constellations, vaguely recognizable ones. The sky had never held much interest for her, being in the opposite direction one must look if one was to enjoy a book, but now she wished she had taken some time to study the scattered jewels of the night sky. If only she had access to an astronomy book. But it didn't matter. This meant that in a sea of the absurd and impossible, there was something real and anchored to work with. She only had to apply the cipher and assign the constellation characters a value.

Ivy's neck was stiff and her eyelids dry, but she worked as if it was her last day on earth, her father's voice always in the back of her mind. *The key is not to try to find new meaning, but to illuminate what is already there. You can do this, Ivy.*

It was dark and the fire in the grate was nothing but embers by the time Ivy put her pen down and massaged her aching neck. As she glanced through her notebook, the smallest of smiles touched her lips. This was it. This was the most she would remember, and she had in front of her the key to unraveling the manuscript. All that remained was to find an astronomy book and set the translation into work. But what then? Tell Arthur? Try to somehow get to the library and then stay awake all night deciphering it herself? Ivy bit at her fingernail. It had to be now. She could not risk falling asleep or forgetting anything, not when she had the answer right at her fingertips at long last.

Wrapping the manuscript in its heavy velvet cover, she tried to tuck it under the arm of her largest cardigan, but it was still too big, too obvious. She would have to leave it. She didn't know what would happen to it if it were to be destroyed, but something told her it wasn't a simple matter of letting the pages burn. After all, that would be too easy, wouldn't it? Someone long before her would have simply chucked it into the fire and been done with it.

There was something else she was forgetting, something she would need. Ivy stood, her gaze sweeping over the room, but her mind was fuzzy, and there was no time to try to remember; it had to be now.

When she had placed the manuscript prominently on the desk, she doused a handkerchief in water and held it to her face. Then, crossing to the fireplace, she opened the grate and poked at the coals. Embers sparked to life. Carefully reaching in a piece of scrap paper, she let it ignite, flames greedily licking at the edges.

With a flick of her wrist, Ivy watched as the paper landed at the base of the curtains. In only a few moments the flames were gobbling up the velvet, and smoke was spreading. There was nothing to be done about her clothes and other meager possessions, but they were a small price to pay for her freedom.

Removing the cloth from her mouth, she ran to the door and began screaming and pounding. "Fire! Someone help, there's a fire!"

Almost instantly there was a key in the lock, the door swung open, and a large, red-faced man with wild eyes burst into the room. "Oi, get out o' there!" He pushed her aside, frantically scanning the room. "Where is it?" But he'd already spotted the manuscript and was lunging to save it from the encroaching flames when she slipped through the door.

And just like that, she was free.

29

Shoes. Why hadn't she thought to dress and put shoes on? Ivy's feet ached with cold as she ran down the hall, her thin nightgown twisting and wrapping around her legs. Though she didn't know where she was going, a vague map took shape in her head. This was the east wing, and there was an armory, a second-story gallery somewhere. But more importantly, there was someone she was supposed to find, someone in trouble. But who? A gold band on her finger flashed in the lamplight as she ran. No, not Arthur. She had to avoid her husband at all costs. There was someone else.

By now there were servants running with buckets of water and a constant alarm of "Fire! Fire!" rang down the halls. No one noticed as she rushed in the other direction, down the main stairs and into the great hall.

She stopped when she reached the library. Animal instinct told her to stay far away, but she desperately wanted that astronomy book, the last piece to solving the manuscript. Smoke was curling down the stairs, and it was only a matter of time before the flames followed. There was no time for second thoughts; she pushed the doors open and plunged inside.

The books danced and shimmered around her, a maze of shelves that stretched endlessly into the murky dark. Blindly, Ivy began pulling books down. Smoke was spreading, and she had to bury her nose in her elbow as she searched. Shouts rang out from the hall, growing closer. She couldn't risk it; she had to leave off her search. With only the faintest notion of where she was going, she fled down the servants' stairway.

The kitchen was deserted, everything tidy and unused. Above her rang the pounding of footsteps and muffled shouts. As her gaze swept over the bare wooden table and the white china lining the wall, flashes of memories came back to her: a broad-shouldered man with haunted eyes sitting at the table, trying to protect her from an attack. Blood spreading across the tiles. A heart she hadn't realized capable of breaking any further, tightening in on itself and threatening to implode.

Ralph.

They had bludgeoned Ralph and taken him somewhere, along with Mr. and Mrs. Hewitt. How long ago had that been? Days? Weeks? Months? Everything was lost, floating in a shapeless fog. Perhaps Ralph and the rest of them were long dead. Perhaps she had attended their funerals, Arthur with a tight grip on her arm as the vicar read the final rites. But those were just dark anxieties, not memories, and so she had no choice but to believe that they were somewhere, alive.

Ivy's head was pounding, her lungs filling with smoke. Desperately, she ran down the hall, passing empty servants' rooms until she came to a locked door. She threw her weight against it; pain shot up her shoulder, but it remained unbudging. She tried the next one and the next one, until, straining to hear over the commotion from upstairs, she could make out a rustle of movement. Her heart beat faster.

"Ralph, are you there? The door is locked, can you open it?"

"If I could fucking open it, the bloody thing wouldn't be locked, now would it?"

She could have wept with relief. Ivy dropped to her knees in front of the lock and reached to fish a pin out of her hair before remembering that Arthur had confiscated them.

"Stay there, I'll be right back," she shouted through the door as she scrambled up.

"Not sure where you think I'd be going," came the dark mutter from the other side.

She raced back to the kitchen where she found a small knife and then stumbled back down the hall. Fingers made clumsy with adrenaline, Ivy pried the knife in the lock until there was a click. Her slick hands grappled with the doorknob, and then the door swung open.

The stench hit her first, a stomach-turning combination of stale sweat and despair. There was a small, ground-level window which might have let in some light, had someone not pasted newspaper over it. A washstand with an empty basin stood in the corner next to a bucket draped with coarse cloth, and on the cot sat a very disheveled Ralph, his hands bound together and loosely tied to the metal bed frame. Even with a finger's-length of beard, the sharpness of his jaw was pronounced, and his clothes hung loose, ill-fitting.

At her widening eyes, Ralph quickly cut his gaze away, a touch of color on his gaunt cheeks. "Don't just stand there staring," he said gruffly. "Cut these, will you?"

Ivy sprang into action and obliged. "How long have you been in here?" she asked as she worked to sever the ropes.

"Seventeen days."

Over two weeks! That meant she had been captive for that

long as well. No sooner had the ropes fallen away, than his arms came around her with surprising force. She stiffened in surprise, but then found herself dissolving into him, her body responding to some memory that her mind had forgotten.

"Ivy, thank God," he murmured into her neck. Rough fingers ran through her hair, excruciatingly tender and intimate. "Did they hurt you?"

She didn't know. Her body was unbruised, but how could she say for certain what had transpired while she was locked away with the manuscript? When she didn't say anything, he wrapped her into his embrace even tighter. She could smell woodsmoke and warm stable leather beneath the peppery sweat, the familiar scents tugging at something deep in the recesses of her mind.

"I thought of you, every day. Seeing you again was the only light in the darkness."

Why was he talking to her like that, like she was his sweetheart, or more? Had his time in isolation addled his mind even more than it had hers? Yet in the refuge of his arms with his breath warm on her neck, Ivy didn't care. Words choked in her throat, but she didn't need them. This felt right. More than right: destined. They stood entwined for what felt like hours, the sound of his heart strong and steady under her ear.

But then reality came snaking back. "Is that smoke?" he asked.

"There's a fire, upstairs." It must have been spreading rapidly, because already the pounding of footsteps had been replaced by an eerie silence above them. "What about Mr. and Mrs. Hewitt? Where are they?"

He jerked his head in the opposite direction. "Next door," he said. Gingerly removing her from his embrace, Ralph cursed as he lost his balance and nearly fell into the washstand. Ivy rushed to offer him a hand but he brushed her off. Instead, he staggered out the door, his long legs gradually steadying.

Grimacing, Ralph led her next door. Ivy worked the knife in the lock, feeling more than a little proud when it sprang open under Ralph's appraising gaze.

"Wait," he said, stopping Ivy's hand on the knob. "It might not be..." He trailed off. "I'll go first. Just in case."

With her heart in her throat and the smoke curling ever thicker around them, she stood back as Ralph opened the door.

"Christ," Ralph muttered when it had swung open.

Ivy couldn't quite conjure memories of the Hewitts' faces exactly, but she remembered a dignified couple that took pride in their work, distantly polite. The man and woman that sat huddled on the bed together had papery skin, sunken eyes, and looked as if they hadn't had a proper meal in ages. At their entrance, Hewitt sprang up, putting his thin frame between them and his wife.

"It's me," Ralph said gruffly.

The butler stood down, but his wan face darkened as he took in Ralph's loose clothes and the dried blood in his hair. "Barbarians," he said, his words heavy with contempt. "Apparently the gentleman's code goes out the window when the Mabrys are involved." Turning, he helped Mrs. Hewitt to stand.

A purple bruise bloomed across her left cheekbone, her eye swollen like a boxer's in a fight.

Ralph's jaw tightened. "They struck you," he said.

"I'm fine," Mrs. Hewitt insisted, brushing off their fussing. "Just a little worse for the wear." Her gaze turned wary as it passed to Ivy. "How much does she remember?" she asked Ralph.

"I've no idea. Haven't had time to chat."

"And the manuscript?"

"It's in my room," Ivy told her, one eye watching the encroaching smoke at the door. "Or, it was. I believe one of the Mabry servants has it."

Mrs. Hewitt made an attempt to push into the hall. "We have to go get it before—"

But Ralph stopped her. "They'll have gotten it by now and taken it somewhere safe. We need to get out of here."

"You'll have no argument from me," Hewitt said, coughing into a soiled handkerchief. "Live to fight another day, that's what I've always said."

With Mrs. Hewitt's weight on Ralph's shoulder, they slowly made their way out of the servants' hall. Ivy would have liked to have had the security of Ralph beside her, drinking in the warmth of his body, but Mrs. Hewitt needed him more. The electricity had gone out, the corridor cast in smoky shadows. They formed a surreal procession, the old couple, the young man with the limp, and the girl with no memory. But even with both the Hewitts and Ralph accounted for, Ivy had the sense that there was somebody missing, a light step, and a small frame in a blue service dress that should have been beside them.

"Agnes," Ivy said, coming to a stop. "Where is Agnes?"

"I sent her home the night of the party," Mrs. Hewitt told her. "And thank God I did."

Continuing, they emerged out of the servants' entrance to an artificially purple sky, the smell of damp earth and acrid smoke rising up to greet them. To one side lay the drive, and to the other, a path leading into the gardens. In the gravel drive, a chain of people had formed, water buckets passing down the line to the fire. No one noticed the huddled foursome as they limped past, clinging to the shadows like thieves in the night. From across the lawn, Ivy could hear Arthur yelling instructions as servants scrambled to find more buckets.

The gardens loomed ahead of them as sharp gravel bit into

Ivy's bare feet. "What will become of the abbey?" She had stopped, awestruck at the sight of black smoke pouring out of the windows of what had been both her prison and her home.

Mrs. Hewitt gave a weary sigh as she paused to catch her breath. "It will survive this. It has weathered greater storms before. And knowing the Mabrys, they will have protected the library. As for the manuscript, it will protect itself."

They came upon a cottage, set safely away from the abbey toward the back of the grounds. In the darkness, Ivy could just make out a thatched roof and brambly rose garden. Hewitt opened the door and ushered them inside. Despite the stale, unused smell that greeted them, it was neat as a pin, homey, and a cat jumped down to greet them with loud, indignant meows.

Mrs. Hewitt caught Ivy's wandering gaze and nodded. "This is our cottage. They'll be too busy with the fire to spare us a thought. We should be safe here, for now."

"How long do you think we have before they start looking for us?" Ivy asked. It all still seemed more like a strange dream than reality, time blurring into an endless string of moments.

Hewitt moved around the small drawing room, closing the curtains and lighting dim lamps. "Not long," he said grimly.

Ivy sank into the worn sofa, leaning back and letting her eyes drift closed. She'd been awake for who knew how long, and keeping herself from slipping into exhaustion was becoming a losing battle.

"Oi!" Ralph was leaning over her, patting her cheek. "No sleeping, d'you hear me?"

Her eyes flew open. She hadn't even been aware that she'd shut them. The next time that happened, she could awaken with no memory of where she was or how she'd gotten there, never mind anything about the manuscript.

With the doors bolted and Hewitt armed with an ancient

hunting rifle, Mrs. Hewitt hobbled to the kitchen to put on tea before Ralph stopped her and took over. Outside, the shouts and clanging of bells drifted through the night, a surreal backdrop to an even more surreal situation.

"We need to secure the manuscript. This might be our only chance to take it back," Hewitt said. He was standing beside the couch, one hand braced on the armrest as he swayed slightly, the other gripping the rifle.

"Won't you sit down?" Ivy asked, concerned that the older man might faint away at any moment.

He bristled. "No, my lady. Not in your presence."

"Harold," Mrs. Hewitt admonished, "I do believe we are past that. Sit down."

With obvious reluctance, the butler lowered himself to the couch, his hindside barely perching on the edge of the cushion.

"They'll have found it by now," Ivy said. "I'm sure of it." She darted a glance at Ralph, trying to discern by his expression if he was disappointed that she had chosen to save her own skin at the cost of risking the manuscript. But he was busy carefully pouring and handing out mugs of tea, his expression blank and miles away from their discussion.

"We have the advantage of chaos on our side. The house will be in disarray, and the library will be unguarded," Mrs. Hewitt said, raising her cup to her lips with shaky hands. "They'll assume that we are dead, locked in our rooms and killed by smoke or fire. Lady Hayworth is the only one who is at risk right now."

Hewitt shook his head. "I doubt the fire would have done much damage down in the servants' quarters. It's only a matter of time before they realize we aren't where we're supposed to be."

Staring into her tea, Ivy willed her eyes to stay open. It was dark and cozy in the little cottage, and it would be so easy to give in to exhaustion, closing her eyes and letting sleep take her. A giant weight had been lifted off her shoulders now that she had escaped her imprisonment; didn't she deserve to rest? But that was just her body trying to persuade her to sleep; her mind knew better. "I deciphered it."

All heads swung toward her, Ralph finally coming out of his daze.

"That is, I cracked the code. I didn't have time to actually set the translation into work, but I think I could."

"My God," Mrs. Hewitt whispered. Hewitt crossed himself. "All these years, these centuries, and no one has been able to get close to it, let alone figure out how to read it."

There was little time—or point—in celebrating Ivy's success. It was a hollow victory, won of desperation. She hadn't found an astronomy book, so the translation wasn't complete anyway.

Ivy sat bolt upright. "My notes! I left my notes in my room." Closing her eyes, she slumped back against the sofa. Out of all the things to forget, how could she have let herself leave her precious research to the fire? She couldn't even rightly blame the library or her lost memories, she had just plain forgotten in the heat of the moment. Her tongue darted over her dry lips as the full weight of her realization settled on her. "What would happen if Arthur were to find them and decipher it himself?"

A heavy glance between Mr. and Mrs. Hewitt. "It...would not be good. The manuscript unleashed is one matter, but under the control of a madman is another altogether."

"I'll get them," Ralph said, slowly standing. In the low-ceilinged cottage he was still large, imposing, but there was a frailty about him now, and the way his shirt hung off him made Ivy want to gently sit him back down and wrap him in warm blankets with a proper cup of hot tea.

Mrs. Hewitt shot to her feet. "Absolutely not. You can barely stand."

"I'll go," Ivy said. "It's my fault I forgot them, and—"

"*No,*" Ralph said, the force of the single word nearly enough to send her back to her seat.

"But I know where they are, and what they look like. I—"

"And what? You're going to walk into a burning building and just walk out again? How will you get past Arthur and his servants?"

"The same way you would, I suppose," she shot back. Ralph's old querulousness was returning and she felt herself heating at the exchange. The embrace in the servants' room had been a fluke, a tender moment born out of desperate circumstances. "I'm going," she ground out.

"No, ye are not, and that's final." His Northern accent broadened and deepened, his nostrils flaring. A flash of the old Ralph shone in his eyes, feral and stormy, commanding despite his weakened state. Even with her scattered memories and spotty knowledge of her chauffeur, Ivy knew that there was no dissuading him; it would only serve to further his determination.

Mrs. Hewitt must have sensed this too, because she gave a resigned sigh. "Very well," she said. "But at least have a proper bite to eat before you go, or you won't even make it down the garden path."

Ralph wordlessly obliged, slowly chewing the stale bread and hard cured meat that Mrs. Hewitt had found in the larder. He might as well have been a condemned man eating his last meal before the gallows, and Ivy had no choice but to sit back and watch, knowing that she was the one sending him there.

When he was done, Ralph pushed the plate away and stood up. "What do they look like?" he asked Ivy.

"It's a red, leather-bound book," she whispered, hardly able to meet his eye. "They'll have taken the notes, or else they were destroyed in the fire in my room. I'm so sorry, my mind is so foggy and I didn't think—"

But Ralph held a hand up and the rest of her words died in her throat. "You did what you had to do."

It didn't make her feel any better. "What if Arthur catches him?" Ivy asked Mrs. Hewitt, her worst fear spilling into the silence of the room.

"There is one thing you could tell Sir Arthur," Mrs. Hewitt said quietly, looking down at her hands in her lap. "Tell him you're a Hewitt. He won't touch you if you're one of us. It's the agreement between our families."

If they had explained to Ivy why this was the case before, she had long since forgotten. "He locked you in the basement to rot," Ivy pointed out, her heart further tightening at the memory of coming upon Ralph caged like a broken feral animal.

"To keep us out of the way," Hewitt clarified. "They wouldn't have killed us, not intentionally."

A small comfort. Ivy helplessly watched as Ralph donned one of Hewitt's old coats, the sleeves too short, the front too baggy. "I'll be back. I promise," he told her, finally meeting her eye. The glint there was hard and determined, and she had no choice but to believe him. He was strong and capable, so why did it feel as if she was sending a piece of her heart into the burning abbey with him?

The door had not been shut behind him for five minutes when Ivy threw herself off the sofa and began pacing. A clock ticked on the mantel, the air grew heavier. Outside chaos still rumbled. "I need to stay awake," she announced to Mr. and Mrs. Hewitt. "And I need air. I'm going to take a walk."

"My lady, you can't possibly think to go out and—"

Ivy stopped Mrs. Hewitt. "I'll go toward the moors and stay

out of sight. If I keep sitting here waiting for Ralph, I'll surely fall asleep and I can't lose my memories right now, I just can't."

Mrs. Hewitt looked too tired to argue, and nodded.

Ivy left the Hewitts to their rest, and made sure they bolted the door behind her when she left. Smoke hung acrid in the air, the underbelly of dark clouds illuminated in the dying orange flashes of the fire. Cold air bit into her, reviving her flagging spirits. Ivy followed the little path out behind the cottage and onto the restless moors, before throwing a last glance over her shoulder, and then taking a sharp left and doubling back toward the abbey.

30

The library doors stood ajar like two crooked teeth, welcoming Ivy inside with a sinister leer. She picked her way over the debris with soft steps, her feet stinging from her journey across the grounds. Burnt rubble sat smoldering in piles in the dark hall, but aside from some smoke stains and the occasional fallen timber, the walls stood intact. Mrs. Hewitt had been right—Blackwood had withstood worse before, and it would be standing long after this.

With footsteps made hesitant by a deep sense of foreboding, Ivy gingerly pushed open the creaking doors the rest of the way and slipped into the library. It was dark. A drifting flake of ash landed on her hair and she flinched before swatting it away. As she moved slowly along the shelves, a long-forgotten song came back to her on threads and tattered moth wings. It was a medieval tune, and though she couldn't remember how she knew it, the meaning was clear as crystal. People had once believed that when one died, their soul must make a perilous journey over the course of a single night, avoiding demons and darkness, before eventually reaching the safehold of Jesus's arms. *This ae nighte,* rang the dark and mysterious refrain. Ivy was a lost soul without the anchors of memory and hope, adrift in the night, unsure of what morning would bring.

Somewhere in the bowels of the house, Ralph was hunting for her lost notes, vulnerable and alone. How would he be able to outrun Arthur or his servants in his state if they came upon him? Would they hurt him, even if he claimed he was a Hewitt as Mrs. Hewitt had instructed? It was no use dwelling on what-ifs and worst-case scenarios; Ivy would either find the books she needed and Ralph would find her notes and together they would rein in the Sphinxes and the manuscript, or Arthur and his club would continue to wreak havoc on the abbey and what was left of Ivy's life.

The predawn light glowing from the window was just enough to make out the murky outline of shelves and tables haphazardly pushed out of the way in the aftermath of the fire. Ivy didn't know what she was looking for, other than an astronomy book that might shed some light on the riddle of the constellations in the flowers.

"What are you hiding?" Ivy murmured into the darkness.

The lingering smell of smoke hung heavy in the air as she slowly made her way forward. Her step stopped as a glowing ember leapt from a pile of ash. But as she jumped to beat it out, it rose up higher in front of her, not in the erratic pattern of a rogue ember, but the intentional movement of a sentient being. No bigger than an apple, it glowed rosy gold, casting the shelves behind it in flickering shadows. Ivy watched as the light rose higher still, bobbing and floating like the disembodied flame of a lantern being held aloft by some unseen hand.

Her eyes were playing tricks on her. Exhaustion had finally overtaken her, and she was hallucinating, dreaming. Yet all the same, she moved toward the light, drawn like a hungry street cat to a warm bowl of milk. It wanted Ivy to follow, and in her dreamlike state, it only made sense that she would oblige.

This ae nighte, this ae nighte,
—Every nighte and alle,
Fire and fleet and candle-lighte,
And Christe receive thy saule.

Was this the end for her, the culmination of her soul's journey? She probably should have been scared, or at the very least, wary. But when one was kicking aside the burnt rubble of an evil library that stole memories, well, she could only muster curiosity and a reluctant sense of acceptance.

She was tired, so tired. But forcing her weary feet through the debris, Ivy followed the light. It would stop, hovering and bobbing as if waiting, and then dart ahead, deeper into the shelves.

For all the damage wrought by the fire and water used to put it out, the books were remarkably unharmed. Shelves had collapsed, and the red velvet drapes were nothing more than threadbare shrouds, but the worst damage to a book seemed to be some singed corners and spines strained from falling to the floor.

The light stopped, gently bobbing in place, in front of a shelf where most of the books remained untouched by smoke or water damage. It looked as if until recently the shelf had been flush against the wall, but was now pulled aside, revealing another row of books behind it. Even in the surreal landscape of the fire-damaged library, Ivy was certain she had never seen this shelf before. The light drifted closer to the books, illuminating the spine of a simply-bound tome before circling back to her. It was so close that she could have reached out and touched the glowing orb if she had been brave enough.

Then it flickered, and vanished, leaving her in the stillness of the library.

Outside, a chaffinch sang its first morning song, a flippant trill that cared nothing for the horrors of the previous night. Ivy had come looking for an astronomy book, but this seemed more important now, so with one last lingering glance for the orb, she pulled down the book.

It took her a moment, her eyes blinking against the poor light, trying to make sense of the words that stared back at her. When they did come into focus, her breath caught in her throat.

The Life and Dreams of Ivy Radcliffe, the Lady Hayworth. 1903—
The book fell from her hands as she stumbled backward, tripping on a charred beam. Something sharp dug into her back, but the pain was far away and inconsequential. She closed her eyes and then opened them again, sure that this was a result of too little sleep and nerves stretched to fraying. But her name stared back at her, the year of her birth and everything between then and now trapped in a simple little hyphen.

The library turned inward eyes on her, the shelves pressing in around her. She should go, run back to the cottage and drink tea with the Hewitts. They had warned her about the library, its insatiable hunger for stories and memories, but seeing evidence of it in black and white was another thing entirely.

Her curiosity turned morbid. With shaking hands, Ivy fished the book out from the pile of rubble where she had dropped it, and, crouching near the window, she read by the light of the gray dawn.

Her hands were trembling so badly that it took her three tries to open the book and flip to the first page. There was no author, no publisher's address, just a chapter heading then dense blocks of text.

She took a deep breath and forced herself to read.

The book knew everything. It detailed her early life, the small flat in which she'd lived as a child when her father taught at Cambridge, then the squalor of the East End after he'd lost his job. The courtyard children who had first mocked Ivy for her love of books, then had begged her to tell them the stories inside the covers when their curiosity had gotten the better of them. It told of her and James's exploits playing Swiss Family Robinson. There were moments in her early life that she had completely forgotten, her first memories of her parents. *She is a darling baby, and her doting parents cannot help but watch her even as she sleeps. The whole world waits for her, but for now she is content at her mother's breast... Her mother smells of warm milk and talcum powder, the sweetest smells in the world to little Ivy.* Unable to see through the tears gathering in her eyes, Ivy flipped ahead to a random page and forced herself to read the words that awaited her.

"Well, I was telling thee the story of the Mad Monk. Everyone in Blackwood has grown up hearing it."

The familiar feeling grows stronger, but it is still fuzzy and indistinct. Ivy nods that Agnes should go on, though a peculiar fear has begun to take shape deep in her gut.

Outside the rain pelts against the windows in unforgiving sheets, the wind groaning. "It was in the days when Blackwood Abbey was a real abbey, a monastery, with monks and priests and the like living here," Agnes says. "There was a monk—no one knows what his name was—that was obsessed with...what is it called? When metal turns into gold?"

"Alchemy," Ivy murmurs.

"—that's it. Anyway, he began to take up darker interests. Things like life and death, and how it was that dead things could come back again. Said there was a fountain of youth, but instead of water springing from it, it was the blood of virgins. He did experiments, terrible experiments, and recorded everything in a great big book. There was

girls that went missing from the town, and even though there was lots of accusations brought against him, nothing was ever proved...

"When King Henry came 'round to burn all the monasteries, the monk disappeared. Some people say he was bricked up alive in the walls somewhere, but most people think that he ran off and went to Italy. The one thing everyone agrees on is that he hid the book somewhere in the abbey, and that his spirit haunts Blackwood, guarding his book and its power, hoping for someone to find it and release him from the bonds of death."

Ivy digests this. Agnes is a good storyteller, and the vivid details make it feel familiar. But it would be quite a stretch to say that she's heard it before—twice.

"You really don't remember?"

The book went slack in her hands then fell to the floor, and she balled her fists against her eyes, rubbing away the imprint of the words on her eyelids. The conversation came flooding back, not just that one, but every iteration of it. This was a trick, a joke. Someone in the house was eavesdropping on her, writing everything down. But no, the passage knew not only what she had been saying, but her thoughts as well. Were they really her thoughts though? What did she remember, and what was a dream, or even an invention of this anonymous author?

Picking up the book as if it were a hot coal, Ivy forced herself to flip ahead.

Ivy stumbles going up the stairs and accepts Ralph's hand, heart pumping fast and hard. She has seen the way he looks at her, the possessive yet yearning glint in his eye. It frightens and excites her, and she wants to see where that look will lead next. She is rewarded with a light kiss, which soon deepens and leaves her legs wobbling and core aching. She craves Ralph with a burning want that she can't quite name. Needs to be closer to him, needs more of him.

But he pulls away, breathing hard, his eyes glassy and dangerous. "We can't do this again," he tells her. He is fingering the gold ring *on her finger. Is it her wedding band, or her old false ring, meant to deter the attention of men?*

Ivy reaches for Ralph, her fingers closing greedily on the open collar of his shirt. "Why not? If it's about my title, my position, then I don't care. No one expects conventionality from me. They already think I'm an outsider, a pretender."

He shakes his head. "That's not what I mean."

Despite her protests, he gently unhooks her fingers and strides away, back to the stables.

Ivy put the book down. Something hot and throbbing unspooled low in her belly. Wanting, aching. Whatever was on the page had never occurred in real life, yet she could almost smell Ralph's scent of warm leather, feel the taut muscles of his chest beneath her fingers. Were these unfulfilled wishes and fantasies? Could the library read her every desire, know things about her that even she didn't know herself?

A yawn overtook her despite herself. Outside, a smoky pink was beginning to touch the edges of the gray dawn. As she warred with herself to keep reading, her eyes grew heavier. With sleep would come more loss, more forgetting. But her body demanded it, and she could no longer fight the inevitable. Perhaps this was what dying soldiers felt on the battlefield, the helpless resignation that once they closed their eyes and succumbed to the darkness, it was all over. But close their eyes they did, and Ivy likewise surrendered to the dark unknown.

31

Someone—or something—was approaching.

The scraping sound of footsteps slogging through debris shattered Ivy's rest, and she sat up, rubbing the sleep from her eyes. Why was she in the library of all places? Rolling her stiff neck, she tried to gather her bearings until the footsteps were almost upon her.

Instinct told her to hide, and no sooner had she crept behind a shelf, than voices accompanied the steps, becoming clearer as they approached. "...and the library, it will still know to feed from her, and her only?" the first voice asked.

"Yes, I am sure of it," answered the second voice. It was a man, coolly confident and very familiar. "I've read through her notes extensively. Once I enter my name in the ledger I will be in control, but it will still feed off of her. It will always revert to Hayworth blood, given the chance."

Ivy peered around the shelf. The man with his back to her smelled of cheap tobacco, his big arms strapped with unforgiving muscles. Beside him, she could just make out the pro-file of another man. He looked familiar with his dark hair and handsome features. He might have been a film star if not for the hard set to his mouth, the frenzied glint in his eyes.

"Christ, this will be a fortune to clean," he muttered as he kicked at a fallen beam.

The world was saturated with the smell of heavy smoke and damp wood. *A fire. There had been a fire.*

"My father will need to have all the staff from Mabry House come here and work round the clock. Everything will be run out of Blackwood from now on."

Arthur Mabry. His name came back to Ivy in a nauseating flash. The handsome young man from the bookshop who had befriended her and taken her under his wing in Yorkshire. But why would he be here, and what did he mean that everything would be run out of Blackwood?

Someone else was coming, and the men broke off in their conversation at the sound of footsteps. Ivy craned her head around the shelf, trying to catch a glimpse of the newcomer, but they had all moved just out of view.

"You! What are you doing here?" Arthur demanded, his voice suddenly pitched shrill.

The response was too low for Ivy to catch, but judging from Arthur's response, he was not on friendly terms with the interloper.

"Would have been a good deal more convenient if you had not survived the fire," Arthur said.

Another low response tickled at the back of Ivy's mind.

"No, stay your hand, Mercer," Arthur instructed. "He may be useful yet. Ivy slipped her guard when the fire broke out. I am most anxious to retrieve my wife, and he may be able to help."

A palpable tension filled the ensuing silence. There was a

clatter and a new voice joined the group. "My lord? You're needed, your father said they are ready for the girl."

There was some low conferring, and then the hasty retreat of footsteps. But a heaviness, a vital presence still hung in the air, and Ivy knew that she was not alone.

She groped at the debris until she found a heavy piece of wood. Slowly uncurling herself from her hiding place, she took a deep breath and sprang out into the open prepared to meet one of Arthur's men head-on.

But the face that looked back at her was all perfect angles, cut jaw, and deeply concerned gray eyes.

"Ralph." The wood clattered to the ground and she stumbled toward him, stopping short when she saw his stormy expression.

"What are you doing here? You're supposed to be back at the cottage."

"I couldn't just sit there waiting. You didn't find the notes, did you," she said.

Ralph confirmed what she already knew with a shake of his head. "You're safe. That's the only thing that matters."

"Come on," he said, finally closing the distance between them and taking her by the hand. It was not the gentle, reassuring touch that she had expected, but rather a demanding invitation that brokered no argument.

"Where are we going?"

"I don't know. Away from here, anywhere." For a moment she was carried away on a wave of romance, and she envisioned running far from Blackwood and starting a new life with Ralph. But then she realized he was looking at her not with the same longing that sat heavy in her chest, but simply with concern and determination.

Ivy dug her heels in, bringing Ralph up short. "What are you doing?"

"I'm not leaving," Ivy protested.

"Oh yes you are."

She yanked her hand out of his grasp with a force that surprised them both.

Ralph ran his hand through his hair, then kicked at a shattered piece of the wooden railing. "Ivy, don't be daft. There's nothing for you here." A stricken look crossed his face. "Don't tell me you—you have feelings for Sir Arthur."

"What? No, of course not. How could you think such a thing?"

His body relaxed a little. "Then what?"

The library was quiet, eerily so, as if waiting for her answer. "I—I just can't." Something tugged deep within her, something unpleasant. "It was something Mrs. Hewitt said. I can't remember it exactly. But I think if I leave, something terrible could happen."

The guilt on Ralph's face passed quickly, so quickly that she almost missed it. "You know," she said. "Tell me. What happens if I leave?"

"The library will find someone else to feed from."

Her eyes fluttered closed as the weight of her situation came round her like iron manacles. "I can't do that to someone."

"For God's sake, look around you, Ivy. It would be Sir Arthur or one of his men. Leave them to their bloodthirsty schemes and save yourself."

But she stood fast, her feet rooted on the charred rug, as if she was as much a part of the library as the shattered marble busts and burnt books. "I can't," she repeated, quieter, but with just as much conviction. "I can't explain it, but I can't leave."

"I could put you over my shoulder and toss you in the auto, drive far away."

"You could, but you won't," she said absently. "I just need

time. I solved the cipher to the manuscript, and I can do it again."

Ralph glanced at the door through which only moments ago Arthur and his men had disappeared. "Time is something we don't have right now."

Ivy picked at the lace collar of her nightgown, trying to reach whatever was inside of her calling her to stay. Whatever it was, it was deeper than the library, older and more insistent.

"Come with me," he said suddenly.

She shook her head. "I already told you, I'm not leaving."

"I know you're not. But I'm not going to let you sit here like a lame duck either." When she still hesitated, he extended his hand. "You can trust me."

Ivy's mind told her that she was not supposed to trust Ralph, that she'd been explicitly told as much. Yet her heart was in vehement disagreement. Swallowing the last of her misgivings, she placed her hand in his. His fingers closed around hers, gentle and warm.

He was leading her up and down a shelf, looking for something, when a voice echoed in from the hallway.

"I left him in here," Arthur was calling to someone. "He can't have gotten far."

Ralph stopped short, Ivy nearly toppling into him. "It's Arthur—he's come back," she whispered, as if it weren't obvious.

But Ralph was already tugging her along, urgency in his step as he began pulling books down one after the other.

"What are you doing? We don't have time for reading, we—"

Ralph shot her a withering look as he pulled another book down, and suddenly there was the creaking mechanism of a door swinging open. Standing back, he gestured to the passage that had appeared. "After you."

Throwing one last glance back at the library doors, she stepped into the dark passage. Immediately the air changed, a stale, dusty smell replacing the smoke and damp wood. "They already took the manuscript," he told her as the passage spilled them out into a small chamber. "This is the last place they'll look."

The ceiling was high, but the corners were probably only two arms' lengths from each other, the air cool and musty. It was dull and inhospitable, but something tickled the back of Ivy's mind; she'd been in this room before. There were no windows, and save for a slot in the door, nothing that suggested the existence of a world beyond the tiny room. An empty lectern, a desk, and a chair comprised the furnishings.

But no sooner had the door closed behind them and Ralph pushed the chair against it, than Ivy realized her mistake; she was alone with Ralph. His closeness was intoxicating, and she was so very tired, so very weak. Sitting on the floor, he draped his arms over his knees, leaving the chair for her. For all of her forgetfulness, she was unable to shake free of the dream she'd read in her book, and it clung to her like a stubborn cobweb.

Silence settled heavy around them. The details of her day-to-day life and past were foggy at best, but memories of the library as it had been before the fire stood out clear as day in her mind. She could picture the grand crenelated window at the far end, the way the lazy Yorkshire light filtered in on sunny days, the comfortable chair upholstered in worn purple velvet. She wanted her library back, her life back.

"It happens overnight, when I sleep," she said, more to break the silence than anything else. "That's when I seem to lose everything." She stifled a yawn, as if reminded of the fact that she hadn't slept more than a few hours in the past two days, then slumped against the stone wall, the coldness a welcome discomfort to keep her awake. "What am I doing?"

she murmured into her hands. She couldn't leave the abbey, but she couldn't stay, either. She couldn't remember anything of importance, and Arthur and his men had the manuscript anyway. She was in purgatory, without the hope of release.

"Ivy. Look at me."

Her eyes had drifted closed, but now she opened them again to find Ralph crouching before her, the intensity of his gray eyes stealing the breath right out of her lungs. He took her hands in his, squeezed them. "It will be all right. I don't know what will happen, but I promise you, it will be all right. The abbey can burn, Arthur can have his library, but I will die before I let anything happen to you."

A little thrill ran through her at his heady pledge. He was a knight kneeling before his lady, giving her an oath, and she didn't for one moment doubt that she would be safe with Ralph nearby. He took his job of protecting the abbey seriously, and she supposed that included her as one of its tenants. If only he wanted to protect her for different reasons.

All the same, she was mesmerized by the fervency in his eyes. The room was small, and he was so, so close. It would only take the smallest leaning, the merest hint of movement to bring them together. If she was sound of mind, she would have pulled further away, but her mind was decidedly not sound, leaving only a body quavering with raw desire.

Ralph was the first to take the leap, his finger gently tracing the line of Ivy's jaw, bringing her lips just shy of his. But just as her eyes drifted closed in anticipation, he pulled back suddenly, breaking the spell.

She bit down on her lip, hard, but not before an involuntary cry escaped her. She'd almost given in to a desire she didn't even understand. Had she misinterpreted his intentions? She stared at the spot at his collar where his throat met his chest, blood still pounding hot in her head. "I—I'm sorry. I don't know what came over me."

There was no answer. When she chanced a look up, Ralph was looking intently at her—no, not at her exactly, but her arm. "Ralph? What is it?"

"Your shoulder," he said, still entranced by whatever he was seeing. "What's that under your sleeve?"

"What are you talking about—Ralph!"

He slipped the loose nightgown sleeve from her shoulder. "You have a tattoo," he said, his eyes sweeping over her upper arm.

"I don't have a tattoo. Don't be ridiculous."

But Ralph didn't seem to hear her. "What is it?"

"Oh for goodness sake. I don't—" But her words died in her throat. As she inspected her arm, a dark smudge against her skin caught her eye. Tenderly touching her finger to the raised skin, she sucked in her breath. The light was poor, but Ralph brought the solitary lamp close and she twisted her shoulder to get a better look. It *was* a tattoo, fresh and still a little pink around the edges.

Even with its crude lines and uneven application of ink, it was obviously some sort of flower, with five petals unfurling to reveal a swirling center spangled with dots.

Ivy stared at it until her neck cramped and her eyes began to cross. What could be important enough that she would have defaced her skin, and in such a crude manner? And that was assuming that she had been the one to do it. What if someone else had done it? Held her down and forcibly tattooed her for some reason?

"It's new," Ralph said, confirming her suspicion. His fingers traced around the edges, featherlight. "It looks medieval, like a rosette on a church pew. Except..." He tilted his head to get a better look at it. "Except there are stars inside of it."

At his words, a floodgate opened, and it all came back. Weeks, days, hours, minutes, seconds of her life, that had been spent in isolation. Holding a sharpened pen nib to her flesh, etching in the key to the manuscript, so that it would not be lost, no matter what.

"It was the flower," she said, shivering from his touch as much as from the cold air on her exposed skin. "The key was in the flowers, the stars. But I needed an astronomy book to put the cipher into action. We have to go," she said, stumbling to her feet.

A wave of dizziness overcame her, and Ralph jumped up to steady her. "You haven't slept in days, and who knows the last time you ate. Sit down, rest. The manuscript can wait."

"I can't—I'll forget…" But even as her words turned into a yawn, she knew that she was in no state to walk, let alone spend hours hunched over and concentrating on a code.

"Here." Ralph took her by the waist and gently brought her to the cold floor. "Sleep. I won't let you forget when you wake up."

"What about you?" Ivy asked. Her eyelids were heavy as her head fell against his shoulder.

The only answer she got was Ralph murmuring something into her hair, and soon she was drifting off to sleep.

A rustle, and a shimmer of light on the wall.

Ivy sat up. She was still in the cell, yet it wasn't the cell. She stood stock-still and watched, breath held, as the light rippled across the stone walls. It was the same light born of the embers in the library that had guided her before. Not the monk, but a benevolent anomaly in a sea of dark powers.

"You," she said on a breath. "Who are you?"

The light didn't answer; Ivy hadn't expected that it would.

But it did float toward the desk, growing brighter and brighter until the room was bathed in white light.

When the flash had subsided and Ivy had uncovered her eyes, she found the dark stones had fallen away, bright, white-washed walls in their place. A window looked out over the courtyard garden, sun spilling in and catching the light of a gleaming wood crucifix hanging over the desk. Birdsong drifted in on a gentle breeze, the smell of lavender and other herbs hanging in the air.

And in this strange waking dream or hallucination—whatever it was—Ivy was not alone. A woman dressed in a dark robe of coarse linen and a white scarf gathered over her head and around her neck sat at the desk, gaze trained faraway through the window. She didn't look scared or surprised like Ivy, rather, her face was a mask of serenity, the smallest furrow between her straight brows as if in deep thought. Dipping a brush into a small dish of ink, she began writing, her hand moving slowly but surely across a piece of stretched vellum.

"Who are you?" Ivy asked again.

The woman didn't answer, and Ivy would have thought that she had not heard her if she had not inclined her head the smallest bit toward the page, inviting Ivy to look.

With shaking legs, Ivy got up and approached the desk. The woman had no smell, no heat, just a gentle, residual glow of light about her. Leaning the slightest bit over her shoulder, Ivy watched the brush leave a stream of script in its wake.

Ivy had seen that handwriting before. It was neat and flowing, soft juxtaposed against the scratchy scrawl of the other hand. This was the author, the person who had penned the manuscript. The woman dipped a brush into a pot of vermillion and began painting graceful arcs, a flower slowly taking shape in the margins.

Drawing back, Ivy continued to watch, fear subsiding into

intense curiosity. There was nothing dark or untoward in the woman's countenance; could she have truly produced something so powerful, so evil as the manuscript? She seemed to be a wise woman who had chosen isolation in which to complete her work.

Turning in her seat, the woman leveled a serene smile on Ivy, as if sensing her thoughts.

"I have waited these six hundred years for a woman to inherit the abbey," she said. Her voice was inside Ivy's head, musical and sweet, and Ivy stood transfixed, never wanting it to end. "There is that which is not meant for the eyes of men. These words, this knowledge..." Her face broke into a beatific smile, and she spread her hands. "They are seeds that have been germinating these past centuries, waiting for the right gardener to help them bloom."

She didn't know what made her the right person, or what sort of fruit the nun's knowledge would bear, but a drowsy sort of peacefulness came over Ivy. She had a purpose, she was an important piece of a larger puzzle. This was the pull she had felt to the abbey, the inexplicable tug that told her she was meant to be here. But then the nun was fading away, taking the sunlight and birdsong with her.

"Wait!" Ivy threw herself at the chair, but her hands only clasped empty air. She sat with the revelation of the nun who had lived centuries ago and written a compendium of sacred and mystical knowledge. What good did knowing any of this do her now? She would awaken, forgetful of the nun, the manuscript, and why she was here. Ralph had sworn he would help her remember, but even he could not know the essence of her dreams. And so it would go until her weary body could no longer support a mind made of dust.

Tears welled up and overflowed, hot and cathartic. Ivy had not given way to tears and rage when her family had died, each death marked only by a solemn and internal grief. She had not mourned the academic life of which she had always dreamed but would never be possible. But she raged and cried now, against the injustice of it all. Her body would give way to exhaustion and soon whatever memories had sown and bloomed would be lost to the unforgiving reaping of the library once again.

The room grew colder, darker. Ralph was still nowhere to be seen. Any comfort the nun had brought was gone, replaced instead with a palpable disquiet. Small spaces had never bothered Ivy before, but now the four walls threatened to close in on her, crush her like one of the spiders that spun their webs in the shadowed corners.

No gentle light preceded the monk, no soft birdsong or scent of aromatic herbs. It took Ivy a moment to notice that the room had changed at all, since much was the same. The same dark walls, the same dismal lack of light, the same cold, hard paving-stone floor. Only the occupant was different.

He sat at the same desk as the nun had, the manuscript laid out before him. The window that had let in light and birdsong was now boarded and covered. The air smelled of stale incense tinged with something like burnt hair. Smoke stained the wall behind the lamp, as if many hours had been spent working beside a dwindling flame. Any moment he would turn around and this time there would be no human face, no recognizable emotion except for death. But he did not turn, did not show any acknowledgment of Ivy's presence; this was a tableau, set for her benefit.

By his wrist sat a small piece of unrolled parchment, a familiar pattern of stars sketched on it; the cipher of the manuscript. He had cracked the code, centuries before Ivy. His quill scratched away, and though her fear would have rooted her to her seat, her curiosity was stronger, propelling her forward to glimpse his work over his shoulder. Where the nun had painted blissful pools of aquamarine, he colored over them in red, turning water into blood, flowers into twisted and thorny monstrosities. Young women with crimson slashes across their throats. Dissections performed in the darkest corners of the abbey. All in the name of not science nor God, but the perverted glory of one man.

What had started as a silent parade of images on the parchment was now an assault on Ivy's senses: the metallic scent of blood mingled with burnt hair. Rotten meat and fetid water. Despair.

"What—what do you want from me?" Ivy forced the words from her dry throat. "You already have everything, why come here and terrorize me just to—"

The monk turned in his seat, leveled malicious eyes on her. To witness him was chilling, but to be the object of his hateful attention was downright terrifying. "I always visit my guests toward the end of their tenure, pay my respects to the great family that has sustained me these five hundred years. You are no exception, though unremarkable girl that you are. I thought that you would last longer, but I suppose there have been some unusual circumstances."

Ivy didn't say anything. Maybe if she didn't move, didn't speak, he would grow bored and leave her.

Unperturbed, the monk continued. "Your life has been short and rather unexceptional, but it is your dreams that interest me. Such dark horrors that haunt your sleep! They have made a brilliant addition to the library, and keep me endlessly entertained."

He was not a man, and not yet a ghost. He was everything that was dark and twisted and wrong. Anger rose in Ivy's body, words spilling out of her despite her sense of self-preservation.

"Haven't you anything better to do? Why must you torment my family and the people of Blackwood? You take and take and take, and still it isn't enough." She must have been dreaming, because she would never be capable of having such a level conversation with the spirit of a monk who had lived and died centuries ago and was now stealing the very fibers of her being.

The monk moved about the small cell, his crimson robes trailing behind him as he ran his finger over the empty desk before turning his attention back to her. "The pursuit of knowledge is the pursuit of the divine. How can we profess to know God without understanding all that he knows? And how can we attain that knowledge in but the brief window of time we are given on this earth?"

"You didn't answer my question," she ground out.

"Didn't I?"

Her eyes were grainy and tired, her mind dizzy and unmoored. *Wake up, Ivy. Why can't you wake up!* "I wish you would just leave," she said, her voice coming out small and childish.

"I'm sure you do," he said with a smile that revealed sharp, uneven teeth. "But that is not how it works, not how the conditions are met."

"What conditions?" she asked warily.

"It always starts with a desperate plea, doesn't it? The first Lord Hayworth was granted Blackwood by King Henry for service in his army fighting against the Scots. He was a man haunted by his memories of the atrocities he had committed on the battlefield in the name of his king. Our needs dovetailed nicely, his memories and knowledge in exchange for a gentle decline, much more respectable than taking his own life. But he did not consider the long-term implications, or if he did, he simply did not care about the generations that were to come after him. For you see, the bargain was not just for him, but for all his family to come. I knew better than to bind myself to just one soul, a finite resource. Someday when the last of the Hayworth blood has run dry, when every book is complete, I will be reborn, infinite and immortal. You ask why I don't just leave you be? Because we are both of us bound to a pact drawn in blood and executed in flesh. Could I finish you now, drain you completely and move on to the next in line? Of course. I could do any number of things with the power I possess. But instead, I take what I want, and give back scraps and slivers, just to keep you a little longer. Fresh memories are always so much sweeter, so much more vivid on the page. In short, you exist at my leisure, remember what I want you to remember."

There was no rhyme or reason, no underlying logic. "What happens if I take my life into my own hands?" she asked. "What if I end it, and there are no more Radcliffes or Hayworths left?"

The monk turned a sharp gaze on her, a flicker of provocation deep within his dark eyes. "Why, your mortal body joins your decaying mind, of course," he said. "I will find someone else, I always do."

He was capable of being irritated, and irritation was a sign of a chink in his armor. She would follow the chink, prying until it opened and spilled out what she wanted to know. "And what became of *your* mortal body?" she asked.

The monk's temper was shortening, a twitch pulling his lips downward. "I rest in glorious repose until one day my body can rise again, my mind alive and nourished with all the knowledge and dreams that the library has to offer. It would behoove you to put a stop to all these questions, lest you learn something you wish you hadn't. I am not here to entertain the questions of a silly girl."

She had gone too far, she knew she had, but she couldn't

stop. Maybe she would forget it all tomorrow, but for now, she had to know, had to have every tool at her disposal if she had any chance of survival. "Why *are* you here, then? To terrify me? To gloat of your contract and your cleverness? Because if everything you say is true, then it doesn't matter. After all, I am just a silly girl."

In the time it took her to blink an eye, he was beside her, a flash of darkness blacker than any night, the smell of hellfire on his breath. And then just as quickly, he was gone, a book in his place.

The cell grew quiet, Ivy's heart beating furiously, her breath echoing in the dream space. A dark presence filled the air, growing by turns hot and cold, whispering against her skin. The book called to her, begging to be opened, to be released.

The Life and Dreams of Ivy Radcliffe, the Lady Hayworth. 1903— She reached for the cover with shaking hands, but before she could even pick it up, the cover flipped open.

She jumped back as the pages of her life whipped past with supernatural speed, the nightmares spilling out, early ones first, the forgotten anxieties of a small child. Being left alone in a crowd with her mother nowhere in sight. Monsters lurking in the shadows under her bed. The coal man who always grinned at her with missing teeth and told her he had a special present for her if only she would follow him to his cart. Sounds of the neighbors upstairs fighting, a man's raised voice and then a woman's scream, a sickening *thud* and the fraught silence that followed. The walls crawled with bedbugs, the floor undulating with the bodies of rats.

"Please stop," she begged, dragging her nails down the door.

But still they came. A frantic nurse in a hospital, her white uniform painted in blood and vomit, too busy to spare a moment for a distraught young woman. Ivy at her mother's bedside, watching helplessly as the fever ravaged first her mind, then her body, until her beautiful mother was nothing but a rasping corpse.

Clambering to the chair, Ivy grabbed the book and began ripping out fistfuls of pages. If there were no words, no memories on the pages, then they couldn't haunt her. But no sooner had she torn out a page than it materialized again, ink appearing as if written by an unseen hand. Blood oozed from her fingers as they razed against the paper, her heart racing to unnatural speeds, slamming against her rib cage. Air. She couldn't get enough air—

"Ivy! *IVY!*"

The voice calling her name came from far away, an echo in a distant cave, but still she tore at the pages. Someone grabbed her wrists, and she flailed against them, certain it was the monk, his bony hands skittering across her flesh, in search of her heart. But when her vision cleared and her heart slowed, it was not a robe drenched in blood that her face was pressed into, but an ordinary shirt, covering an ordinary man.

"Ralph?"

At his name, he relaxed his grip on her. "You're safe, you're safe."

"Where were you? The monk, he was here, and you were gone." Her pitch rose as her sense of relief was replaced with betrayal. "You said you would be here, that I could trust you and you left."

"You were dreaming. You were thrashing about in your sleep." He ran his hand through her hair, leaving her scalp tingling in its wake. "I didn't leave. I would never leave."

Her breath slowed, and she glanced about the cell. No torn pages, no lingering stench of death. It was just as it had been when she'd laid her head on Ralph's shoulder and fallen asleep. "It was so real," she murmured. "He told me about the manuscript, about the pact that gave him his power." As she recounted the dream, more of the horrors came back to her, like pulling a thread that unraveled an entire blanket. "And the nun!" She told Ralph how the nun had been the original author of the manuscript, all the precious knowledge she had gathered in the hopes of preserving it for future generations. The monk was everything dark and evil, had perverted the nun's words, twisting them for his own vile purposes. Whatever mystical knowledge she had committed to the pages had been powerful perhaps, but not harmful. The manuscript as it was today was a corruption of the original. And now the monk held the library and the manuscript in thrall, living off the knowledge that it gave him.

Ralph listened, his fingers idly twining through Ivy's hair as she spoke. "So, what now?"

It took a long while for Ivy to answer. They had been dreams, yet the messages they had contained had been real.

"I think we can stop it," she said, finally.

"Stop what?"

"Everything. The monk, Arthur, the Sphinxes. And we don't even need the manuscript. We don't even need to leave this room."

32

The stones were cold, unyielding. If they had secrets beneath them, then they were loath to give them up.

Ralph watched as Ivy got on her hands and knees and ran
her fingers over the edges of the slate floor. "What are you
looking for?"

"I'm not sure, but I'll know when I see it." Rocking back
on her heels, she let her gaze roam over the small room until
it landed on the lectern. The floor was uneven beneath it, one
of the large paving stones just barely protruding. She tested
the stone with her fingers, but it wouldn't budge.

"Here." Ralph crouched beside her, his arm brushing hers
as he pushed aside the lectern and crooked his fingers under
the lip of the stone. "Bloody thing is heavy," he muttered. He
had her move to the other end. It was cumbersome, her arms
screaming in protest, but together they were able to find just
enough purchase, and the stone scraped away, inch by inch.

When it was free, Ralph hoisted it the rest of the way and pushed it to the side.

Realistically she'd known that what she was looking for wouldn't be right there, but Ivy still felt a pang of disappointment as all that greeted them was a floor made of hard-packed dirt. A bug skittered away as the lamplight fell upon it, and Ivy took a fortifying breath. "We're going to have to dig."

They fell to work. Fingernails full of dirt and arms on fire, Ivy was just about to admit defeat, when the glint of glass shone up at her. Hurriedly brushing away the rest of the dirt, they stared down into the dark recess. The smell of death and rot rushed up to meet them, filling the cell.

"Shit." Ralph scrabbled backward, but Ivy just stared at the foggy glass coffin and the visage that grinned back up at her.

The monk looked like the skeletal reliquaries of the Roman Catholics, reclining with his mouth ajar, coins resting in his sunken eye sockets. Emerald and ruby rings hung loose on his bony fingers, and his crimson hood was as vibrant and soft as the last time he donned it. Someone, perhaps the first Lord Hayworth or one of the other monks, had taken some extraordinary measures to preserve him, send him off into the hereafter in extravagance. Yet there was something not right about the skeleton. The bones that should have been dry and white instead glistened, and the sagging skin was wet with sticky brown blood. A faint humming rose from the grave, low but persistent.

Ralph murmured something too low for Ivy to hear, and her stomach turned over on itself. Fighting the urge to replace the stone and pretend as if they had never found it, she leaned down, sliding her fingers under the lip of the coffin lid.

"Ivy," Ralph warned, but his voice was faraway.

The humming grew louder. It was the sound of a thousand voices speaking, words pouring over each other so quickly that she could barely catch one before another drowned it out. Stories, memories, dreams. A frantic chorus of forgotten lives. Here was the epicenter of the storm which brewed in Blackwood, the words winding around the skeleton, each story preventing any further degeneration of flesh. It was not blood which pumped through his desiccated heart, but stolen memories. The monk would never stop feeding, never stop searching for the words and stories that would sustain his suspended state of rest.

All of the death, the stolen lives and dreams, the grief. All of it because of one man, and his selfish, twisted beliefs. Ivy yanked off the glass lid, rusted hinges giving way with a groan and then she was face-to-face with death incarnate. Without so much as a second thought, her hand closed around the femur, wet and repulsive to the touch. With a yank, she pried it off. Next came the head, smashed to the floor, the golden jaw flying off. The arms, the ribs, one by one the bones came off, sinew and flesh protesting, but no match for Ivy's frenzied state. The humming built until it was a storm of words and screams, swirling about with no page to land on.

When the bones lay shattered on the floor along with all the gold and jewels, she finally allowed herself the chance to breathe. The humming voices had gone quiet, but there was still a prickling tension in the air. Then light, slowly building, like the sun breaking free of clouds on a stormy day. The cell filled with it, warming her skin and bringing her to a place and time that was at once beyond the scope of her memory, yet intensely familiar. The tolling of a single bell echoed through the chamber, the spicy scent of incense wrapping around her. The world went still, and Ivy could feel not just the absence of evil, but a loving presence hovering just out of sight, like a mother watching her child from the doorway of another room.

The sound of Ralph calling her name gradually came back

to her, his hands around her waist, pulling her back from the edge of the grave.

"It's over, Ivy. It's over."

She sagged against him, wanting more than anything for him to be right. If it was truly over, then the tugging in her heart would slacken, and she would be free.

"No," she said, as much to force herself to accept the inevitable as to convince him. "It's not. We have to stop Arthur from whatever it is he plans to do."

Ralph scrubbed at his jaw, looked as if he wanted to argue, but he finally nodded. He put his ear to the door, listening. "I go first," he said sternly. "If it's clear, follow me."

Ivy had assumed it was morning, but as they passed through the hidden door into the library, the sky beyond the window was an ashy gray, the sun just slipping below the horizon. Had they been in the cell for hours, or had an entire day passed? Feet still sore and blistered, she let Ralph help her pick her way through the burnt rubble.

"Wait." Among the overturned shelves and burnt beams, a book lay face up, a splash of white in the darkness. "I've seen this book before, in my dream," she told Ralph as she rummaged the book out of the debris and brushed ash from its cover. "It—it knows everything about me, all my dreams and memories."

The book sat heavy in her hand. Here was the sum of her life, the dreams, both good and bad, that filled her mind. The salty summer days spent in Brighton, the blanket forts and evenings reading by lamplight. Wandering the stacks of the library as her father tunelessly hummed while he worked. All those precious memories and so many more, the patches needed to fill a moth-eaten quilt, all lay within the book.

But before she could read even one page, the book quavered in her palms. Pages flipped open on their own accord, the words fading faster than she could read them, as if erased by some invisible hand. Throwing it down, Ivy backed up into Ralph, and they stood together, watching as her memories disappeared. The monk had been the sinew that held together the body of the library, the memories and dreams the pumping blood in a symbiotic relationship. But now the monk was gone, and there was nothing to hold it all together.

Soon a cyclone of pages was whipping through the air. Somewhere deeper in the library all the books of every Hayworth and librarian must likewise have been evaporating. Where would all those stories, those memories, go once they were no longer condemned to the pages of the monk's collection? Ivy braced herself, waiting for her memories to come flooding back, but there was no great flash of light, no moment of complete enlightenment. Ivy felt the same as she had a moment ago, moored to reality by the strange encounters in the cell, but unable to grasp any threads of her past, except for whatever the monk had thought fit to leave her with. The rest had disappeared into the ether with the monk, gone forever.

33

The air hung heavy with anticipation, as if the house itself was holding its breath. Waiting, watching.

With every determined step through the shadowed halls, Ivy's nerves grew stronger, though Ralph insisted on walking in front of her, stopping at every little sound, making sure that it was safe before proceeding. Signs of the fire were everywhere: the beautiful tapestries were singed and sooty, the windows shattered. But she hardly noticed. There was a gaping chasm in her heart; seeing the story of her life disappear in front of her should have been freeing, after all, it no longer belonged to the library. But all she felt was a numbing sense of loss, that there were memories and entire chapters of her life that were never coming back.

They did not have to search long. As soon as they reached the front hall, they came upon a group of about two dozen or so men gathered around something, their backs to Ivy and Ralph. There was a strained hush to the group, and the electric lights had been turned off, in their place hundreds of glowing candles lining every surface and step. Occasionally a gust of wind would come through one of the holes in the roof still gaping from the fire, sending the flames flickering sideways and casting strange shadows.

Beside her, Ivy could feel Ralph tensing, as he reached for her hand. Using the deep shadows as cover, they slipped unnoticed behind the men, then up the stairs to the gallery where they could look down from the safety of the marble balustrades. They huddled like two soldiers in a trench, conferring in whispers about going over the top.

"What's your plan?" Ralph asked her. "I assume you have one?"

"We need to tell Arthur that the pact has been broken, that the monk is gone. He'll have no choice but to leave Blackwood. My book was erased and the monk is dead. Well, more dead," she amended as she tried to see what it was that had the men so captivated below them. "What are they doing, I wonder?"

"Stay here," Ralph ordered as he started to stand.

Ivy pulled him back down by the arm. "What? Where are you going?"

"I'm going to go tell Arthur that it's over. To go home. That's what you want, isn't it?"

It all felt so anticlimactic, so simple. All Ivy wanted to do was curl up somewhere safe, feel a hot cup of tea in her hands, know that all of this was behind her.

"I'm coming with you," she told him. She was prepared to argue, to press her case for being the one to send Arthur on his way, but Ralph wasn't listening. "Ralph?"

He was half-crouched, his knuckles white as he grasped the banister, looking at the scene below them. There had been a shift in the atmosphere, a hum of excited expectation rising from the group. "Don't look, Ivy," Ralph said, his voice dangerously low.

"What is it?" She started to stand, but he pushed her away with surprising force, causing her to stumble back further into the hall. "Ralph!"

"Stay here."

"I will not!"

"Ivy, you are not to go down there. I forbid it."

"You can't forbid me from anything!" Her voice rose as she realized that her chance to set everything to rights was slipping through her fingers, simply because Ralph felt the need to assert his masculine ego.

In the time it took Ivy to blink, Ralph was in front of her, holding her by the shoulders and glaring at her through the murky dark. "I know you enjoy being contrary, but I am not about to watch you get your bloody head blown off."

Something in his tone snapped her from her adamancy, and she finally noticed the fear flaring in his eyes, the way his fingers were shaking as they dug into her shoulders. Whatever was happening in the hall had rattled him, badly.

She nodded, and he released her.

"Good. Stay here, and don't look. I'll be back."

Ivy watched as Ralph headed for the stairs, fighting the urge to reach out and keep him with her in the cold darkness. Crawling on her hands and knees, she approached the gallery and peeked through the marble balustrades. There was no harm in watching. She hadn't come this far and undergone every nightmare imaginable just to sit back and hope that Ralph sent everyone home with a polite please and thank-you.

But as she stared down, she wished maybe she had listened to Ralph after all, and stayed put. There should have been little left to shock her after what she had experienced, yet all the same, as she stared down at the scene below her, she felt as if she was witnessing some strange waking dream unfold.

A stone pool had been brought into the hall—lord only knew how, it looked like one of the huge fountains found in a London park—and the men stood around it, transfixed. It was a strange sort of baptism, with Arthur standing in a white robe in the center, hands clasped in prayer before him. For it was not water that came up to his knees, billowing the robe out around him—it was blood.

Where had the blood come from? It was so much blood, more than simply that of a slaughtered cow or pig. Bile rose in Ivy's stomach, the antiseptic smell of hospitals rushing back to her. Blood slicking the hallways, men missing limbs, the putrid stink of flesh rotting on the bone. The blood in that pool was human, she was sure of it. She knew it just as sure as if she had read it in a book, because she had. Arthur was recreating the illustrations from the manuscript, bringing the bizarre rituals to life. A cry escaped her throat.

Arthur snapped around at the sound of her voice, then looked up. The candles lit him from the back, casting him in a halo of light, illuminating the shape of his body through the white robe. Yet he looked like nothing so much as a young boy, wading ever deeper into a dangerous current at the jeering encouragement of his friends.

"Ivy," he said, his face blank. "You shouldn't be here."

Movement out of the corner of her eye. Lord Mabry was conferring with another man in harsh whispers, pointing up at them.

Ralph had doubled back at her outburst and was gripping her arm, almost to the point of bruising. "I'll deal with this. Go back to the cottage."

"Isn't this why we're here?" she retorted. "I can end this now."

"Not if it costs you your life," Ralph hissed, tightening his grasp.

"Lady Hayworth," Lord Mabry said, as he began the slow ascent up the stairs, one of his men close behind. "You are a slippery one, aren't you?"

Ivy wrestled her arm free. On one side was Ralph, all restless, dangerous energy, and closing in on the other, Lord Mabry.

"It's over, Arthur," she called, slipping from Ralph's grasp and skirting round the edge of the gallery, putting more distance between her and Lord Mabry. "The manuscript doesn't hold any power anymore, or the library. The monk is dead, gone. Whatever you are trying to do, it won't work."

"It's never over," he responded. He appeared cool and determined, but there was a slight tremor in his voice. "It can go on forever. We are eternity. If the monk is gone, even better. It means that the library is ready for a new master. My father thinks that it could be me."

"You don't really believe that, do you? What has your father ever done for you? What do you have to gain from this? Please, come out," she begged. Arthur had betrayed her in every sense possible, treated her like a child, a prisoner, a sacrificial lamb. But under the bravado and hard veneer was a scared little boy who wanted to please his father.

There was the faintest ripple in the blood as his body swayed, but then he set his jaw, shaking his head. "This is for the glory of the Sphinxes, of the Crown. Britain can once again take her rightful place as the greatest empire in the world, but first we must make sacrifices."

Lord Mabry's man—big, with a crooked nose and bulging neck muscles—had reached the top of the stairs, and made a clumsy lunge at her.

Running along the railing, Ivy easily evaded the advance, Ralph intercepting him instead. Behind her she heard a fist connect with meaty flesh. She prayed it was Ralph who had landed the blow. "It won't work! It's over, truly over," Ivy called down. "The curse is broken."

"You're trying to deceive me," Arthur said darkly. "My father was right about you."

"What do you think this will achieve? Nothing good can come of this."

"What will it achieve?" He let out a laugh, a delighted, if not manic, sound. "Why, *everything*! Eternal life, the rejuvenation of broken bodies, the ability to amass knowledge unlike anything man has ever seen."

It all happened so quickly. One moment Arthur was looking up, past her, as if searching for some unknowable sign in the stars just visible through the damaged roof. Then his body was tensing, and with a gurgling plunge, he was under the surface.

Darting down the opposite staircase, Ivy rushed to the fountain. "Arthur!" She lunged, grasping for fingertips still just visible above the blood, but one of the men had caught up to her, pulling her back by the waist.

A hush fell over the hall, even Ivy going still as she watched. A handful of weak bubbles peppered the surface, spreading in rings.

She measured the ensuing silence in the rise and fall of her own chest. *One breath, two breaths, three breaths…*even if Arthur were to hold his breath, by now he would have been forced to come up for air. But his body did not resurface, and he stayed below, drowned in the elixir of life.

The man holding her had loosened his grip as he watched everything unfold, but Ivy was likewise too transfixed to try to run.

"You killed your son," she let out in a choke when the last bubble had burst. Lord Mabry had come to stand on the other side, staring stone-faced at the pool. "You killed your own son, you monster! And you just stand there!"

The remaining Sphinxes exchanged glances, cleared throats. Some wore expressions of shock, others of polite embarrassment, as if they had not actually expected something so vulgar to occur. An acrid breeze swept through the hall, candles guttering in its wake. Nothing else happened: no grand celestial event, no light bursting forth from the fountain, no heavenly chorus of angels.

Lord Mabry finally dragged his gaze from the blood fountain and met Ivy's eye. He looked old, the bags under his eyes more pronounced, the corners of his mouth drooping into what might have been a frown or a grimace, or just age. There were thousands of fathers in England who had lost sons, but none looked as utterly beaten down as the old general did in that moment. She thought he might be in shock, the reality of what had just occurred belatedly setting in, but then he was reaching into his waistcoat pocket, drawing out a gun.

"I can't risk you going to the authorities," he said, leveling the pistol at her. Her captor immediately stepped away, releasing her so that her only bond was the threat of a bullet tearing through her flesh.

"But you *are* the authorities," she said. She didn't know all of the men who comprised the secret society, but she knew that most of them were wealthy aristocrats, and wielded power both in Parliament and among the nobility. No officer or barrister would dare to go against them.

"There will be questions," one of the Sphinxes said. "She's a lady, and her death would draw undue attention."

Ivy's eyes darted to where Ralph was standing. He was looking past her, eyes locked on the pistol trembling in Lord Mabry's liver-spotted hands. "Ralph?"

He stood still as a statue, his eyes glazed as if witnessing something only he could see, throat working compulsively. At his side, his fingers twitched. He looked young, scared.

"Never mind him," the general sneered. "He's war-addled."

Ivy dragged her attention back to where the argument over her life was raging.

"We can't let her go free. It will be over for us," another man countered.

"Then put her in the cell. Let her live out her days there. The love of her life died and she went mad, became a recluse. It's an easy enough story to peddle," Sir Alfred said.

The pistol wavered in Lord Mabry's hand and Ivy held her breath. She should run, at least try to make an escape, but she found herself rooted to the ground, unable to tear her gaze away from the pool lest Arthur miraculously resurface.

"You truly are a credit to your father's legacy," Lord Mabry said, thoughtful. "I always felt badly that we had to see him removed from his position at Cambridge, but it wouldn't do to have the manuscript fall into the hands of someone like him, someone who didn't understand it the way we did. He got close several times, even going so far as to correspond with his cousin, the late Lord Hayworth. Can you imagine the damage they could have done? It would have been the end of a dynasty, the waste of the culmination of centuries' worth of knowledge."

"You...you knew my father?"

"I wouldn't say that exactly, but I knew enough to see that he had to be stopped. I was only too glad when I learned that he'd enlisted and would no longer prove a threat to us."

The smell of blood filled Ivy's nostrils, her lungs, her very being. Her father's demise, her mother's broken heart and subsequent decline, it had all stemmed from this man and his obsession with the manuscript. She was frozen in a moment in war where a soldier must decide if he is to stay in a foxhole, or take his chance going over the top. Ivy's vision narrowed to the pistol, a dangerous glimmer of metal in the candlelight.

No one was expecting it, least of all her. Lunging forward, she hurtled her body into the old man, knocking him off balance and sending the pistol clattering to the floor. She snatched it up, scrambling to her feet and pointing it at Lord Mabry with trembling hands.

"Put the gun down, girl," Lord Mabry instructed.

She felt light-headed and far away from her body, as if she was still on the gallery looking down at herself. "The blood," she said, gesturing with the gun to the fountain. "Where did the blood come from?"

The old man's lips tightened. "How should I know? Arthur was responsible for all that."

She swung around in a wide arc, men shrinking back as the gun passed over them. "Where is the blood from?" she demanded before turning the pistol back on their leader.

"I—I believe there was a girl, a maid," a thin man in wire-rimmed spectacles volunteered in a shaky voice.

She closed her eyes. Agnes. All this time, Agnes had been dead, and Ivy had been none the wiser. Had they imprisoned the girl, keeping her alive until just before the ritual? Had it been fast, a merciful killing? Or had they drained the blood from her in a slow, steady stream while she was still alive? Bile rose in Ivy's stomach, acid filling her mouth. But it was so much blood, more than from just one person, surely. "Who else."

Several of the men exchanged looks. "Pigs, my lady. When it became clear that it…that it wasn't enough, we—"

"Stop." She wavered on her feet, tightening her grip on

the smooth pistol handle. "You killed Agnes, an innocent girl. And for what?"

"How little you understand," Lord Mabry said, unrattled by the pistol trained on him. "Men die by thousands in war for the greater good. What is one girl when it is for the good of our nation? Our race? You think of only what you see before you, of the present moment. But I see the larger picture, a world where war can be fought on paper instead of distant battlefields. How many people did you lose to the war? Would you deny the mothers of the future their children's lives?" The earl's long face twisted in a sneer. "Of course not. You are selfish and small-minded. This is why someone of your station is unfit to hold a title, to be responsible for the purity of English blood. You were a means to an end, but I was never pleased about my son taking a wife from the gutter."

She was going to kill him. Ivy's finger tightened on the trigger, the cool metal inviting her to release all her anger and rage. Was this how James and her father had felt on the battlefield? What a terrible burden to hold a man's life in the balance, even if the man was evil incarnate. The rush of power shamed her, yet her heart beat fast, her finger tightening on the trigger. Memories, hidden ones that she had always kept close to her heart, smoldered and flared like lightning striking a tree.

James, crouching at the edge of the pond in Regent's Park, crooked grin on his face as he watched the ducks and geese. Too young to die.

Tightening.

Her father, spectacles askew as he held her on his knee, showing her the manuscript he was working on. The world robbed of a great mind, a loving man.

Tightening.

Her mother, kind and generous and warm, who could fill a grimy London flat with music more beautiful than any orchestra, lying in a hospital bed, unable to afford a doctor who cared enough to try to save her.

Tightening.

Ivy Radcliffe, no longer a girl, but not quite a woman yet. Alone in the world, without a purpose or a place, forced to find her way without the love of her family.

Pulling.

34

A ringing *bang* echoed through the hall.
Candle flames jumped at the sudden disturbance of air, and Ivy's hand flew to her mouth as she watched the old man recoil. The pistol clattered to the ground with a sickening finality. He couldn't possibly be dead, could he? But then a spot of red was blooming on the general's white shirt, spreading as the man fell first to his knees, then face forward, with a terrible groan.

For a moment everything stood still, an audience holding its collective breath before the curtain dropped. Blood seeped out across the stone floor, an echo of the vignette of the pool behind them. Somewhere beyond the open roof, a night bird let out a melancholy cry. The world seemed to have called a truce while the shock of the moment settled in. But then there was a stampede of bodies as everyone came back to life.

"He's dead!"

"Get the girl!"

A press of bodies and then hands grabbing for her, the smell of gunpowder choking the air. Anger rose off the men like steam off a lake in winter. Ivy's fingers were stiff from gripping the gun, but she clawed the group off, buttons and shirt collars coming off in her hands. Someone grabbed her hair, another an arm. She might have been a lady, but her title would not save her now, not against men who had until moments ago believed they would hold the key to eternal life, only to see it snatched away.

Her vision blurred as she fought for air against the press of bodies. But just as suddenly as they had fallen upon her, the men fell back, air rushing in where she had been suffocating. Someone was lifting her, not with hungry, clawing arms, but strong and gentle ones. When she felt rough wool beneath her cheek, she knew that she was safe. Holding her against his chest with one arm, Ralph wielded the pistol in the other.

"I'll start shooting and I won't stop. I don't care if you're a bloody duke or the king himself, I'll kill you all and be glad to do it."

It was like a dousing of cold water, the mob instantly falling apart. Most made for the doorway, but a few lingered, unsure if they should avenge their leader or not. In the end, it was self-preservation that won out over loyalty, and the hall emptied.

The candles were burning low, and all Ivy could see of Ralph was his tense posture, a stormy expression. Whatever had caused him to freeze, he seemed to be released from the spell. Taking her chin in his hand, he made a quick inspection of her. "You're in shock," he said.

She hadn't realized she was shaking until he draped Hewitt's coat over her shoulders and she heard the chattering of her own teeth.

"Come on," he said, tugging her along.

Ivy cast a glance back at the abandoned experiment. Arthur was somewhere under the surface, a premature slumber born of desperation to please an impossible father. "We can't just leave him there."

"Oh, yes we can," Ralph said without looking back.

He pulled her along, and secretly she was glad that she wasn't forced to see Arthur's body, wasn't privy to the outcome of whatever the Sphinxes had been trying to accomplish. Outside, motorcars were pulling out of the drive, flustered chauffeurs scrambling to pull them around as the rest of the Sphinxes fled back to the safety of their estates and castles.

"Do you think they'll come back?"

Ralph didn't say anything as he navigated her behind the drive and to the stables by the light of the full moon. Inside, it was warm and safe and smelled of sweet hay and horses. Feeling was slowly returning to her tingling hands and feet, and she was able to follow him up the steep stairs that led to the loft.

Ivy watched as he moved about the small space, lighting old oil lamps and getting out stacks of folded blankets. *I've killed a man*, she thought, *and now I am in Ralph's bedroom*. Laughter bubbled up inside her at the absurdity of it, and she swayed back and forth like a lunatic.

"Sit," he instructed, guiding her to the bed. Her laughter gradually subsided as she perched on the edge of the quilt, suddenly aware that she was still in her nightgown, with only an old coat draped over her shoulders to afford her any sense of modesty.

Ralph's quarters were sparse, but homey: a neatly made bed, an old chest of drawers, and gingham curtains pinned to a small window which looked out onto the abbey. So this was where he slept and dreamed while she had pottered about the big empty house. Given the choice, she would have rather made her home here, curled up with a book in the little loft, watching the seasons change from the window, the gentle sound of the ponies whickering below.

She thought he might sit beside her, but ever the gentleman, he pulled up a wood chair and perched with elbows on his knees, fingers tented in thought. She shifted her weight on the creaking bed, watching as his stormy expression faded into something else, something softer but that sent chills racing along her arms.

He let out a curse, pushing his hand through his hair. "Christ. Ivy—" He broke off.

Below them, a horse stamped in its stall and whinnied to its neighbor. Ivy desperately wanted him to say something else, to give words to whatever it was that was spiraling through his mind. But whatever it was, was too heavy, and stayed lodged in his throat.

"Mr. and Mrs. Hewitt," she finally asked, "are they all right?"

"Both still resting at the cottage, assuming they have any sense."

She nodded. "What now?"

Ralph hitched a shoulder, eyes trained on the burnt visage of the abbey through the small window. "That's up to you," he said. "Rebuild, or..." he paused, gave an uncomfortable swallow, "or leave."

Could it really be that simple? After every kind of imprisonment and tether that had bound her to the abbey, could she just simply leave it all behind? Where would she go? And did she even want to? Her body still ached, her hands fidgety at the memory of the pistol in them.

"Are you sure that it's truly over?" she asked. "The other members of the club won't press charges against me? They'll leave me alone now?"

"They'd be bloody fools to try," Ralph said. "The curse, or whatever it was, is broken, there's nothing left for them in the library. Their leader is dead." He paused, his hands clasped tight as if he did not know what to do with them. "Will you—will you stay?"

All the lovely dreams of Ralph that she had read of in the book were nothing more than that—dreams. A painful lump sat heavy in Ivy's chest. She was a widow now. She had made her choice with Arthur and look where that had gotten her. There was no denying that Ralph was a good, upstanding man, but the Ralph of her dreams was not the man who sat before her.

"I'm staying," she said, her decision crystallizing as the words came out of her mouth. "We'll rebuild everything that was damaged, restore it to an even higher standard than it was before." The only way to push the memories of the hellish night out of her mind would be to throw herself into a new project, one that would require all of her time and attention. This would be the fresh start she had been denied the first time around. Besides, there was something that still bound her to the abbey, though she could not name it.

Ralph's shoulders relaxed a little. "Right," he said, his voice a storm cloud with just a hint of sunshine peeking through. Pushing back the chair, he stood and shrugged into his old work coat.

"Where are you going?"

"To clean up that mess," he said with a grimace.

Ivy started to sit up, but one look from Ralph told her that her presence would thankfully not be tolerated.

"Get some rest," he instructed. He hesitated by the stairs, then doubled back and dropped a featherlight kiss on her temple. Before she could blink her shock away, he had gently tucked a quilt around her and then was descending, the steps creaking under his weight.

35

Four months later

Ivy emerged into a brilliant spring day with a sky as blue and sharp as cut crystal, tender green buds and pink petals spangling the bare tree branches. The smell of damp earth and sweet pollen had never felt so decadent before, so liberating. The previous four months had been spent supervising repairs and renovations at the abbey, and Ivy would fall into bed each night exhausted by the work required to bring her vision of a restored abbey to life. Ralph had taken care of the remains of the Sphinxes' bloody experiment, though he refused to divulge to her how he had done it or what had become of Arthur's remains. "It isn't for you to worry about," is all he would say, and Ivy was glad not to know.

When she and Ralph had brought the Hewitts back to the cell to show them the monk, all that remained was a pile of dust and jewels. "He's gone back, then," Mrs. Hewitt pronounced with a taut nod of her head. "To think, his evil bones were under the floors all these years, taking and sucking like a leech." She toed a gold bracelet studded with rubies on the floor. "If we had known that he could be stopped, that it didn't have to be like this…" Her words trailed to nothing.

"Does that mean that you're free of your part of the pact now?" Ivy asked.

"Free of the library and our dark charge," Hewitt said. "But not free of Blackwood, never free of Blackwood. The pact may have been broken, but our service to the family transcends all that."

"It's in our blood," Mrs. Hewitt explained. "It's as much our home as it is yours."

Now as Ivy stood on the abbey's front steps, the ancient stones beneath her feet and the battlements silhouetted against the sky above her, she finally understood what they meant. It was not just memories and bloodlines that tied them to this place, but a deep sense of stewardship. She was as much a thread in the tapestry of the history of Blackwood as all those who came before her.

Ralph had brought the car around and was holding open the door for her, dressed in his deep green livery, brass buttons shining in the sun. Her heart did a fluttery dance in her chest as she stopped just short of him. She could still feel the light brush of his lips on her forehead, though neither of them had spoken of it. In fact, she had hardly seen anything of Ralph the past months, let alone spoken to him. He was a constant presence in the abbey, and she would often hear him overseeing the construction workers, but whenever she went to seek him out, he would suddenly be otherwise engaged or mysteriously just on his way out the door. But that morning he had sought her out in the library, and asked if he could drive her somewhere after tea. All he had said was that it was a surprise, a place that he thought she should see.

Ivy studied the back of Ralph's neck as he drove, where the starched white collar met his lightly tanned skin. It felt strange to share such a small, intimate space with him and yet not have the slightest clue what he was thinking, what was causing his shoulders to hunch just a little.

Eventually they crested a peak, and a valley scattered with ruins came into view, glittering in the sunlight trapped between the rolling hills. Ralph parked the car near the bottom, and helped her out.

The sun warmed her cheeks as she lifted her face to follow the stones into the sky. Here were the romantic ruins that she had envisioned when she'd first come to Yorkshire, rugged nature cradling something beautifully fragile yet defiant against the passage of centuries.

"It's beautiful. What is this place?"

"Rievaulx Abbey," he told her. "Didn't fare so well as Blackwood after the Dissolution. Been in ruins for centuries."

While it might have been a skeleton of its former self, it was a graceful decay. Arches made of honey-colored stone soared up into the clear blue sky, and birds sang their cheery sermons from the airy pulpits. A herd of disinterested sheep watched Ivy and Ralph as they scrambled over the rocks and through half-standing doorways. Ralph took Ivy's hand firmly in his, helping her navigate the uneven terrain.

By the time they had made it to what must have once been the transept, Ivy's color was high and her lungs were burning from the effort of climbing and scrambling. It felt wonderful. Later in the spring, the abbey must have been favored by local artists, easels set up to capture the romantic sprawl of ruins. But on this mild, early March afternoon, it was deserted save for the two of them, their footsteps and voices echoing off the shallow valley walls.

Ralph was gazing up at a pair of birds on one of the soaring walls, hands jammed in his coat pockets, a small furrow in his brow.

"Penny for your thoughts?"

"They aren't worth that much."

"Ralph," she insisted.

He scuffed at a paving stone with the toe of his shoe. "I want to read something. What book would you recommend for me?"

The question caught her off guard, but the soft edge of vulnerability in his voice even more so. Ivy regarded him, the dark gray eyes and hard cut of his jaw, the invisible armor of sarcasm and bluntness that he draped around himself. Under there somewhere there was a scared boy who had been sent off to war, forced to witness things that Ivy could only begin to imagine. "A novel, something with some adventure in it, but also a love story. I think you may be a romantic at heart."

She thought he might protest her assessment, but he just nodded. Running her fingers over the pitted stones of the wall, she pondered what story would make Ralph feel safe within its pages. "*The Count of Monte Cristo,*" she said finally. "It's long, but worth it, I promise."

"I'd like that."

She was lingering in an archway, marveling at the moss that thrived on the undersides of the cold, damp stones, when suddenly Ralph was taking both her hands in his, gently pushing her up against the stones and pressing his body into hers.

She froze, his sudden heat making her drowsy and excited all at once. "What are you doing?" she asked in a whisper.

Ralph's eyes searched her face, tender and hopeful. He skimmed his hands downward, letting them rest on the swell of her hips through her cardigan, and a jolt of heat shot through her.

"You kept it," he murmured.

She could hardly think straight. "Kept what? What are you talking about?"

"The muffler." He brought one hand up and gently ran it along the wool. "I had hoped you would."

Frowning, she touched the muffler at her throat. It had felt cooler when she'd woken up that morning, and she hadn't realized she was still wearing it. "This? I don't even remember where I got it."

"No?" Some of the warmth left his voice, but he was still holding her so tightly against him that she could feel his arousal. It made her dizzy and hungry for more, so much more.

"I... I don't think this is appropriate," she murmured, despite the hammering of her heart. Was this the Ralph of her dreams? Or the Ralph who usually showed nothing but contempt for her, antagonized her? He had been milder, more agreeable since Arthur's death, but this was different. This felt like a continuation of something she didn't remember, something she may never have been part of. "I'm so grateful for everything you've done to help me, but—"

Cool air wrapped around her as he drew away, and she wished that she'd held her tongue even just a moment longer. "Ralph? What is it?" He had shed his cap and was running his hand through his hair, the afternoon sun catching the strands of gold. The man looked tortured. "I don't understand," she whispered.

"You don't remember," he said, his voice heavy with heartbreak. "I knew it was possible, but it had been a few months and I had hoped..." When he looked up at her, his face was a portrait of a man on the brink of despair.

Some foreign emotion cracked deep within her. Why was

his pain making her feel as if she was the one falling down a deep, dark well? Why did the hurt in his eyes make her want to rush to him and cradle him like a small child, hushing away all his troubles?

"What, Ralph? What don't I remember?"

The sun had slid behind a cloud, a cold edge sharpening the air. He shook his head. "It doesn't matter."

The inexplicable tug at her heart again. "Whatever it is clearly means a great deal!"

"It once did, and to me, but clearly not to you."

"You can't say something like that and then not tell me. If something happened and I don't remember it, it still happened. Tell me," she urged. "I feel as if I were robbed of my own life. I don't know how much time I've missed, *what* I've missed. If you know something, then I am begging you to tell me, even if it is hard to hear. I need to know. I need to rewrite my life."

Ralph's hands fisted and uncurled at his sides. He let out a long breath and then nodded. "I have to show you. Please," he said, the single word holding a lifetime's worth of pain, so that she had no choice but to give a jerky nod and let him continue.

He was taking her by the shoulders, tilting her head back, his piercing silver gaze fixed on her. "Ralph! What are you do—"

His lips met hers and shock quickly faded into something warm and familiar, and she found herself responding to the kiss, even as her mind raced to make sense of what was happening. The stones at her back were cold, and as she pressed herself into his heat, some long slumbering part of her began to awaken. There was something deeply familiar and comfortable about the kiss, yet it felt exciting and new at the same time. He fit her body perfectly, her arms easily coming around his neck as his thigh gently nudged her legs wider beneath her skirt. Even the Ralph of her dreams could not compare with the man of flesh and blood whose touch was leaving her breathless. With hesitant hands, she ran her palms down the hard contours of his chest, tracing his muscles and memorizing the way his moans felt on her tongue.

When he at last pulled back, an involuntary whimper escaped her throat. Raising her gaze to his, she found something almost tender lurking beneath the feral gray eyes. "Do you remember now?" he asked, his voice husky.

"I—" she started, and then stopped. At first it was a soft patter like summer rain against a window, hazy images slowly clearing from the back of her mind. A hand held out and accepted on a foggy moor. Stolen looks and discreet brushes of fingertips. Then it was sharp and painful, as if a bullet were being dug out of her flesh with the blunt end of a knife. A longing so acute that her chest hurt when she lay alone in bed at night. A stolen kiss. What she had thought had been dreams, wishful, beautiful, hopeful dreams, had all been real.

Her breath caught deep in her chest, threatened to stop completely. "Oh, Ralph," she managed to choke out. "I didn't... that is..." What was there to say? Questions piled up one on top of the other faster than she could ask them. "We were lovers, weren't we? For how long? When?"

If her finally remembering brought him any pleasure, it didn't show on his face. He looked haunted, tortured even. A soldier whose mind was still in the trenches, despite being hundreds of miles away from battle.

"Not lovers, not really," he said, the faintest spots of pink appearing along his cheeks. "But friends with the promise of something more, from nearly the beginning," he told her. "I tried to keep my distance, but I couldn't... I couldn't stay away from you, Ivy. I tried to protect you, to keep the worst from you. I knew what would happen with your memory, just like with all the others. But you wouldn't go, and by then it was too late. The forgetting began, and you got engaged. It seemed like after the fire you started to remember more things, but I guess not us."

Her mind raced to make sense of the timeline, but it was hopeless. How could she finish a puzzle when she didn't even know what pieces she was missing? She shook her head. "I'm sorry, I don't."

"Maybe some things are more important than others," he said, a touch of petulance in his voice.

"That's not fair."

Ralph kicked at a rock, sending it skidding down the steep embankment. "None of it is."

"I don't remember my marriage to Arthur, and really, how can you even call it a relationship? He used me, lied to me and manipulated me. Even if I thought differently at the time, there was never any real love between us."

Ralph flinched, as if she had struck him. "Don't say his name. I never want to hear that name again."

She watched him, moving between the shadows and the light, all restless energy in the shape of a man. "He was part of my life, even if it was a dark part," Ivy said evenly. "I can't simply choose to forget him, and truthfully, I don't want to. I've come to realize that my memories are precious, even the bad ones."

Ralph had turned away, was recklessly climbing back down the rocks, heedless of his limp.

"Ralph, wait."

He stopped, but it was only to help her over the rocks. Once they were back at the auto, he let go of her hand and wordlessly opened the door for her.

"Here," she said, unwrapping the muffler. "Take it."

"I don't want it back."

"Don't be silly," she said. "It's clearly yours, you should have it."

With a dark look, he finally accepted the muffler and threw it onto the front seat. Then they left the abbey behind, the setting sun throwing the ruins into stark shadows and quiet obscurity once again.

36

The library had once again become her escape.

But this time it was not ghosts or the banal duties of being a lady from which she sought refuge, but Ralph. They had not spoken since the kiss on the ruins the day before, and really, what was there to say? Knowing that she'd had him and then lost him without so much as a memory of their friendship was somehow worse than never having had him at all.

Lucky for her, there was endless work to be done to salvage the books after the fire. Shelves needed repairing, books needed to be dried and aired after being damaged by water, and cataloging had to be started from scratch. Mrs. Hewitt pulled books from the shelves, gave them a dusting, and then handed them to Ivy who noted them in her ledger. They worked quietly, but companionably. It was pleasant, working with a shared purpose, a fire crackling in the grate and a tray with warm tea and biscuits between them. The headaches that had once plagued her were things of the past, and she no longer dreaded the aftermath of her time spent in the library. All of her plans for restoration came back to her, and she had the time now to dedicate to making the library as beautiful and welcoming as it was important. The lending library in the village was all well and good, but people deserved to experience the magic of a library like Blackwood, to have doors opened to them and be welcomed into a place of learning.

Dusting the spine of a book and about to hand it to Mrs. Hewitt to shelve, Ivy let out a little sound of surprise when a slim packet of letters slid out from between the pages and onto her lap.

"My lady, what is it?" Mrs. Hewitt asked.

Unfolding the envelope, Ivy shook her head that she didn't know. She quickly scanned the lines written in an unfamiliar hand.

To my kin and heir,

I write this with heavy heart, in a rare moment of clarity. If you are reading this, then perhaps you will already understand why I say that, or perhaps you have no idea what I am talking about. I hope that it is the latter, but in case it is the former, then I hope you are in a likewise lucid moment.

Firstly, my apologies. For everything. I know the Radcliffes are struggling, and many times I have battled myself in whether I should shed my cloak of anonymity and step forward. But in the end, I am a coward. My only consolation is that by remaining anonymous, that my misfortune and ill-luck shall not stalk the next generation of Hayworths. Perhaps my solicitor shall not be able to find you, though I doubt that will be the case with the dogged Mr. Duncan.

Regardless, if you do find yourself at Blackwood, I beg of you, run. There may be consequences, but these pale in comparison to what you will endure should you choose to stay.

Ivy paused in her reading, aware of Mrs. Hewitt watching her expectantly. Poor Lord Hayworth. He seemed well-meaning, but could he really have been so naïve as to think that the next Hayworth heir wouldn't succumb to the same fate as all the others? She tried not to think of what would have happened if she had found this letter earlier in her tenure at Blackwood, all the heartache it might have spared.

"It's a letter, written by Lord Hayworth," she told Mrs. Hewitt. "It seems he had a stroke of consciousness and wanted to warn me, or whoever came after him, about the library."

Mrs. Hewitt let out a heavy sigh. "I often felt like a warden of a man awaiting the scaffold. It was my job to guard him, make sure that he stayed so the library could feed, but it didn't mean that I didn't feel compassion for him. He was a good man, a little aloof perhaps, but always even-tempered and kind to the staff."

Ivy didn't say anything. Mrs. Hewitt may have just been doing her job and holding up her end of a centuries-old agreement, but it was hard to feel sympathy for any grief on her part.

Ivy turned her attention back to the other paper in her hand. It was a letter posted from London, the return address their old flat. Hungrily, she unfolded it the rest of the way and drank in the familiar, yet long-ago handwriting of her father.

Cousin, if what you say is true about the library, then of course I am both shocked and sympathetic, though I fail to see how I could be of assistance. Work and family obligations preclude me from traveling to Yorkshire at present, but when next you are in London, pay me a call, and we can discuss it further if that will ease your mind.

Ivy leaned against the shelf, read the brief letter again. Her father hadn't just known of Lord Hayworth and Blackwood, he'd known about the manuscript and library, and it seemed the curse that went along with them. Lord Mabry had said something about having her father removed from his job at the university; had her father actually met with Lord Hayworth at some point and seen the manuscript for himself? What had he made of it? He must not have believed the stories of curses surrounding it, or perhaps he simply thought there was no chance that he or anyone in their family would actually inherit Blackwood someday.

Mrs. Hewitt, bless her, was making a study of a book, giving Ivy time to hastily wipe her eyes and fold the letters back up.

"Is everything all right?" she asked presently.

"Yes. No, I don't know," Ivy admitted. "It was a letter from my father to Lord Hayworth." She didn't elaborate, and Mrs. Hewitt didn't pry.

The housekeeper pressed her lips, clearly fighting with herself about what she was about to say. "I don't want to add to your troubles, my lady, but there is something you should know."

"I suppose you had better tell me now while my handkerchief is still out," Ivy said.

"Ralph found Agnes."

For a moment a delirious happiness overtook her. "She's alive? What happened, I—" But then she saw the look on Mrs. Hewitt's face. "Oh, no," was all she could manage to say.

"It is my understanding that there was...well, there was not much of her left, from what Ralph told me." Mrs. Hewitt picked up a biscuit, put it back down again. She'd gone a little green. "Ralph said that there was evidence that the rest of the blood didn't just come from pigs as they claimed."

The implication settled between them; there had been others. The Sphinxes had tried to recreate the monk's experiments, trading in blood for eternal life or whatever it was they thought they would gain.

"We should call on her family, pay for a memorial," Ivy said. Poor, sweet Agnes. Her family could never know what had become of their daughter; it would devastate them.

"And it was all for nothing," Mrs. Hewitt responded with a shake of her head. "Those villains should rot for what they've done."

"I believe Ralph would shoot every one of them if he were given leave," Ivy said. She still felt as if she were holding her breath, waiting for Scotland Yard to come to investigate Lord Mabry's and Sir Arthur's deaths, and haul her away in handcuffs.

"That's just what I fear," Mrs. Hewitt said, bending to retrieve a book she had dropped. "He would do anything for the people he loves, even if it means landing himself in trouble." She squared a knowing look on Ivy.

Ivy's cheeks burned as she concentrated on pouring a cup of cool tea, her lips pressed tight. The silence grew heavy and prickly.

"He cares for you, you know. And I think," Mrs. Hewitt said, pretending to inspect the book, "that you have some affection for him as well, do you not?"

Pages flipped by in Ivy's mind, detailing embraces that she did not remember, kisses and hoarsely whispered promises that might have been dreams for all she knew. "Apparently," Ivy said. "Though it was built on gestures and words that I don't remember. Besides, I've had enough of men. I was hardly a bride and now I'm a widow."

"What on earth are you talking about? You're no more a widow than I am."

"But Arthur is dead." The teacup trembled in Ivy's hand as a cold panic started in her fingertips, spreading up her arms and through her chest. "Are you telling me he's not dead?"

"Of course he's dead, and I'm quite sure he's somewhere

far warmer than here, where he belongs. What I mean, my
lady, is that you were never married."

"But… I saw a photograph. Arthur showed me our wedding portrait."

Mrs. Hewitt actually had the nerve to laugh. "Did he now?
I'll not pretend to know how he managed *that* trick, but mark
my words when I tell you that Arthur Mabry died a bachelor."

"Are you certain?"

The housekeeper raised an affronted brow. "Quite certain. As soon as you announced your engagement, I wired
Mr. Duncan, the estate's solicitor, and informed him not to
draft a single document, unless instructed to do so by your
ladyship herself, in person. I didn't want that snake Mabry
having wills and documents drafted in your name while you
were wasting away under the effects of the library. He told
me that a friend of yours had come around his office, and was
concerned for much the same reasons as I was. In any case, I
heard from him shortly after—" here Mrs. Hewitt broke off
and gave Ivy a meaningful look "—that night. He wanted to
know if the engagement had been broken, as he hadn't heard
a word from Lord Mabry, Sir Arthur, or yourself."

Ivy sat in stunned silence. "And you didn't think to tell me
any of this?"

"I hadn't the foggiest that you were under the impression
you were married, my lady."

Ivy slumped back into her seat. She wasn't married. She
never had been. All the unpleasant places her mind had
gone trying to fill in the blank spaces of an unremembered
marriage…none of it was real, none of it mattered anymore.
Instead, she was left with a vast, unwritten page, one where
anything was possible. One where she wasn't bound to a ghost,
one where she was free to write her own story with whom-
ever she wanted.

She took a long sip of her tea when she realized Mrs. Hewitt was watching her expression with keen interest. "It doesn't matter," Ivy said a little too quickly. "It doesn't change anything between Ralph and I."

"Doesn't it? Well, I will tell you one thing," Mrs. Hewitt said. "My first duty is to Blackwood, but I will guard that boy's heart as if it were my own."

Desperate to change the subject, Ivy chanced a sidelong look at the housekeeper and put down her tea. "You care for him," she said. "More than just as a friend or fellow servant."

The book lay forgotten in Mrs. Hewitt's hand as she stared out the window at the gathering rain clouds. She quickly whisked a tear from her eye and stared down into her lap, her thin fingers wound around each other. The silence grew long, but something told Ivy to stay her tongue, that Mrs. Hewitt was building to something. "Ralph is our son," she said finally.

Ivy's cup hovered beneath her mouth as Mrs. Hewitt's revelation settled around her. Had she known that, or was it a secret? There was a certain similarity between the firm set of their jaws, the serious gray eyes, but she wouldn't have noticed unless she was looking for a resemblance. "Ralph never told me," she murmured. "Or, if he did, I don't remember."

Mrs. Hewitt looked up sharply. "He doesn't know."

Was he the product of an affair? Were the housekeeper and butler not truly married, and had had a child in a clandestine relationship? How could three people—a family—work together their whole lives, and one not know that they were related to the others?

As if reading her thoughts, Mrs. Hewitt gave a ghost of smile. "It's nothing like it sounds. It was the war, his memory was..." She made a futile gesture as she searched for words. "Ralph came home different. Broken. He used to be such a good-natured lad, still is, I suppose, but without that spark in his eyes. He was such a spirited boy, always getting into trouble around the abbey. Bringing toads into the kitchen and giving the cook the fright of her life. I remember one time he put on a play for the whole staff, acting out each part himself," Mrs. Hewitt said with a misty-eyed smile. "But all that was gone after the war. I suppose some of it was just growing up, but I can't help but feel the war stole the rest of his youth."

Ivy slouched back in her seat, closing her eyes. Ralph was missing pieces of his life too. And not just memories, but the knowledge that he had a family that loved him.

"We were so careful," Mrs. Hewitt was continuing. "Even with our family history, we made sure that he was never about the library too much, or even in the house too long for that matter. But then the war came, and he insisted on fighting. It broke my heart as a mother, but I couldn't stop him. You know Ralph. And then he came back..." She dabbed a handkerchief at her eyes. "My sweet boy came back so...so *angry*. He didn't remember what happened to him, and there were these big black spots where he couldn't remember entire chapters of his life. He knew that he used to work at the abbey, and he remembered the library and its secrets, but he didn't recognize us as his parents anymore. He'd go into rages at the smallest things, and the longer it went on, the less we felt we could tell him the truth. It wasn't until you came that he began to calm down, though he still carries that anger, still doesn't have a name for it."

Ivy quickly cut her watering gaze away. Watching the usually stoic housekeeper fight the tremble in her lips gave Ivy no pleasure, but she had seen how Ralph hungered for companionship despite his hardened demeanor. "Don't you think he would have wanted to know, even if it was painful?"

"We thought it was better this way," Mrs. Hewitt said. "Mr.

Hewitt and I are bound to the abbey, the library. We didn't want that for Ralph. We didn't want to burden him."

"Burden me with what?"

Both women snapped their attention to the door where Ralph was standing, an army-issued canvas sack hefted over one shoulder.

Mrs. Hewitt shot to her feet. "Ralph."

Slinging his bag to the floor, he moved further into the library. "Burden me with what," he repeated without inflection.

Mrs. Hewitt looked about the room as if she might find an escape route, as Ralph's energy heated and seeped into the library.

"Maybe I should leave," Ivy said, rising from her chair.

She could just make out their voices as she waited outside the library doors. Ralph did not seem to be taking the news well. There was shouting, then a teary rejoinder from Mrs. Hewitt. Ivy was just considering going back in to act as peacekeeper, when the doors flew open and Ralph stormed out, Mrs. Hewitt's voice calling out behind him.

Ivy chased after him out to the cold March evening. Raindrops were starting to fall, a thousand silent witnesses to Ivy's desperation. "Ralph, wait." Her hand caught the edge of his coat, only to have it slide through her fingers.

"Will you talk to me?"

"What good is talking?" he growled without turning around. "Words don't seem to mean much around here."

Still, she followed him out through the back gardens and to the edge of the moors, ignoring the sharp raindrops falling in her hair.

"Where are you going?" He still had his bag over his shoulder, and she had a terrible feeling that she already knew.

"I'm leaving."

She stayed her step, nearly losing her footing in the uneven heather. "What?"

"That was always the plan. I'm not needed here—the work on the abbey is almost done."

"What are you talking about? Of course you're needed here. I don't want anyone else. Ralph?" She scurried in front of him, planting her hands on her hips. "Tell me what's really wrong. I demand it. And don't tell me it's what Mrs. Hewitt said—I know it must have been a shock to learn the truth about your origins, but you had your bag with you before that."

He hitched the bag higher on his shoulder, gazing out into the dark rain. "You wouldn't understand," he muttered.

"Hogwash."

His voice was low, made even harder to hear by the wind and rain. She moved closer to catch his words. "I—I swore to protect you. And then I failed you, when you needed it the most."

"I don't understand."

Color touched his ears. "Lord Mabry," he said. "You were forced to shoot him, because I was too... I was..." His words trailed off into miserable silence.

She blinked away the rain from her eyes. "That's what all this is about?" She could have laughed. This was fixable, a question of a man's pride.

"You think I'm being foolish."

"No, no of course not," she hurried to reassure him.

"When that gun came out, it unlocked something, something I would have rather not remembered. And I... I couldn't get out of my own head. I was frozen. It was as if I was back in France again, and..." His words faded off as he swallowed whatever horrors they had contained.

"Oh, Ralph." Ivy moved closer still, put a tentative hand on his chest. His heart was beating hard despite his stillness.

"I've seen firsthand what the war has done to men, and I don't think it helps to bottle it all up and keep it inside of you."

"Christ, Ivy." He regarded her with deeply haunted eyes, but did not move away. "That's why we fought, for people like you, sweet girls who have their whole lives ahead of them, so that you'd never have to know the hardships of the world."

"But I want to know you, and if you truly want to know me, then you have to trust me. I seem to remember placing my trust in you even when I was told not to."

Shaking his head, Ralph looked past her toward the abbey. "You can be bloody convincing with those big brown eyes, you know."

"I know."

He let out a snort that was a hair away from being a laugh. "I'll make a deal with you. You can ask me whatever you want and I'll give you an honest answer, but in exchange I can ask you anything as well."

"Fair enough. I'll go first." She took a deep breath, the cold air bracing her for asking a question she wasn't certain she wanted an answer to. "Why won't you give me another chance, now that I can remember? You must know—" She broke off, swallowed. Put her messy thoughts in order. "You must know that I have feelings for you. That everything that happened between us I remember, but only as the most wonderful dream. I didn't dare think it could have been real. And now that I know it was real, I can't go back to a life without you."

Rain fell between them, a veil through which Ralph's gray eyes watched her without a hint of what thoughts might be lurking behind them. Plunging her hands into the pockets of her thin cardigan, Ivy shifted her weight. Cold was creeping through her shoes and the wind nipped at her nose. She could bear it all if only he would say something, but he just stood there, immovable and silent as one of the busts in the library.

"Please," she whispered into the cold air, "please say something."

A dark movement in the murky gloaming, and then he was in front of her, radiating heat and that exquisite scent of woodsmoke and leather that transported her to cozy and safe spaces in her mind. Shrugging out of his coat, he draped it over her shaking shoulders and she closed her eyes.

"It wasn't a dream," Ralph said. "It was real, every stolen minute of it." Pulling her into the refuge of his embrace, he clung to her as if drowning. "Ivy, I didn't make sense until you came here." His voice was a hoarse whisper against her hair, sending reverberations through her body. "I felt like a sheepdog without sheep," he continued. "Something in me... I wanted to protect, to guard. And then you came, and you were so good and sweet, and actually *cared*. I would do anything to keep you safe."

"You're a Hewitt," she said against his chest. "You were born to protect the library, but your parents never told you. All that instinct had to go somewhere. I never needed protecting though," she felt compelled to add.

A shudder of his chest, and she realized he was laughing. Pulling back, she marveled at the way the dark shadows that usually haunted his face instantly cleared. He was a beautiful man, but when he laughed, a sort of brilliance shone through him.

"Of course not, you're Ivy Radcliffe, a force of nature, a titled lady who would rather ride a bicycle through a rainstorm than ask her own chauffeur for a ride. Now it's my turn," he told her.

Ivy stiffened in his arms, loath to end the lovely moment. Gently cupping her face in his hands, he brought her gaze up to meet his. "What are you afraid of, Ivy?" he asked softly. "You say that it was all a wonderful dream, but you wouldn't kiss me back, wouldn't even let me touch you, and that was real. Even the bravest soldiers harbor some secret fear, and there's something that you're afraid of. Is it me?"

She looked away, unable to bear the desperate sadness in his eyes where only a moment ago had been laughter. "I suppose I'm afraid that I'm not the person you fell in love with, that I don't remember who she was or how to be her." The truth of her confession hadn't fully settled until she'd said the words out loud. At least when she had thought it a dream, she had been safe from the risk of disappointment.

"I see." He squinted up into the rain, deep in thought. "Do you still love books?" he finally asked, bringing his gaze back down to rest squarely on her.

"Of course," she answered, puzzled.

"And would you still go out of your way to defend a friend in need, or help an injured animal?"

She frowned. "Did I help an animal?"

"You brought me a barn swallow with a broken wing," he told her. "We were able to mend it. So, would you do it again?"

She didn't remember that, but she answered without hesitation. "Every time."

"Are you still the most beautiful woman in Yorkshire—no, in all of England?"

Her cheeks heated. "I—"

"No, don't answer that, I can see that you are."

She gave him a sardonic look.

"Are you still stubborn as a bloody mule?"

"I am not stubborn! I'm—"

He stopped her with a raised brow. "I think I already know the answer to that one, too."

At her indignant expression, he drew her closer to him, his

hands strong and sure as they clasped her at the small of her back. "If there's one thing the war taught me, it's that we can try to forget and push away memories all we want, but we are still the same, damaged people. Those forgotten memories shape us as much as the remembered ones. Everything that we shared, whether you remember it or not, brought us here. So I suppose the question isn't if you are the same girl that I fell in love with—because you are—but if you will have me, broken and unpolished as I am."

She didn't answer him, instead fingering the edge of his collar, wishing that she could follow the trail of heat down his chest. "Where was our first kiss?"

His brows rose at the sudden change in subject. "Out on the moors, the day I found you running like your life depended on it. I'd been drinking whiskey, and you came crashing through the heather all pale and breathless, and..." He scuffed his boot in the mud as if suddenly self-conscious. When he spoke again, some of his old gruffness had returned. "And I decided I had to kiss you, right then or die from the wanting."

At his words, a key clicked into place, and out tumbled a precious cache of memories. The loss of time walking back from the moors. Whiskey-warmed breath on her lips. The electric brush of Ralph's stubbled jaw against her cheek. The cold and rain fading away until it was just Ivy and Ralph clinging to each other, a lonesome island in the rolling mist.

"Take me there."

With a searching sidelong glance, he looped her arm through his, guiding her further out of the grounds until the heather grew wild and the dead grass brushed at their legs. The patchwork view of rolling hills and valleys was familiar, the trees all crooked lace with branches feathered against the dark sky.

She stood still, closing her eyes, the breeze sweeping off the moors and invigorating her. "I remember," she whispered.

"You were standing close to me, but you felt so far away. I was scared, but that wasn't why I stayed."

Ralph's breath hitched beside her, his arm tightening around her waist. Spinning to face him, she planted her palms flush against his chest, savoring his stability, his realness. "Kiss me, here. It will be our first kiss, again."

He pulled her closer, obliging. "I would forget everything every day if I had to, just for a lifetime of firsts with you," he murmured.

"Let's hope it doesn't come to that," she said, lifting her mouth to meet his. The world stretched out before her as sweeping as the rolling moors, as promising as fresh sheets of paper just waiting to be filled with words. And she would savor every unfolding moment of her story, every gentle touch, every look from Ralph. Every cup of tea and joke shared with Susan. But most of all, she would carry her family's legacy with her; James's sense of adventure and endless encouragement, her mother's warm love and practical advice, her father's brilliant mind. She was the best parts of all of them, and they would live on, through her.

Darkness was creeping in, the rain becoming too persistent to ignore. "You're cold," Ralph said, unlooping his muffler and gently wrapping it around her neck. It smelled of sweet straw and leather, of gusty moors, of Ralph. It smelled like home.

She laced her fingers in his, his warmth, his vitality, traveling up her arm and spreading through her chest like a bird coming home to roost. "Come on," she said. "Let's go warm up in the library."

PRESS RELEASE FOR THE UNVEILING OF THE BLACKWOOD MANUSCRIPT AT THE BRITISH LIBRARY, 1931
THE BLACKWOOD MANUSCRIPT, C. 1350 ANON.
TRANSLATED BY DR. IVY HEWITT (NÉE RADCLIFFE), THE LADY HAYWORTH

Discovered by Lady Hayworth in Blackwood Abbey, the Blackwood Manuscript has been hailed as a momentous find by both academics and occultists alike, and sheds light on the study of astrology and herbology in the fourteenth century. Much of the knowledge within the brittle pages was hitherto lost to time, and will greatly advance not only our understanding of life in the fourteenth century, but also herbal remedies and their applications today.

Though the artwork is crude and vernacular in style, the text is written in an incredibly sophisticated cipher, one that might have gone centuries without decryption if not for Lady Hayworth's indefatigable will and singular skill with code-breaking. Lady Hayworth credits her late father, Dr. Matthew Radcliffe, as both her inspiration and mentor in working with codes and ciphers. His oeuvre is currently enjoying a renaissance among the medievalist community, and several exhibits and catalogs are being planned to coincide with the unveiling of the Blackwood Manuscript.

Perhaps the most enduring mystery of the manuscript is the missing pages. Lady Hayworth explains that it was not uncommon for manuscripts to be re-bound over the years and lose pages in the process, yet the torn vellum feels intentional. This hints that there was perhaps other knowledge bound within this book that was removed for whatever reason, be it censorship from the Church, or simply a long-ago owner who thought to take the job of editing upon themselves. But whatever became of these pages is unknown, and will most likely remain a mystery. What is known, is that the Blackwood Manuscript will leave an indelible mark on the field of medieval history, and is a jewel among medieval manuscripts, both in Great Britain and abroad.

Those wishing to view the manuscript can do so at the British Library where it currently resides when not in use by scholars. Lady Hayworth has also graciously opened the Blackwood library to visitors, and welcomes anyone and everyone to experience her incomparable collection of books and manuscripts.

★ ★ ★ ★ ★

ACKNOWLEDGMENTS

A bittersweet thank-you to Brittany Lavery, who championed my work for five years and made each and every one of my books what they are. I feel extremely lucky to have had the opportunity to work with such a warm, caring, and talented editor.

Endless gratitude to Lynn Raposo, who gracefully and competently stepped in at the eleventh hour and got me to the finish line.

It's been a strange and wonderful journey to get here, and I couldn't ask to end up in better hands than those of Sara Rodgers; I'm so excited to see what the future will bring.

The team at Graydon House, Harlequin. I couldn't ask for a better group of people to bring my books to fruition. Erin Craig and Mary Luna for the exquisite cover. Sophie James and Leah Morse for their tireless work on the publicity end of things. The eagle-eyed copy editors who make it look like I actually understand grammar and can spell. Thank you.

Jane Dystel for being a stalwart ally and champion of my work for over six years now.

Trish Knox and Jeanne Hilderbrand for being there, from the earliest drafts through all the doubts and dead-ends to cheering on the final book. Your friendship and support mean more to me than you can know.

Chris Davis for his help and expertise in creating the anagrams for the manuscript.

Authors Susanna Kearsley, Constance Sayers, and Rachel McMillan for their generous endorsements, as well as Paulette Kennedy, Kris Waldherr, and the rest of the members of the Gothic and dark fiction writers' group.

Agatha Andrews for her continued support, and everything she does for the Gothic writing community.

The booksellers, librarians, bloggers, and Bookstagrammers who help put my books in readers' hands.

My readers, who make it possible for me to keep doing what I love to do. Thank you, from the bottom of my heart.

And lastly, my little team, which grew to three this year. All my love to MF, FF, & PF.